Sign up for our newsletter to hear
about new and upcoming releases.

www.ylva-publishing.com

Other Books by Lee Winter

Standalone
Hotel Queens
Changing the Script
Breaking Character
Shattered
Requiem for Immortals
Sliced Ice (anthology)

The Truth Collection
The Ultimate Boss Set (box set)
The Brutal Truth
The Awkward Truth

The Villains series
The Fixer
Chaos Agent

On The Record series
On the Record – The Complete Collection (box set)
The Red Files
Under Your Skin

The Villains Series:
Book 2

Chaos Agent

LEE WINTER

Acknowledgments

My beta readers stepped up once more in book two of my *Villains* duology.

Thanks to Órla Smith who made me swoon over her menu suggestions for the O'Brian dinner parties, among other essential Irish input.

Sandy Unger's knowledge of lovable saftas is matched only by her insights into delicious Jewish treats.

Astrid Ohletz reminds me as always of what's missing as well as when I've overdone it. I'm so grateful.

A shout-out goes to my fave doctor, author Chris Zett, who helped me rough up then treat a character—and gave hilarious advice about how soon it could be before "fun" could commence.

My wonderful content editor, Alissa McGowan, sharpened her red pen again. Thank you!

To my readers—I love you for sticking with the last half of the journey to see how Michelle's redemption turned out. You inspire me every day.

Dedication

For my Michelle Hastings muse, narrator, and friend, Angela Dawe.

Chapter 1
Office With a Name

The first time Eden Lawless vanquished an archnemesis, she had just turned thirty-six and was not exactly expecting it. After all, no one had ever beaten Francine Wilson at *anything* before. But not only had Eden become an unlikely nemesis vanquisher, she'd somehow scored a new job out of it, in Washington DC, at a top-secret organization called The Fixers.

Eden had never been more surprised in her life—and that included the time she'd seen her mother naked on the TV news wearing only fake blood at an anti-fur protest. Never let it be said River Lawless didn't fully commit.

But of all the bizarre events that had filled Eden's professional activist life to date, working an office job for the first time was way up there.

It was in an *actual* office. With a glass desk, a swirly chair, a hot boss, and everything.

Whoa. Her brain screeched to a halt. Scratch the hot boss thing. That was wildly inappropriate.

Michelle Hastings, said boss, had hired Eden after appreciating her work on a small, ten-week subcontracted job in Eden's hometown of Wingapo, Maryland. That was the entire extent of their involvement. *Super* businessy.

Besides, even if Michelle *did* like women, an *if* based entirely on point five of a second's reaction on a Skype call weeks ago, the woman wasn't about to act on it. Because Michelle had always been, from minute one, a consummate professional.

But that didn't mean Eden couldn't appreciate the view. If she leaned back in her chair, she could see her, in profile, working at her desk. Well, by "see" it was more like her pale wrist, a bit of blue sleeve, and a slice of face that was entirely nose, mouth, and chin. Still, even that was a nice view.

Eden groaned. A bit of focus wouldn't kill her. Well, she'd focus when someone gave her some work. Her phone pinged with a text from her best friend.

Omg I can't believe you have an OFFICE job! YOU?!! Good luck for Day One. omg #endtimes

A new text landed: *Also next time ask my advice BEFORE accepting coz this is weird. You+Office=crazy*

Then: *Our friends have a betting pool on how long you'll last in a corporate job. Most betting a few days. I'm down for a month coz I know about Hot Boss. Don't let me down. Winner gets beer.*

Not for the first time, Eden wished she'd never mentioned Michelle's hotness to Aggie.

One last message landed with a picture of Aggie grinning idiotically in her new 'Kevin the guinea pig' pajamas.

Eden's recent birthday gift had been received as "the greatest creation in the entire course of fashion history, no kidding." While her "Find Kevin a Companion" list was apparently "genius." Aggie called it "Tinder for guinea pigs" and vowed to use it soon.

Aggie and Kevin looked adorable in the photo.

Something to print out & stick up on your desk to laugh at when you're drowning in the horrors of working inside 4 walls

Eden grinned and looked around for a printer.

"Tilly," Michelle called, "of our unassigned cases, are any...good?"

"Good?" Ottilie Zimmermann, Michelle's sixty-four-year-old personal assistant, settled into the visitor's chair and steepled her fingers. "Define *good*."

"The opposite of evil. A case where you might think, 'Well, that's something good we're doing.'"

Tilly stared at her as if she'd lost her mind. "No."

"What about...*less bad*?"

"There's the banker who wants his boss's job and wants us to leak the man's kinks to upper management to embarrass him into resigning. That impacts only one person."

Michelle winced. "Kinks shouldn't be used to shame people."

"And yet we've been planning to do just that for weeks now." Tilly eyed her.

"Yes." Michelle knew this, of course. "Only one person being impacted doesn't mean it falls into the category of *not* evil."

"Okay, what about that businessman, Yin? He wants to get his daughter away from the syndicate before she gets drawn deeper in. Wants us to get them off grid so they can't be hunted."

"Definitely not evil, but it's overseas. Think American assignments. Better yet, DC ones."

"Okay...Hank Brewer?" Tilly's expression twisted into disdain. "If you tell only half the story, it looks good."

Michelle brightened. "Perfect."

"May I ask why?"

"Ms. Lawless has joined our organization as of today." Michelle schooled her features to neutral.

A sharpness entered Tilly's eyes. "It'd be easier to just tell her the truth than try to manipulate our assignments to make us look good."

Sometimes Michelle hated how astute her PA was. At least Tilly hadn't asked why Michelle had hired the "panda" full-time for their emporium of sharks and snakes.

"She's a potentially valuable resource," she began justifying anyway, even though Tilly hadn't spoken. "However, she'd run for the hills if she knew the truth about us. I want to tap into that resource for now. Brewer is the perfect job to occupy her while I find her something more useful."

At Tilly's dubious look, Michelle added, "Look on the bright side: when was the last time we took on an effective employee who didn't make your skin crawl just a little?"

"Good point. And how disturbing."

Michelle chose not to dwell on that any more than she would dwell on the fact she couldn't wait to see Eden Lawless in the office, five days a week.

"Good morning, Ms. Lawless," Tilly said as she stopped at Eden's desk. "I trust everything is in order with your working space?"

Eden immediately sat up a little straighter in the face of the woman's no-nonsense tone. Her accent sounded faintly German—which made sense with a surname like Zimmermann—even though her choice of words was all English and proper. Eden felt entirely sloppy by comparison. "Yep, all good. Great view." She beamed.

"So glad you approve." Tilly paused and eyed the photo stuck on the partition at Eden's desk.

Eden followed her gaze and grinned. "Meet Aggie and Kevin."

"There's a 'no personal items on desks' policy at The Fixers," Tilly said briskly. "The workspace must remain clean and professional at all times."

No looking at Aggie and Kevin all day? Damn. Office life was harsh. "The Fixers' loss," Eden said with a small grin as she plucked the photo off the small divider.

Tilly slid a folder across her desk and then dropped a slip of paper on it. She gestured at Eden's computer. The top-of-the-line iMac was so new that Eden could still smell the plastic wrapping it had been ripped from.

"Your login and password details." Tilly tapped the paper.

Eden studied two random jumbles of letters and numbers and asked, "Which is which?"

With the tiniest of tuts—Eden wasn't sure if it was directed at her or IT—Tilly wrote "password" and "login" next to the relevant codes.

"Additionally," Tilly said, "speak to our cybersecurity department about getting a secure laptop for use outside the office." She pointed to a list of phone extensions. "Ask for Snakepit."

"Seriously?"

"Mmm."

"Okay." Probably some ex-hacker. Eden's geek side was fully pumped. "Great! What's next?"

Tilly flipped open the folder. "Your first job. Well, first in-office job."

Eden glanced at the cover sheet inside. "Hank Brewer? The multimillionaire?"

"Billionaire," Tilly corrected. "He had a good second half last year."

"Isn't he the guy who blew up native land for a gas-expansion project? And his demolition work caused a landslide that wiped out thousands of homes in Ecuador?"

"He has a checkered history, yes."

"And isn't he the guy who said college kids are 'entitled jerks pissing away Daddy's dough just to sound smart'? And educating girls outside of home economics is pointless?"

"He's not the most…evolved…man." The edges of Tilly's mouth threatened a smile.

"So, are we helping him fix the awful stuff he's done?" Eden offered a hopeful look.

"No." Tilly hesitated. "Well, not yet. The problem is, because of his past deeds, no one wants to be associated with him, even when he genuinely wants to do good."

"I don't blame them." Eden shuddered.

"He actually *does* want to be better. However, he doesn't want his rivals to think he's gone soft. So he's asked The Fixers to find a way to donate to worthy organizations but without anyone finding out he's behind it."

"Then he should tell charities to treat his donation anonymously," Eden said. "He doesn't need us."

"He does actually. He's already tried donating all over the place, but he's so toxic that they send his money back. They're terrified of being skewered on social media if it ever came out they accepted his blood money. So, your job is to donate *this* sum in a way that doesn't trace back to him." Tilly tapped a number.

Eden stared at all those zeroes. "Hank must be feeling *really* guilty. And sure, I'd be happy to help."

"Excellent." Tilly turned to leave.

"Um, hey, so when does Michelle get a break?" Eden asked casually. It wouldn't hurt to check in with her new boss, would it? For…reasons.

Hell. I am so lame.

"Did you wish to make an appointment to see Ms. Hastings? If so, go through me. She has a tight schedule." Tilly waited, eyebrow poised. "Why do you need to see her?"

"Um…" Eden panicked. "I thought I could debrief about Wingapo."

"No need. She approved your report as sufficient." Tilly waited some more.

Eden thought wildly for another excuse. "Do you think she'd like a green tea?" she asked weakly.

"No. But if she suddenly decided to take it up, she'd ask *me* to get her one. As her PA."

"Look, I just want to catch up with her," Eden finally admitted.

"Ah." Tilly considered that. "Well, she takes a coffee each day at nine and three. If you were to appear with one at five minutes to three, she'd be unlikely to refuse." She scribbled on a piece of paper. "Her Starbucks order."

"Thank you!" Eden grinned, gave a double thumbs up, then felt ridiculous. She blushed.

"Mmm." Tilly said thoughtfully as amusement glinted in her eye. "You know, I'd genuinely love to witness you two attempting a conversation. Marshmallow and acid, I'm thinking."

"Nah, I'm not *that* acidic." Eden's grin widened.

And this time, Tilly laughed.

The receptionist—the art lover Eden had met during her job interview—was the one assigned to giving her an office tour about an hour later. Her name was Daphne, which she pronounced <u>Darf</u>-knee, as if she'd just stumbled off the set of *Downton Abbey*. Apparently, she was an office manager too, as well as phone answerer, snooty visitor ignorer, and occasional art critic.

"We're on the top floor," Daphne said, "which may not be apparent since the elevator doesn't have numbers."

"Yeah. That's weird."

"The letters make perfect sense if you know what they mean," Daphne said with a sniff.

She reminded Eden a lot of a contrary Siamese cat. She walked like one too, reeking of grace and attitude. Today she wore a crimson suit and matching lipstick that looked gorgeous against her dark skin. The outfit was probably designer. And those glossy, peep-toe heels had to cost more than Eden's whole van.

She and Daphne were nothing alike, but Eden would never let that stand in the way of making friends. You just had to get people talking. Find common ground.

"Have you worked here long?" Eden asked.

"Yes."

"Do you like it?"

Daphne rolled her eyes. "Who says *no* when you ask them that? What a question!"

Good point. She tried again. "How many people work at The Fixers?"

"That's not the right question either." Daphne shot her a long-suffering look. "I mean it's difficult to answer with any precision because we use a lot of freelancers." She waved at Eden. "By the way, it's exceedingly rare for one of them to get promoted to full-time staff." Daphne lifted her impeccable eyebrow as if to imply that was clearly an error she trusted would be corrected.

"Okay, how many full-time staff work in this building?" Eden persisted.

"We don't really see ourselves as one building. Every floor is treated as an entirely self-contained ecosystem. We prefer it if staff over different floors don't mix because sharing too much can lead to leaks, so it's all contained by department."

Overkill much? Were the nondisclosure agreements the staff all signed not sufficient?

"So, top floor is us." Daphne waved at the open-plan floor. "We're home to the admin department—the CEO and her staff—along with Political, Business, and Diplomacy, or POBUD. Apparently, you fall under that umbrella, although no one has yet assigned you a title. These are our networking divisions that get things done via negotiating or low-level maneuvering." Daphne's lips pursed. "These are clever, clever people, so watch your back."

"Um, why would I have to watch my back from my own colleagues?" Eden asked. "That makes no sense."

For the first time, Daphne's mask dropped, her face transforming from aloof to outright surprise. "Oh my *God*." She poked Eden's arm lightly.

"Hey!"

"Just had to see if you're real or I'm dreaming. An actual *idealist* in our building. If I had pearls, I'd be clutching them. Where *did* you spring from?"

"Wingapo?" Eden shrugged.

"Regional backwater? Of course." Daphne shook her head as if erasing that thought like an Etch-a-Sketch. "Anyway, also on this floor we have Protection and Security, PROTSE for short."

"Shouldn't that be PROSE?"

"It should, but you can be the one to tell our scary head of security that he now works in PROSE." Daphne looked amused by the idea. "I suspect O'Brian would dangle you off the rooftop."

"He sounds nice." Eden chuckled.

"He's as nice as a colostomy bag, but he has some charm *if* he likes you. Him liking someone is about as commonplace as stylish Crocs. Anyway, O'Brian's department is the physical kind of security, not computers. Cybersecurity is on the next floor down."

"Let me guess, CYSEC for short?" She was getting the hang of this now.

"No. *Cybersecurity*." A hint of devilment entered Daphne's eyes. "They think their name sounds cutting edge. If true, that's the only cool thing about their department. Trust me. I've met those boys."

"I'll have to visit."

Daphne side-eyed her. "Good God, *why*? And did you miss the part about not mixing with other floors?"

"I love computers and comparing notes with geeks on tech. It'll be fun. I assume it's allowed that I go down there if I don't share what I'm working on?"

"Cross-pollination of staff across floors is frowned upon as far as discussing cases goes, but if it's just to talk about little nerdy things, I doubt it matters."

"Great."

"If you say so. Underneath Cybersecurity is Counterintelligence and Espionage. That's two different departments, so no fancy acronyms, and they don't play well with us or each other. Secretive little creatures, one and all."

Eden stopped cold. "Say what?"

Daphne frowned and turned to look at her. "*Counterintelligence and Espionage*," she repeated, drawing the words out as if speaking to a stupid child.

"Do The Fixers do *spy* work?" Eden lowered her voice, gaze darting around. "Like with actual *spies*?"

With a snort, Daphne said, "We do *whatever* is required. If that means finding out who's stealing tech designs, then that's what we do. We'll set up someone on the inside to work out the culprit."

Oh. *Defensive* espionage didn't sound so bad. Or illegal. Eden reminded herself that the contract she'd signed for the Wingapo job had clearly stated she couldn't do anything illegal. So, it wasn't like The Fixers staff were running around breaking laws or toppling governments. They weren't the CIA.

"Right," Eden muttered, having nothing better to say.

"So, under the *spies* floor," Daphne punched Eden's word in amusement, "is Mass Communication, Message Branding, and Trend

Development. That's mainly publicity and managing social media for clients in a deviously clever way. MassMess for short. They think that nickname's funny. Of *course* they would; they live on Twitter." She rolled her eyes. "That's everything."

"But what about all the other floors? I mean, this building is *huge*. You've only mentioned four floors."

"I never said each department only has one floor. Cybersecurity, for instance, has six. Their servers take up most of that."

Six floors? Just for the IT department? Oh, wow, Eden had to get an eyeful of that. "So how many employees are there for all those departments? The full-time ones? In total?"

"Forty-eight."

"Is that all?" Eden gazed around the gleaming office in astonishment. "I thought you were much bigger."

"We are. We hire hundreds of staff worldwide in a limited-contract capacity. It's cleaner that way. No paper trails. Easier to cut loose later. So, as I say, it is exceptionally rare that one of the disposables…"

Eden blinked.

"Sorry, *freelancers*, is brought on board to the staff. It's…not only rare, it's quite shocking." Daphne's gaze raked her body, expression genuinely confused. "Okay, what is it *you* have that's so unique that you got promoted from disposable to staff?"

"No clue. My assignment in Wingapo was creatively done? I'm good at thinking on my feet when presented with problems?"

Daphne studied her, seeking a lie, then seemed to give up. "All right, this way. I'll show you where the kitchen is."

A moment later, they stepped into a large room with a fridge, sink, microwave, and a swanky Italian coffee machine.

"Hey, that's a nice one," Eden pointed at the shiny beast in mint condition. "Takes pods *and* has a bean grinder? Fancy!"

"Don't even *think* about it. That's reserved for CEO use only." Daphne all but pouted, a flash of envy in her eye.

"Does Michelle enforce that rule?" Eden asked in surprise.

"*Ms. Hastings*," Daphne stressed, "doesn't have to enforce anything. She's obeyed. Unquestioningly. That's it."

"You make her sound like an ogre." Eden laughed at the absurdity.

"She is our CEO and should be treated as such," Daphne said firmly. "Now, then, the fridge is for all top-floor staff use, but label your food and hands off anyone else's. As you can see, we take security of food seriously here." Amusement laced her tone as she waved at the fridge.

On its face, stuck by magnets, was a handwritten notice.

If anyone eats my lunch, I will garrotte you.—O'Brian.

Garrotte was crossed out and, in different handwriting below it, was the word *dox*. That had also been crossed out and replaced with *blackmail*. Down the page it went, with different people leaving different, funnier threats.

"Your staff is pretty creative," Eden suggested. "If a little violent."

"They're both," Daphne deadpanned. She flicked her wrist over to study an elegant gold watch. "I have a meeting. You're on your own. Email me or Tilly if you get stuck on the basics. Golden rule: Don't touch anyone's desk or anything on it, *ever*. And for the love of God, stop calling our CEO by her first name!" With that, Daphne spun around on her gorgeous heels and took off at a fast clip.

Eden called after her, "Honorifics are classist!"

Daphne's derisive snort was loud and disbelieving.

Eden smiled.

At five to three, Michelle looked up to find Lawless hovering at her door, holding a coffee mug. "Are you lost?"

"No." Lawless scampered over and placed the mug on her desk. "I made you a coffee. Thought you might want some."

"You made it?" Michelle asked in surprise. "I usually get mine from Starbucks. Well, Tilly does."

"Well, that seems un-environmentally friendly." Lawless frowned. "There's a perfectly good kitchen in this office that even has a top-of-the-line coffee machine. Apparently one that only you can use, and yet you don't. Why is that?"

Michelle lifted her eyebrows at the temerity of the question. She was not required to explain herself to anyone. Still, unlike Eden, no one else had dared to ask. "The last CEO ordered it and insisted on it being just for him. He only ever drank this dreary light-roasted blend—the cupboards are still full of expired pods of the stuff. I hate it. Starbucks is easier."

"Well, I did find a pod in the cupboard of a different blend that sounded interesting, which I hoped you might like." She gestured at the cup. "Sorry, I didn't notice how it old it was."

Michelle took a small sip. The flavor was actually good—surprisingly so given how long it had sat in the cupboard. "That is not terrible."

"Well, if you decide you want more, I think we should discuss how pods go straight to landfills and don't break down for seventy years." Lawless's big wide eyes were so earnest.

"You don't say," Michelle said, trying not to laugh. "How…awful."

Lawless rolled her eyes. "I'm just saying you can get reusable pods for these machines. It's not hard. Or, even more sustainable, use ground beans. Your fancy machine actually does both." She bounced a little on her heels. "I could look into options for you, if you like."

"Or, I could resume having a Starbucks and not worry about the former CEO's god complex *or* his exclusive little coffee machine."

"Well, if that's what your plan is, why not let everyone use it?"

"Ah. Do *you* want to use it? Is that what this is?" Disappointment filled her. Not even a full day into her new job and Lawless was now trying to use their prior connection to wheedle favors out of her.

"That is *not* why I asked." She actually looked offended. "But I know from talking to people that staff would love access to it. And if you don't care, why can't they use it? Wouldn't it be more productive, too, to save them all having to leave the building to get a coffee?"

"Did Daphne Silver put you up to this?" Michelle regarded her. "I'm well aware she covets my machine even more than invites to Gucci launches."

Lawless folded her arms. "Why must everything be some sneaky, underhanded scheme? A manipulation? Can't a person just see a problem and want to fix it? Off their own initiative? Without any agenda? I was brought up to believe a happy group is a productive group."

"You understand, don't you, that *everything* we do here has an agenda?" Michelle said quietly, taking in the other woman's radiating hurt. She sighed inwardly at Lawless's sad face. "I didn't intend to besmirch your noble reputation."

"Apology accepted." She instantly lost the defensiveness and grinned.

"I wasn't aware I *had* apologized."

"Close enough." Lawless flapped a careless hand. "So yes or no on the office use of your coffee machine? And I have no dog in this fight. I don't mind a good coffee, but I don't need it the way some do. I just like clear answers."

"Fine." Michelle said, indifferently. "You may tell the office's caffeine addicts the machine is now open for their use."

"Awesome." Lawless smiled widely, as if thrilled to prove her belief that Michelle wasn't some petty overlord.

Seeing that smile felt good. No one around here ever seemed to smile without it meaning something sly had just occurred. Yet Lawless was utterly delighted that a bunch of strangers would get a treat that she wasn't that invested in herself.

After another sip of coffee, Michelle asked, "So, anything else, or you just came to bend my ear about making my coffee machine un-classist?"

Lawless laughed. "I admit my egalitarian self was getting hives over it. But, yes, I have another question."

"Uh huh," Michelle said, tone wry. "Well?"

"You know I'm a tree-hugging greenie, right, so I say this with love." Lawless stopped and a cute blush covered her cheeks. "I mean, I say it with great respect," she corrected hastily. "But why are there no plants in your building?"

"Plants?" Michelle frowned. "Why do we need plants?"

"Michelle!" Lawless looked at her in genuine outrage. "You have the good taste to put an *original Degas* in your office and a nude—*entirely nude,* by the way—designer sculpture in your outer area, but you don't understand the value of living, breathing greenery that makes the soul rejoice?"

Michelle hid her smile behind her coffee mug. "Soul rejoicing? That's not exactly on my to-do list for staff this month."

"It should be." Lawless's expression transformed into her 'mentally making a list' look.

"Ms. Lawless, I'm not going to justify to the board the expense of filling an entire building with vegetation. They'll think I've lost my mind."

"If it cost you nothing, you'd say yes?"

"How could it cost me nothing?" Michelle asked in confusion.

"You know my background. I have *so* many contacts. There's this one horticulturist I know who's amazing. He owes me big time. I first met him at a rainforest protest in Brazil."

"Of course you did," Michelle murmured.

"Besides, employees think more clearly with plants. It's all that oxygen. And it'll help Tyson most of all."

Michelle thought hard, skimming through all her departments, before conceding she had no idea who this Tyson individual was. "Who?"

"How can you not know Tyson? You see him every day in the foyer! The security guy?"

Oh. *Mr. Marshall.*

Lawless continued: "Do you understand how soul destroying it must be for Tyson to have nothing to look at but a wall of heavily tinted glass, one couch, and two elevators all day, every day? He needs plants as a matter of *urgency*. I just can't with the cruelty to the human spirit." Her eyes widened at the horror of it all.

"Cruelty? Because he doesn't have a stick with leaves to look at?" Michelle had to take a gulp of coffee to keep from laughing outright. "Poor man."

"I see you think it's hilarious, but I'm telling you, you'll change his world." Lawless brightened with enthusiasm. "Come on, let me do this. It won't cost you a cent. Productivity will soar. And the air in here won't taste like stale air-conditioner."

"It doesn't now."

"You've been here too long because I assure you it does." Lawless lifted her eyebrows. "So? Plants for The Fixers?"

"Far be it for me to get in the way of employee soul rejuvenation," Michelle drawled. "But if you bring in some exotic nonsense that makes us look in any way ridiculous, I'll throw them all out the window, the way I did your cheap champagne."

"You did not," Lawless said with a chuckle, looking delighted nonetheless by Michelle's agreement.

"Oh? How do you know?" she asked imperiously.

"The windows in your building don't open."

Ah. Lawless had her there. Michelle finished the coffee. "This was acceptable. Ask Tilly to bring me this daily instead of my usual Starbucks order in future."

"No, I don't think so." Lawless bit her lip.

"Ex-*cuse* me?"

"Michelle," she said reproachfully, "I made you that flavor because I found it in the cupboard already. But it's not a fair-trade coffee. Not organic, either. I truly can't endorse its ongoing consumption."

"Oh, for God's sake." Michelle shot her a warning glare. Ordering coffee shouldn't feel like a hostage negotiation!

"But we *can* work around that," Lawless said hastily. "I'll make a list of the good stuff you can choose from, okay? No need for you to drink earth-destroying evil coffee when you can just as easily have the alternative. Let me get back to you on that."

Of all the cheek!

"Please?" She looked hopeful.

Damn her. "I'll consider your list." Michelle waved at the door. "Now, I have work to do. I'm sure you do too. I'm fairly certain that Hank Brewer can't redeem his blackened soul if you're busy debating ethically sourced coffee with your boss."

"No problem." Lawless leaped to her feet. "Although, I finished that assignment half an hour ago."

"But he wanted to donate to a *dozen* charities." Michelle eyed her. "You've solved this already?"

"Yes. I thought about who to donate to as much as how. I picked charities he'd never want to be linked to. Like college scholarships for poor kids, rainforest protection groups, domestic violence shelters, STEM advancement foundations for women, that sort of thing. So the best part is, if it ever got leaked he was behind the money, no one would ever believe it. I've used a good friend who runs an NGO charity as a go-between. I gave him the money as a 'donation,' which *he'll* then spread around to all my chosen charities. Best part is, you can even use our 'donation' to his NGO as a tax write-off."

She beamed, looking so proud.

And... *Fuck*.

"Thank you. Now, I'm really very busy." Michelle pushed the empty coffee mug away. "Please return that to the kitchen when you go." She faced her monitor.

A puzzled expression crossed Lawless's face, but she collected the mug and turned to leave.

"Send Tilly in on your way out," Michelle added.

Moments later, Tilly appeared. "Ms. Hastings?"

"I believe our newest recruit has overshot the runway on her assignment. She's chosen charities which Hank Brewer would never, ever want to be associated with. And a third party was paid to ensure anonymity."

"Oh dear."

"It's impossible to leak it now. Even if we did, Brewer would deny it was him with vehemence." Michelle sighed. "We'll have to eat the cost on this one. Chalk it up to the perils of not properly briefing the employee."

Tilly's expression reeked of 'I told you so.' "From Ms. Lawless's point of view, she completed the assignment to the letter."

"Unfortunately." Michelle sighed. "Well, what's next?"

"We tell her the truth."

"You want me to explain that Hank Brewer really *did* want to be exposed as a secret good guy? That this was to rehabilitate his image?"

"Or feel free to explain to her that we do the devil's work," Tilly said, tone dry. "And that occasionally the stars align and the work performed is less bad, but generally it's about giving people with power or money more of what they covet."

Michelle pursed her lips. "Give her the Langley job next. Brief her better this time, so she can't make any more accidental errors. Factor in that she's too creative and clever for her own good…and ours." She turned back to her paperwork. "I trust you'll know precisely how much of Langley's secret to tell."

Tilly looked thoughtful. "It's curious, isn't it? How many secrets we know."

"Well, I *am* the secrets keeper, after all." Michelle offered a small smile.

"No, you're the secrets trader. I've never seen you waste a good secret when you can trade it for something better."

"True." Michelle wondered why that settled so oddly in her stomach.

Tilly gave her a curious look. "You *are* good at this. That's enough, isn't it?"

"Yes, of course. Why wouldn't it be?" The lie slid so smoothly from her lips.

Tilly gave an indulgent smile. "Exactly. That's worth remembering."

Eden looked up to find Tilly at her desk, sliding another folder across to her.

"Your next assignment." Tilly flipped open the folder.

Inside was a picture of a tanned young man with bright, happy eyes and curly hair. The bio next to his photo said his name was Jason Langley, aged nineteen, from Washington DC.

"Jason Langley is a young man with big dreams," Tilly began. "He plans to do a charity walk from coast to coast across the US to raise money to get more braille books in public libraries. His little sister is blind, so he wants to help her 'experience more adventures,' as he calls it."

"How wonderful." Eden loved this assignment already.

"There's been some tension with his father, Robert Langley, a top political lawyer in DC. Jason believed his father wasn't supportive of his dreams. To show his support and mend their relationship, Robert made a sizeable donation to his son's charity walk GoFundMe—enough to cover costs for a support team and much more."

"Okay," Eden said, curious as to where this was going.

"Things were fine until Robert sat down with Jason to learn about his plans for the walk in detail and discovered they're a mess. He's very concerned his son is going to kill himself through dehydration or sunstroke or some other means because he hasn't thought it through properly."

"Ah." Eden had met a few dreamers like this in her time.

"Robert has sent his son various intermediaries to talk some sense into him. Experts to help him budget his expenses, work out routes, and factor in weather and conditions. His son rebuffed all efforts, dismissing the intermediaries as 'suits with negative energy.' Jason believes he's being undermined, not helped. Tension has returned between father and son."

"How can I help?"

"Jason needs a reality check but won't believe the source unless it's from someone he can relate to, not a stuffy suit. If he heard about the risks from someone who understands fighting for a cause, he'd be more inclined to listen." Tilly looked pointedly to Eden. "I'm quite sure when you pull up in your…Gloria…he won't mistake you for a bean counter."

Eden grinned, understanding dawning. "Nope. No chance of that."

"Now, I cannot stress this enough: Jason's father, who is our client, wants you to ram home to his son every possible negative consequence. No sugar coating. The young man must understand the risks and everything that can go wrong. It's not your job to help Jason believe he can do it. He already believes. Show him what he *isn't* thinking about. Once he knows all the worst-case scenarios, only then will his father consider him ready."

Eden nodded. "I'll start researching immediately—from blisters to full-blown disasters."

"Good. The main issue is Jason's such a 'head in the clouds' type that he thinks he can wing it with shortcuts. Scare him if you have to. Remind him his little sister won't thank him if he's dead."

Ouch. But true. "Consider it done."

Tilly smiled. "Excellent. You'll find his contact details in the file." She left.

Eden flicked through the paperwork, noting the man's proposed route—well, routes, as he'd listed ten possibilities—and then got to work.

Chapter 2
The Pandafication Begins

Ten days later, Michelle eyed the enormous jungle engulfing the building's foyer when she arrived at work. She stepped around a towering potted palm and glanced up to find trailing ferns dangling from the ceiling. Pea-sized beaded greenery fell between them—String of Pearls, if she recalled correctly. The effect was magical and eerie against the glossy, forbidding black surfaces.

Her gaze fell to the security guard, a dark-skinned man with bulging muscles beneath his navy-blue uniform.

"Quite the change of scenery, Mr. Marshall."

"Yes, Ms. Hastings." He shot her a worried look.

"May I assume you're okay with being relocated to deepest, darkest Peru?" she asked lightly.

"Oh, yes, ma'am. Most surely." His relief was palpable. "I love it, ma'am." He flashed her a grin. "Ms. Lawless and her rainforest friend came by at seven this morning with a team. They unloaded a truckload of plants. Here and upstairs."

"Did they, now?" Michelle wondered what awaited her on the top floor. And "rainforest friend"? Trust Lawless to have friends nicknamed according to various nature biomes. Michelle strode toward the elevators.

"Please thank Ms. Lawless for me," Marshall called after her. "I… it's…"

She turned at his stuttering.

His eyes glowed with happiness. "*Incredible.*"

"Thank her yourself. It wasn't my doing." She stabbed the elevator button, assuming her usual hard-ass persona. "It cost me nothing, so I don't care."

"Yes, ma'am. By the way, I didn't take you for a Paddington Bear fan."

Ah. The deepest, darkest Peru reference. The question was not only unexpected but way out of character for the man who'd only ever been monosyllabic in her presence before. Apparently, vegetation had shaken his tongue loose.

"Nor I you." She stepped inside the elevator. "Carry on."

Michelle's office contained a cascade of greenery. Peace lilies had won a coup—they were on every surface. String of Pearls dotted the windowsills, showing off their dangling green tails. But the plant that captivated her most was a mystery to her. She leaned in to smell its violet flowers and rich burgundy leaves.

"That's my favorite too," came a familiar voice. "Well, aside from the peace lilies, which do the goddess's work."

Michelle straightened, annoyed to have been caught admiring the plant. Then she felt annoyed she was annoyed because it was *her* office and she could do whatever she wanted in it. "The goddess's work," she said sarcastically, to hide her self-consciousness. "So…you're religious?"

"More…spiritual." Lawless spun around. "Doesn't your office look amazing! So that one you were smelling is an oxalis. It's so elegant, isn't it? Bees love them."

"We're *inside*, Ms. Lawless."

"True." Lawless chuckled. "And peace lilies do the goddess's work because they're great at oxygenating rooms—so much so that astronauts took them into space. My friend Francisco got us a ton, so soon we'll be sucking in sweet, sweet air instead of ick."

Ick was hardly scientific. And Michelle still couldn't smell the stale air Lawless claimed permeated the office.

"So," Lawless asked hopefully. "Do you like it?"

Michelle folded her arms. "No." How could she admit something so vulnerable as the fact the beautiful greenery captivated her? It made her office feel less sterile for the first time in the nine years she'd inhabited it.

Doubt flickered into Lawless's eyes, but she rallied. "Maybe they'll grow on you."

"Was that a plant pun?" Michelle moved to settle behind her desk.

"Me? Pun you? Nah. You'd be merciless." Lawless grinned.

"I'm not kidding." Michelle's tone and look sharpened. "I did not give you permission to overrun *my* office with plants. I allowed you to put some around the various floors, but in here..." she tapped her desk, "you've crossed a line. This is my *private* office. You don't get to invade it on a whim." Anger rose at the thought of how Lawless's actions would be perceived outside this room. Would her staff call her weak?

"I'm sorry," Lawless said, looking remorseful. "I didn't understand."

"I can see that. Now, clear it out. Immediately."

Lawless nodded, embarrassment coloring her cheeks.

Within fifteen minutes she was done. Starkness greeted Michelle once more, and her heart fell at the sight of it.

Lawless plucked the oxalis off her desk—the last plant—and turned to go.

"Wait." Michelle inhaled. "Not that one."

Returning it to the desk, Lawless risked a hopeful grin.

"Tell no one," Michelle warned her and shifted the plant to a side table, out of public view.

"Lips are sealed. Well, I gotta go. There's a meeting for The Fix, and I've got to prepare."

"The what?"

"Didn't you get my email? I CCed all Fixers staff in the building."

She had *what*? That was a major protocol breach. *Another one!* Only managers should be sending announcements to the whole staff.

Grimacing, Michelle made a mental note to get Tilly to go through office protocol with Lawless. Clearly the protester life hadn't prepared her for the nuances of corporate employment.

"So," Lawless began enthusiastically, "I've started a new club for coffee lovers at The Fixers, called The Fix—as in getting a caffeine fix?"

"You've started a *coffee club*?" Michelle stared.

"Sure. After I told people they had permission to use the coffee machine, do you know what happened next? They all flung open the cupboards and began plowing through those old crappy pods. They're all expired, aren't fair trade, and aren't recyclable."

"Oh dear," Michelle deadpanned.

"Right? So The Fix is a friendly way to introduce them to better coffees. Every meeting, club members will learn about a new flavor or two and the villages helped by buying those beans."

Michelle grimaced. "Did it even occur to you to ask my permission before instituting our building's first club?"

"*First club?*" Lawless's eyes widened. "I didn't think I needed to. I'm not holding meetings during office hours."

"You truly haven't worked in an office before, have you?" Exasperation filled Michelle.

"I don't understand why it's so different. People are people, you know? A group of office workers, a group of protesters…it's the same."

"It's also clear you have no understanding of office etiquette."

"But why should—"

"No." Michelle sighed. "It's not just about protocol. How do you think it makes *me* look that you just run around doing whatever you want here? An employee who has been here only five minutes? It'll look like *I've* lost control. That *you're* in charge."

"No, it won't, because everyone's terrified of you." Lawless frowned, clearly mystified. "I'm sorry, though. I didn't mean to overstep."

"Well, you have." Michelle gave her a dissatisfied glare.

"Want me to cancel the club?" Lawless asked quietly. Her eyes were now everywhere except on Michelle.

Do I? "If I cancel it now, I become an ogre," Michelle said. "Well, more of one. Which I admit *is* tempting." She took in Lawless's hangdog expression. "No, don't cancel. Besides, I doubt there'd be much interest anyway. Why would anyone join a club to sit around and talk about coffee?"

"Don't be so sure." Lawless suddenly grinned. "I have Fixers staff inquiring from all floors. I'm excited to meet people from the lower levels. Do you think the Espionagers might come?" She gave a tiny chuckle. "And if so, do you think they'll turn up in trench coats?"

Michelle wondered if anyone would actually turn up at all. "They might be less interested once they see the prices of those exotic coffees you'll be introducing them to."

"Nah. I'm paying for all the coffees we try. And if people want to keep drinking them at work, I'll pay for those too. I'm a big believer in putting my money where my mouth is."

Michelle's stomach knotted in dismay. Now her staff's interest in Lawless's little club became clear. They saw her as a sap to use for free coffee and then would mock her behind her back. Was she the office joke already? Someone should tell her before she threw away her money on manipulative colleagues who would abuse her guileless enthusiasm.

"Ms. Lawless, the employees here are…" *Sneaky, slippery bastards.* "…not the usual people you mix with at your social justice gatherings. They're cynical. Half are ex-FBI, NSA, CIA, or worse. They'll take advantage of your kindness."

Lawless shrugged. "We'll see. Mom always said the secret to making the world a better place is to fix one small thing and go from there. Maybe it's a hopelessly optimistic plan, getting a bunch of cynical former agents interested in ethical coffee. But I'd like to try."

Michelle didn't want to imagine how it would be in a month's time when Lawless heard the office mocking her. Anyone perceived as soft, naive, or kind was ripe for ridicule. Michelle knew that better than anyone. She opened her drawer and drew out a business card. "Here," she said. "Take this."

Lawless frowned at it. "You think I need a money manager?"

"I do. If you're blowing all your Wingapo assignment's payment on free coffees for staff, someone should talk to you about ways to at least retain some of it in an investment portfolio before it's all gone."

"Thanks for your concern, but money should be spent. On *people*." She pushed the card back. "I'd much rather make my colleagues smile than shovel all my cash into investments."

Michelle sighed and returned the card to her drawer.

"So," Lawless said, hope returning to her eye, "is it okay for me to hold The Fix?"

"*Now* you're asking?"

"Yes?"

"If anyone asks, tell them I threatened you with bodily harm if we have even a one percent drop in productivity," Michelle said.

"What? Oh…you're joking?"

Michelle wished she were. Rumors had started over less. If not about her allowing the club to go ahead or granting access to the coffee machine, then certainly for endorsing a plant invasion. She fixed Lawless with a long, cool stare. "That's what you tell them. Understood?"

"Um…" Lawless blinked. "Okay."

Finally. "Good."

"Right, um, I brought you this." Eden pushed a page across her desk. "As promised, these are all fair-trade organic blends for you to try."

There were hundreds, including some ridiculous titles. Golden French Toast? Orange Indulgence White Tea?

"So, I'll leave those with you," Lawless said. "Email me your top ten and I'll magic you up some whenever you're in the mood." She paused, cheeks reddening slightly. "For *coffee*. Because that came out weird."

Michelle smirked.

"The first Fix meeting is after work tonight. You're very welcome. Check my email for details."

"I'll pass." Michelle grimaced.

Lawless's expression faltered.

"No one wants their boss at these things," Michelle explained.

Lawless grinned. "I do."

More proof she didn't have a clue who Michelle was, but the sentiment felt unexpectedly nice. "How goes the Langley case?"

"Finished. I'm just writing up a report. I've got Jason prepped within an inch of his life for his charity walk."

"Prepped?" Michelle asked slowly. "You've explained to him everything that could go wrong?"

"Better than that." Lawless beamed. "I reached out across my network and found someone who'd done the same trek. Dylan's this old greenie dude who did the walk barefoot, with no support crew. He had tons of cred with Jason. Dylan took him through everything: how to prepare and how to not die, basically. So now Jason's as close to bulletproof as any nineteen-year-old about to walk 2,339 miles can be. He's already flown into Brunswick with his support team. That's his starting point to take the shortest route."

"He's ready now?" Michelle whispered in horror.

"Definitely! He finishes in San Diego. He's been training hard with Dylan."

"When does he leave?" she asked weakly.

"Tomorrow." Lawless pulled out her phone and tapped a few buttons. "I'm sending you a link to a story on him." She put her phone away again. "Don't worry. Dylan'll make sure he's safe. He's walking part of the way with him, to ease him into it. That's good, right?"

"Yes," Michelle forced out.

"Great. I better get back to it. Things to do." Lawless grinned and left the office, a woman on a mission.

"Tilly," Michelle stabbed the intercom. "I need a minute."

Her PA entered, and Michelle crooked a finger to get Tilly to come to her side of the desk. Michelle hit "Play" on the video she'd cued up from Lawless's link to a Brunswick TV news report.

Jason Langley was telling a small pack of reporters how he couldn't wait to raise money for braille books in libraries. "I want my sister to experience just as many adventures as I do!" His face glowed. "Maybe one day she'll walk with me too, but for now, she's only eight and loves to read about adventures. Wouldn't it be cool if she and other blind kids had a thousand books to enjoy?"

Tilly's eyes widened. "He's *doing* it?"

"Apparently. Yet Robert Langley assured us that if his son genuinely understood the risks and hardship, he'd quit. He said his son was weak." Michelle waved at the screen. "Does *that* look weak to you?"

Jason had just dropped to the ground to do a few push-ups, then sprung to his feet to do star jumps as he announced between puffs that he was in the prime of his life. Then he looked at the camera and said: "I couldn't have done any of this without my expert guide, Dylan. He made my dream possible. I would have quit fifty times over if not for him." He punched the air and added, "Whoo!"

"Oh dear," Tilly said faintly.

"His father will be furious." Michelle's head started thudding. "The whole *point* of this assignment was to scare Jason, not embolden him. The boy was supposed to get intimidated and back out!"

"I know," Tilly muttered. She inhaled. "Robert is to blame for underestimating his son's willpower."

"Or Lawless decided this was a worthy cause and went out of her way to make it happen."

"If that's the case, we should have told her the true objectives. That we had to sabotage Jason's walk."

"And why would Lawless want to support that?" Michelle asked. "Robert won't want to pay us a cent, and I'm now going to have to argue that Robert didn't know his own son and that that's on him. I'm sure *that'll* go down well."

"He may refuse to pay," Tilly said. "That will be twice now Lawless has cost us money."

"No, twice she's fulfilled her assignment to the letter of her briefing because she didn't know its true purpose. And it's happened twice because we underestimated her. We're not harnessing *who* she is properly. Lawless thinks in a way we don't, so we can't predict what she'll do next because it's so far out of our usual realm. She could be a valuable resource because she has networks in areas different from ours. Instead of using that resource, we're working against her, not with her."

"The only way we can work *with her* is by telling her the whole truth," Tilly argued.

"If we do that, we lose the resource entirely. Unacceptable." Michelle rubbed her aching temples. "We're smart women, Tilly. We should not be defeated by a clever employee who happens to think a little differently. It's on *us* to predict her actions better, assume she'll always try to find the nicest, win-win solution, and oversee her accordingly. But first, it will be on *you* to brief her in such a way that gets us the results we need. Understood?"

Pursing her lips, Tilly said, "Yes, Ms. Hastings."

"You're certifiable," Daphne told Eden as they headed to the office kitchen for the first meeting of The Fix. It had just turned five. "Paying for everyone's coffees? They'll eat you alive." She made a Hannibal Lecter slurping noise. "Fresh pickings."

"Michelle said kinda the same, but nicer."

"Ms. Hastings does not do nice," Daphne said. "You're delusional as well as certifiable. But anyway, just prepare yourself to be mobbed by greedy monsters, your bones picked clean."

"Ye of little faith. And that was kind of gruesome."

In truth, Eden was nervous. Her first goal was having at least five people show up. Her next goal was that they didn't walk out in boredom when she started getting into the social conscience side of her chosen coffees. Beyond that, she just hoped there'd be enough interest for a second Fix meeting, or this would be humiliating.

"I happen to think it was realistic." Daphne sniffed. "And could you stop calling our supreme leader by her first name. It's weird."

"Why?"

"She's terrifying, so humanizing her is seriously unnerving."

"Why's she terrifying?"

"Because she's the boss villain in a building full of nasty, evil little henchmen and women."

"She's not a villain!" Eden scoffed. "That's nuts." And evil henchmen? *What the hell?*

"It's not nuts. Our CEO has a terrifying reputation. I hear she's done things no one else would dare. So, I give her a wide berth and full respect because she scares the scariest people I've ever met. You should too."

Before Eden could digest that, they arrived at the kitchen. *Oh wow.* There was a crowd of well over thirty people.

In the middle was the most enormous man, with a nose wrapped halfway across his pockmarked face, who looked like he could pull the limbs off a bear with ease.

"Oh, damn," Daphne hissed, eyes on him. "It's O'Brian. He's the worst of them all. He'll make your life hell. It's not too late to call this off."

"Never." Eden grinned. "I love a challenge. And what everyone seems to forget is I've spent a lifetime working with idealists, anarchists, disruptors, and dreamers and getting them all on the same page. What's a bunch of Fixers after that?"

Eden pushed her way into the middle of the gathering, meeting their curious gazes. "Hi everyone," she began. "I'm Eden Lawless. Newest POBUD employee, founder of The Fix, and..."

"A complete rube!" O'Brian cut in. "Or a complete asshole, if there's a catch. We're all dyin' t'know which it is." His Irish accent competed with his American one, making Eden wonder which country he'd been in longer.

"Ahh, a cynic!" She laughed. "Okay, fair enough. But there is no catch."

Suspicious gazes greeted her. Then came a round of "yeah sure," "not likely," "who gives away free coffee?" And on it went.

"Oh, for God's sake!" Daphne growled. "Shut the hell up and let the woman speak! And I can assure you there's no catch because she's from... *Wingapo*." Daphne said it as if Eden had just rolled in on an Amish buggy. And it was freaking hilarious.

Eden wheezed with laughter, not feeling the tiniest shred of embarrassment. Which started the room off laughing too.

"Fine, fine, so I have zero chill," Eden admitted cheerfully. "I don't care if I'm cool. I just want to talk about coffee. The good stuff. I'm sure most of you have traveled the world, dined in some pretty fancy restaurants, had some of the best beans there are, am I right?"

That got plenty of nods. "But you haven't lived till you've tried *these* blends. I'm talking flavors that'll blow your cosmopolitan minds. Blends from the far corners of the earth, little villages elevated from poverty by their crops of coffee beans." Eden reached into her bag and pulled out a packet of beans. "You'll learn about the tiny collective of women coffee farmers who changed the fortunes of their villages in Dak Cheung in Laos. But that story's for another meeting. Tonight, I have a real treat."

The room had fallen silent. Eden grinned at everyone's anticipation. Even O'Brian looked interested. The suspicion had gone from his cool eyes.

"First up, we're all gonna be experiencing the glory of Laughing Man's Ethiopia Sidama." Eden ripped open the beans and poured them into the machine. "It has notes of bright citrus, bergamot, hints of lime. So, yes, it's sweeter than normal for an Arabica coffee. But it's also *intoxicating*. Line up your cups on the benches, everyone, and I'll tell you all about the Sidama people while we brew some of it. Oh, and by the way, this one's kosher, in case that's important for you."

Eden launched into her tale as the coffee brewed, then started filling up and passing out mugs like she was running a production line. "And that's when my mom, absolutely *enraged* by this point, covered in mud, *still* chained to the tree, told the Ethiopian official, 'And *that's* why you're single!'"

The room erupted into laughter. By now, they all had their coffees and were sipping on them. Story over, they began talking amongst themselves.

A hulking shape approached. "Lawless," O'Brian rumbled. "I just found out you're behind the vegetation that's been plaguin' our office."

Eden looked up (and up) at him. "That'd be me. Once a tree-hugging hippie and all that."

"Christ," he snorted. "Just what the world needs more of. Hippies."

"You don't like your fiddle-leaf fig?" Eden asked. "I picked it out especially for Security. I figured you guys might need something with big leaves. Could come in handy as cover."

She held her breath waiting to see whether he was about to fling her against a wall.

He threw back his head and laughed. "Fuck me! And I never said I didn't like it. I only asked seein' as the missus wants one for home.

I showed her a photo. She wants the name of it." He looked at her intently. "So, fiddle-dee-dee what now?"

"Fiddle-leaf fig. Give me your cell number and I'll text you its botanical name and where to get it from."

He dug into his pocket. "Right. Here's my card. Text me. By the way, your coffee wasn't shite."

"Glad to hear it."

"But next time can you not do *notes* of *delicate* flavors? Especially anything *fruity*?" His face screwed into a grimace.

"What's wrong with fruity?" Eden asked, lifting her eyebrows playfully. "I'm ninety-eight percent fruity myself." She prayed he wasn't homophobic as well as obnoxious. But for some reason, her gut told her he wasn't entirely the bastard he so clearly liked playing. He seemed more for show. Eden really wanted to see if she was right.

"Of *course* you are," he said, as if it were the final piece of the puzzle. "Addin' it to the hippie, greenie, ethical-coffee-fangirl deal you got going. But no, seriously woman, can we get somethin' *meaty* next time? Deeper? An angrier roast, like?"

Next time? That boded well, didn't it? Her staunchest critic would be back?

He must have mistaken her silence for disapproval because the security head suddenly added politely, "If...you *wouldn't mind?*"

Three neckless men within earshot all shot startled looks O'Brian's way. Daphne's eyes widened to dinner plates. A shy young man from IT, Snakepit, almost dropped his mug in surprise.

"Sure thing, O'Brian," Eden said. "Can do. I have *just* the blend. So, same time next week?"

"Right you are," he said. He clapped her so hard on the shoulder, a vibration ran through her. "Hell, Lawless, you might be some hippie-la-la, woke, PC rube who's probably got rainbows on your pajamas, but you're okay by me!"

"I'll take that as high praise," Eden replied with a grin.

He frowned at her. "Well, of course you oughtta. How else could you take it?"

She laughed hard. Everyone else started laughing too. Eden really hoped they were laughing *with* her.

"Right," O'Brian announced. "Who wants to roll on outta here to the local for drinks? Lawless is buying!"

This was greeted with a roar of approval.

"Hey!" Eden protested. "I bought your coffees, now you want me to buy your booze too?"

"Yes!" The cries were good-natured, at least.

"Fine, fine. First round's on me," Eden said. "Then it's on O'Brian." She slapped him on the stomach. "Cause I'm sure he wouldn't volunteer anyone to do anything he wouldn't do himself."

And this time when the room burst into laughter, there was no doubt they weren't laughing at her.

Tilly brought in her paperwork and gave Michelle a weighted look, her signal that she expected to be told it was time for them to call it a day. Given the clock was nudging seven, it was a reasonable expectation.

"I think we're done," Michelle relented. "But before you go, I know you'll be aware of what happened."

"Happened?" Tilly's eyebrows lifted.

"Lawless's touchy-feely coffee group."

Tilly smirked. "I wondered how long it'd take for you to ask."

"Well?" Michelle made a *get-to-it* gesture.

"I stopped by to get the lay of the land."

Of course she had. Tilly saw all. "And…"

"Mr. O'Brian was there."

"Ah." Michelle winced. "Tell me he behaved? Did he heckle her?"

"Funny you should say that. But first…attendance was a surprise."

"How many?"

"Thirty-eight, not counting me."

"Thirty-eight!" Michelle reeled in shock. "Our staff must be bored."

"Or deprived of caffeine. I think most just wanted to try the CEO's mythical coffee machine. Some wanted to meet the curious woman who'd talked you into making it available to all. And then there was Mr. O'Brian."

"How many times did he mention his pet peeves of precious snowflakes, drama queens, and leftie hippies'?" Michelle asked, bracing herself.

"More than once. Fewer than three times. For something different, though, it was almost affectionate.'

"Unlikely."

"No, it was. He also wanted details from Ms. Lawless about the plant in his office."

"Are we still talking about *the* Phelim O'Brian? Who can make grown men wet themselves with just a look?"

"The very same. Of course, he also couldn't resist getting a jab in about her 'woke PC brigade.'"

"How did she handle him?"

"She promised to text him the botanical name of the plant and…" Tilly waited a beat, "she teased him."

Michelle was too startled to breathe. "Well. I assume the meeting broke up by way of him throwing the fridge?"

"Actually, the meeting broke up by way of everyone heading off to the Black Rabbit for drinks. Mr. O'Brian volunteered Ms. Lawless to buy the drinks, to much cheering."

Michelle's stomach tightened. *Of course. Vultures.* "They couldn't resist taking advantage of her generosity."

Tilly lifted a finger. "Not so fast. Ms. Lawless agreed to buy the first round, but then she volunteered Mr. O'Brian to pay for the second. She did it in a way he couldn't say no."

"How…is Eden Lawless even still breathing?"

"A mystery we'll await to find out another day, because I returned here and they headed out."

"So, all in all, the coffee club experiment was a success?"

"Indeed. Especially when she told us about where the coffee we were trying came from. How it was changing lives. It was a tale well told. It almost made me want to donate to someone."

"You?" Michelle arched an eyebrow.

"Well, I said *almost*." Tilly's eyes danced. "She is entertaining, that one. Clever. She had the room eating out of her hand. I'm also pretty sure Snakepit has a crush."

"Good luck, Snakepit." He'd need it. If Lawless ever looked twice at that unworthy man-child, Michelle would eat her oxalis. She forced back the ridiculous slither of jealousy. "I suppose this club will be a regular thing?"

"Mm. I'm pretty sure it will."

Would wonders never cease? "Lawless will be insufferable now. I warned her they wouldn't have the best motives. Turns out The Fixers staff *can* play well at times. To think I was worried our panda would be mauled by the snakes and sharks. It turns out they should have been afraid of *her*."

Tilly tilted her head. "Maybe we all should. Things worked efficiently before. Now…it's a little more chaotic." At that, she prodded an oxalis leaf on Michelle's desk and added, "I'm going home."

Chapter 3
Spies Like Us

The weeks had flown by. Eden was getting the hang of her new job, and each day at five to three, she presented a new coffee to Michelle to try.

As Michelle sipped it, Eden would give her the story of where it had come from and a couple of notes about the flavors. After the first few days, Michelle had even stopped looking surprised to see her. It was just routine now. Tilly certainly seemed to appreciate not having to go fetch a Starbucks twice a day.

On the topic of Michelle's PA, there had been a curious conversation earlier today when Eden had asked her what her secret was.

"My secret?" Tilly's pale blond eyebrows gently lifted.

"How do you manage to get Michelle to call you by your first name? Why is it Mr. or Ms. for everyone else except you? Is it because of how long you've worked together?"

Tilly regarded her for the longest moment. "No."

"Then is it just because it's *you* that you get called by your preference in name? She likes you enough to do it for you?"

"I never said Tilly was my preference."

Wait, what? "I don't under—"

"My preference is my actual name—Ottilie, or Ms. Zimmermann."

Eden's mouth fell open. "Why don't you tell Michelle?"

"Ms. Hastings is the CEO and can call me Tilly if she wishes."

"But—"

"No. Let sleeping dogs lie." She gave Eden a firm look. "And don't you start calling me by my preferred name now, knowing Ms. Hastings will notice and ask why. Leave it be."

Eden sagged, wishing she could help with this.

Six hours later—as was now The Fix's habit after each meeting—most of the members had wound up back at the Black Rabbit for a meal and a few drinks.

Okay, it was more like a *lot* of drinks. Eden had planned ahead and reserved an upstairs room for their party of thirty so they could swap stories in privacy instead of talking in code as they had at previous Black Rabbit sessions.

Eden was feeling particularly merry two beers in. Or was it three? She found herself announcing to her new friends: "I love you all! I'm not just saying that because I'm a little bit drunk!"

O'Brian roared with laughter. "Lemme get you more booze then if you're only a little drunk." He lurched off, headed to the bar downstairs.

"Woman, you are not a little bit drunk," Daphne declared. "You are a *lot* drunk." Then, abruptly, she cheered. Which set off the rest of the group in equally merry cheers.

Eden smiled a bleary smile, and suddenly time sped up and O'Brian was back at her side, thrusting a beer in her hand. He grabbed her by the back of her jacket as she did a startled wobble. He plonked her onto a chair.

"Oops. Thanks. Didn't even realize I was standing."

"Honestly, woman, you can't hold your drink. Typical woke, liberal-assed hippie," O'Brian muttered. "Knew you'd be hard work."

"Ha!" Eden clapped him on the chest. "You love me. Y'know, you remind me of this kick-ass anti-nukes protester from Budapest…"

For the next hour, Eden regaled the group with tall tales from her protester life, sparking ample laughter. She heard a few stories in return, snippets about what her new friends had seen and done. Many had lived remarkable lives all over the world.

A manicured man in a beautiful suit leaned in. Eden didn't know him. He barely spoke to the group, just sipped his wine and listened. Eden suspected he was "family."

"Tell us about Wingapo," he said, his long-lashed eyes warm and interested.

His colleague, a raven-haired, amply curved woman in an expensive skirt-suit, leaned in as well. "Yes, Eden, you *must*." Her voice was faintly Indian accented, rich and inviting, but she seemed far too practiced. Almost…too charming.

Ah! This had to be the pair from the Espionage floor.

Eden had outsourced the job of running The Fix membership and updates to Daphne after Tilly had sat her down and explained how she'd breached office email protocol in about fifteen different ways. Yesterday Daphne had told Eden in a breathless tone that two "Espionagers" had just joined The Fix. "And," the office manager concluded, sounding highly suspicious, "they never join *anything*."

"You want to know about my hometown?" Eden asked the man in confusion.

"No," the woman purred, "my colleague wants to know *how* you brought down its mayor."

"Who said I did?"

"People talk," she said, "even though the powers that be would have you believe there's no communication between floors. We know that was your assignment. And since Wingapo's mayor is now Ronald Boone, we know you were successful."

The table had fallen silent. All eyes fixed on Eden.

"Am I *allowed* to talk about it?" It was hard to keep a clear head right now.

"Not outside the office, no," the elegant man said. "We've all signed NDAs, though. No one here will tell a soul."

Eden glanced at O'Brian. As the most senior member of The Fixers in attendance, he'd know if she was allowed to share. He gave her a small grunt of affirmation, then added, "No client names."

Of course. She wouldn't have divulged that anyway.

Eden launched in. She made the story more exciting than it was as she outlined the scavenger hunt, clue by clue. Before long, everyone sat engrossed as Eden spun her tale. She was at clue number six when the Espionage woman murmured, "It's a zodiac hunt, isn't it? That's your theme. How clever."

Eden gave her an impressed look. "Yes."

All the others groaned at not having worked it out.

Eden grinned and finished the story. That earned a smattering of delighted applause and cheers.

"Well, don't leave it there," O'Brian declared. "Who was behind the Bubba Bros PAC?"

That launched a chorus of debate.

"No one knows," Eden eventually said. "I asked a well-connected friend to find out, but he came up empty. Guess we'll never know."

"But it's obvious," the Espionage woman said. "Is it not?"

Eden blinked. "What do you mean?"

The woman glanced at everyone else who had gone silent. "You all see it, don't you?" She received blank stares. Then she looked at her colleague. "Liam?"

He nodded. "Yes. I see it." He reached for his phone. "I can probably confirm it with polling data. Meanwhile, why don't you tell them, Mia?"

Liam and Mia. Eden filed the spies' names away.

"I will." The woman looked at Eden. "In exchange for something I want to know." A small smile curled the edges of her lips. "I promise it's nothing difficult."

"Oh?" Eden wondered what on earth she knew that this clever woman didn't know already.

"Tell us: How did you get our illustrious leader to part with exclusive access to her coffee machine?" Mia asked. "Answer that and I'll reveal who's behind the PAC."

"You first," Eden grinned.

"All right. It occurred to me your arrival in town didn't go unnoticed," Mia began, her sensuous voice captivating. "Anyone who knew of your past, disrupting Wilson's ambitions, would have been aware you'd try again. Someone smart and devious would also be opportunistic. When that tacky ad came out, the mayor saw its potential immediately. She set up her own PAC to make it go viral and attack herself, to ensure no matter what you came up with, she'd get a sympathy vote. She used Bubba Leighton's misogyny to capture the women's vote."

"No," Eden said, "that doesn't track. She sent my dad to find out if I was behind the PAC. He said she was furious."

"My dear," Mia said, "the mayor is ruthless, as evidenced by how she tried to use your own father against you. He was a distraction. She sent him in to make it seem as if she were not responsible for the PAC. The worst outcome possible would be you working it out and making it known she was calling *herself* a cunt."

Silence fell. *Well, shit.* That *did* sound like Francine. The former mayor's boldness and ambition were next-level.

"It was an insurance policy; ultimately ineffective, but it was a good try," Mia finished. "I'd have thought of that myself if I were her." She glanced at Liam. "Well?"

"Poll numbers, before and after the PAC ads, confirm Wilson got an additional swing from women voters of twenty-two percent. It would have been enough except data shows that after the final scorpion clue went up, she was sunk."

Mia smiled. "It was a clever preemptive strike. Wilson clearly hoped whatever you had planned wouldn't be as good as it was." She tilted her glass Eden's way. "And, my dear, it was indeed good."

"It was," Liam agreed. "If you ever want to leave the kiddie table that's POBUD and dive into the dark side, you know where to find us."

A couple of defamed POBUD staff howled at him over that dig.

Eden chuckled. "I don't really think that cloak and dagger stuff is for me, but thanks."

"Yet it's *already* you." Mia smiled beguilingly. "Anyway, pay up. How *did* you get Ms. Hastings to share her coffee machine with the hoi polloi?"

"Well," Eden began. "You won't like it."

"Oh?" Mia's eyes took on an interested gleam, as did everyone else's. Eden lowered her voice to a confidential whisper. "I *asked* her."

Mia frowned. "And?"

"What do you mean *and*?"

"What did you promise in return? Did you bribe her with something?" Her eyebrow twitched up in amusement. "Or...blackmail her?"

That caused roars of laughter.

"Bribery? Blackmail?" Eden snorted. "You people act like these machines cost a fortune. I simply *asked*. I caught her in a good mood. But if she'd said no, I'd have bought one for you all anyway. I've learned from my protester days that while an army runs on its stomach, creative types run on coffee."

Mia frowned. "But *how* did you ask? Was there pleading?"

"Why is it so difficult to believe that I asked and she said 'okay'?"

"Because it's our scary overlord," Daphne cut in. "I told you two months ago that she's terrifying. No one just goes up to Ms. Hastings and asks for things. That's just stupid."

"Why, thank you," Eden drawled. "My stupidity got you all coffee machine access, need I remind you?"

"And I, for one, worship at your stupid, unfashionable, vegan-leather-wearing feet," Daphne said. "Between our boss and *these* evil little reprobates, I declare you The Asshole Whisperer!" She lifted her glass and smirked at her colleagues amidst good-natured cheers and boos.

That seemed as good a time as any to call it a night. "Right, this Asshole Whisperer is heading home." Eden then turned to the Espionage pair. "Mia and Liam, it was great to meet you both."

"Likewise," Mia purred. "It was most *educational*. And I don't just mean for the Guatemalan coffee blends." The duo rose to go.

Daphne also stood, snatching up her Gucci purse. "I meant 'assholes' as a compliment," she told Eden too loudly. "Honestly. People are so touchy." She rolled her eyes.

"Daphne," Eden informed her cheerfully, "you're hilarious."

The group was now breaking up, heading for the door. Eden spun around, looking for the biggest person in the room.

"O'Brian…" She headed over to him. "Please tell your wife that it's a yes to dinner next week. In answer to her question, I'm a vegetarian—not a vegan, although Mom's still trying to lure me to it—and I'll bring her a fiddle-leaf fig in grateful thanks for a home-cooked dinner. It's so lovely she offered."

"Shall do." He beamed. "She's fierce excited to meet someone from work."

"Surely she's met others before me."

"No, of course not. D'ya think I want her knowin' about the kinds of folks I work with?" He chuckled. "At least with you, she'll think I work with sweetness and light."

"Thanks. I think?" Her brows knitted. "Am I being used for propaganda purposes by any chance?"

"Too right you are."

"You know, on this topic, there's something I have to know. And I'm asking you because you seem to be the only straight shooter around here." Eden paused. "Well, aside from Daphne, but she's more insulting than honest—actually, maybe dramatic's a better word. I never know if she's being factual or just amusing herself."

"Is there a point buried somewhere in there, Lawless?"

"Right. Sure." Eden laughed. "Why does everyone act like The Fixers is evil and filled with awful people? I've only seen it do good. And everyone I've met so far is lovely. Yet, there's this in-joke you all do. Like the note on the fridge, promising all these dire punishments for food theft. What gives? Why's it a running joke that everyone is violent and shitty?"

"Ah." O'Brian tugged his ear and glanced away. "You asked the boss that?"

"No. She never gives me straight answers either. That's why I'm asking you."

He shifted from foot to foot. "It's true it's a runnin' joke. And it's true we carry on like we do the most evil shite." O'Brian folded his arms. "But I'll tell you one thing for a fact: my job is security chief, and the boss has a standin' order for me to avoid paperwork at all costs."

"What does that mean?"

"It's her code for, 'Don't make me have to bail your ass out of jail cos you did somethin' illegal.'"

"Really?"

"Yes. She doesn't mind me walkin' up to the line, bein' all menacin' and so on. Which I know how to do pretty well, bein' a former boxer and all. I'm not goin' to lie to you, Lawless, I've done some time on the inside too. Stupid stuff. But Ms. Hastings rescued me from a bad spot once and has my loyalty. So, if she wants me makin' people shit-scared but not layin' a finger on 'em, then sure. I'll not be givin' her any paperwork."

"So you're saying everyone's all bark, no bite?" Eden exhaled in relief. "Good to know. I was starting to question my sanity for a moment. My assignments are all so benign, yet everyone's acting like we're doing the worst. It didn't make sense."

"I imagine it wouldn't," O'Brian murmured. "Look, I better get home. I've already asked my missus to pick me up. Can't keep her waiting." He fumbled around his pocket and pulled out a bunch of keys. Attached to the ring was a beautiful wood-carved snow leopard.

"Oh," Eden exclaimed. "I *love* snow leopards. And that's so gorgeous."

"Thank you. Worked pretty hard on it."

"Wait, *you* did this? You're a carver? That's so beautiful."

And then the most astonishing thing happened. Phelim O'Brian blushed. It was impossible to miss against his pasty-white skin. He scratched the back of his neck and muttered, "It's nothin', still learnin'..." but Eden knew she'd found the man's secret passion.

"You're very talented, Phelim," she told him sincerely. "Don't ever quit your carving."

He smiled then, and it seemed so odd on his asymmetrical face, with all its imperfections. But in his love for his hobby and appreciation of the compliment, Eden thought she'd never seen anyone look more handsome.

A thump against her shoulder jarred her into him. "Whoa, sorry," she gasped, straightening.

They both turned to see who'd hit her. It was a tall, impeccably dressed man in an Italian suit, with attractive features, a strong jaw, and a jagged scar bisecting his cheek.

O'Brian's eyes narrowed in recognition.

The stranger offered an insincere smile and lifted his hands. "Oh, my mistake." The words belied his radiating menace.

Eden, immediately anxious, leaned a little away from him.

O'Brian glowered at the interloper. "Got some fuckin' nerve showin' your face in here. You know this is The Club's bar. You're as welcome as a fart in a submarine."

"As eloquent as ever, Chewbacca," the man said. "Say *grrr* for me." He made a clawing motion.

"Who *are* you?" Eden asked.

His penetrating gaze swept over her with interest but not the sexual kind. It was as though he were pulling her apart, molecule by molecule, assessing. His gaze turned dismissive.

"Me? Oh, I'm…leaving." He smiled, his expression shuttered, and stalked to the exit.

The moment he was gone, Eden asked, "Who was that?"

"Trouble," O'Brian grumbled. "Used to work in my department. He knows better than to be here. It was no accident. He didn't just *happen* to be here."

"What's his name?"

"Baldoni." O'Brian glared as he said it.

Baldoni. The name pinged around her brain before it finally registered. Alberto Baldoni. Michelle's ex-husband.

Michelle's grandmother had told her about him and how dangerous he was. Hannah's dislike of him had been obvious. Eden understood why now. There was just something about his smug, cold face that made her want to punch it repeatedly.

O'Brian shook himself. "Best be gettin' home. I'd say home and *to bed*, but that Death Wish coffee you poured into me is really kickin' in. Sleep's goin' t'be a fantasy tonight. How'd you talk me into *three* cups of the stuff?" His eyes twinkled.

"By saying, 'No, O'Brian, that's insane, don't do it, you fool.'"

"Yep, sounds about right." He chuckled and headed to the door.

She followed.

They passed through the main bar and reached the exit with no sign of Baldoni.

"Hey, Lawless." O'Brian turned as he opened the door. "Want a lift home? My missus could drop you off somewhere if it's in the same direction."

"No need." As they stepped outside, Eden pointed at her van parked down the street. "I'm already home. One of the perks of Gloria. I live where I drive."

O'Brian took one look at the vehicle and laughed his ass off. "WhaddidIsay? Fuckin' crazy hippie. Goddamnit!" He clapped her cheerfully on the back, almost knocking her off her feet. "Shite! You're a fuckin' classic. Ya drive a *wokemobile*."

"Yeah, yeah. No insulting my ride. Go home, Riverdance, you're drunk."

"No, don't you call me that." He glowered playfully. "If that catches on, I'll have to kill ya, and that'd piss me off because you'd miss dinner, and my wife's lookin' forward to meetin' ya."

Chuckling, Eden said, "Fine. I promise, no Irish dancing nicknames for you. Night, Phelim."

"An excellent, life-enhancing decision." He grinned as she headed off.

A gust of cold air bit through her. Eden shoved her hands into her pockets. The action made the usual crinkle noise from all the receipts she kept in there, because sorting receipts was a *some-other-day* project.

Then she felt it: a small plastic object. She pulled it out. A USB thumb drive.

From Baldoni? He *had* bumped into her. Okay, what on earth had the former Fixers employee and ex-husband of the CEO given her? Dread mixed with burning curiosity swirled inside her.

It was followed by a bigger question: *Why me?*

Chapter 4
Paper Trail

THE MOMENT EDEN HAD SECURED herself inside Gloria, she booted up her laptop and plugged in the USB.

A lone *password* box appeared.

She frowned and exited the screen, searching for a back way in. After that, followed hours of frustration and failed workarounds. At three a.m., barely awake, she conceded defeat.

Trying to sleep failed, however. So, four hours later, Eden drove to Colin's place and begged him to tackle it. Aggie's long-suffering not-boyfriend had forgotten more about computers than she had ever known.

After poking at the thumb drive for a while, Colin gave her an apologetic look and ran up the white flag. "That's got more encryption on it than the CIA's network. Your only option is knowing the password. Sorry, I have to get to work."

Eden dragged her exhausted self into work thirty minutes later. She offered a wan wave at Tyson, hid her wince at his over-bright greeting, and almost nodded off waiting for the elevator.

It finally occurred to her, after her first cup of coffee, that she was wasting a valuable resource. Surely The Fixers' in-house geeks would be the best of the best?

She headed down to Cybersecurity. Snakepit brightened at the sight of her. Literally. His cheeks turned a rosy red as he waved her over to his desk.

Eden grinned. "Hey, Snakepit." She slid the USB stick across to him. "So, I—"

"Oh!" he said in surprise. "It was for you?"

Her tired brain tried to decipher his words. "For me?"

"Yeah." He nodded. "When I was told to back up a bunch of files, I wondered who it was for. Now I know." He glanced at the drive, then back to Eden.

"Oh, yep," Eden agreed, not wanting to tip him off that there was no way she was the authorized recipient. "I'm here because I'm having a little trouble getting in."

"You didn't get the password?"

"Was it, um, separate?"

"It's usually written down and supplied with the drive. Not much point putting it in a file *on* the drive, is it? What's the point of encrypting it, hey?" He laughed.

Written. She remembered the crinkling noise when she'd put her hands in her jacket pockets. What if the password had been in there too amid all her old receipts?

"I'm not allowed to give anyone our files without them being encrypted up to their eyeballs," Snakepit continued. "Even though it's authorized that you got them, I still have to have the files locked down; password only."

"Right." She smiled. "Of course."

"If you didn't get the password, just ask for it again from the employee who supplied you the thumb drive." He looked a bit uncertain. "I'm not allowed to give it out myself for security reasons. Sorry."

"No, of course." Eden inhaled. "Thanks anyway. I'll just ask for the password again." She made to go.

"Um, thanks for The Fix club. I really like the—" he gazed at her. "Coffees."

"I'm glad," Eden said, ignoring his blush. "I'll see you next Thursday, then!"

He nodded hard. "Hells yeah."

Eden headed to the ground floor, mind tumbling. Based on Snakepit's clues, the thumb drive must contain Fixers files. An authorized employee had ordered him to create them, and somehow the files had ended up in the hands of Alberto Baldoni, an ex-Fixers employee. But how? And why was Baldoni giving them to her?

Eden raced to Gloria and flung her clothes around looking for last night's jacket. Her hand fell onto the black vegan leather, and she yanked it out. She rummaged through the pockets and pulled out the scraps of paper. Receipts galore, a shopping list, a theater stub from six months ago, and... *a handwritten password*. Not written by Snakepit, because she knew his illegible scrawl, and this was actually neat.

Eden booted up her laptop, shoved the drive in, and entered the password. Her laptop screen turned blank.

For one horrible moment, she thought it was a virus. But, no, Snakepit had said he'd made this for work.

VERIFYING

The word jumped on the screen. Okay, that was promising.

Finally a new screen appeared with a bunch of folders that had numbers for names. Dates? She clicked one at random.

It was a case file. Her mouth fell slightly open as she read. The Fixers had been tasked with artificially inflating the price of a new cancer wonder drug to ensure a pharmaceutical executive got promoted.

Eden googled the drug. Its price had jumped a thousand percent overnight and demand had skyrocketed when its reputation was cemented as a miracle treatment.

Her stomach turned. How disgusting.

Eden randomly picked other folders, absorbing the contents with growing revulsion. The Fixers' reach was astonishing: all fields, most nations, no job apparently too big or small when it came to the rich and powerful.

She recognized hundreds of client names. Most used The Fixers to bury secrets or become more powerful by harming someone else. One case stood out as having only recently happened. It involved a senator's husband committing statutory rape on a young male volunteer—in plain view of the office security cameras. The Fixers had been tasked with burying the husband's indiscretions to further his wife's White House ambitions. At the bottom of the file was a line: *Caseworker: J. Jennings. Supervisor: M. Hastings.* So not only weren't The Fixers the good guys, but Michelle was up to her neck in dirt.

And surely that was the case that had rattled her—about the older man taking advantage of his young lover? At least Michelle was capable of horror over what she did but, still. The case was sickening. All of them were.

I helped them. I. Helped. Them.

Eden was about to exit the drive when she noticed one folder had letters, not dates, in the file name. It also had a more recent date stamp compared to the others. Had someone added it after getting the drive from Snakepit?

Opening it, Eden found a business transaction: the purchase of an apartment for The Fixers' CEO.

Eden blinked. Michelle lived in a *twenty-million-dollar* luxury apartment overlooking the Potomac River. She looked up the address and found a photo of it. Not far from the Watergate Hotel. Like attracted like when it came to vipers' nests, it seemed.

Michelle's building had a low, wide edifice that was beautifully designed, with architecturally stunning chrome and glass balconies.

The Fixers' board had bought the apartment for Michelle four years ago. *Four* years ago. Eden slumped at what that meant.

Michelle oversaw everything The Fixers did. Every single shitty, underhanded, immoral case was on *her* watch. She greenlit them all, and some were supervised personally. She'd had been CEO for nine years. That meant her apartment wasn't some perk she'd received as part of her promotion. The gift was too recent for that. It meant this was a performance bonus; something she'd earned for being good at her job.

Eden stared at the ostentatious address. Wow. Michelle Hastings was apparently *excellent* at being evil.

Eden couldn't be sure how long she sat in her van. Long enough that her phone rang a few times. Daphne. Then Ottilie. Then Michelle.

All those people. Those funny, smart, charming people she'd toasted the night away with had done truly terrible things. No wonder it was a running joke how bad they were. Eden was the idiot who'd had no clue. Maybe they'd all been laughing at her the whole time.

Yet the jobs Eden had been assigned had all been good. That had to be deliberate. Michelle and Ottilie had been playing her so she never knew what was really going on. Fury coursed through her. *I'm a sap!*

To what end, though? Why hire her at all?

Michelle had claimed it was because Eden was creative and clever. Well, from what she'd just read, there were forty-seven other people in her building who were far more creative and cleverer and who didn't have their hands tied by pesky ethical concerns. Not to mention hundreds more on freelance contracts. This made no sense.

Should she consider the source? Alberto Baldoni obviously had an axe to grind with his ex-wife. O'Brian had said Baldoni used to work in his department. The man's specialty, therefore, had to be in physical security work, not computers. Even Colin hadn't been able to get into the files, and he was a legend at computers. So, it stood to reason the files she'd received had been unaltered by Baldoni.

Snakepit had been ordered to produce the USB backup. Who by?

Her gaze fell on the slip of paper with the password. She studied it again. The handwriting seemed familiar, now she really looked at it. Something pinged at the back of her brain as she studied the cursive writing, but try as she might, the answer didn't materialize.

Eden's brain was too tired for this.

Betrayal suddenly swamped her at the reminder of how much she'd been enjoying spending time with Michelle. Their coffees were the highlight of her day. Michelle always injected something more into the conversation—acerbic observations that were clever and amusing, that felt like they were just for Eden.

Her knowledge, intelligence, and experiences were intoxicating to unearth. Eden had been delighted to be the recipient. She'd told Michelle more than once that she loved all her stories.

Each time Michelle had looked lost for words. As if she hadn't realized she'd shared a story. Then, usually, while looking confused, she'd order Eden out of her office and tell her to do some work.

Eden always laughed and did as ordered. Their interactions had felt sweet and genuine, as if they'd had a connection. Eden had been transfixed by how unusual and unexpected Michelle was. Unpredictable and on the edge of unknowable. How true *that* had been.

Couldn't she have warned me? About who and what she was? About what The Fixers do?

Of course she couldn't. If Michelle had warned her, Eden wouldn't have set foot inside the building. It's why she had lied by omission, using Eden's assumptions.

What of O'Brian? She'd thought he was a straight shooter. He'd known, hadn't he? When she'd asked him so naively the previous night about the running joke at The Fixers. "There's everyone acting like we're doing the worst and it didn't make sense," she'd told him.

"I imagine it wouldn't."

I imagine it wouldn't. Because it didn't make sense unless you knew the truth. How cleverly he'd parsed his words without outright lying. Eden was a fool.

Michelle was the architect of all this. The schemes, the cons. The hacks. The spying. And the bribes. So, so many bribes.

The USB drive only contained nineteen cases. That was a drop in the ocean for an organization that had been running for decades. How many more injustices had The Fixers perpetrated? Were they even worse than this?

What do I do now?

Quickly, Eden ran through her options. One: Resign. Good choice. Like hell she wanted to return to that building ever again. She definitely didn't want to help them do a damn thing now.

Two: Fight. Either stay on and work out how to hurt them or resign and hurt them. But fight them somehow.

Three: Do nothing when emotional. Not to mention when exhausted.

That one. Eden ran a shaky hand across her face. Her brain was a fried mess. She should call in sick and take the day—along with the weekend, since it was Friday—to examine her options.

Except, the handwriting on that password niggled her. She felt sure if she was at her desk, the answer might come to her.

Decided, she forced herself out of her van and headed back to the building, the thumb drive and password safely in her pocket.

How normal everyone looked. Eden's gaze followed colleagues, seeing them with new eyes as she walked to her desk. People smiled at her, as if they weren't doing despicable things.

Hadn't Daphne dubbed her the Asshole Whisperer last night? That tracked. In fact, Daphne had been the only one telling her the unvarnished truth from the moment she started here.

"Hey," Daphne called. "Where'd you get to? Ms. Hastings wants to see you."

"Yeah," Eden muttered, her mood darkening.

Probably has more lies to spin me. Oh, that's right, Daphne had also given her the head-up on Michelle. *Alpha villain. Whom all her evil henchpeople are afraid of.*

Then there was the fridge notice! Everyone had openly admitted their evil specialty for all to see! From garroting and blackmail to doxing.

And what had Daphne said when Eden joked The Fixers' staff seemed "creative but violent"? She'd *agreed*.

"Eden?" Daphne frowned as she passed. "You okay?"

"Sure," she lied.

"Hangover, huh?" Daphne rolled her eyes. "You're just too sweet to hold your booze. You look like shit."

"Shit," she repeated morosely. "No one's perfect."

"Especially not around here!" Daphne snorted.

Again with the truth telling. The woman was a freaking billboard for the truth, and Eden had never noticed.

"You got that right," Eden said. And, because that sounded mean, she attempted a smile.

"Sit for a minute," Daphne called. "I'll find you a hair of the dog. It'll get you back on your feet."

"No, thanks." Eden dreaded to think what sort of cure someone around here would invent. Probably had six kinds of toxins in it.

"Suit yourself. Suffer in silence. I'll put an Advil on your desk anyway." Daphne's tone was compassionate, as if she was decent and thoughtful and not the gatekeeper for an *actual evil organization.*

Eden continued on autopilot to her desk and sat.

She wondered why Michelle wanted to see her. Maybe she'd found a new assignment for her. Like channeling money to an orphanage in some remote village. Because that sounded un-evil, didn't it? Were the good deeds something she could point to and say, "See, we do good?" Or was it just to distract her? Either way, the joke was on Eden.

She flicked quickly through her paperwork, trying to find anything handwritten. She ruled out Daphne first.

Michelle's messages were all typed emails. Then Eden remembered the envelope her contract had been in—Michelle had scribbled her Skype username on it. She closed her eyes and pictured the handwriting. Squishy. Slanted.

No match. Unsurprisingly.

Eden resumed rummaging. Then she saw it. No wonder the writing had pinged something in the back of her head. It actually had the word *password* written on it, beside *login*. From Ottilie, on the first day on the job.

She pulled out the scrap from her pocket and compared it to Ottilie's version. Identical.

What the hell? Ottilie seemed so loyal to The Fixers. She was efficient, kind, and radiated a grandmotherly vibe. The woman was so gentle, she didn't even want to make waves when Michelle had misnamed her for *nine years.*

So why would she give such damning information to Eden? Maybe someone had stolen it from her?

Eden stared at the two identically written "passwords" for so long that her brain ached. She sat through Daphne stopping by, sliding an Advil and water onto her desk, telling her she looked like a "checked-out zombie, not even one of the cool ones," and leaving. She sat through her phone ringing twice.

An hour later, she caught sight of Ottilie walking her way. Eden's gaze scoured her, desperate to find answers from the sight of the unassuming woman.

Under the scrutiny, Ottilie paused in her stride. As their eyes locked, the older woman's expression shifted from mild to sharp.

Eden lifted the USB drive into her sight line. Ottilie's gaze turned to flint, and she pointed to the elevator.

With a nod of agreement, Eden shoved the drive deep into her pocket, grabbed her passwords, and went to join her.

They were sitting in a small coffee shop close to work. Ottilie sipped a tea, Eden a coffee. They still hadn't spoken, aside from giving their orders.

Eden glanced at the tea. "I thought you liked coffee." Ottilie had been at the inaugural Fix meeting, after all.

"No."

"Oh."

"How did you know?" Ottilie asked curiously.

Eden appreciated she hadn't made up some lie to cover herself. She reached into her pocket and slid the matching passwords onto the table.

"Ah." Ottilie's neutral expression was impenetrable.

"Why?" Eden asked.

Her eyebrows lifted. "Isn't it obvious?"

"Are you trying to bring down Michelle? Given what I do for a living, maybe you want me to expose her for what she does while keeping your own hands clean?"

"Goodness no!" Ottilie's eyes widened in shock. "Ms. Hastings has my support. Besides, most of the cases on that drive happened before she was CEO."

"Then why?"

"I want you to quit."

"Quit." Eden blinked.

"Yes. Could you do it sooner rather than later?" Ottilie clasped her fingers in front of herself, gaze earnest.

Eden frowned. "I didn't realize you disliked me. I actually liked you a whole lot. But you hate me enough to want me gone?"

"I don't dislike you," Ottilie said. "I dislike the baggage you come with. I suspect it's not even *possible* to dislike you, judging by your stealthy pandafication of our entire building in only two months."

"My *what*?"

Ottilie's eyes held an amused glint. "Ms. Hastings calls you a panda. Your imprint is now all over the building, from the plants to the coffee club, to the fact O'Brian tolerates you—and he tolerates very few. Ergo: the pandafication of our office."

"Why panda? Does she think I'm slow, simple, and hairy?" Eden asked, mystified.

"She thinks you're innocent, hapless, and lacking a conniving bone in your body. An endangered species around DC."

Eden stared. Apparently she'd failed some cynical standard The Fixers preferred in its employees. Why on earth had Michelle hired her if that was her true feeling?

"And *cute*." Ottilie pursed her lips at the word. "Look, clearly you're not disagreeable, unlike most of our employees, but you're making my life impossible. So, yes, the files were slipped to you so you'd see who you're really working for and want to quit. I even personally included something on the apartment our CEO owns in case you were part of that 'destroy the rich' crowd."

"Wait, how am I making your life impossible?" Eden asked, lost.

"I'm sixty-four years old, Ms. Lawless. I only have a year until retirement. I have been looking forward to it for some time. Winding down the clock. What I don't want in the last year of my working life is chaos. And you, sweet summer child, are nothing but a chaos agent."

"How do you figure?"

"My job used to be so simple." Ottilie sighed. "I had no friction or problems with anyone that I couldn't manage. Then you come along. Suddenly, I'm expected to find you *not-evil* jobs. However, this invented busywork must not in any way tip you off as to the truth of what we do. I have to share enough of your mission to make you productive, but not so much that you learn the true objective, and not so little you can't complete the assignment."

Eden's mouth fell open. "You're kidding."

"Your first case, that billionaire? He was *supposed* to have his donations leaked, but you were a little too effective at hiding them. I had to run around and *creatively account* for the millions we had to swallow on that job in such a way that Ms. Hastings wouldn't be forced to answer to the board for the loss."

"Oh." Eden's mind reeled. Suddenly it all made sense. As if *Hank Brewer* would ever decide to become charitable after decades screwing over everyone and everything.

"Jason, the charity walker? His father wanted us to scare the daylights out of the young man, not furnish Jason with an expert to help him do it!"

"Why?" Eden asked, shocked. "Why wouldn't he want his son to succeed?"

"The father ran up a gambling debt but couldn't ask for his extremely large GoFundMe donation back without admitting his problem or damaging his relationship with his son. If the walk was canceled, the funds would have been returned to all donors."

"Oh no."

Ottilie gave her a grim look. "The hours of extra work dealing with you are annoying on their own. But now I'm forced to tiptoe around you and ensure others do as well. I was tasked with *suggesting* employees not tell you what we really do. You were to be kept in the dark."

Eden scowled.

"Ms. Silver, however, could not seem to remember to tone it down. But that didn't matter because you apparently took as a joke everything our forthright office manager said. Fortunately, the rest of the staff took the hint and avoided mentioning our company's methods or goals in your presence, as per Ms. Hastings' instructions."

So, Eden was definitely the office joke. She went cold.

"What made everything worse was you wouldn't contain yourself to one floor like everyone else. No, you decided to magnify your presence with your company-wide emails and that coffee club." Ottilie huffed.

"Now I was expected to run around and ensure no one in the *entire building* gave away our core objectives."

Eden muttered: "That must have seemed weird to everyone."

"More than that." Ottilie's lips drew into a sharp line. "The Espionage team became *so* fascinated by this new edict that they actually joined your coffee club just to meet you and find out what made you unique."

Humiliation flooded her. Well, that explained it.

Ottilie looked exasperated. "That was the final straw. Managing you is almost a full-time job. So I ordered a selective files backup from Cybersecurity and called in Alberto to deliver the drive. He doesn't know what's on it, but all he had to hear was getting it to you would annoy his ex."

"And your hands would be clean," Eden concluded.

"Yes. I assumed you'd never tie the drive to me."

"Sorry to disappoint."

"That *was* an unexpected wrinkle." Ottilie took a sip of tea. "You've always been hard to control. To be fair, it's not entirely your fault. Ms. Hastings is the one adding to my workload. The way she treats you as a special case is so frustrating."

"Special case? You mean treating me like a mushroom—kept in the dark." Eden glared.

Ottilie snorted softly. "That's not what I meant. You're as bad as she is. Denial runs deep, clearly. Honestly, in any other circumstance, it might even be sweet, the two of you circling each other like clueless idiots. However, as I said at the start, I just want an easy final year before retirement. That's not too much to expect, surely?"

Circling? Denial? Sweet? It almost sounded like she thought Michelle and Eden were...No! "Michelle barely even notices I exist except when I bring her a coffee!"

"My ever-expanding workload says otherwise. That and the fact I have to step around your precious plants all day. Trust me, that's not something that's ever happened before: Ms. Hastings acceding to the whims of an underling spreading their hobby all across the building. Or, hobbies, if you include the coffee club. She cares about your wishes in ways she does no one else. So, Ms. Lawless, please, could you resign so I can go about my business in peace? I'll even have her write you a lovely reference, if that's what you want?"

Eden's head hurt. "How can she possibly care about me or anyone? She's a *villain*."

Ottilie snorted. "There'd be a lot more single entrepreneurs, media manipulators, and politicians if that were true."

"I mean...why would someone like *her* have any interest in me?"

"Why, because you're *so* good and pure?" Ottilie's eyebrow lifted.

"Of course not." Eden scowled. "Come on. Why would anyone who does what she does have any...romantic...interest in someone who thinks the opposite?"

"My dear, that's what makes it so, so painful." Ottilie sighed deeply. "The heart wants what it wants even when it's baffling. And even though Ms. Hastings has yet to even realize what's happening under her nose, it's easy for me to see it because I know her so well. I went through all the drama about Ayers too. I've seen it all before."

"Ayers? What's that?"

"*Catherine* Ayers?"

"The journalist?" Eden recalled the infamous woman whose career had blown up in DC about a decade ago. "Didn't she end up doing a gossip column in LA or something?"

"Yes. Did you never wonder why?"

Eden tried to remember the case. It had been on all the news channels. "She got a big story wrong, I think?"

"A Fixers hit was put on her career. Ms. Hastings, who was back then a rising star at our organization, had to bring her down so Ayers wouldn't write about things the client didn't like."

"How did she do it?" Eden asked.

"Seduced her until Ayers trusted her implicitly. Then Ms. Hastings fed her a false news story to report on, implicating many powerful men. When it emerged that the story was fake, it ruined Ayers."

Horror closed Eden's throat. Michelle had used someone's affection for her to destroy them?

"Now, what happened next is what's interesting. At least, to me." Ottilie regarded her thoughtfully. "Her husband, Mr. Baldoni, whom you met last night, was jealous and enraged. He claimed Michelle had fallen in love with her target. He spread that all over the office. There's no greater slur in our organization than to be seen as soft or weak."

Eden inhaled. "*Did* Michelle love her?"

"She put those rumors to rest in a most cruel way: Ms. Hastings ghosted Ayers and laughed about it. It was so cold and calculating. The office conclusion was that no one who loved someone could do that, therefore Mr. Baldoni was just bitter and making up malicious gossip. Shortly afterwards, Ms. Hastings was promoted to CEO."

"Michelle used Ayers to get promoted?" Eden's stomach roiled. "How despicable."

"That's the prevailing tale."

"Why do you say that? Don't you believe it?"

"I know Ms. Hastings better than anyone, and I wonder if Mr. Baldoni had a point. It's possible she did love the reporter."

"Then that makes her worse!" Eden's voice rose in dismay. "It's one thing to hurt someone you don't care about. It's far worse to love them and do it anyway."

"It is, isn't it?" Ottilie studied her tea mug. "And that's where she earned her terrible reputation around the building—because either way she was needlessly cruel. She crossed lines no one else would have and didn't seem to care."

Eden felt even sicker. "What happened with Alberto? He obviously no longer works in our building."

"Divorce came first. It took some time before Ms. Hastings got him out the door at work too. You see, all hirings and firings must have board approval, so she couldn't just toss him out on the grounds he'd tried to humiliate her. She had to prove to the board he was also incompetent."

"So, my hiring was board-approved too?"

"You're a special case. *Naturally.*" Ottilie rolled her eyes. "Our CEO slid you into a probationary category. If you'd lasted three months here, then Ms. Hastings would have put an argument to the board to hire you permanently. That's another reason I acted when I did; I don't want you permanently hired, and you've been getting closer to the three-month mark." She paused. "It is rare to do a backdoor, probationary hire, but Ms. Hastings knew the board would say no if you hadn't been trialed first. You don't fit our criteria."

"I don't?"

"Your credentials are not flattering. Your humanitarian causes would make you a high risk. You're literally too good for us." Ottilie's tone turned faintly taunting. "Isn't that right, Ms. Lawless?"

"I never said that!"

"But you did. It's in your every look and tone. You're also much better than Ms. Hastings, who is terribly wicked," Ottilie mocked. "Correct?"

Eden clamped her mouth shut. No argument.

"So, that's everything." Ottilie finished her tea. "Shall I expect your resignation by day's end?"

"I have to think about this." Eden's brain was too full. It was too much.

Her mind jumped between Michelle's cruelty and the revelation her lover had been a woman, to how Eden had been duped by her entire office, and the fact all her colleagues did terrible things. Shame at her foolishness, rinsed with red-hot anger, threatened to swamp her.

"What's there to think about?" Ottilie asked, sounding astounded. "You hate everything we stand for. You make extra work for me, which I can't abide. And your so-called *evil* boss has an inappropriate, sexual interest in you, even if she's deep in denial. Could this *be* a more toxic workplace? You don't belong here and you know it. Do everyone a favor, including yourself: Quit. Today."

Eden gave her a mutinous look. "Or I could stay," she said silkily. One thing she hated was being told what she *had* to do.

"Why? You'd be miserable. Angry." Ottilie leaned in, tone warning. "Just walk away. I'll even process a nice exit bonus for you. I have that authority."

"You're offering *me* money?"

"I'm merely covering all my bases. Just in case." Ottilie straightened. "I'll take your righteous outrage as a no."

Was that all anyone cared about? Money? What about justice? Not hurting people?

What would her mom do? Not stroll off into the sunset as if she hadn't just uncovered a corporate hellscape, that's for sure.

The worst part of all this was just how casually awful everyone involved was. They came into work each day, joking, and befriending her like what they did was nothing! All of them knowingly carried out evil and didn't even care. Well, fuck them all.

Ha, she thought sourly. Maybe that's exactly what she should do. She lifted her chin.

Ottilie gave her a wary look. "My dear, if you're planning some secret operation to bring us down, don't bother. A few have tried, all failed. Why? Because they signed a binding NDA, just as you did. Our thousand-dollar-an-hour lawyers will crush you if you even breathe too loudly about what you know. Those case files I gave you mean nothing without proof. They're just a list of times, names, places, assignments."

Eden leaned back and eyed the other woman. She gave a tiny smile. "Tell me something: How uncomfortable would it be for you if I told Michelle all about this?" She waved a finger between the two of them. "You leaking me files via her hated ex. Trying to get me to quit? There had to be a reason you didn't want me to know you were behind this. Would it mess with your sweet retirement plans, perhaps?"

Ottilie's eyes narrowed. "You wouldn't dare."

"No?" Eden regarded her. "Lots of people tell me that. They're always wrong."

"You were supposed to be disgusted by us and quit on the spot. Not stay to…play games." Ottilie shot Eden a disgruntled look, apparently for not sticking to the script. She gritted out: "What do you want?"

"For The Fixers not to exist." Ottilie's eyebrows shot up, and Eden waved her hand dismissively. "But I can see I'm not going to get that. However, I'll do you a deal. Whatever you see or hear about me in coming months, you *didn't* see or hear it."

Ottilie stared at her so hard, Eden could practically hear her cogs whirring. "What do you mean?"

"You will have no opinion on me at all to Michelle. You won't talk about me or drop thoughts into her head, at all, speculating about what I'm up to."

"What makes you think I do now?"

"You hate coffee but went to The Fix meeting. You're Michelle's eyes and ears."

Ottilie inclined her head.

"Right. So, if you see something you think I'm 'up to,' then from this moment on, you didn't. Even if she asks you outright, your answer is 'No idea, Ms. Hastings.' In return, this meeting and what led up to it, never happened."

"I don't know what you have planned, but need I point out that if you turn on your employer or try to reveal what we do, Ms. Hastings will come after you with everything in her arsenal. She has before. I don't just mean calling in the lawyers. No, she takes betrayal personally. She rains down punishment that's swift, harsh, and ongoing. You've met our staff; you know what they're capable of. They'll be sent after you. And for what? So you feel some good came out of the fact you grubbied yourself by working with us? To soothe your wounded pride? It's not worth it."

"Forget all that," Eden said, voice low and even. "Forget everything but what I'm proposing."

"Ms. Hastings *will* destroy you," Ottilie warned. "Don't think her feelings for you will stop her. She destroyed Ayers. That reporter was a wreck after Ms. Hastings was finished with her. It took the woman *years* to rebuild her career. Is that what you want? To be a wreck? You will be."

Eden didn't rise to the bait. "Let *me* worry about Michelle. If she wants to sic the lawyers on me or declare World War III, that's between her and me. I'm talking about *you*. Ottilie, I can see you're clever. Given you are the CEO's personal assistant, you are powerful, too—probably far more than anyone gives you credit for."

Surprise darted into her eyes, followed by agreement.

"I'm no fool, although goddess knows I feel like one today," Eden continued. "I don't want to fight another powerful woman as well as Michelle. All I'm asking is you stay out of it. *If* it becomes a fight. I might do nothing. I'm keeping my options open right now. But from this moment on, you're neutral as Switzerland."

"Only it isn't."

"What?" Eden blinked.

"Switzerland has never been neutral. The Swiss Government has been one of our biggest clients for decades when it comes to message massaging and manipulation. But for argument's sake, I'll take your intent on board." Ottilie gave her a skeptical look. "How would that work, you insisting I stay silent? You won't know what I'm saying in the office."

"Oh, don't think I won't find out. I've made some good friends and allies. For instance, The Espionage team and I have become quite close."

A good bluff never hurt. The advantage of the Espionage department's lack of socializing meant Ottilie was unlikely to be friendly enough with them to know that Eden was full of BS. "They tell me they know *everything* that goes on in our building. Probably have the place bugged in some clever way to get around the white noise. They seem capable of it. Tell me, do you think such equipment is possible?"

Her startled expression told Eden she knew for a fact it was. Sighing, Ottilie finally growled. "Switzerland, you say?"

"Yep."

"And if I agree, you'll quit today?"

"Yes."

"Then we have a deal."

They finished up in silence, paid separately, and walked back to the office together.

"You're smarter than I gave you credit for," Ottilie observed after a few minutes. "Not many people even stop to consider that I might be a threat too."

"PAs always are. They know where the bodies are buried. And who buried them."

"True."

"I *really* hope we're talking about metaphorical bodies here," Eden said.

Ottilie smirked.

"Does it bother you?" Eden asked quietly, as they waited to cross a busy street. "What you do? Aren't you a villain along with your boss? Accessory to evil?"

Ottilie gave a faint snort of laughter. "Oh dear. Just when I think you might actually be impressive, you revert to this juvenile nonsense again. You're so binary, aren't you? Everyone's *good* or *evil*. Who in this world actually uses the word *villain* to discuss corporate maneuverings? No one's any *one* thing. Well, except to you."

Eden's jaw worked at Ottilie's characterization. It sounded far too close to what her father had warned her about. They were both wrong, though. Some people were so far gone that only *villain* fit. "Just answer the question."

"No, it doesn't bother me what I do. Because all I can see when I look around the office is the day I'll retire. And at that time, these people I put up with, the high-maintenance clients...*and* employees..." she shot Eden a look, "even the boss who has unintentionally wrongly named me for years, *all* of this will fade into the background while I have a beautiful, quiet life."

Eden digested that.

As the lights changed, Ottilie's eyes crinkled. "And in the end, that's all I've ever wanted."

Eden stabbed the Send key on the email to Michelle containing her resignation, blind copying Ottilie. The subject line was *Resignation—Effective immediately.*

She'd just risen to leave when the CEO strolled toward her from the elevator.

Speak of the devil. Literally.

Michelle's expression was its usual blank mask. For a split second, though, it dropped away, replaced by pleasure at the sight of Eden. Then it was gone.

Was *that* what Ottilie was talking about? How Michelle treated her differently? Eden's stomach lurched at the thought this would have meant everything to her a day ago. Now? It was all so wrong. Everything was.

"You're here at last," Michelle said, her voice low and smooth. "You missed my call, and I'd started to wonder if last night's events had claimed you as a victim too. I just passed O'Brian, who keeps clutching his head and looking ready to end it all." She offered a rare smile.

Eden nodded, unable to speak. How do you go from pleasantries to "Oh, by the way, I found out you're evil; shame on me for being so trusting. Also, check your inbox: I quit." She said nothing.

Michelle's sharp gaze took her in. "You all right?"

"Why wouldn't I be?"

"You look as though there's something foul smelling in here."

There is. "Tired, I guess. Last night ran late."

"Well," Michelle said thoughtfully, "don't make a habit of scheduling your Fix afterparty on weeknights. We need all our operatives on their game."

I'll bet. Eden's nostrils flared at being called an operative.

This time Michelle shot her a look of true concern. "No, really, what's wrong?"

"I think I do need an early night," Eden said. "I might be coming down with something."

"Do you require assistance?" Michelle asked. "I can send around our company's physician if you need a house call." Her lips ticked up. "Or *van* call."

"No. Thank you." Eden was appalled to discover tears in her eyes. *Oh, hell no. Not now!* But how depressing was it discovering a woman you liked, *really liked*, was the absolute worst?

Alarm filled Michelle's expression. She hesitated, then stepped in closer. Lowering her voice, gaze darting around as if to make sure there were no eavesdroppers, Michelle said, "Just send me the Benson file whenever it's done and go straight home. If you need anything, text me and I'll have someone drop it around."

Eden swallowed. "Thanks," she said thickly. "But no need. The Benson file is done. You'll have it soon." She stepped back, out of that unsafe space. Like hell she'd supply the Benson file. Who knew *what* its true purpose was?

Michelle's expression was pensive. "I don't care about the Benson file," she admitted. "I want you well. I…um…want all my staff at peak operating efficiency, of course."

Why does she have to look at me like that?

Michelle had been reinforcing their professional distance for months. *Now* she decided to show her human side? It was cracking Eden's equilibrium.

"Take off now," Michelle was suddenly saying. "Email me the file if you can, and if not, well, Monday is fine too."

Eden nodded and grabbed her things. For her own mental health, she didn't look back as she headed for the elevator. She passed Daphne at her desk.

"Hey! Headache any better? And where are you off to in a rush?"

"Michelle wants me to do a thing."

"Oh, right. And it's *Ms. Hastings*," Daphne declared so dramatically that it'd be funny if it wasn't the last time Eden would see her.

Instead, she just felt teary. She sniffled.

This was ridiculous, Eden thought as she pressed the Down button and waited. Except, the truth was, she was going to miss them all. From the clever, all-knowing Espionagers and blushing IT kid to the hilarious, arch receptionist and bombastic Irishman who could carve animals of such beauty, it was astounding.

But she'd especially miss Michelle. Who by now would be reading her resignation email.

Michelle…who is a villain.

Eden hardened her resolve. No, she'd been right the first time.

Fuck. Them. All.

Chapter 5
Just Being a Good Boss

Ordinarily, Michelle didn't concern herself with the well-being of her staff beyond ensuring the appropriate department paid their wages and medical benefits on time and as required.

Eden Lawless, therefore—the bubbly little burst of ridiculousness who'd burrowed herself into the office and refused to blend in—should not have been a special case.

But it was clear she was. Michelle shouldn't care, shouldn't notice, shouldn't a lot of things. However, she'd seen Lawless's expression and was gravely worried. The other woman had been holding back tears. Rage curled through Michelle at the thought someone had evoked that response.

Had something happened last night? That could be it. And if something had happened at a work function, even one held outside office hours, that fell under Michelle's purview, didn't it? Of course it did.

She'd ask O'Brian to fill her in, once he got over his hangover.

Or now. *Right now.* She snatched up her phone receiver.

O'Brian rallied manfully despite his sore head. "You wanted t' see me?"

"Did something happen to Lawless last night?" Michelle asked.

"Happen?" He peered at her. "Well, she got a bit cheerful. We all did."

"Aside from that?"

He slowly shook his head, then a flash of something crossed his face.

"What?" she demanded.

"Probably nothin'." He shifted uneasily. "A long, tall, piece of shit made an appearance. He crashed into her."

"A long, tall, piece..." *Oh.* O'Brian reserved that designation for only one person. "Alberto was there? He *hurt* her?"

I'll kill him.

"No. Bumped might a better word. She wasn't hurt. Then he insulted me, I insulted him, and he was gone."

"He didn't say anything to Lawless?"

O'Brian scratched his jaw as he thought. "I don't think so, no."

Michelle glared, hating the impreciseness of his answer. "Why was he there? He knows the Black Rabbit's a Fixers hangout. He's not welcome."

"He still has a few buddies around. Might have been catchin' up with one."

"I've warned our staff to stay away from him. He's been undermining us forever." *Well, me.*

"Yeah, but people think he's harmless..." He threw up his hands. "Anyway, I don't think last night had a lick to do with Eden."

Eden now, was it?

"Ah, Lawless," he corrected.

"You two seem close," she suggested silkily.

"We get on okay." He shifted. "I'm, ah, havin' her round for dinner with the missus when Shauna calms down over how late last night ran."

He was *what*?

O'Brian, Michelle knew for a fact, had never invited a single colleague home in his entire career at The Fixers. Not even his own deputy.

At her shocked look, he gave a faint laugh. "Yeah, I know it sounds ludicrous, but I like the kid. She's good, y'know? Hell, that's rare. And

I wouldn't want to take someone bad home to the missus. She might get a clue about what we're doin' here. Lawless doesn't even know, does she?"

No wonder Michelle had never been invited. Her stomach tightened at the reminder she was apparently seen as toxic by her favorite manager. "She is unaware, yes."

"We were all talkin' 'bout that last night, when Lawless went downstairs for drinks, and we think it'd be for the best if she never knows." He met her gaze. "We don't think she'd take it well. I reckon Tilly's right. She's been sayin' the same to us: keep a lid on it."

Exactly as Michelle had instructed her to do.

"And we…ah…agreed: we want her to stick around." His smile was sheepish.

"Well, of course you do," Michelle said snidely. "She's your provider of fancy coffee and free booze."

"No, boss, that's not it at all. We *like* her." His expression brooked no argument. "She needs protectin' from certain…ugly truths. And if there's one thing we're all good at, it's protectin' shit. Even the Espionage team agreed—and when have those creepy spooks ever agreed with us on anythin'?"

Surprise flooded her. "What on earth were they doing there?"

"The power of coffee?" O'Brian shrugged. "Or the power of Lawless. She's hard to say no to."

Impossible to say no to, more like. "The panda strikes again," Michelle muttered. "Sweet and clueless, so everyone wants to protect her—even the worst of the worst. Baffling."

"Pretty much." He chuckled. "Hey, I saw her wokemobile last night. That van she lives in? That's a helluva thing. I've no clue how someone like her wound up workin' here."

Don't remind me. Michelle gave him a dark look.

He scratched his chin. "So, anyway, to answer your question, nothin' happened last night that I know of that'd have upset Lawless. She was fine when we left. I kept an eye on her after we parted, to make sure she got in that van of hers okay. She did."

"All right. Thanks."

"So what's wrong with her?" O'Brian asked, sounding worried. "She okay?"

I wish I knew. Michelle's roaming gaze fell on her email inbox. And there, under Lawless, E, was the subject header: *Resignation—Effective Immediately.* A chill of dismay flooded her. *No.*

"What's wrong?" O'Brian asked.

"She just resigned."

"What?" He sprinted to Michelle's side of the desk, and they both stared at the email.

Ms. Hastings,

I am resigning, effective immediately. My time working for you was really interesting, but I need to get back to my protesting work. Besides, you'd be the first to agree I was never a good fit for office work.

Look after everyone.

Goodbye,

Eden Lawless

"She called me *Ms. Hastings*," Michelle said softly, feeling the words stab at her. She'd have been warmed in a different context. But this wasn't about respect. It felt…distancing.

"Yeah." O'Brian looked at her sideways. "What the hell?"

Look after everyone. That sounded nice as a platitude, except it felt strange coming from Lawless. If anything, Michelle would have expected something personal and inappropriate like, *Look after yourself.* Or: *Take care, Michelle.* Or: *I'll miss you.*

Her heart tightened at the last one. It was hard to know where the awful began and ended—the fact Lawless hadn't done her usual line crossing, or the fact she was gone.

Why had she gone? Surely not because she wasn't a "good fit" for office work. Hadn't she won over the entire staff by being herself? No one had commented on her lack of regard for rules or etiquette. They hadn't blamed Michelle for not keeping a tighter rein on her. It was like they understood you couldn't fight a force of nature.

Michelle slumped. *You didn't have to go. You do fit.* In her own eccentric way, she did. Everyone at the coffee club had agreed, hadn't they? They wanted to keep her. Wanted her to stay.

I want her to stay.

"Something's happened," Michelle said curtly. "Start over and tell me everything about last night that you left out the first time. No matter how small."

O'Brian screwed up his face in thought and then launched in.

Michelle listened for half an hour as he went over the minutia. Despite this being a specialty of hers—finding clues from mundane conversation—she couldn't see the answer. Whatever had set Lawless off didn't appear to have happened during the staff drinks.

Finally she held up her hand to stop him. "I can't see it. But now all I can wonder is if she *knows*."

"Yeah. I thought that too. But I can't work out how she found out about The Fixers between getting in her van last night and arrivin' at work this morning."

"Then if it's not that, it must be something else."

O'Brian shrugged. "Or maybe she really does want to get back to protestin'?"

"And not tell us all about it? All the pros and cons, and the people and projects she's missing? She's an open book, O'Brian. Does skipping all that sound like her?"

Confusion filled his face. "No."

No. Michelle waved her head of security out and then shot off a text to Lawless. It wasn't long, merely inquiring about her well-being.

She was just being a good boss, of course. Well, ex-boss now.

The text was ignored.

―――――⇢◇⇠―――――

Eden parked outside Aggie's. She was exhausted, pulled by the enormous weight of emotions overloading her, demanding attention. She couldn't think of where else to go and was dying to pick everything apart with a trusted ally. But the NDA still applied, and these were dangerous people she was dealing with. It wouldn't be safe for Aggie.

Her best friend, as always, flung open her front door, squealed, and raced to the van in welcome.

"Hey," Eden said tiredly. "Can I crash for a few days?"

"Is the Pope Catholic? Do slugs have four noses? Is Kevin the cutest guinea pig in existence?"

Eden smiled wanly. She'd look up that slug thing later. "Thanks."

"Edie, what's wrong?" Aggie started helpfully hauling her out of Gloria. "You look terrible. Are you sick? Why aren't you at work?"

"I quit." Well, that sounded a whole lot more real, didn't it? "Effective immediately."

Aggie opened her mouth, but Eden shook her head. "Not here."

When Aggie shut the front door behind them, Eden sagged onto the couch, feeling safer already.

"Right, spill."

Eden didn't know where to start. It was overwhelming sifting through what she could and couldn't say.

Aggie jumped in instead. "I thought you liked it there? Hot boss, smoking bank account, great medical and dental benefits. Your colleagues even loved your coffee club."

Eden willed herself not to cry. "My boss is ugly."

At Aggie's astonished expression, Eden added, "Inside."

"Okayyy." Aggie dropped to the couch beside her. "Why's Hot Boss suddenly ugly?"

"I can't tell you—legally—but it's scary, evil stuff they do there."

Aggie blinked in surprise. "I see. So what *can* you tell me?"

"Almost nothing," Eden said, voice flat. "Do you mind if I take a nap? I'm beat."

Aggie gave her a concerned look. "Of course. I'll get some pillows. Sleep as long as you want." She left.

"Thanks," Eden whispered to the air. She really wanted to curl into a ball and cry. Why did she feel so hollow and sad? She was pining over losing a woman she hadn't even known! How pathetic could you be?

Ottilie's comments about Michelle's affections played on her mind, but the woman was wrong. Michelle couldn't really care about her. If that were true, it meant she had a heart. And people with a heart didn't do what Michelle did for work. They didn't, for instance, seduce a reporter just to destroy them.

Eden could barely wrap her brain around the enormity of that cruelty. Who did that to another human being? How heartbroken Catherine Ayers must have been. To have felt loved and safe and happy with Michelle, only to discover it was all a lie.

Deep down, if Eden were being honest with herself, she'd wanted to have Michelle's attention and affection. What did it say about her that even now, she couldn't shake that craving?

Maybe what was worse was she hadn't even suspected the truth. She'd always thought she was good at reading people, and she'd spent more than four months getting to know Michelle, from daily Skype calls to coffees in her office. At most, she'd thought her former boss was closed off because she'd been deeply hurt at some point, but glimmers of a warmer side had been creeping through the cracks. Eden had felt special to be the one to catch glimpses of the real Michelle.

But that real, warm, wonderful Michelle didn't even exist. She was a fantasy in Eden's imagination. And still, *still*, even knowing that, Eden missed her already. The other, *not*-real, Michelle.

Way to go, Eden, you idiot. You just catfished yourself.

She cared for someone rotten to the core. Worse, Eden had helped her do her dirty work.

A small cry caught in her throat. Why did Michelle have to be like that? She'd made Eden feel like she was doing good. She didn't have to do that—make her feel so stupid.

She'd been laughing at her, hadn't she? How could she not? Maybe they all were. Even O'Brian, who'd sounded so genuine when he'd invited her to dinner. Guess he really *did* want someone too naive to give the game away to his wife about what he did at work. He was as cynical as Michelle.

I'm such a stupid idiot.

She was crying softly into her arms by the time Aggie returned.

"Oh, Edie," Aggie said sadly as she slid the pillow under Eden's head. "Want me to stay?"

"N-no."

"Okay, I'll be here if you want to talk. I'll just be in my office working, but interrupt anytime. I won't mind. We can talk about anything you like. Revenge plans. Swapping recipes. Kevin's Tinder short list. Whatever you want."

Aggie's supportiveness was the absolute best thing about her. Gratitude just made Eden's eyes leak more. "Sorry. I'm a mess."

Aggie shook her head. "I'll never understand why people apologize for having feelings. You're not a robot, you've been hurt—you get to cry now. Or rage if you want. You're allowed to *feel*. Don't be sorry."

"Thanks." Eden offered her a watery smile. "I think I'll just sleep now."

"Good plan."

When Eden woke hours later, it had gone dark. Aggie was rummaging around the kitchen twenty feet away.

"Wha…time is it?" she sat up and rubbed her eyes.

"Six. You were out all day." Aggie turned, holding a bag of corn chips. "Comfort nachos time."

Eden whimpered. "I'm not sure my stomach can face those tonight."

"Well, it's that or an expired can of soup—flavor unknown because the label came off last month. And I told myself I'd remember what was in there, but…gone." She made a whooshing motion. "Then, for something completely different, I kept forgetting to go shopping, and now, here we are. I'm a disgrace to my heritage. If Mom could see me now, failing in my hostly duties, she'd be so ashamed." Aggie grinned.

"I can't face food, so your honor is safe." Eden attempted a grin back. "Cook whatever. I don't care."

"All right. Hey, you should know I put your phone to charge in my room coz it was almost out of juice, and I thought you might need it. It's been blowing up with texts and missed calls."

"Not interested." Eden rolled over onto her side. "They can all go to hell."

"They?"

Eden scowled. "Ex-colleagues. Turns out I was a joke to them. Ha ha, let's laugh at the naïve activist blind to what's going on under her nose. You were right. I wasn't cut out for office work. Especially *that* office."

"Hon?" Aggie came over and crouched next to her. "I'm the first to tell the kids who call my helpline that not everything's always as it seems. Maybe you could talk to her? Or them?"

"No. They're evil." Tears pricked her eyes again. Even her nice co-workers were all in on it. Even sweet Tyson in the foyer probably knew.

"Every single person in an entire building is evil?" Aggie asked quietly.

"Yes."

"Wow. So, why'd they recruit you?"

Eden stared at her in utter confusion. "I seriously have no idea." She blinked back tears. "I wish they'd just left me alone, though. I'm not built for this."

"This?"

"Betrayal. Mockery. Pain." She thought about Michelle and sniffled. "My boss pretended to be someone decent and normal like anyone else. She pretended I mattered to her too, and it was all a lie."

"It feels awful getting lied to," Aggie said kindly. She snatched a few tissues from the box on the coffee table, handing them to Eden. "You know for a fact they set out to lie to you? It wasn't an accident?"

Eden scowled. "They knew. I found out today that not only did they know, but Michelle had her PA running all over the building ordering staff to lie to me."

"Ouch." Aggie slumped. "That seriously sucks."

"I'm done talking about this." Eden wrapped her arms around herself, as if that could push down the bleakness.

"Cool. So what's your next plan? In your post-corporate life?"

"I'll pretend the last four months never happened. I never returned to Wingapo. Never faced the mayor again. Never took an office job. Never worked for *her*."

"Never reconnected with your dad again," Aggie said gently. "Never had the money to pay off your student loan. Never had a crush on your fascinating boss."

"Crush?" Eden shook her head—hard. Appreciation, yes. *Crush*... sounded uncomfortably more than that.

"I'm not blind, Edie." Aggie's eyes radiated sympathy. "I've been watching you fall for her for a while now. She's all you talk about. You light up whenever she contacts you. You crumple when you two fight. She's been the center of your universe for months."

"No." Eden scowled.

"Denying it doesn't make it less true." The microwave dinged. "Eden Celeste Lawless, I'm your best friend. Best friends admit inconvenient truths to each other, even if they don't to themselves."

"*Really*," Eden snapped, hating how exposed she felt. "How *are* things with Colin?"

Her friend didn't look in the slightest bit aggrieved and simply rose and headed for the microwave. "I'll tell you what," Aggie said as she pulled her plate out. "You get a few days to wallow, but then we talk about this properly. On Sunday. We'll talk about it then."

"But..." Eden faded out when Aggie turned to face her, eyes determined.

Biting into her nachos and chewing for a moment, Aggie said thoughtfully, "Nice goo-to-crunch mix." She returned and offered her plate to Eden. "Sure you don't want some? Extra cheese cures *everything*."

"I'm not sure *that's* possible," Eden said miserably.

"Well, maybe just take the edge off, then." The plate did a little waggle under Eden's nose.

Eden shoved the pillow over her face. "I'm not there yet. All I feel are edges."

That evening, Michelle took to the balcony and gazed out at the stars she usually enjoyed with her grandmother, Hannah, beside her. It was that time of the year when her safta took off for a few months to Florida. Officially it was to catch up with her oldest friend, Rosemary; unofficially it gave Michelle her space.

Hannah had mastered texting...after a fashion. Michelle had gotten the gist, though: her safta was fine and happy and not missing Michelle at all.

Well, to be fair, she'd probably invented that last part.

Michelle sighed. Even though she craved alone time, now she had it, she missed her grandmother's constant presence. If she'd been here, Michelle would be tempted to ask her about Eden's mystifying disappearance. As it was, she had no one to talk to.

It was an odd feeling, a need for someone. That was new. Hell, she'd survived an entire marriage while remaining self-sufficient.

Her husband had been the same. Besides, Alberto, eternally away on security missions, was rarely around enough for her to tire of him. And yet, tire of him she had.

Michelle clutched her glass tightly. She sometimes wondered where and with whom she'd have ended up if the FBI hadn't recruited her in college where she'd been studying political science. She'd still have a relationship with her parents at least. Not this…eternal silence.

Michelle gave her gin a swirl, remembering when life hadn't been silent. It had felt full of possibilities back then, just before everything changed. Michelle had been at the FBI four years, a field agent capable of "extracting information from targets in social settings." Or, in layman's terms, a mixer at parties who could flirt and schmooze and relieve people of information before they realized they'd shared it.

One night a powerful target had worked out how she'd played him for information and sent one of his men to follow her outside. The assailant flattened Michelle against a wall. Suddenly, a sharp-featured man with cold, dark eyes had stepped from the shadows and neutralized him as a threat.

Her rescuer was a man with a special forces background who'd gone into private enterprise. Alberto Baldoni had been thrilling. Dangerous. She couldn't even fathom the depth of power he had. It was deeply attractive. Michelle felt so safe knowing he was by her side. She'd needed that feeling of security desperately back then, because she hadn't felt safe at work.

"It's just a body. An effective means to an end." Her boss's favorite line. He'd used it to convince Michelle to sleep with a bomb-building, neo-Nazi terrorist for information.

A newspaper photograph of the two of them having intimate drinks at a bar had alerted her family that she'd been palling around with a domestic terrorist.

At Thanksgiving, two months after the photo's publication, her father pulled her aside. "You were my little girl," he began, sounding bereft. "And you had to go and do that."

Michelle swallowed. *Of course* he'd know the truth. He had high enough security clearance to pull her file and investigate why she'd been with a neo-Nazi. And worse, exactly what role she was performing undercover within his terrorist cell. "Girlfriend" was nothing any father would want to see. "If it hadn't been me, it would have been someone else's little girl."

"You didn't have to volunteer, though. That's the real disgrace of it. Your ambition should have some limits."

"What?" Michelle gasped in disbelief. "I didn't *want* that assignment. I certainly never asked for it!"

"Michelle," her father said in an admonishing tone, dripping in condescension, "I know it's not edifying what you were asked to do, but don't tell me you didn't volunteer. Usually on assignments requiring sex to gain access, a prostitute is brought in. For an agent to be asked, it has to be a high-stakes case, needing skill sets beyond a civilian's abilities, and it *has* to be voluntary. The FBI can't just order agents to prostitute themselves." Her father folded his arms. "I know better."

"Well that's nice in theory, but it *wasn't* voluntary," Michelle gritted out. "My boss manipulated and emotionally blackmailed me about how many lives were on the line. He wore me down until I agreed. I hated every minute of it."

"He'd never do that," her father said sharply, eyes narrowing. "I can understand your embarrassment at being caught out like this, and, frankly, the FBI should have prevented that photo ever being published, but don't lie to me. I know Slater. He's a good man, decent. Excellent tactical mind, not emotional or illogical. He's even been agreeable when I've had to turn down funding for his pet project. He conceded we have to be pragmatic about our work. I can see no basis in fact for your claims that he manipulated you. That's just not who the man is."

Fury scorched Michelle. White lights went off behind her eyes, signaling the start of a migraine—the first she'd ever had.

"You're wrong." She squeezed out the words as a sick, sticky dread filled her. How could her father believe a scheming underling over his own daughter? "He's a snake and a bully. He ordered me into a terrorist's bed and there *wasn't even a bomb*!"

Irritation flooded her father's face. "He couldn't have known that!"

"He *should* have! His intel was laughable—those revolting little terrorists were never even remotely close to having the capacity to make a bomb. Your *decent man* took the easiest, laziest path—just throwing me in to find out—instead of protecting me. Or, hell, maybe it wasn't laziness at all, but payback for you not approving that pet project? He did tell me I had to be *pragmatic*!"

"That's absurd!"

"Is it? I don't know. All I know is I debased myself and went through hell for nothing! And you're standing there, taking his side while looking at me like I'm a cheap whore." Michelle's head pounded at the betrayal.

Her father straightened. "Well, I'd say about the only thing we agree on is that you debased yourself." He glowered. "The bottom line is that assignment *was* voluntary. *You* chose not to say no. Taking out your buyer's remorse and shame on your boss is irrational and unprofessional." He sighed. "And now, when I look at you, I can't unsee what you did. I can't even tell your mother—who's beside herself, as you well know—that you only screwed that evil bastard to get ahead at work. Although I doubt she'd react much better knowing the truth."

Silence fell. Long, awkward, and pained.

It was like being slapped out of the blue by someone you loved and trusted completely, then waiting for the sting to fade, knowing nothing would ever be the same again. How could it be?

Tears welled up, but Michelle squeezed her eyes shut to stop them. She wouldn't give her father the satisfaction of thinking he'd won something.

Finally, she asked acidly, "So where does that leave us? Given you can't even look at me anymore?"

"I…don't know." His face was a map of obstinance and pain.

Suddenly Michelle despised him. Not only didn't he believe her, it seemed that her worth as a daughter was only as deep as her "virtue" to him.

She shook her head, turned on her heel, and left.

That had been that. Polite, stilted meetings with her parents followed in the next few months. Those gradually turned into only calls, and then, eventually, nothing. Enter the silence into her life.

Alberto had been distracting for a time, especially helping her escape the FBI to The Fixers, but he never filled the space left by family. The void had stayed empty, quiet, and deep until Catherine Ayers had come along.

When Catherine kissed her out of the blue on their third meeting, Michelle had absolutely had no clue. The clever journalist who had DC in terror of her wit was a closeted lesbian? And she wanted *Michelle?* That had been rather convenient since it was mutual, and Michelle's assignment had been to get close to her.

She'd never felt anything as consuming for Alberto. Had he guessed? Probably. It explained his rage that persisted even nine years later. He still could be counted on to stir up trouble for Michelle whenever the opportunity presented.

Michelle took a deep sip of her drink, savoring the iciness of it sliding down her throat.

Sometimes in her mind's eye, when she wanted to torture herself more than usual, she watched it all play out again—the assignment, the affair, the destruction.

She had no doubt Catherine believed exploding her career had cost Michelle nothing. It had cost her everything, not just her marriage. Hell, Michelle didn't even need Alberto to feel safe by then. No, it had cost her herself. Her soul.

After that, Michelle hated herself a little more each day. She occasionally fantasized about turning back time and choosing differently. Picking Catherine over the job.

Those taunting dreams abruptly ended when news of Catherine's engagement and later marriage to Lauren King had reached her.

In some ways, that helped. Things had become simpler without the ridiculous fantasy of one day seeking out Catherine and repairing the damage—and maybe reconnecting in other ways. Michelle had the certainty now of knowing it would never happen.

That had made her even calmer. Icier. She was distilled more into the essence of who she was: cool, intellectual, sharp, and incapable of being ruffled. She was devoid of emotion. Empty. Silent.

Except for when she escaped into a rage room for release. Only then did she allow herself to fully feel every emotion she had.

But outside? Well, what *was* there to feel, anyway? She could certainly never be like Eden Lawless, whose emotional state, thoughts, and feelings broadcast to the whole room like CNN.

The reminder of Eden plummeted her mood. *Damn it.*

No, Michelle didn't need to feel. Besides, these days, she was used to the silence.

With that, she drained the rest of her drink and took herself to bed.

Chapter 6
A River's Course

Colin came over to hang out with Aggie on Sunday, which was a relief as it gave Eden some space without feeling the weight of questions left unanswered.

How could she answer Aggie when she didn't know herself what she felt, what her plans were, and how to deal with her inconvenient attachment to a woman who had betrayed her?

Eden vaguely listened to them discussing the short-short shortlist of Kevin's possible live-in buddies. They had to take Kevin somewhere for a compatibility test and make sure he liked his potential housemate. If one guinea pig didn't hide from or tackle the other, that meant they'd probably be fine with each other.

Humans were so much more complicated. Eden both wanted to tackle *and* hide from Michelle, which was the problem. She'd never dealt with someone like this before. Complicated people, manipulators who had layers and secrets, were a new experience. The worst part was she desperately missed Michelle. Her text, asking if Eden was okay, had sounded so worried and sad.

Eden had several missed calls from her too. Also some from O'Brian, Daphne, assorted members of the coffee club, and…Mia. The Espionage woman had texted her "concern that office rumors are true and you've faked your own death."

Well, that's tempting.

"Or you've just quit," Mia had continued. "Which would be a loss for us all." She actually sounded like she meant it. That was nice. Although Eden knew fishing when she saw it too. Apparently no one believed she had a burning urge to return to protesting.

Later in the afternoon, after Colin had left and Aggie was cleaning up in the kitchen, Eden's father surprised her with a call. He chatted about little things and then reminded her he loved her no matter what.

Which prompted her to burst into tears. She hung up before he could work out she was upset.

Aggie appeared, arms wrapping around her. "I'm sorry you're struggling. Hot bosses are the worst, clearly."

Eden laughed through her tears. "Gah, I'm a terrible friend." She sniffled. "All mopey. Dad says hello, by the way. Asked after Colin too."

"Nice he remembers us." Aggie lifted a surprised eyebrow. "Your old man's really sorted out his stuff, hey?"

"He's getting there. He'll never make up for everything—it's hard to forget all he's done. It's a long road."

"I don't think you'll ever forget, but maybe it'll hurt less as time passes. He's trying, though, right?"

"Yeah. He is."

"Besides, no one's perfect." Aggie's eyes crinkled. "Not even me."

Mom is.

Eden almost said that. She'd never seen her mother fail any moral challenge. She always did what was right. No doubt, no thought, she just *knew*. Suddenly that was all Eden wanted: clear direction. Absolute certainty on the right course.

"I'm..." Eden cleared her throat, "gonna call Mom."

Aggie's brows knitted into confusion. "Isn't she in the middle of the North Sea?"

"No, she got back on land last week."

"Say hi from me."

Eden headed into Aggie's office, closing the door behind her. It had been three months since they'd last spoken. Hopefully, her mom wasn't busy at...Eden mentally converted time zones...nine at night in London.

"Darling!" River answered. "What a nice surprise!"

"Mom? I can hardly hear you!"

"Oh, we're doing a march. Let me find somewhere quieter."

Of course! Why waste a perfectly good night when you could protest? Eden smiled and waited.

"Sorry about that. There's an odious MP who made some ignorant comments about women being best suited to staying in the kitchen, and we just had to do a march on his home."

"His home? I pity his poor neighbors."

"I pity his poor wife," her mother shot back. "Stuck with him in the fifties? And his neighbors will survive a night of shouting and bullhorns. That's what you get for living next to a sexist pig."

"Right." Eden was pretty sure that wasn't the neighbors' fault.

"Thanks for the donation! That was astonishing. I'm still working out what's worthy to use it on. So many people and causes need help. Do you have a preference?"

Oh, right. Eden had sent her mother most of the money from her Wingapo payout. She figured there'd always be something River could use it for to improve lives. "No preference. Whatever you think needs it most." Eden braced herself. "Mom, I have a question: If you uncovered a secret organization doing terrible things, what would you do?"

"Expose it, obviously. How's that even a question?"

"I mean the boss is someone I…" *Liked? No!* "Someone who would retaliate."

"Sounds like you're making the right kind of enemies," her mother said. "I'm *so* proud you're exposing the big boys."

"Well, I haven't yet."

"Why not?"

"I only just found out."

"And are you frightened?" River's tone became serious. "Afraid you might be hurt?"

"Physically? No."

"Then I don't see the issue. All you need is willpower. We have a duty not to overlook injustice just because it's inconvenient. You saw where that got your father."

"Speaking of Dad," Eden said, "I caught up with him a few months ago. He's stopped drinking. He's living with the Boones, running a shed for men, and teaching shop in school."

"Waste of a good medical degree," River grumbled. "Damn him! He could be working at Médecins Sans Frontières, making a difference. I'm sure the students of Wingapo High could cope without him."

Eden blinked. An alcoholic giving up drinking was not something to be dismissed lightly. Her father had been working hard. "But he's just getting back on his feet."

"He needs to think about more than just himself. We all do. The world is bigger than us, Eden Celeste. The world is all we have, and we must do everything we can, not just the bare minimum."

"It's a lot, Mom."

"That's why we have to *do* a lot. What's more important? Ask yourself that. Then you'll know what you have to do."

"I'm struggling with what's ahead. I'm dealing with powerful people. Senators and billionaires are on their books. This organization can easily destroy people in a lot of ways. They could shatter me if I expose them. I might not be okay if I take them on."

"Eden, listen to me: you have to be strong. Stronger than them. *Fierce.* Isn't that what I taught you? That's all there is to it. Now, I have to go." She hesitated. "It's not your birthday, is it? Is that why you called?"

"No, Mom." Eden slumped. How could she not remember?

"Good. Time flies so fast. All right, I'd better get back to it. The marchers are at the MP's house, and the police are here. Go make me proud. Love you."

There was a series of shouts and the line disconnected abruptly.

Love you too.

Eden stared at her phone for the longest time, the unease in her stomach growing. On the one hand, her mom had made it pretty clear what the right course of action was here. On the other...did the danger Eden might be in matter to her at all? She'd just blown straight past that as if she hadn't given it a passing thought.

Maybe she hadn't? After all, her mother was no hypocrite, as her father pointed out. She held herself to the same high standards she held everyone else to. River never gave any thought to the risks she put herself in either.

So. Eden's choice was pretty clear. Do the right thing and make her mom proud. Or do the safe thing.

She even knew just the person to help implement her Bringing Down The Fixers scheme. Not only did she have Colin for the IT side, and he had political contacts, but she knew just the journalist. A few words in the woman's ear about Fixers cases every few days, and before long Michelle Hastings' evil little cabal would be in a world of hurt.

Until they realized Eden was behind it, at least. Then it might be Eden hurting…

Her stomach roiled.

It was ironic. Eden was ideally suited to the job of bringing down The Fixers when Michelle had argued she was ideally suited to working *for* them. The only question was whether she had her mother's courage.

Well, you only lived once. Time to fix The Fixers.

Chapter 7

Snake Catchers

Senator Phyllis Kensington burst into Michelle's empty building late in the evening, fire in her steely blue eyes. Michelle looked up from behind her desk and made a mental note to rescind her open-access privileges and only allow her entrance by appointment in future.

In her most appeasing tone, Michelle said, "Something on your mind, Senator?"

Phyllis didn't need much of an invitation to unload. "Let's start with the security leaks! Your cases coming out in the press? Am I to be next?"

Ah. The leaks.

No one else seemed to have noticed, due to the fact few people at The Fixers knew who all their clients were. But somewhere out there was a snake. Stories Michelle had kept a lid on for years had suddenly started surfacing. Somehow Phyllis had put two and two together and come up with the truth.

Given the timing of Lawless's departure and the appearance of the stories, Michelle had initially wondered if she was behind them. Except Lawless had next to no security clearance and no way of knowing about any of these cases, some of which went back decades.

So—not Lawless. As Phyllis kept ranting, Michelle glanced at the oxalis on her side table. *Not her,* she reminded herself, plucking a tiny curl of dried leaf from its pot, then crunching it between her fingertips.

She'd grown absurdly fond of the little plant in a short time and had been doting on it. It was a tangible reminder of her lost employee. *Ex*-employee.

And not lost. Lawless had simply moved on.

Probably doesn't miss us at all.

Phyllis leaned over and slapped the desk in front of Michelle, shocking her back to the present. "Pay attention!"

Anger flooded her. But one look at Phyllis's face revealed the senator was absolutely terrified of having her career derailed by leaks.

This was not good. Michelle swung into management mode and began expertly manipulating Kensington to doubt her accusations.

Phyllis eventually ran out of steam and took a long, contemplative look at Michelle, seated calmly in her chair in her primmest navy business suit. The senator did have a terrible weakness for uptight women in charge.

Michelle drew in a breath, wondering if she should use this. Distract Phyllis with sex. Send her on her way again, having forgotten her outrage at The Fixers' failings. It was so cynical though. Michelle had crossed so many lines in her work, she wondered why she was hesitating at this one. It would be so easy.

Phyllis suddenly kicked off her high heels, reached under her dress, and slipped her hose and a black thong to the floor.

Michelle had better decide now. How far was she prepared to go to make a client happy?

A client whose body she had enjoyed fucking rather a lot.

A client she'd sworn off fucking because of the senator's dubious ethics surrounding her husband screwing his underage intern.

Phyllis had clearly noticed Michelle's lack of protest at shedding her undergarments because her questioning look turned predatory. She stepped around to Michelle's side of the desk, sliding her scarlet sheath dress up her thighs.

Sitting on the edge of the desk, she spread her toned legs, giving Michelle an X-rated eyeful. "I know you're lying to me about the cases being linked."

Andddd so went the theory she'd successfully manipulated the woman about the security breach. Michelle's mind raced, sorting through her options. Desire washed through her, and she tried not to think about her body's hormone-driven response.

"I'll let you off with a warning and your commitment that you're fixing your security problem, if you take care of my pressing situation." Phyllis's expression was dark and hungry.

There was so much danger there. Someone capable of anything. Michelle found that thrilling. *Usually.*

"Failure to agree to my compromise will mean I notify the board of your security breach," Phyllis continued, tone businesslike, as if she wasn't sitting—legs spread, arousal on display—four feet away. "Something I'm quite sure you haven't done."

"You don't even know who's on the board." Michelle's eyes narrowed, brain finally focusing.

"Is that really a risk you're prepared to take?"

Michelle's jaw worked. And from many options, she was now down to one. She supposed she *could* take her chances with the board, but Michelle was still unsettled by Tilly's subtle warnings that they suspected Michelle had leaked two cases and were watching her.

Besides, it really *wasn't* a hardship to fuck Phyllis Kensington. She looked like Glenn Close's frosty lawyer Patty Hewes. There was no denying her icy appeal.

Michelle paused, realizing she was trying to talk herself into this. That was unacceptable. *She* was the one in charge here. To hell with Phyllis!

"Blackmailing someone into sex isn't a good look on you, Phyllis dear," Michelle drawled. "Especially since I don't believe for a minute you know any of our board."

"You sound so sure."

She studied Phyllis. Everything in her experience told Michelle that the identity of The Fixers' five board members remained its biggest secret. Even she hadn't figured out who the fifth man was despite nine years of digging.

"You're bluffing." Michelle lifted her chin. "Besides, I have every intention of notifying the board. In *my* time frame. But I will not be blackmailed."

Phyllis's blue eyes went hard and assessing.

Michelle did not flinch.

Suddenly Phyllis offered a sweet smile that was all charm and home-cooked recipes. The smile that got her slippery Republican ass elected in a landslide every election.

"Now what?" Michelle asked, warily.

"Let's forget the stick and try the carrot," Phyllis purred. Her hand slid down and she began to slowly stroke herself. "See to my needs now and I'll stop highlighting your failures to my network."

"How's that any better than your previous offer?" Michelle demanded. "That sounds a lot like the stick."

"Fine. I'll let you do *anything* to me." She lifted her now-slick hand. "Do whatever wicked little thought comes to you. Won't that be delicious?"

And that was the moment Michelle went cold. No. It wouldn't be delicious. It was no better than how she'd been maneuvered by the FBI. Just a body for someone to use or get off on, regardless of her own thoughts.

Revulsion crept into her. Michelle was so done. Done playing power games, moving all the pieces around the board for slight advantages, looking for the traps, laying traps. In fact, she was suddenly exhausted even by the idea of games of any kind. Because this was where it got her: Back where she started. *Just a body*. Something someone else manipulated and used.

No one should be treated like they're nothing. *Not even me.*

Michelle's breath caught. She'd lived with self-loathing for so long it was unnerving when her brain rejected it as faulty reasoning.

That just left one other thing to reject. With a chilly look, Michelle met Senator Kensington's eye and said the truest thing she knew. "You're not that special. I'm not interested in your proposal. Not now. Never again."

Phyllis stared at her in shock, then rose and pulled on her thong and stockings in sharp movements.

Michelle looked away, unwilling to watch. Phyllis undressed, taunting, game-playing, and living for her power-tripping diversions was a constant reminder of the woman Michelle used to be. A skin she was no longer comfortable in.

When had that happened? *Why*? Surely it wasn't that her disgust for Phyllis's husband had transferred to his wife?

No. She inhaled. Not *just* that. Michelle had felt out of sync with her own body for a while. Her migraines and churning stomach had been screaming at her to notice. Her way of surviving each day was something her body barely tolerated now, let alone wanted.

Maybe she'd *never* wanted it?

Michelle almost choked. Had she just escaped to The Fixers because it was the only face-saving option after being destroyed at the FBI? She did her work because she was good at it, not because she *wanted* it?

If that was true, why had she only noticed now? What had changed?

Phyllis and her sexually hungry ways were not new. Michelle's home life was unchanged. Work was still its usual series of problem-solving challenges.

Why couldn't she see the damn answer? She was well aware her skills at denial ran deep. It was always easy to push inconvenient ideas down and never reassess anything. Well, until the day you can no longer avoid the mirror and seeing what you've become.

Was *that* why she so loved breaking mirrors?

"Tears?"

Michelle snapped her head up.

Phyllis was watching her, smug as a self-satisfied cat.

"What?"

"You're crying."

Startled, Michelle lifted her hand to her eyes and was shocked when her fingers met wetness.

"I'll add that to my blackmail file," Phyllis said with a cool chuckle. "Can make even the icy Fixers queen cry after saying no to a good, hard fuck from me."

Michelle stared. She understood now, with her arousal gone and her head clear, that all she felt for this woman was loathing. She'd thought she was done with her before, but this time she *knew*. Phyllis could blackmail her all she liked, but never would Michelle touch her again.

Because Michelle was *not* just a body. Not some piece in a clever game—even if she'd designed the game herself. She was no longer interested in playing. Michelle was worth more. And right now, she couldn't think of anything worse than being touched sexually by someone who didn't care for her. Which meant, of course, she'd no longer be touched by anyone.

"What?" Phyllis asked with a sneering laugh. "You look so disgusted. You don't like being turned on by me? Is that it? Hate yourself for it a little? A pity you said no. God, how I love hate-sex."

Michelle's lips thinned. "You can go. I'll handle the other matter we discussed."

Senator Kensington's eyes narrowed. "I can *go*? The pet poodle has been *dismissed*?"

Michelle lifted her chin. "Yes. Dismissed. For good. I'm sure you'll find someone else to get your power kicks off with. Maybe one of those sweet church ladies you fantasize about? Or I can find you a list of discreet escorts if you'd like."

"I don't think so," Phyllis snapped, eyes blazing at the "church lady" crack. "I'm not sure I trust your idea of *discreet* anymore."

"You should," Michelle said with a confidence she didn't feel. "Not one word has leaked about your husband or how little you care about how low he goes."

The senator paused. "Is *that* what this little tantrum of yours is about? That I don't care my husband is a bastard? I knew it when I married him. He never pretended to be a nice guy. I didn't want some solicitous fool pretending to be a gentleman. I wanted someone in *my* world. Who understood it."

"He took advantage of an underage teen! Broke his heart!"

Senator Kensington straightened. "Maybe look in the mirror sometime."

Michelle froze. "What do you mean?" She couldn't possibly be talking about Ayers. No one outside of The Fixers knew about that, except for Ayers and her wife.

"You're not the only one with a network of spies. I hear things. And your ex talks too much. You might want to fix him while you're fixing all your organization's other little issues? Hmm? Oh, and Michelle? I don't want to hear of one more case leaked from this building."

Michelle glared at her.

Phyllis met her gaze with an imperious one of her own. "You don't get to judge me. You're as ethically bankrupt as any. Your soul could sour milk and, honestly, *that's* why you interest me. You don't have a drop of cloying sweetness in you." She leaned in, her mouth beside Michelle's ear lobe as she whispered, "But you're not better than me. We're *exactly* the same. Except for one thing: I embrace my darker impulses, while you fight them. You fight yourself so often you're exhausted, aren't you?"

At Michelle's flicker of shock, Phyllis said, "I think I actually feel sorry for you. You hate yourself instead of owning it." Phyllis's hand cupped Michelle's breast, rubbing her nipple through her blouse, making it harden again. "And that hatred means you'll always push away what you need. You'll always be alone because you can't be honest with yourself. So, fuck you, my dear, *most sincerely*, for thinking you're better than me. At least I like who I am."

With that, she spun on heel and left, pulling her phone to her ear, barking for her driver.

Michelle watched her to leave, the words burning into her.

At least I like who I am.

You'll always be alone.

Michelle dragged out her phone.

"Alberto," she drawled. "It seems you've been leaking like a sieve."

"*Shelly*," he said, using her hated nickname. "How lovely you remember I exist."

"Give me one reason not to drag you through court for breaching your NDA!" Michelle snapped. "And you *know* I have the power to ensure it's a closed court with a judge of our choosing, so don't bother threatening me with exposing The Fixers."

"Ahh but how did you know *I* did it? Anyone could have put it in her pocket. Like Chewbacca, for instance?"

Pocket? Chewbacca? "What on earth are you talking about?"

There was a small silence, then: "What are *you* talking about?"

"Phyllis Kensington."

"Oh. That was months ago. She was cashed up and I was short—so sue me. I only gave her small stuff. Nothing compromising operations or that'd get the board upset."

"I might *well* sue you." Michelle ground her teeth. "Our NDAs aren't for show. They have teeth."

"You haven't sued me yet for any of my other minor breaches. Anyone would think you're terrified of who I'd subpoena as a witness. Catherine Ayers? You'd have to sit there and listen to all the ways your lover was betrayed by you. You'd have to sit there squirming, pretending you don't care, when we both know you care so much that it kills you. And I'd happily email the transcript of my case to all your staff to remind them of your weakest moment. Nine years is an eternity. I'd hate for them to forget."

Alberto's goading was infuriating. He was right about why she hadn't gone after him: She didn't want another war with her ex after he'd almost ruined her reputation at work. He might succeed this time.

Michelle pivoted to a safer topic. "What did you mean by the pocket thing? Chewbacca is what you call O'Brian, isn't it? Because he's big and you can't understand a word he says?"

He snorted. "The man's accent is like picking spinach from your teeth it's such hard work. And you'll find out what I meant sooner or later."

She turned that over. Hadn't Alberto called O'Brian "Chewbacca" on the same night her ex had bumped into Lawless?

Bumped. Into.

Pocket.

Christ! Oldest trick in the book. She wanted to slap herself. "What did you put in Lawless's pocket?" Michelle demanded.

"You know, I'd love to tell you, but Peaches here charges by the hour." He hung up.

Alberto was winding her up again. She knew he had no interest in prostitutes. No thrill of the chase. What *had* he been up to, though?

Michelle's jaw tightened as the entire evening threatened to overwhelm her. It was tempting to disappear into a rage room. Except Michelle realized she suddenly had no desire to look at mirrors.

Not even broken ones.

Chapter 8
The Fall of Eden

It had been a month since Lawless had quit, and Michelle's office was in disarray. Employees were cranky, mistakes were being made, and everyone seemed to silently blame her for the absence of their favorite colleague.

As if she didn't have enough on her plate than dealing with her staff's disappointment. As if Michelle didn't miss the woman every single day and wonder where she was and how she was doing. And most especially, *how* Lawless could have left without a goodbye.

There was a widespread rumor that Michelle had fired her because she hated the plants or the coffee club. On the latter, Daphne had taken over running The Fix and was now prone to shooting Michelle petulant looks each day that Lawless's desk remained empty. If Michelle didn't understand the loss so well, she'd have fired her for impertinence.

According to Tilly, the club had turned into some weird tribute to its founder, given attendees didn't have the first clue about fair-trade beans. So they talked about coffee they *thought* Lawless might like. O'Brian was the most adamant the group continue.

Michelle suspected they just liked the reminder of Lawless. Michelle did not. It was hard seeing signs of her everywhere she turned— such as the enormous plant with giant, floppy, green leaves in Security they'd named *Ralph*.

Some days the reminders were so strong that Michelle wanted to hurl the oxalis from her office. Instead, she'd regretfully dust its little leaves and check the moisture levels in the soil and promise to keep it safe.

This was getting ridiculous. Michelle snatched up her phone and called O'Brian. "I want you to return the office vegetation to sender."

There was a startled "What?" Then: "Aww, hell, do we have to?"

"Yes!" Michelle scowled. He knew better than to second-guess her.

"Why are you askin' *me*?" O'Brian asked, not unreasonably.

"Because I'm reliably informed that you're friends. Didn't Lawless go to dinner at your place?" she asked acidly. "Your wife cooked for her, you said?"

O'Brian sighed. "Lawless canceled it, same day as she quit. When I told Shauna dinner was off, she said, 'Oh hell no' and got her number off me and called direct. Told Lawless somethin' about how she'd been really looking forward to meetin' someone from my work and it'd mean a lot to her if Lawless could come. My wife's *awful* persuasive. Still, it took a fair bit of negotiatin' and all, but it's on for next week." His delight was clear.

Michelle blinked. "Did she say why she resigned?"

"'Fraid not. But one thing was loud and clear: she ain't coming back. I asked if she would. Place ain't the same without her hippie, woke ass." O'Brian's tone deflated.

Michelle slid a disappointed glance to her perky oxalis. *She won't be back,* she told it. Well, thought at it.

A wave of how wrong everything felt without Lawless inserting herself into every corner of Michelle's working life overwhelmed her for a moment. And that just kicked off the start of yet another vile headache. She'd been having so many lately.

"Back on topic: get rid of the plants," Michelle told O'Brian, now grumpier than ever. "Get her rainforest man to collect them, or whatever it takes. Make sure they're gone by Friday." She slammed down the phone.

It was Wednesday morning. Surely Lawless could figure out how to get her plants removed in a day and a half. And if not, finally Michelle would have an excuse to talk to her. Her mood lifted and she returned to work.

The plants were gone.

Michelle had arrived early on Thursday morning, officially to finish a report, but unofficially she hoped Eden would be in with Rainforest Man, frantically removing them.

Too late. The foyer was sterile. It made her heart ache. Michelle stared at the empty reception area, then her gaze flicked to the security guard. "When?"

"Last night, just after you'd left."

Was Lawless watching? Waiting for me to leave?

"Came in herself along with a friend called…" he tapped his screen, "Agatha Teo."

Not Rainforest Man then. The best friend instead.

Michelle glanced again around the foyer, bereft in some way she'd never expected. *So cold.*

"I escorted the two ladies around and oversaw them while they put the plants on a trolley they'd brought," Marshall continued.

"Trolley? Singular? How long did it take them to clear the building of plants?"

"Three hours."

Three hours? "I'm sorry you had to stay so late. Submit an overtime request. I'll see it's approved."

He nodded. "I was sad to see them go. I mean the plants as well as Ms. Lawless. And, uh, I sort of thought you liked deepest, darkest Peru." His tone was tentative, as if unsure whether she'd appreciate the joke.

"No, Mr. Marshall," Michelle said grimly. "As it turns out, I do not."

When Michelle reached her building's top floor, she looked for even a hint of greenery, but there was nothing. An awful thought occurred, and Michelle began to stride quickly toward her office. She hadn't told O'Brian to leave her oxalis! She'd meant everything *else* should go except…

Not…

Michelle burst through her office door and ran to her desk. She stopped dead.

It was gone.

Fuck.

Michelle sank into her chair, misery overtaking her as she stared at its empty spot on the side table. She spotted a tiny curl of leaf that had been left behind and picked it up. Studying the lone little leaf, sadness swallowed her.

What if she texted Lawless to ask just for that plant back? Would that look too pathetic?

That horse had bolted, hadn't it? She *was* pathetic. She could barely run her office. Her staff were in open revolt. Cases were being leaked to the media. And everything was unraveling.

Tossing the pitiful leaf onto her desk, Michelle spun around to gaze at the view. She stared so long that the sun inched higher, the city coming alive below. Her phone pinged an email alert. Michelle glanced at it. From Fixers client and famous author RM Fox.

Michelle clicked it and found a link to an article about how Fox had only made the shortlist in a prestigious writing contest thanks to a bribed judge's vote. The fuming author's accompanying email was an overwrought six-page screed demanding to know how the story had leaked.

She wished she knew. But, based on the unedited spray he'd just sent her, the article was right to call Fox an undeserved finalist.

Her phone pinged again. The email's subject header was "RM Fox."

> *So much for fixing your security breach. Consider our partnership terminated.— Phyllis*

The termination was not entirely surprising. Kensington no longer needed The Fixers now her husband had been brought to heel. A new email landed.

By the way, I can't possibly be the only one to notice. Consider this a friendly warning.

Michelle's stomach tightened with annoyance at her high-handed decrees. She made an instant decision: Time to rein in the senator. The woman's potential to leverage what she knew about The Fixers was now a real danger.

Michelle grabbed her desk phone and tapped an extension.

"Liam Pendrelli," came the smart reply. The Espionage staffer had contacts deep in DC's political circles, deeper even than Michelle. "What can I do for you, Ms. Hastings?"

"Is anyone doing oppo research on Phyllis Kensington?"

"Brown and Curtis. They're prepping in case she runs for the top job in eight years. They've been trying to get up a file on her for some time, but they're getting blocked."

Brown, a Republican researcher; Curtis, a Democrat. They were both as cunning and immoral as each other, collecting dirt on various rival candidates for possible future use. And they were getting blocked because Maurice Wagner, a.k.a. board member Number Four, had deemed it so. She made a mental note to inform Four that the Fixers' protection deal for Phyllis and her husband was done.

"I want you to supply Wagner and Curtis the essentials from Kensington's Fixers file," Michelle said. "All the cases on her husband we've covered up."

"You want her out of the running?" Pendrelli asked in confusion. "Even though she's a client?"

"No longer a client, Mr. Pendrelli."

"They probably won't release the dirt even if I give it to them," Pendrelli said. "Not yet. They'll sit on it for blackmail, closer to her presidential run."

"Tell them the condition of them getting it is, at the bare minimum, telling her they have it. She needs to know that she's finished. One other thing: Redact the name of the intern, Troy Plymouth, before you send it. I want his identity protected."

"Can do. When do you need it done?"

"Today. Kensington just terminated her services with us. Our protection ends *now*."

Play with fire. Get roasted.

"Understood, Ms. Hastings."

"Good." She ended the call. When this came out, Phyllis would figure out it had come from her. Michelle didn't care. It wasn't about payback. Not exactly.

One, Phyllis should *never* be president. What a self-serving, immoral, corrupt administration that would be. Two, she was explaining who had the power. That Michelle might have enjoyed fucking the senator on occasion, but Phyllis didn't have any rights to her. And she deserved retribution for attempting to blackmail the CEO of The Fixers.

Oh, and it had nothing to do with a few home truths she'd slung at Michelle on the way out the door. Nothing whatsoever.

For a while, Michelle lost herself in the view again, thoughts scattered and disturbed.

A throat cleared, and she turned. The young hacker from Cybersecurity stood in her office, shifting anxiously from foot to foot.

"Yes, Mr. Snakepit?"

"Sorry to intrude, ma'am, but I had intel I thought you should know about?" His weedy voice cracked.

"Are you asking me or telling me?" she snapped.

"Uh, telling, m-ma'am."

"Well?"

"It's about the…breach in security." He inhaled. "How our cases are getting out into the media?"

"Yes." She bared her lips. "I'm well aware. Somehow a journalist keeps hearing about our clients' misdeeds."

"Thing is," Snakepit said, "I've noticed a pattern?"

That got her attention. Her gaze sharpened. "Go on."

"Every case released was on the USB drive I created. *Only* cases that were on the drive have been leaked; no others."

"What USB drive? Why did you create this?"

"Um, I was ordered to? It came through a standard job request. Matched the protocols and codes. I created the drive, put it in a secured pouch, and it got collected."

"Who created the job order?" Michelle demanded.

"I don't know. Like all my work requests, it was just a bunch of numbers, and it matched the authorization code. It's done that way for security reasons."

"Then how does that help me, beyond knowing we have a traitor inside my building who ordered that USB drive?"

"Um, coz Ms. Lawless came to see me and she was holding it?"

Shock battered her. "How could *Lawless* have ordered it? She doesn't have clearance!"

"I know. I thought it was odd too, but she definitely had it. She was acting like she'd been given it and didn't know how to open it. I told her she had to use the password supplied by the person who ordered the drive. And if she didn't have it, she should ask for it again from them."

"Did she say who that was?"

"No. Um, ma'am."

"Then what happened?"

"She thanked me and left."

"When was this?" Michelle demanded.

"Uhm, the fourteenth of last month?"

The *fourteenth*. Michelle inhaled. The day Lawless had quit. So *that's* what Alberto had given her when he'd bumped into her? No wonder she'd resigned. Obviously, she'd found a way into the files.

Who had given the drive to Alberto? Sneaky as he was, he had zero access to the building. But hadn't O'Brian mentioned Alberto still had friends at The Fixers? Who?

Anger that anyone had helped Lawless learn all their ugly deeds made her head pound. "Mr. Snakepit, can you go over the job order and see if there's anything identifying the source of the job request?"

"I did, ma'am, already. And…well I'm pretty sure…the request came from your office."

"Mine?"

"It had *your* code at the end."

Michelle slumped. "Someone copied my code."

"Yeah." He swallowed. "Sorry. I didn't know it wasn't legit. Everything matched." He gulped.

"Thank you, Mr. Snakepit. Tell no one about this. I'll follow up myself."

He nodded, looking relieved—probably shocked he hadn't been fired.

Michelle spun back around to stare outside. Who knew her authorization code? As far as she was aware, no one. But her entire office was full of clever, slippery people. Any one of a dozen people had the ability to find a way to access it if they were desperate enough.

But why would they go to this effort only to give it to Lawless? What was gained? Lawless's reaction had been predictable: a social justice crusader like her would consider it her duty to go after The Fixers. Was that the traitor's aim? To hurt the company?

Of course, Michelle's own reaction would be predictable too: She had no choice but to go after Lawless. A company-wide vendetta would be implemented in order to both stop and punish the ex-employee.

Maybe *that* was the traitor's aim? To hurt Lawless?

Right now, though, motive didn't matter. There were bigger things at stake. Her entire company, for instance. Phyllis was right about the constant drip of leaks: "I can't possibly be the only one to notice."

Lawless had to be stopped. If it was war she wanted, she'd get it. Michelle's gaze fell to the oxalis leaf. With a snarl, she brought her hand down on it with a furious slap, then scrunched it to a pulp.

Chapter 9
'Tow' to Tango

GLORIA WAS A SORRY SIGHT, leaning to one side where Eden had parked her a few blocks from the Smithsonian's National Zoo. Two punctured tires. It was the third time this week. The first time, Eden had been perplexed. The second time, suspicious. Now she knew.

She supposed she should be grateful The Fixers had stopped at two flats today. Eden sighed and opened the back where her spares were. A jungle of peace lilies swatted her in the face.

She hadn't been able to get all The Fixers plants somewhere safe just yet. Aggie could only plant-sit so many until Francisco was back in the country. Michelle's order to clear out the office had sure showed her how little the plants and Eden mattered, hadn't it?

She pulled out a pair of tires. Eden had taken to keeping four spares these days.

As frustrating as this campaign of tire destruction was, it seemed like an almost innocuous revenge, given all the power at The Fixers' disposal. Hadn't Ottilie promised vengeance, lawyers, the worst of the worst?

Maybe this was the starter dish, and they were just getting warmed up?

"This vehicle yours, ma'am?" a uniformed man in a fluorescent vest called. "I'll need you to clear the lane ASAP."

"Why?" she asked.

He pointed at the road edge. "You're in front of a curb cut, restricting access to pedestrians and wheelchair users crossing the street."

Eden stared in astonishment. This wasn't where she'd parked. Gloria had been moved a little. Those scheming…

"Are you refusing to comply with a Washington DC Parking Enforcement Officer?"

"I can't—I've got two flats."

"Failure to comply with a reasonable request means I'll have to write you a ticket."

"How is this reasonable?" She waved at the tires.

"Not my problem, ma'am." His eyes seemed shifty. The man reached for his pad.

She folded her arms. "How much are they paying you? And did *you* move my van?"

"Are you suggesting a DC Parking Enforcement Officer has been bribed and interfered with the egress of pedestrians?"

"Yes." Eden frowned. "I am!"

"If you continue with this abuse, I'll call the Metropolitan PD." He began scribbling. "Is that what you wish? A visit from police?"

"No." Eden gritted her teeth. "I'll change my tires now and be on my way."

"I'm afraid that won't be possible, ma'am. It'll take you too long to clear this sidewalk blockage. I'm calling a tow truck."

"You can't!"

"Are you telling me how to do my job?" he asked as he scribbled. "That would be a grievous error."

Screw you. And screw Michelle.

"Don't," Eden muttered, the wind going out of her sails. After paying off her student loans, buying coffee from all over the world, paying Colin for his IT help, and sending her mom a big donation for her next cause, she didn't have any spare change left from the Wingapo job. "I can't afford to—"

"Not my problem." He shoved the tickets at her—definitely more than one—then reached for his phone. "Tow needed," he barked, then rattled off the address.

Before Eden could protest further, her phone rang. *Aggie.*

"Hey," she answered.

"Come home."

"Can't right now." Eden darted a look at the man. "See…"

"I don't care," Aggie cut her off. "Come. Home." Then she hung up.

Alarm pierced her. Eden opened her van and hauled out any essentials she wouldn't risk with a tow company. Bag packed, she called for an Uber, then turned to face the officer.

"Which tow company did you call?" she asked.

"Can't recall. Guess you'll have to work that out for yourself."

"Asshole," she muttered.

"Are you insulting a DC Parking Enforcement Officer?" he asked sweetly, reaching for his pad again.

He didn't have the power to do whatever it was he was threatening, but Eden was out of patience…and money. "No," she ground out.

He mock saluted and walked away.

Bastard. She glared.

Eden jumped out of the Uber outside Aggie's house and stared in astonishment. "The hell?"

"Goons came by," Aggie replied bleakly. "At first I thought they were cops; they had on suits and mirrored sunglasses and were done before I knew it."

Crime scene tape crisscrossed the front lawn. "That's it? Just tape?"

"Yes. But it's *how* it was done."

Eden glanced at the gathered neighbors gossiping behind their hands. "Is this a…threat?"

"I think it's supposed to be intimidating. Or make us the talk of the neighborhood?" Aggie eyed her. "This is your ex-boss, right? What's next? A body outline on the drive?" Her fingers tightened into fists. "They were so professional, like they were CIA or something. They scared me half to death even though they were only here ten minutes."

"I'm so sorry," Eden said, fury rising. "I'll take care of this."

"How?" Aggie asked. "Don't do anything crazy. They looked dangerous."

"I know who to talk to. Tear down that stupid crime tape. I'll be right back."

Eden stepped away from the throngs. She pulled out her phone and called a man she'd once thought of as a friend. "O'Brian? What the hell? That was my best friend's place you just made look like a crime scene!"

"Lawless," the head of security said with a sigh. "I know *that*. Orders are orders."

"Did you have to make the place look like it's home to a terrorist cell?"

"Yes, actually," he said. "I don't tell you how to your job, now do I?" He paused. "Well, former job. Shit, did ya have to wind up bein' a traitor?"

"O'Brian," Eden said tightly, "just tell me one thing: Are you planning follow-through? Upsetting Aggie's family or something?"

Silence fell.

"Come *on*," she urged him. "Aren't we friends?"

He stayed silent.

"Please? Phelim?"

"Look it wouldn't be very good psychological warfare if I answered that, would it?" he said, sounding peeved she'd even asked.

"Well don't answer. Just don't go near my friend or her family, okay?"

More silence.

"Phelim?"

"I wasn't going to," he muttered. "Those weren't my orders. I was told to make a point to you that we know where ya live—well, half the time it's where you live—and if we wanted to, we could mess things up but we're choosin' not to fer now. Still, though, I'm really pissed off at you for this. I *liked* you!"

"And I liked you too! But I'm following my conscience. Thanks for hurting Gloria."

"That wasn't me. But, yeah, it *was* us. Orders and all."

"No kidding."

"Look, Lawless, you absolute eejit, what'd you think'd happen if you crossed the boss lady? Hastings has long arms, a long memory, and she's fit to be tied. She's so damned upset it's you behind this. Just be thankful she's decided you're getting the fleas not the bear."

"The what?"

"She wants you attacked by a million fleas to piss you off in every *little* way. If it was a bear attack, you'd lose phone, power, internet, credit cards, all of it. Your wokemobile would be found at the bottom of a cliff somewhere."

Eden digested that for a moment, then said quietly: "So *is* this the end of it?"

"It's called *fleas*, Lawless, not flea. Whaddya think? And don't cross her again, or she'll swap us to bear mode, okay? That's my free advice because I like you, Lord only knows why, you crazy-assed tree hugger. By the way? When you get your van back, check under the seat. Oh, and this conversation never happened."

Eden sighed.

"But, hey, while you're on the phone," O'Brian added, tone warmer, "we still on for dinner on Wednesday? The missus was thinkin' of making her mam's authentic coddle recipe. That's this one-pot casserole with potatoes and boiled pork sausages and carrots and beans and cider, and it's probably the greatest dish on earth. I'm not just sayin' that. Don't worry, we'd skip the sausages on account of you bein' a vegetarian and all. Or her Plan B is boxty. That's like a potato pancake thing?"

Eden stared at her phone and then laughed. Because, hell. Just... wow.

"Lawless?" O'Brian asked hopefully. "Was the hysterical laughter a good or bad sign?"

"Fine. Yeah, sure, why not?" Eden shook her head. "And either vegetarian dish sounds great."

"Good."

"Hey, I'll still bring the fiddle-leaf fig I promised."

"Now *that's* good news."

She could picture his grizzled, pockmarked face beaming and couldn't stay mad at him.

"See you Wednesday. I'll text my address. Bye, Lawless." The phone clicked off.

Eden shook her head again. That exchange probably passed as normal in O'Brian's world. Messing with people on orders was just business to him. He'd compartmentalize and go home to his wife, whom Eden already loved based on one warm and funny phone call cajoling her into dinner. The woman clearly had no clue what her husband's evil day job entailed.

Eden's anger returned at the reminder. She wondered just how far Michelle would go. Aggie's frightened voice came to mind. Eden texted Michelle furiously.

Do what you want to me

She accidentally sent the text before she could add the rest of her comment, *But leave my friends out of it.*

The phone beeped half a minute later.

Oh Ms. Lawless, I intend to. I've only just begun.

Eden glared at the bill given to her by the impound lot employee holding Gloria hostage. "Four hundred twenty-three bucks?" she growled. "Seriously?"

"And fifty cents," the woman added, her tone bored. "I can itemize it for you if you want." She tapped a few buttons on her keyboard. "A hundred thirty-six dollars for the boot fee…"

"Gloria wasn't booted!" Eden protested.

"It was when the towing vehicle arrived," she replied, eyes sliding down the list.

"I'll bet," Eden said.

"Tow fee, one-forty; tow dispatch fee, sixty-seven fifty…"

"Never mind." Eden passed her credit card over. "Was there any damage?"

"Apart from the two flats? No." She took the card and processed payment.

As the receipt spat out, Eden wondered whether baked beans for every meal was in her future. "Is that everything?" she asked.

"We have the issue of the vandalism."

"The what now?"

"You said your vehicle was called Gloria." The woman pursed her lips. She swiveled her monitor around and hit a button. Black and white footage of a fit woman in black could be seen shimmying down the wall and then pulling out a spray can. In large letters, she painted "Free Gloria" over the roller door. She repeated it again on the side of the building, then patted Gloria affectionately before slithering back up and over the wall.

The woman lifted her eyebrows. "Costs to repaint that were three hundred. If you settle up now, we won't put your name on a police report."

"Three hundred? But that's not me! I can't scale a ten-foot wall! That's a complete stranger!"

"How did a complete stranger tap your exact vehicle and know its name?"

"I'm being set up."

"Uh-huh. The police, or pay up?"

"You have no evidence!"

"She seems about your height," the woman nodded at the screen. "Same basic dimensions..." she waved in the general direction of the ninja's chest.

"Not me."

"Police or pay," the woman repeated.

"Police," Eden said. Then she stopped, remembering how the traffic enforcement officer had been on The Fixers' payroll. What were the odds they knew people on the police force too? Someone who'd escalate things and add charges and...

Damn it.

"Pay," Eden growled out. "But I want it on the record I did not do this."

"Sure, hon." She shoved a piece of paper her way. "Write your objections down right there. I'll get the receipt from the graffiti removalists."

By the time Eden finally slid behind the wheel of Gloria, she was mad as hell. She flapped away a fern frond that side-swiped her from behind. The oxalis, Michelle's former desk plant, looked up at her from the seat beside Eden.

"Screw Michelle!" Eden told the plant as she pulled out of the lot. "Sorry oxy, nothing personal."

A rattling, grinding noise started. Eden slammed on the brakes. *The hell?* She jumped out and popped the hood, looking for signs of damage or tampering. Now she'd have to call in a mechanic and…

Wait. O'Brian's warning came to mind.

She popped the driver's door and felt around under the seat. Her fingers hit something round and metallic. Gingerly, she retracted it and discovered a rattling old paint can. Using the tip of her car keys, she levered off the lid and discovered a massive pile of old bolts. Loud and clangy.

Screw Michelle.

―――•⊙◇⊙•―――

Eden perched on Aggie's front step at sixty-thirty on Wednesday, despondent at losing Gloria to the impound lot yet again—this time a stealthy tow-and-go hit job. Eden was unable to get her van back tonight as the lot was shut.

She'd texted O'Brian that dinner tonight would have to be postponed since she'd lost her wheels and her funds were too low for cabs thanks to all the towing fees. Aggie and Colin were out, so they couldn't take her.

He'd texted back, *Stay right there.*

Twenty minutes later, he roared up in a retro pickup truck, leaned out the window, and called, "Hey, hippie! Need a ride?"

Eden laughed at the absurdity of the man who'd *caused* her to be ride-less offering her a ride. But, again, she filed that under "makes sense to O'Brian's brain" and scrambled to her feet.

"Ain't you forgettin' somethin'?" He gave her a hopeful grin.

Oh. Right. "One sec." She ran inside, grabbed the fiddle-leaf fig she'd promised him, and headed for his truck.

"Oh yeah," he said happily. "It's the same one from Security. We called him Ralph."

"Yup, I set that one aside just for you." Eden gave it to him to put in the back. "You seemed to really like it."

"Nah." A redness crept up his neck. "Just the missus was fond of it—from the photo."

Eden clambered into the passenger's side. "Thought you'd be a better liar, Phelim." She grinned. "No one names plants they don't like."

He shook his head and laughed, pulling away from the curb.

Over dinner, it didn't take long for Eden to understand why *she'd* been chosen for the rare honor of being invited to Phelim's home. His wife and kids were the sweetest people. Optimistic and generous, they saw good in everything.

"Can you tell us what Da does at work?" O'Brian's littlest boy asked, mouth full of green beans.

"Sure can," Eden said.

O'Brian shot her a worried glance.

"Your dad glares at people and pretends to scare them so they follow his boss's rules. But he's just a big ole teddy bear."

O'Brian looked scandalized at this characterization, but Shauna and his kids—two little boys and a girl—nodded happily as if this made perfect sense.

"And what do *you* do at Phelim's workplace?" Shauna asked. "He never tells us anything."

Now Phelim's expression turned fretful. He'd obviously not told his wife that Eden had quit.

"I've just left, actually."

"Oh?" Shauna said in surprise, darting a glance at her husband. "Goodness, that's sudden. Phelim tells me everyone loves you at work. Why'd you leave?"

O'Brian's forehead began to glisten with a sheen of sweat.

"I wanted to get back to my protest work," Eden said. "I want to make the world a better place. It's hard to do that from inside a corporation." *Especially that one.*

O'Brian visibly relaxed.

"Did you know Da used t' be a boxer?" his youngest, Thomas, asked.

"I did, yes," Eden said.

"And a carba," Thomas added.

"A what?" Eden frowned.

"Wood carba." He pointed at an intricately made wooden bowl containing salad.

"Carver?" Eden stared at the glorious bowl. "That's so beautiful."

"Yeah. Da's amazing."

"True," Shauna agreed, eyes twinkling. "Amazin' at everythin' except housework and cuttin' the grass."

O'Brian scratched his ear. "Never said I was perfect. I'll leave that to you, my love." Then he went bright red.

Eden chuckled. "Don't worry," she assured him, "your secret's safe with me that you're as mushy at home as your wife's mashed potatoes."

Shauna laughed. "He truly is a teddy bear. It's astoundin' to me anyone's scared of him, but I hear sometimes folks are."

"Fancy that," Eden said. "By the way, I have to say I officially love boxty." Her dish of buttermilk potato pancakes came with a selection of delicious salad sides and the most glorious pumpkin arancini.

"Do you, now?" Shauna jerked a thumb at her husband, "I told *that one* you would. You're such a well-traveled woman who's probably tried dishes from all over. Figured you'd like to try something from my home."

"You know I'm well-traveled?" She'd never told O'Brian that.

"Well, of course. You're a protester, just like your mam." Shauna smiled. "Can't do that from one place!"

"You've heard of Mom?" Eden asked in surprise.

"Oh, yes! That's why I wanted to meet you so much." Shauna chuckled. "I'm such a fan of River's fight to stop overfishing by super trawlers off the UK. Once our fish reserves are gone, they're gone."

Eden shot O'Brian a triumphant smirk along the lines of *See! Your wife likes us protester types.*

Bafflement filled his expression, as though this were news to him.

Hilarious. "I'm really proud of Mom. All hail woke hippies, hey?"

Shauna lifted her glass of wine. "Cheers to that." She elbowed her husband.

Dutifully he lifted his beer. "To woke hippies," he drawled. "Always said that's what the world needs more of."

Eden laughed her head off.

Hours later, after dinner wrapped up, Eden gave her hostess a hug, agreeing not to "be a stranger." She ruffled the hair of three adorable little O'Brians, who called out an enthusiastic "Night, Eden!" And she slapped O'Brian on the back as he guided her to his truck for the drive home.

"That was a fantastic meal, my friend. Your wife's a superb cook."

"She is." He unlocked his truck. "I'm also glad you still think of me as a friend. You know what happens at work ain't personal to me, right?"

"I know. No hard feelings."

He exhaled in relief and dug something out of his pocket. "Here. A little thing I made. Don't go makin' a fuss, but I just thought you'd maybe like it. I felt bad about the shit you're goin' through, even though it's *totally* self-inflicted. Still…" He handed her a small package, roughly wrapped in tissue paper. His cheeks were flaming bright red.

Eden discovered, nestled within, the sweetest carved panda.

"Oh, it's so cute!" She loved it. "You're really talented." Eden met his shy blue eyes and hid her smile at his squirming. "Why a panda?"

"I thought you knew? It's the boss's nickname for you."

Oh, right. Ottilie had said. "Because I'm vegetarian and hairy?" she deadpanned.

"Sweet and harmless," O'Brian corrected.

"Fun fact," Eden said, "pandas aren't harmless. They've been known to attack people. Not often, but don't push them." She grinned.

"Well then, it's an even better nickname for you than the boss knew." O'Brian eyed her for a beat. "She really misses you. She hides it well and thinks no one knows, but I can tell."

"Misses me so much she had her whole building stripped of my plants. Francisco's out of the country, so I've had to store them anywhere I can until he comes back. Aggie's taken in as many as she could. But I've had to put the overflow in my van. Haven't you thought it weird there's a jungle in Gloria every time you tow her?"

"Okay, first," he said, "the towing of your wokemobile is not my department. Second, yes, I noticed you've got greenery shootin' out all your windows these days. Thought you were bein' eccentric."

"No, I'm being 'I can't force any more plants on Aggie' considerate."

"Want to leave some with us? I'm sure Shauna'd be only too happy. She's gotta green thumb an' a half."

"That's really kind. I might take you up on it when I spring Gloria." Eden blinked for a moment at the absurdity. Phelim was working for the people forcing her to drive around with a van full of plants in the first place! A van that was impounded because, again, Phelim's people. Or his boss, to be specific.

Who missed her.

Wait… Her brain caught up with that comment. "And I don't think Michelle misses me. She's furious with me."

"So furious she doesn't like lookin' at leafy reminders of you all day. Besides, you *can* be mad at someone and miss them too."

"No you can't!" That was nuts.

"Sure can." O'Brian started the engine. "By the way, I was wonderin' how long you're planning on releasin' Fixers' secrets for?" he asked as they accelerated away.

"Why?"

"Cos my life ran a lot smoother when you and Hastings were on friendly terms. It was the nicest mood she's ever been in. Now it's like a Cat-5 hurricane circlin' the building, not lookin' like it's ever gonna blow out. It's givin' me an ulcer."

"Sorry you're suffering, Phelim. But I have to do what's right."

He huffed. "Thought you'd say somethin' like that."

As they pulled up at Aggie's place, O'Brian said with a smile, "Take care of yourself. And remember: It's totally a thing to miss someone you're mad at. That goes for you *and* the boss."

"There's *no way* I'm missing Michelle. Be sure to let her know."

O'Brian chuckled. "Oh, *sure*. Not like I want my head to stay where it is or anythin'. Catchya 'round, hippie."

Chapter 10
Where Else to Go

It had been almost two months since Eden had quit. Also two months since she'd last seen Michelle.

That last fact bugged her in ways Eden didn't really want to examine. Because while the woman was loathsome, detestable, a villain...it was also possible O'Brian was right. Eden missed her. Just a little.

The attack of fleas persisted and were, as promised, small, frequent, and highly irritating.

To date, Gloria had gone through multiple flat tires, one missing license plate, two broken brake lights, and one Saran-wrap attack which had seen her and a tree made one—clear plastic film had been wrapped around both van and tree hundreds of times. Poor Gloria had been left like that for hours probably until the neighborhood's giggling kids had knocked at Aggie's door to inform Eden. At least none of the van's plants had been harmed during that ordeal. O'Brian and his wife had taken possession of them weeks ago.

Time taken to unwrap Gloria: twenty-three minutes. The shame: a lifetime. Largely because video of the wrapped van had gone viral. All part of The Fixers' service.

Michelle had even sent a goading text: *we've barely begun.*

She wasn't lying. Gloria's dashboard clock regularly showed a different time by random amounts. Off by fifteen minutes, then three hours, then seven minutes.

Eden's email inbox was filled with newsletters and ads from the Flat Earth Society, the NRA, pro-nuclear groups, and one organization standing *with* China against Tibet.

Solid points for originality came from learning she was now a member of the 501st Legion, a volunteer group for *Star Wars* Stormtrooper costume enthusiasts. That subtle dig about Eden joining the dark side made her wonder how much her ex-boss was involved in these flea bites.

Did Michelle sit around coming up with more twisted attacks on her? Or did she never think of Eden at all, outsourcing punishments to minions?

"Your van's getting towed again," Aggie called from the kitchen, mouth full of toast. "Y'know, at this rate, it'd be cheaper to set fire to it than to keep getting it back and fixing all the crap done to it."

"And then Michelle would have won," Eden shot back, snatching up her phone, keys, and wallet and racing outside.

"Hey!" She waved to the tow-truck driver. Oh great. *Ted*. He'd towed her several times and always seemed happy about it. "It's legal for me to park here."

"Had complaints." Ted leaned out the window. "Your vehicle has been abandoned on someone else's property for more than ninety-six hours without permission."

"I *have* permission!" Eden protested, waving toward Aggie's house.

"Not *that* house. That one." Ted pointed next door.

Gloria's nose was barely three inches over the property line. It blocked nothing, not the neighbor's drive nor their view.

"I'll move it." Eden jangled her keys. "Right now."

"No can do, ma'am. You're too late."

"Don't suppose you're open to a bribe?" she threw out in frustration.

"You can't pay me more than I'm getting."

She hadn't meant it seriously. The glint in Ted's eye was real, though. No way his employer had put it there.

Screw Michelle.

"At least give me a ride with you to the towing yard," Eden tried. "I'm sure Dominique must be missing me. It's been all of six days since I last paid her to spring Gloria."

He shrugged. "Sure, why not? No skin off my nose."

Eden ran around to the passenger seat. Ted tossed a few old motor-racing magazines and drink bottles from the seat to the floor.

They roared off up the street with Gloria looking about as dignified as a beached whale behind them. Eden sent her an apologetic look in the side mirror. *Sorry, girl.*

"So," Ted said with genuine cheer, "you must have pissed off someone pretty high up."

"The highest," she agreed forlornly.

"Thought so, since I've got a standing order to pick your van up whenever I see even the smallest infraction. I get a fat bonus every time I catch you out."

Of course. "What would have happened if I'd called the police to protest any of this?"

Ted's easy smile turned amused. "By the time they arrived, I'd have already left with your vehicle. And if not, I'd have explained how you'd blocked your neighbor's driveway for a week and only moved it when I arrived."

Eden frowned. "How do you sleep at night?"

"Sleep fine." He shrugged. "Your war's nothing to do with me. It's helping me put my girls through college, though. I'm appreciative. So, when a certain third party tells me to jump, I jump."

"Doesn't it bother you I'm innocent in all this?"

"No." He honked suddenly and leaned out his window, shouting, waving an arm. "Go round!"

"Why not?"

"Coz no one's innocent if they're dealing with that particular organization."

"How do you figure? That organization does the bidding of the rich and powerful."

He glanced at her. "You're serious?"

She nodded.

"Lady, they don't punish for no cause. You clearly did wrong somewhere along the line, and until you do right by them, we're gonna keep on meeting up."

Eden glared. "I'm not going to do right by an evil organization."

"Then my girls thank you for their college tuition."

They traveled in silence for the rest of the way.

Blue Plains Auto Impound Lot sat next to an asphalt plant and a Metrobus parkway and was around the corner from a giant concrete business. Scenic as hell.

Ted stuck his head out the window. "Hey, Dominique! How's my favorite girl?"

A familiar round face poked her head out of the office and sized him up. "Just peachy," she drawled, immune to Ted's charm. "And I ain't been a girl for thirty years." Her eyes flicked to Eden, who waved sheepishly.

"Not you again." Dominique sighed, her massive bosom rising like the ocean swell under her uniform shirt.

Eden climbed out. "Would you consider a frequent-towee discount?" she joked. "Because I'm getting tapped out here."

"Lord," Dominique said with a tut, "it'd be cheaper just to nuke that thing."

"So I hear." Eden exhaled.

"Your timing's lousy. I'm about to go on my break," Dominique said. "I take an early lunch. Come back in an hour and I'll release her."

"Can't you just do it quickly now?" Eden asked hopefully.

"No, ma'am. I've been here since seven-thirty! I've earned my break, so don't go giving me those big sad eyes." Dominique folded her arms.

Ted finished unhooking Gloria, jumped back in his truck, gave an obnoxious honk, and started up the road.

So cheerful at her expense. Eden glanced back to Dominique. "What's there to do around here for an hour? We're in the middle of nowhere."

"Beats me. That's a 'you' problem. See you in an hour." She returned to her office, flipping a sign on the door from *OPEN* to *BACK IN 1HR*.

Eden trudged out to the road, taking in the empty, industrial wasteland. So much black wrought-iron fence enclosing vacant land.

Her stomach grumbled and Eden remembered she'd skipped breakfast. It was now late morning.

She pulled out her phone and had a hunt around for food places. Okay, the nearest was two miles away, Fort Carroll Market—Groceries, Beer, and Wine—right next to a Unity of Love Praise Temple, whatever that was.

Google's Street View images showed lots of peeling paint, tattered curtains, and security wire on both the market and the church. Empty lots were on either side, and aside from a dry cleaner across the road, there didn't seem to be much else around. Still, beggars couldn't be choosers.

She tapped a few more buttons, noted it was a thirty-eight minute walk each way, and set off. She could use the exercise. Besides, anything was better than hanging around an impound lot. At least where she was going had food at the end.

Eden's stomach growled again. *You act like you've never been fed in your life,* she told it. *Are you a cat?*

She laughed at her own absurdity and glanced up. Spotting the food market, she quickened her pace.

"Gotta light?" The low male voice was only feet away.

Eden started.

A tall, solid figure in a gray hoodie and jeans leaned against an open gate in front of one of the empty lots. She had the oddest sensation he was wildly out of place. He wore thick-soled black boots. The expensive kind. Military looking. There was a casual power in his frame. His stance said he thought he was important.

Important? Around here, with all the shredded signs and cracked windows? He *was* out of place.

Fear rippled through her. "I don't smoke, sorry," she said, voice tight, and made to jog toward the store.

She didn't even make it two feet when the first blow smashed the back of her head. Shock rattled her. Eden didn't feel any pain—at first.

Her fingers clawed at dirt and cement. How had she wound up down here? She had no memory of falling.

The man grabbed the back of her jacket and dragged her deeper into the empty lot, toward a distant stand of trees.

Out of sight.

Fight!

Eden struggled furiously and opened her mouth to shout.

One huge, heavy boot hefted into her ribs. Then it slammed into her stomach, crushing the breath from her body. She gasped in agony, trying to find air.

Her assailant resumed dragging her.

After another minute of Eden wheezing and gasping, the hand let go of her. She slumped to the ground, and he loomed over her from one side.

Eden gazed up. She couldn't even hear the road now.

"Just knew you'd be trouble," he said.

Why is his voice weird? Wait, how is it weird?

She tried to make sense of it as fear scorched her. She wheezed too hard, and her aching ribs protested. Eden clutched them.

The man studied her impassively, a backlit, hulking shadow. The hoodie, pulled over his head, blanked his identity into nothing.

"Who are you?" Eden tried. His voice was odd. *Not…right.*

Why do I think that?

The man dropped to crouch over her, bringing into view dark sunglasses and a snarling lip. *Caucasian. Clean-shaven. Older. Cheap aftershave.* He backhanded her across the face.

Eden's nose exploded in blood, which flicked up into her eyes. "Ow! Why!" she gasped as the shock hit her again.

He looked at her like a bug he was about to stomp.

Adrenalin surged, mixed with terror. She was frozen. Her throat closed in panic.

Straightening, he lined up to kick her in the ribs again.

Instinctively, Eden clutched her sides tightly to protect herself from the incoming blow. At the last second, his foot deviated and went straight for her head.

Oh hell, Eden Celeste, her brain whispered at the sight of it. *You're in trouble now.*

Black sole was the last thing she saw before her world went dark.

It was icy cold and dark when Eden woke. She peeled her eyes open. They felt puffy and seemed to unstick rather than pop open. Her head was throbbing under her fingertips.

Eden gingerly touched the rest of her body, assessing. Even shifting that much, pain jagged her ribs. Had she broken one? More than one?

Her arms and legs and everything else seemed untouched and in basic working order.

She contracted her stomach muscles to sit up and experienced another ripple of pain. *Christ.* Her ribs were in a miserable state.

Slowly, painfully, she managed to sit. Her brain swam, thundering against her skull like a herd of elephants had been kicking it for hours.

Hours? How long *had* it been? Eden reached for her phone only to find it missing. Her hand brushed metal on the ground—and there it lay. Shattered, as though ground under heel. Carefully, she put the pieces in her jacket pocket and zipped it up. Maybe the SIM card could be salvaged later.

Okay, so she should hunt down a cab and... Eden stopped and rummaged her clothes, wincing again in pain, then looked around. Her wallet was gone.

Shit!

All right, she'd just go to the store, borrow their phone to call Aggie, and then...*Shit!* She had no clue what her best friend's number was. It'd only ever been a name on her screen to tap.

Goddamnit. No. Okay...focus. The store—they'd help. Somehow. She staggered back to the empty road and headed toward the shop. Every step jarred her ribs and sent pain spiking through her.

The old, paint-flaked market door was closed and locked. Fear and panic rose.

What if her attacker was hiding somewhere, lying in wait? Eden started peering fearfully into shadows, her hands becoming slick.

That was irrational, wasn't it? He'd attacked her when it was daylight. Now it was dark. Why would he sit around for hours waiting for her to come to? He'd be long gone.

Wiping her hands down her jeans, she forced herself to relax. Her mom's voice filled her head: "How you deal with setbacks reveals character. Either get busy panicking or get busy doing. But only one of those solves anything."

Right then. *Get busy doing*. Eden forced her worst fears away. What time was it? She peered at the store's sign. It closed at seven thirty nightly. So…after seven thirty.

A dog barked in the distance, and a chill shuddered through her from the crisp night air. Should she find a hospital? She had no idea where any were around here. Now what? She struggled to order her thoughts. Goddess. Even breathing hurt. Flag down a car? Bang on someone's door?

Terror shot through her at the thought of trusting strangers. She wanted to crawl deeper into her jacket in fear. She shuddered.

Okay, my body votes no to that.

Low honking came from somewhere…but it was not a car. It was deep and long, and it pulled at a memory. Tugboats. She was near the river.

It was like a hand reaching into her brain to lay out the answer. *Michelle lives near the river.*

Not just near it. Right *on* it. Good. That meant she wasn't *that* far away, surely?

What was her address?

Eden's disordered mind sputtered to a stop and offered nothing. Well, that didn't matter. She didn't need an address. It was somewhere near Watergate Hotel. All she had to do was follow the river north until she recognized Michelle's building. The facade was so distinctive.

Once there, Michelle would help. Eden knew it in her bones. Besides, Michelle owed her, she thought crossly. She wouldn't even *be* here to be attacked if Gloria hadn't been towed on Michelle's orders.

A surge of righteous indignation kicked in. It was enough to start her moving toward the sound of those boats, while the adrenalin coursing through her kept her going.

Yeah, she'd give the woman a piece of her mind, Eden thought as she trudged…well, *lurched*. She would explain that Michelle was wrong and evil and a liar and that Gloria deserved respect, and Eden was only doing what was best…and…and…other stuff. And then she'd ask her—no, *demand*—how she could do something so terrible for a living.

Eden most wanted to know that part. She sniffed back stray tears. *Stupid shock reaction.* She plodded on.

Her vision blurred. Suddenly it was overwhelming: She wanted Michelle Hastings right in front of her, fixing the mess she'd gotten Eden into. Wanted her taking charge of this the way she did everything: with calm, powerful efficiency. She was such a force, bending the universe to her will.

To suit her evil clients, you mean.

Eden's rage boiled up at the reminder. Okay, so she didn't *just* want Michelle's reassuring competence. She also really wanted to know *why*. Why she'd hired Eden to work in her office in the first place. Why play her for a fool? She'd made Eden the office laughingstock! Why any of it? They could have parted ways after Wingapo. Michelle had prolonged this, not Eden. *Michelle.*

Why!

With that conundrum stewing in her brain, Eden continued to force herself along, ignoring everything else but her anger and confusion over Michelle. Worse was the broken trust. That part really hurt. Because Eden had come to see so much more in Michelle than she showed the world. Someone warm, gentle, and protective of her safta. Someone wry and amusing and so, so smart.

Had that version of Michelle really only existed in her mind? She wiped another tear away.

Honestly, Eden missed *her* Michelle every single day. She'd felt like *Eden's*. They'd gone through things together. Connected. She knew Michelle was private and didn't share herself with others. But she'd opened up about her pain for the teenager who'd been let down by his lover. Eden had seen that; seen *her*. And she missed their connection so much that it ached.

But Michelle also did horrific things. How could both Michelles be real?

Eden gave up fighting and let the tears fall. Because crying over a woman you didn't really know was no better than tears in rain—they didn't count. And the honest truth was that Michelle Hastings circa two months ago wasn't even real.

Except…she had felt pretty real to Eden.

She choked out a sound that was something watery and heaving, which went all the way down to her ribs. The tears kept falling. And Eden kept walking.

Eden had lost track of time. The moon was higher and fewer boats were on the Potomac now, but that was about the extent of what she could process anymore. She was also seriously thirsty.

Fatigue and nausea were kicking in now that the adrenalin had worn off. At least the tears had stopped. Not even thoughts of seeing Michelle filled her anymore. Everything in her periphery became a misty red haze.

Twice she'd had to stop to throw up, and the retching had made her ribs feel like they'd been punched with knuckle dusters. Which was a variation on them aching from the cold. The worn-out corduroy trucker jacket she was wearing wasn't nearly warm enough.

On the plus side, she no longer felt hungry. Just thirsty and sick.

It was much, much darker by the time she saw Michelle's building. She'd know those sleek chrome balcony railings anywhere. With one final, exhausted lurch, she leaned against the heavy glass entrance door and pushed herself inside.

Face to face with the lanky doorman, Eden came to a standstill. It was only at that moment, when his brown, concerned eyes widened at her disarray, that two things occurred in rapid succession.

One, what if he didn't let her see Michelle? What if he thought she was some weird, dirty hobo and kicked her out of his fancy foyer?

And two…her heart tightened painfully at this thought…what if Michelle didn't *want* to help her?

Because why would she?

Her brain suddenly remembered a crucial thing: She had *turned on* Michelle. Had been attacking her organization for almost two months. Now Eden had come to her for *help*?

The guard stepped from behind the desk, frowning. "Can I help you, ma'am? And, er...I think you need some urgent medical attention."

"I'm E—" Why did her tongue feel too big for her mouth? Words sounded so weird coming out—far away. "I'm Eden Lawless. Here t' see Michelle Hastings."

"Is Ms. Hastings a friend of yours?" he asked with frank skepticism. "Or something else?"

"Or something," Eden agreed. It hurt her cracked lips to smile. "Wha'time is it?" Her legs began to fold. "Oh." That wasn't good. "I just need to...to..." She indicated the floor. "I'll sit while you get her."

"It's just after eleven-thirty, ma'am." His face looked blurry.

Eden closed her eyes for a few moments. The red mist in her head was back.

Then nothing.

When she opened her eyes again, Eden's shoulder was being shaken by someone saying her name.

Michelle? It sounded a lot like her. Except the voice also sounded mad. Really mad.

"Ms. Lawless!" The angry Michelle voice snapped. "Wake *up*!"

"H...hey?" Eden peeled her eyes open. "Michelle!" Her wobbly smile of relief—Michelle had come for her!—faltered at the other woman's thunderous expression.

Was it because Eden had just invaded her home? Heart pounding, Eden swallowed hard and whispered, "I didn't know where else to go."

Fury and venom dripped from Michelle's voice as she leaned right in and demanded: "Who *did* this to you!"

Chapter 11
Who Did *This to You?*

Michelle rubbed her eyes and placed the latest report to one side of the desk in her home office. It was almost eleven-thirty. Another late night thanks to Lawless's media leaks. Michelle would be on her knees with exhaustion if she kept this pace up, trying to furiously clean up each spot fire.

Nine. The number of clients Eden Lawless had thus far outed.

The latest leak was catastrophic: A pharmaceutical executive chasing a promotion had artificially inflated a cancer drug's price to keep it for the rich. Michelle had inherited that case and wasn't in the least bit sad to see the man shamed. However, it was a damning blow to The Fixers' reputation for discretion.

She'd planned to inform the board of the security breaches after she'd successfully contained Lawless, so there could at least be some good news. Unfortunately, the woman was damned stubborn, and this was going on too long. Lawless persisted no matter how uncomfortable O'Brian's team was making her life. So Michelle's latest strategy was to focus on stopping the journalist to whom Lawless kept leaking.

The only surprise was that Lawless hadn't outed the existence of The Fixers. Why?

Michelle rubbed her aching temples. It was hard to motivate herself to protect these slimiest of clients. But that was the job, wasn't it? She had always known this was the deal.

Today was difficult to push through, and Michelle had been finding it harder and harder to put her head down and do what needed to be done. Her heart wasn't in it.

Giving herself a little shake, she forced herself to focus on finishing up. Right. In the morning, she'd get someone from MassMess with a flair for publicity spin to deal with the latest exposed client. An expert could gently ease the clients into understanding that their lives were about to be over.

And they deserve it.

Irrelevant. They'd paid well for her services, and Michelle would see they got their money's worth.

Her cell phone rang. Hope flared for a second that it would be her grandmother, distracting her with all her Florida adventures with Rosemary. But there was no way her safta was calling this late. It showed on her screen as her building's security number. "Hastings."

"Ma'am, it's Joe Pearson from the lobby. I have a woman here asking to see you. Eden Lawless."

Her mouth fell open. How had that woman found out Michelle's home address? It was something she protected fiercely. Not even O'Brian knew where she lived.

"I have no interest in speaking to her," Michelle snapped.

"Okay, ma'am. I just thought, maybe since it was an emergency? Because she's hurt and—"

"She's *hurt*?" Michelle shot to her feet. "What happened?" She ran to her apartment door.

"Not sure, ma'am. Looks like she's been beaten up. She's covered in dirt and has these big bruises—"

"I'll be right down." Michelle hung up, stabbing the elevator button repeatedly. What the hell had Lawless gotten herself into now?

Beaten up!

Obviously, it wasn't Michelle's people behind this. Even if she hadn't been explicit in her instructions that O'Brian's team should go softly, softly, she knew none of them wanted to hurt Lawless even a little. They'd been grumbling about the security op against her from day one.

The elevator doors opened and Michelle rushed in. With mounting impatience, she glowered as the numbers in the elevator ticked down slowly. *Faster!*

She came to me. She knows I wasn't behind this.

The thought short-circuited her chaotic brain. As infuriating as Lawless was, as hurtful as it had been that she'd betrayed Michelle, she never wanted a single hair hurt on her beautiful head.

For fuck's sake. Stubborn. *Stubborn* head.

Satisfaction and relief curled in the pit of her stomach as she remembered the point. *She knows I didn't order this.* It shouldn't matter, but it did.

The moment the doors slid apart, Michelle sprinted from the elevator and immediately spotted the guard, kneeling. Next to him lay a lumpy shape caked in dirt and blood. Matted hair stuck to Lawless's unconscious pale face. Her shadowed eyes were closed, and one swollen cheek was badly bruised.

Protectiveness and rage burned through Michelle. Who had done this? Why! Was it random? Did they know her?

Joe shifted Eden's bloodied hair off her face, concern etched on his solemn features.

Michelle sank to her knees beside them, feeling sick at the sight. The fearless woman was like a valiant, bright flower in an empty wasteland. And some…animal…had tried to crush her.

They would pay for this. Michelle's nostrils flared. She knew so many ways to make the assailant suffer. The Fixers staff would gladly do it, even though they also knew she'd betrayed them. They didn't even care.

When it had first come out that Lawless was leaking Fixers cases, they'd all reacted as if it was just in keeping with her eccentric nature. Astonishing.

Michelle had seen vicious vendettas started over stolen lunches in the staff fridge, but Eden's full-on betrayal? *Meh, it's Lawless being Lawless. What can you do?* Cue shrugs.

Some days, Michelle felt like the only one in the office still hurt and angry over what had happened.

So, yes, there would be plenty of volunteers to assist in finding Lawless's attacker.

Grasping her by the shoulders, Michelle gave her a gentle shake.

Lawless's head lolled to the side. Large, sinister finger marks imprinted around her throat came into view. Michelle gasped. Someone had tried to *strangle* her too?

This was not a simple mugging. It was a threat. A show of "I could have if I'd wanted to." Or had the assailant tried to kill her and been interrupted before finishing?

Michelle's breath caught at that, and fury roared in her ears. Shaking harder, she ordered, "Ms. Lawless! Wake *up*!"

"H…hey?" Her voice—while a relief to hear—sounded all wrong. Distant. Rough. Confused. Lawless's eyes met Michelle's and widened at whatever she saw there. "I didn't know where else to go," she whispered.

Michelle blinked in surprise.

Eden looked about ready to slide into unconsciousness again, her eyes rolling back.

With another firm shake to keep her conscious, Michelle demanded, "Who did this to you!"

Lawless's eyes refocused and crinkled into softness and recognition. "It's *you*."

"Yes?" Michelle frowned. "You came to my home. Of course it's me."

"Been so long since I saw you. T'other you."

The other me? Lawless's brain had to be rattled.

With no small concern, Michelle cupped her cheek, a thumb brushing restlessly up and down, the warmth under it reassuring her. "Ms. Lawless, look at me. I'm here. You're okay."

"*Now* I am." She spoke with utter conviction. Her expression was distant, though. Unfocused.

"What happened?" Michelle asked.

"Hurts."

"I can see that. Who hurt you?"

"Stranger. Attacked. Out of nowhere. Empty lot near the food market." A tear slid from her eye, cutting a track through dirt. "Really hurts. Ribs, stomach, head. Kicked me. Dragged me into the lot."

"All right. I'll call my doctor. She may need to take you to her private hospital for scans."

Lawless began to droop. "Don't wanna hosp…ital. Tired. Thirsty. Need sleep."

"I'm not sure that's wise if you have a concussion." Any first-aid training she'd received at the FBI had fled years ago. Michelle peered into the other woman's green eyes as if she could determine what her pupil dilation status meant. She'd seen it in a movie once. "No arguing."

Michelle pulled out her phone and stabbed a number. "Dr. Michelson? I need you at my residence ASAP. I have an injured employee who has been badly assaulted."

"Yes, Ms. Hastings," the doctor replied, sounding mercifully sharp. "Can you indicate the nature of their injuries?"

Michelle glanced back at Eden, taking in the swelling cheek and the way her arms had wrapped around her ribs. "Beaten and bruised. Possible fractures."

"All right, I'll be there in twenty minutes."

"Make it ten," Michelle snapped. Then she sighed. "Sorry. I'm… concerned. Hurry?"

"Of course."

Michelle ended the call.

"Mi…chelle," Lawless said haltingly. "*Ex*-employee."

"What?"

"You said *employee*. I don't work for that…*place*. Could never. Not now."

"I know." Michelle's lips twisted sharply. "You've made that abundantly clear."

"Good." Eden nodded before her eyes fluttered closed and she slipped into unconsciousness.

Panic hit. "Ms. Lawless? Wake up!"

Nothing.

"Come on, stop scaring me. *Eden?* You're supposed to be tougher than this!" Where was her infuriating, fierce fighter?

However, Lawless lay limply on the floor, suddenly so small and damaged.

Michelle shot a look at Joe, who was standing a respectable distance back. When had he moved? "Would you please help me get her to my apartment? My physician is on her way."

"Yes, Ms. Hastings." The man easily scooped Lawless into his arms and tilted his head to the elevator. "Press the button?"

Rushing over, Michelle stabbed it violently. The doors opened and she followed the guard in. She fretted the entire ride up, constantly glancing at the limp body in the man's arms.

How tiny Lawless seemed now, her pale face against Joe's uniform sleeves, messy red hair spilling over his arms. Lawless took up so much room usually—so energized and filled with purpose. Now she seemed to subtract the air from the elevator, making it thin and insubstantial.

Nothing seemed right anymore. Not one damned thing.

Michelle led Joe into her master bedroom, indicating the bed.

He lay Eden carefully down, then backed out.

"Please send Dr. Michelson up the moment she arrives. And thank you, Joe."

He nodded and left, closing the apartment door behind him.

Michelle padded one floor down to her laundry room and located a washcloth. She retrieved a large plastic tub, half filled it with warm water, and hurried upstairs, pausing in the kitchen to grab a bottled water.

Lawless was waking up, looking groggy.

"Don't try to talk," Michelle ordered. "You've been hurt, but you're safe. You're in my apartment."

"Michelle?" Lawless's eyes widened in recognition. She seemed more aware this time. "How did I get here?"

"You came to me, remember? Walked some distance by the looks of things," Michelle said sharply to hide her fear. She unscrewed the lid on the water bottle and handed it to her. "You said you were thirsty earlier."

Lawless gulped down the water.

"May want to slow down a little," she said in alarm. "I promise there's more in my kitchen." Michelle picked up the tub of water and placed it on the bed beside Lawless, waiting until she finished drinking. "Better?"

"Yeah."

"Good." Michelle removed the bottle. "Now I'm just going to get some of this dirt and blood off you while we wait for the doctor. Lie still."

"I can do that myself," Lawless protested and made to sit up higher.

"You really are terrible at taking direction, aren't you?" Michelle lifted an eyebrow. "For once in your life, just do as you're told and let me fix this."

Lawless sagged. "Guess that's what you do? Fix things."

"Exactly," Michelle said, a tiny smile on her lips. "Allow me, Ms. Lawless."

"'Kay." Lawless's eyelids fluttered as the fight went out of her. "But stop calling me that. Hate it."

"What?"

"My name is *Eden*."

Michelle inhaled. "As you wish…Eden. Now lie still." She efficiently drew the washcloth through blood and grime, revealing the awful extent of the bruising on one cheek—possibly broken—a darkly shadowed eye that would almost certainly bloom into a terrible black eye, and a bloodied nose (not broken). Next, she ran her fingers through the red hair on her scalp, seeking any wounds.

"Feels nice," Eden mumbled.

"It's not supposed to," Michelle observed wryly, satisfied to find nothing untoward. "I'm checking for injuries." She slid loose hair out of Eden's eyes. "And I'm trying to make you look less like you've done ten rounds with Frankenstein."

"Frankenstein's monster," Eden said, eyes still closed.

"Hmm?" Michelle moved lower, wiping blood spatters off the woman's neck.

"Frankenstein was the doctor who built him. Monster ha' no name."

"Well, I'm glad to see your brain's still working."

Eden offered a tired smile. "Bet you wouldn't ha' said that 'n' hour ago."

"I have never said your brain was working in an *exemplary* manner," Michelle said with an amused tut.

Eden's faint smile didn't go away, and Michelle was delighted to see it again. She had no interest in arguing with her. Not now.

Michelle eased Eden's jacket off, hanging it on the back of a chair. It made a rattling noise. She investigated and found a shattered cell phone in her pocket.

Returning to her side, Michelle reached for the top button of Eden's blouse and asked hesitantly, "May I? I just want to see your clavicle—it seems there's more bruising there. Or would you rather wait for the doctor?"

Eden hesitated a long time. Myriad emotions flashed across her face, the chief ones being fear and vulnerability.

Michelle pursed her lips and nodded. "That's fine." She understood the woman's reluctance, and her stomach tightened. Half an hour ago, they'd been enemies. It was too much to expect Eden didn't still feel anger—or worse—around Michelle. "Let me throw out this water. I'll be right back."

"No!" Eden's eyes snapped open, filled with alarm.

"I'm just going to the en suite." Michelle indicated the murky water in the plastic tub she was holding.

"No." Eden's eyes grew more afraid.

"Okay." Michelle placed the bowl on the floor instead. "I'll stay. Well. Let me see what else I can do to make you more presentable." She reached for a comb on her dresser.

"Good luck with that," Eden muttered, voice thick. "I know how I must look."

Michelle ran it through Eden's hair, careful not to tug, excising the worst of leaves, dirt, and detritus. "You've been through an ordeal," Michelle said as she finished, setting the comb aside. "I'm not judging."

She made her way to the end of the bed and began removing Eden's footwear. "Well…" She lay the boots on the floor. "Maybe a little: I wouldn't have thought you'd wear leather boots, given all your animal-loving causes." Her lips tugged into a smile to show she was teasing.

"*Vegan* boots. Gift from Mom," Eden murmured. "Not leather."

"Could have fooled me. They look genuine." Michelle turned back to discover Eden's gaze on her. "They're so…sturdy."

"Not like his were."

"His?"

"The man. Military boots. Thick and heavy. Fat rubber soles. Hurt like hell. I didn't see much of him given his hoodie and sunglasses, but I remember those boots. Bastard also got my wallet. Broke my phone."

"We'll find him," Michelle gritted out. "Don't worry. He'll be sorry."

Puzzlement filled Eden's expression. "Why are you being so kind to me? I'm trying to ruin your evil company."

"I'm well aware." Michelle gave her a tired look. "You are nothing if not consistent. A better question is why you came to me tonight. Weren't you afraid I'd ordered this attack?"

"No."

"Not even for a second?" Michelle's eyebrows lifted in surprise.

"No." Wonder filled Eden's tone as the realization seemed to hit her. "I knew it wasn't you."

"All right, but even so, why come here? To me? You said you didn't know where else to go but you would have gone by several open businesses that would have been able to help. Restaurants? Hotels? You bypassed them all to find me."

Eden looked away and said in a small voice, "I was afraid."

"Of strangers?" Michelle suggested. "Hurting you?"

"Yeah." Frightened green eyes fixed on Michelle.

"But not of me."

"No."

Michelle hesitated. "Why?" she asked in genuine confusion. "You know what I'm capable of. God, you knew that and *still* betrayed me."

Eden's eyes flashed. "And *you* betrayed *me*."

What? She'd done no such thing!

"But even so…I knew you would help me," Eden continued, frowning. "When I was in Wingapo and we were fighting, I texted you to say Francine had found out I was behind the scavenger hunt. You asked if I needed security. You were mad at me and you still immediately wanted to help me. You made me feel…safe." She winced at the admission, looking away.

Safe. Michelle warmed. "Eden…" She drew in a breath.

"Don't you dare say you did that because I was your *employee*," Eden snapped. "Don't minimize it. That moment really mattered to me."

"I was *going* to say I wasn't really mad at you." Michelle gave a frustrated huff. "More like feeling hurt. I was blindsided discovering you and my safta had gone behind my back and were delving into my private business that you had no right to discuss." Her voice sharpened. "Of course, that was nothing compared to later, learning *you* were the snake trying to destroy my company. That was a whole other level of betrayal and hurt."

"Well, you hurt me first." Eden's big green eyes filled with tears. "A lot."

Michelle's indignation and annoyance faltered in the face of those sad eyes. "How?" she finally asked.

"I trusted you," Eden said unevenly. "I loved the work I *thought* I was doing with you. I thought I was making a difference. Helping people. It was a lie. Everyone else knew. They were all laughing at me. Who does that to another person?" She swallowed.

Shame flooded Michelle. She hadn't thought about what it would have felt like from Eden's perspective.

Eden's voice cracked. "Imagine how humiliating it was to learn I was just a punchline. Someone for you and the others to laugh at. Everything was a lie."

Michelle wanted to protest that. She hadn't *outright* lied. Not exactly.

"Each time I sat with you, sharing my coffee, sharing *me*, you were playing me for a fool," Eden went on, her gaze radiating pain. "That hurt so much. You broke my trust, and that broke my heart."

Silence fell.

Eden bit back the tiniest sob, then turned away, looking crushed. "Don't you dare dismiss that. What I felt. Realizing I'd been too trusting to see what you were all doing." Eden hugged her ribs, looking utterly bereft. "I just don't know *why* you did that to me. Can you explain that?"

Michelle didn't know what to say, but her mind swamped her in dismay and shame. The lies of omission that Michelle had told, and that others had told for her, must have felt like mockery to Eden, not acts of protection from an ugly truth. Eden had felt foolish and embarrassed. Her beautiful, trusting heart was now bruised. All because Michelle couldn't admit the truth. She wanted Eden to stay in her world. She'd been so selfish.

A knock sounded, making them both start.

"That'll be my doctor." Michelle's gaze was fixed on the wet trails on Eden's cheeks. *I did that to her.* The words *broke my heart* hurt almost as much as seeing her in pain. "Eden," she said quietly, "I promise I wasn't laughing at you. I never wanted to hurt you. All the…misdirections…were to protect you."

"Sure." Eden muttered, her disbelief clear. "Protect *you*, you mean." She turned away. "By the way, this attack happened near the impound lot. I was only there because your people had Gloria towed. *Again.*"

Shock ricocheted around Michelle. "Oh," she whispered. Guilt flooded her.

"Yeah." Eden closed her eyes. "Exactly."

Dr. Michelson had been The Fixers' on-call physician for three decades. She had never been told exactly what the organization did, and Michelle had noted with satisfaction that she was too wise to ask those sorts of questions despite seeing a variety of hard-to-explain injuries. The most she'd ever said on the topic was that it wasn't her business. Smart woman.

The physician sat beside Eden and gently asked her questions as her fingers lightly roamed various body parts, inspecting for injuries.

"You don't look so bad under all these bruises," Dr. Michelson said with a reassuring smile.

The comments went a long way to reassuring Michelle too; her thundering heart rate slowed in relief.

"I think we can do a full set of hospital scans tomorrow since you're so adamant about not going anywhere tonight," Dr. Michelson continued.

Michelle left them to it, closing the door behind her, taking the bowl. Heading downstairs to her apartment's laundry, she poured out the dirty water, washed the tub, and then tried very hard not think about the woman lying in her bed. Eden was a dazed shadow of herself.

Her earlier question sprang to mind: *Why are you being so kind?*

Michelle was not kind. Oh, her grandmother might disagree, but Hannah was the exception. In Michelle's profession, kindness was seen as weakness.

"I'm not kind," she told the shelves above her.

Eden was a woman in trouble, no more, no less. Anyone would have done the same.

You could have called an ambulance and walked away.

Michelle pushed that thought aside and focused on Eden's absolute certainty that she wasn't responsible.

I knew it wasn't you.

How had Eden known it wasn't O'Brian's team? She'd been so sure.

At the reminder of her security chief, she grabbed her phone to call him.

"O'Brian," he said after it rang awhile. He yawned and added, "What d'ya need, boss?"

She appreciated he didn't whine about the lateness. "Cancel all ops on Lawless. Her vehicle is still impounded, so retrieve it and drop it at her friend's residence. Remove our tracker off the van. We'll no longer be alerting the tow company as to her whereabouts."

There was a stunned silence, and then, with obvious relief, he said, "I'll see to it personally. Confirming no more ops on Lawless."

Michelle drew in a breath, hating to break her head of security's rising mood. "Someone attacked her in the street. I want to know who."

He inhaled sharply. "Is she okay?" Concern turned to anger when he said, "Want me to interview her tonight?"

"No. She's being examined, and then she'll need a rest. Tomorrow would be better. She's battered and bruised. I'm suspecting rib damage. She seems okay. Lucid." Michelle paused, remembering Lawless's confusing comments when she'd first gained consciousness. "Well, lucid-ish."

"Where'd it happen?"

"Near the impound lot." Michelle paused to let that sink in for him.

He inhaled sharply. She knew he had to feel as guilty as she did.

"She said something about a food market," Michelle continued. "She was assaulted in an empty lot nearby. I want to know who did it and why. Strangulation marks at her throat make me think a message was being sent."

O'Brian growled. "Did she say anythin' about the attacker?"

"She mentioned he was big, wore military boots, sunglasses, a hoodie."

"Right." O'Brian sounded as if he was taking notes.

"When you investigate, you have *carte blanche* to bring in anyone from work you need in order to be thorough."

"Will do," he said. "And when I find the bastard, I'll let him know he's made a fuckin' enormous mistake messin' with one of ours."

"You do that." Michelle said, too tired to argue Eden was not theirs and hated being seen that way. And yet, O'Brian's comment also felt right.

How can both be true?

"Anythin' else?" he asked.

"Contact that friend of hers—Agatha Teo. She may be worried. Explain Lawless has been hurt but is being taken care of tonight. However, Ms. Teo can meet her at the hospital tomorrow if she wishes. I'll text you the appointment time to pass along when I have one, but Dr. Michelson will likely want Eden there first thing."

"Right." He sounded determined. "On it."

"Good."

The doctor Michelle had sent to look after her was nice, Eden decided. She was gentle and professional and careful not to hurt Eden any more than she was already as she examined her.

"Okay, young lady," Dr. Michelson said in a kind tone, "your ribs don't feel broken, but they may still have a slight fracture or two. A concussion also seems likely. I'll get your ribs and head scanned at my private hospital tomorrow. But overall? It seems like you've been lucky and avoided the worst."

"You have your own hospital?" Eden asked in amazement.

Dr. Michelson smiled. Her gray eyebrows lifted. "I do. That's why your employer likes me. I come complete with a medical facility."

"She's not my employer. Not anymore," Eden said moodily. "And before you ask, not a friend either."

"Could have fooled me. She was extremely concerned when she called."

"She's feeling guilty. I was only where I was when the attack happened because of something she did."

"Trust an old woman," Dr. Michelson said, patting her arm. "I've seen plenty of guilt in my time. Plenty of concern too. I know the difference. Ms. Hastings might feel some guilt, no argument, but she's also very worried about you." She paused and frowned, moving in closer. "Tell me about those handprints around your throat."

"I…the what?"

"There's an imprint of fingers on your neck."

Eden's hand flew to her throat. It was tender. "I don't know."

"No memory of it?"

"No?" Fear shot through her. "It must have happened after he knocked me out. Does that mean he was trying to kill me?"

"Well, he's a bit incompetent if that was his aim, wouldn't you say?"

"He didn't strike me as incompetent at all." Eden swallowed. "He knew exactly what he was doing."

"I see." No surprise flickered on Dr. Michelson's face. "Then the thing to focus on is you're safe now. Ms. Hastings won't let anything happen to you. I've never seen her more protective of anyone in all the years I've worked with her."

A tremble of fear overtook Eden at how easily she might have been killed.

"Will the police be called?" the doctor asked. "I'm asking so I know whether my notes will be needed for a criminal investigation."

Eden stared, astonished she hadn't even thought about police. "I don't know," she whispered. She thought about the strangulation marks. That felt personal. "I…"

"It's okay. I'll prepare some in case. You can decide later. Now then, I have something for the pain to help you get through the night. I need you to follow the directions exactly. This stuff can make you a little loopy. Have some food, drink plenty of fluids, and have a nice, restful night's sleep. It'd be best to have someone around to keep an eye on you. I'm assuming you're staying here?"

"No. I have a friend's couch I crash on when I'm not sleeping in Gloria. That's my van." She scowled. "But she's still impounded."

"I'm afraid a couch won't cut it as a recuperation option any more than a van bed," Dr. Michelson said sternly. "You need to be able to fully stretch out in comfort and heal—while supervised."

Just then a knock sounded, and Michelle poked her head in. "How is everyone?"

"I have a stubborn patient with a mercifully hard head," Dr. Michelson replied. "Come in—I've just finished. She'll need scans tomorrow for her ribs, cheek, and skull, but right now I don't think anything's broken."

A brief smile flashed across Michelle's face. "Well, that's good news. What time do I need to bring her in?"

"Eight would be good," Dr. Michelson said, rising.

"Um, excuse me? I'm right here?" Eden protested, then tried to sit up. "Ow."

"I apologize, Ms. Lawless," the doctor said. "Is eight too early for Ms. Hastings to bring you by?" She turned back to Michelle. "I've already recommended she stays here tonight so she can be observed, as opposed to going to her friend's house, which has a couch she sleeps on and is not ideal."

"Who says Michelle's overseeing my care?" Eden argued. "Or taking me anywhere?"

"Oh, I'm sorry," Michelle said in a low, dangerous tone, "did you have somewhere else to be in your doubtlessly packed schedule?"

"No," Eden muttered.

"Then what's the problem? And thinking I'll let you anywhere near a couch tonight is just ridiculous. You need to heal. You need to be safe. My apartment can offer both."

The doctor looked at Eden. "Your healing must come first."

Eden glanced at each of them and then mulishly tried to fold her arms. Only it made her ribs hurt like Hades, and she cried out.

Michelle's smug expression vanished. "This is what I'm talking about! You cannot be trusted on your own for five minutes!"

"Right, that's it!" Eden tried to rise. "I'm outta here," she said, but the world seemed to wobble.

Concern filled Michelle's face as Eden collapsed back into bed, humiliated.

"You're the most stubborn woman." Michelle eyed her in frustration.

"Takes one to know one." With a small mumble, Eden conceded. "Tonight, then. Just tonight."

Michelle rolled her eyes. "How magnanimous."

Dr. Michelson smiled. "I'll leave you two to it. I'll see you both first thing tomorrow."

Michelle followed her to the door to show her out.

Eden closed her exhausted eyes.

She could make out soft tones as the women talked. Michelle was asking about any other injuries.

Eden sighed. Somehow she'd acquired an unlikely caregiver. Why did it have to be the head of an evil corporation?

Twice throughout the night Eden woke, disoriented and in pain. Twice she had the sense that someone had just been there. Michelle? Checking on her?

The second time she called out, "Michelle?" she did it quietly enough that she wouldn't wake the other woman if she was wrong.

"Yes?" came a soft, concerned voice from the doorway. "Are you okay?"

What a question. She felt confused, strange, and unmoored. Was it the loopy side effects of her drugs or her jangled brain? "I just wondered who was out there."

"Only me." Michelle entered.

There was enough ambient light from the city below to give form to her shadow. Michelle wore a pale T-shirt and shorts. It was the most casual and rumpled she'd ever looked. Eden realized she'd never seen Michelle's hair out of its tight bun before. For the briefest moment, she forgot she was mad at and just stared at those pale, naked legs and unlikely bedhead.

"I thought I was being quiet," Michelle added.

Eden blinked. "I've only been dozing. Even with the painkillers, everything's tense and sharp when I move. I'm also starving. It's been almost a day since I ate."

"Why didn't you say! I'm sure there's some of my safta's chicken soup in the freezer. I'll heat it up. Be right back."

Before Eden could reply, Michelle was gone.

Five minutes later, she returned holding a large mug, flicked on a low wattage table lamp, and handed it over. "It'll cure anything that ails you. Don't believe me, just ask my grandmother."

Eden sat up a little, as much as she could manage, and gratefully drank, savoring the rich flavors of the soup. Her stomach rumbled its appreciation. When she finished, she gave the mug back. "That was good."

Michelle smiled and turned to leave.

"Wait." Eden stopped her in her tracks. "What were you doing in here?" She wriggled and twisted to get in a better position, yelping when her ribs reminded her they were in no condition to be moved.

"Serves you right," Michelle said dryly. "No heroics in bed."

"I know," Eden shot back grumpily. "And you didn't answer the question."

"I wanted to make sure you hadn't taken a turn for the worse." Michelle paused. "Head injuries can really mess people up." Her voice became quieter as she said, "I've seen people stop breathing for no reason; their brain just decides to forget how to make lungs operate. It's awful."

"That sounds horrible." Eden tried to read her expression, but Michelle's face was as cool and neutral as ever. "You were worried about me? That I might be not breathing or something?"

"Just being cautious. I should have remembered you'd be too defiant to die."

"That's me." Eden smiled. "Stubborn as hell."

"Yes. Look, I'm just down the hall in my grandmother's room. Call out if you feel unwell. I'd have told you earlier, but you were already asleep after I showed Dr. Michelson out."

"Okay. Does your fancy apartment seriously only have two bedrooms?" If there were more than two, why wasn't Eden in a guest room? Hadn't this place cost twenty million or something? "And where's Hannah? I'd love to meet her in person."

"My safta's in Florida visiting a friend for a few months. And while I do have a guest room downstairs, I can't very well look in on you easily if you're a whole floor away, especially if you're at death's door." Michelle's lips twitched.

"I don't feel at death's door. But thanks for giving me your room. It's very…" Eden realized she hadn't fully absorbed where she was: in Michelle's private, inner sanctuary. In her *bed*.

With the lamp now on, she took it in. The room was large and elegant with classical lines and sleek white oak closets at one end. Thick, dark curtains lined the windows, although they were currently open. Bedside tables made of polished wood and glass sat on each side of the queen bed and were pinned down by frosted glass lamps. One table had a paperback resting on it. Eden was dying to roll over and see what Michelle was reading, but that would involve twisting, something no longer in her body's repertoire.

"Very what?" Michelle's lips had compressed, as if rethinking her hospitality thanks to Eden's curious gaze.

"Generous of you. And your bed's super comfy."

"Mm." Michelle's shoulders relaxed.

Eden suddenly remembered something. "Hey, in the morning, can I make a call? Aggie expected me back at her place after picking up Gloria. She must be worried."

"Already taken care of. I sent Mr. O'Brian around to see her last night. He explained you'd been mugged and were being looked after tonight. She's been supplied details about your hospital visit so she can see you then if she wants to."

Eden blinked. "You sent *Phelim* around to tell her I'd been attacked?"

"Yes." Michelle frowned. "Why?"

"He's kind of intimidating if you don't know him. She probably thinks you've kidnapped me."

"Why would I want to kidnap the thorn in my side?" Michelle asked, tone dry.

"Because I may have told her fifteen different times and ways that you're evil."

"Ah." Michelle's expression dimmed at the word. Hurt flickered in her eyes. "Well, in that case, I'm sure your friend will turn up at the hospital for a proof-of-life check. You can inform her that you remain free of captivity then."

Eden nodded. "What if I wanted to see her now?"

"Do you? It's two in the morning and you're not on the brink of death. But if you desperately needed to see her, I'd arrange for you to be delivered promptly to Ms. Teo—no matter how medically inadvisable."

Eden turned that over. "Delivered to?"

"I don't give out my address freely," Michelle explained, "so I won't allow strangers here either. Can you bear that in mind and not share my information with anyone else?"

"Uh. Sure." That seemed fair.

"On that note, how *did* you know where I live?" Michelle's expression was tight.

"It was on the USB drive I was given."

Michelle stared. "And you remembered my address from back then? Despite a head injury?"

"Oh, hell no." Eden snorted. "But the day I discovered your address, I looked your place up. Saw photos. Admired the chrome designer balcony. Noticed you were right on the river and not far from Watergate Hotel. So tonight, I just followed the river toward the fancy part of town and kept walking till I found you."

Michelle stared at her. "You recognized the *balcony*."

"Yep. It's very...architectural. Pretty."

"Well." That seemed to stymie her. "And who gave you the USB drive in the first place?"

Eden saw no reason to lie. "Alberto Baldoni."

Based on Michelle's unsurprised expression, she already knew that. "And how did *he* get it?"

Eden shrugged. A deal was a deal. "No comment."

"I see." Michelle's lips tightened.

"What are you going to do to your ex-husband for trying to hurt The Fixers?"

Michelle eyed her. "Aren't you more worried about what I'm going to do to you? Aren't I some terrible villain?" The flash of hurt was back, and this time Eden knew she wasn't imagining it.

There was a lot of hurt to go around apparently.

"Like I said, I felt safe coming to you," Eden said. "Maybe I'm wrong, but the way I see it is, if you were going to mess me up, you'd have done it by now. Everything you've done to me has just been annoying. The money side's the worst of it—finding ways to pay for slashed tires and impound fees."

"Don't tell me you've blown through your Wingapo payment already?" Michelle gaped. "I urged you to take my financial planner's card!"

"Not that it's any of your business, but yeah, the money's gone. All on good causes."

"Like my staff's coffee habits?" Michelle sounded exasperated.

"Partly. I don't regret that. If even one of my ex-colleagues is inspired to stick to fair-trade coffee now, it was worth it."

"You really are useless with money management." Michelle sighed. "Financially crippling you wasn't my intention, but it doesn't change the fact you deserved retaliation from The Fixers. You've been trying to destroy us!"

"Yeah. Because it's a shitty, evil business that *deserves* to be destroyed." Defensiveness rose in Michelle's expression, but Eden jumped in faster. "And I get it's *yours*. You're the boss. But come on, Michelle, it can't possibly make you happy."

Michelle's lips pressed together. "It's so easy for you, isn't it? You're like a wrecking ball, trashing anything you don't agree with."

"Evil businesses deserve to be trashed, Michelle. And I'm sure Hannah would agree with me too."

"Leave my safta out of it." Michelle's jaw ground hard. "This is none of your business. *None.*"

"The *world* is my business, Michelle. It should be everyone's. What we walk past is the standard we accept. I don't accept what you do at The Fixers. Your grandmother wouldn't either. And neither should you."

"Try walking a mile in other people's shoes! Then you'd see. Nothing's quite so cut and dried. Things happen for reasons." Michelle's mouth twisted into a snarl. "I do this job for a reason."

Eden burned with curiosity. "I'd *like* to walk a mile in your shoes. Will you tell me about it? Help me understand how you came to be at The Fixers?"

"Absolutely not! What makes you think you've earned that story? You're actively trying to *destroy* me."

Eden fell silent. "You're right," she agreed. "But point of clarification: I'd never try to hurt you. Just your company. Never you."

That seemed to set Michelle back on her heels. "Why not me?"

Eden sighed. "For the same reason you didn't destroy me when you had the chance. You're only playing with me—like a cat with a mouse. You've never seriously tried to hurt me, have you?"

Michelle frowned. "Why assume that?"

"Because you're showing an impressive amount of restraint for the CEO of an evil organization."

"Don't call it that."

"You don't think it's evil? Michelle, your company is ensuring cancer drugs don't get to poor people."

Michelle rubbed her temple. "I never approved that. It was before my time. I'm not even upset you leaked that case. But I wish you'd stop now. You've made your point."

"The evil you walk past, Michelle, the evil you ignore, the evil you *can* fix but don't: that's all on you. I won't have it on my conscience. Why are you okay with it being on yours?"

Michelle fell silent. Something dark flickered in her eyes. If Eden didn't know better, she'd call it sadness. Or...agreement?

Instead of answering, Michelle clutched the soup mug tightly. "I'll leave you to rest. I'll wake you at seven. Good night."

Then she was gone.

Chapter 12
Full Care Package

Michelle had barely said a word to Eden all morning. Not when waking her up with a soft shoulder shake or helping her out of bed and to the bathroom door or offering to assist her into the shower (although she'd avoided Eden's gaze, her cheeks going slightly pink). Michelle had seemed relieved when she declined the shower-assistance offer.

Eden managed herself, even if it took forever and resulted in Michelle's worried voice asking through the door if she'd drowned.

Not drowned, no. She'd spent most of the time under the blissful, cascading water, head leaning into steamy glass, wishing for so many things beyond her control: To rewind the past twenty-four hours. To have never decided to look for food at that little store. And, most importantly, for Michelle to explain herself.

With a soft sigh at the confusing state of her life, Eden exited the shower.

Back in Michelle's bedroom, wrapped in a towel, Eden found laid out for her some yoga pants, a T-shirt, sweatshirt, and a matching bra and panties still sealed in new bags. Were the undergarments Michelle's? Or had she ordered someone to magic them up somehow before seven? Unlikely, but not impossible.

Next to these lay a new cell phone. In confusion, Eden turned it on, and her usual home screen appeared. *Oh!* They'd salvaged her SIM card? All her phone contacts were safe!

Again, how had Michelle managed it at this hour? Maybe they had spare phones sitting around the office and she'd ordered one be dropped off? Probably.

Eden slid on the panties and yoga pants, ignored the bra as impossible to deal with, given her ribs, and then tugged on, slowly and painfully, the T-shirt and sweatshirt. Both were tight, clearly Michelle's.

After helping herself to more painkillers—following Dr. Michelson's instructions—Eden sat on the end of Michelle's bed and looked longingly at a pair of brand-new socks and her old boots. There was absolutely no way her body was going to contort to put those on without her passing out in agony.

"Hey?" she called softly to the universe.

"Yes?" Michelle's head popped around the door instantly.

Eden pointed at the socks. "I've met my match."

Michelle merely nodded, knelt, and efficiently slid on both socks and boots without another word.

"Thanks for the clothes. And the phone. That's a huge relief."

Michelle inclined her head in acknowledgment and rose. "Breakfast first or straight to the hospital?"

"Can't eat. Too nervous. Your middle-of-the-night soup's still tiding me over."

"All right. We'll go now."

And that had been the entire sum of conversation until they arrived.

The hospital was one of those small, gleaming, no-expense-spared private affairs that dripped with money. Eden was almost blinded by all the shiny surfaces. Paintings in the foyer weren't prints—they looked like originals.

"Degas?" Eden sputtered. "Tell me that's not another one?"

"I owed Dr. Michelson for something. And I always thought her office could use some art."

"So, you gave her a *Degas*?"

Michelle's lips curled. "Well, the previous owner decided he didn't want it anymore."

"Uh…huh." Eden's eyes narrowed, pretty sure there was a lot more to that story. "Did you help him reach that conclusion, by any chance?"

Michelle shot her a mischievous look and didn't reply. Instead, she lowered herself to a seat in the waiting room and reached for a *National Geographic*.

So even swanky private hospitals still had the waiting-room classics, it seemed. At least the magazine wasn't months out of date.

"You should read the article on saving the Great Lakes." Eden waved at the cover headline.

"You've read it?"

"I subscribe. Besides, Mom's quoted in that story." Eden leaned against a nearby column, unwilling to endure the pain of having to sit and soon stand again.

Michelle's eyebrows lifted in surprise.

"She gets around. That's one of her pet projects." Eden tried to shrug and instead winced.

"Edie!" came a joyful cry from near the doors.

Eden turned to find Aggie racing up at a rapid rate, clearly planning to give her a mighty hug.

"No!" she cried out in alarm just before contact.

At the sound of her cry, Michelle's expression shifted from placid to furious warning, as if about to forcefully eject Aggie. At the same instant, the imposing form of Phelim O'Brian stepped out from behind a pillar at the end of the room, hand shifting to a bulge at his hip under his jacket.

Oh, for heaven's sake. While it was good to see his adorably craggy face, the worry in his eyes was clear.

Aggie had come to a screeching halt inches from Eden and shot Phelim and Michelle alarmed looks as she…*gently*…gave Eden a reassuring pat.

"I'm fine," Eden assured Phelim, whose hand dropped. She then shot Michelle a *relax* look and muttered softly, "That goes for you too."

Michelle's hackles slowly went down, but her cool eyes did not deviate for a moment from Aggie.

"Um…hey," Aggie said cautiously. "Sorry to scare you—I wasn't thinking. But your bodyguards just terrified a few years off my life, so I guess we're even."

Phelim grunted and slunk back behind the pillar. Michelle headed over to the front desk.

"So…you weren't kidnapped," Aggie whispered. "I'm relieved. I did think the worst when that big Irish bruiser turned up on my doorstep. I wasn't sure if you'd been offed in a hit job or not."

"No hit." Eden's breath caught painfully. "But I did get beaten up by a goon."

Aggie's gaze darted to Eden's throat. "More than beaten," she hissed in alarm. "You were throttled."

"I was unconscious then." Eden swallowed, forcing down her anxiety.

Aggie's horrified look wasn't helping her nerves. "I'm guessing it wasn't your ex-boss's people or she wouldn't be here now. On that note, I'm scared to ask how long I'd have lived if I'd given you a rib-cracking hug."

"Best not to test it," Eden joked. "Rule is only she's allowed to harass me." Even as she said it, that felt weird. Michelle had been so protective. Michelle, who was also her enemy.

"So…" Aggie lowered her voice. "Why's she being nice to you? Aren't you guys at war?"

"No idea." Eden worried her lip. "But I'm glad she's being nice because I was out of options. No phone, no money, no van. I couldn't remember your number. Her building was the only thing that stuck in my head. I'm lucky she took pity on me when I collapsed in her lobby. I'm not sure if we *are* still at war, to be honest."

"Edie, that Irish bodyguard told me last night she's called off the operation against you. Didn't she tell you?"

Relief flooded her. "No."

"What's more, he parked Gloria out front this morning, and she's gleaming. Cleaned and detailed, looking like a million bucks. Even got the rust spots out."

Eden stared. "That's impossible."

"I know, right? Those rust spots were like freckles."

"But the impound yard doesn't even open till eight!"

"Wait, you think he busted Gloria out?" Aggie's eyes widened. "Is Gloria on the lam?"

Eden laughed, which was no doubt Aggie's intention. "Knowing them, they bribed someone to open up early."

"Right," Aggie said. "So, anyway, Irish Dude scared the ever-loving whatsit out of Colin."

"Colin was there?"

"He stayed over to help me settle in our newest addition to the family." Aggie's face lit up. "Two pounds of longhaired Peruvian guinea pig. She's gorgeous."

"You finally picked a friend for Kevin? That's great!"

"You've got to see her. It's like she spent all day with a hairdryer. Her name's Bacon."

Eden paused. "Wait, your pets are Kevin and Bacon?"

Aggie grinned. "Yes. See, it turns out the guinea pig seller knew Kevin's mom's owner. So, six degrees of Kevin Bacon?"

"No one does that game anymore."

"Oh well. So, anyway, when that Irish goon came by last night, Colin was snoring on my couch, so he didn't have to face him. But when he showed up again first thing this morning with Gloria, he scared Colin so bad, he almost forgot his own name. I think his life flashed before his eyes."

Eden winced. "I promise Phelim's sweet when you get to know him."

"Tell that to Colin. I haven't been able to get a word out of him since, and his voice is far too sweet to lose." Her eyes flicked over Eden's shoulder. "Hey, Hot Boss is coming back your way. Oooh, shit, she's shooting daggers at me, like she thinks I'm standing too close to you or something. Is she the jealous type? Do I need better health insurance?"

Eden snapped around. Michelle was still bent over the counter, tapping it impatiently as she spoke to the receptionist, her shapely ass in tailored-black pants providing an enticing view.

"Made you look." Aggie grinned. "And I wasn't BSing just now. She gave me this look half a minute ago in case I got any ideas of hugging you again. So I'mma just back slowly away and give you some space because I think if anyone could order me to be tossed out a window, it'd be her."

Before Eden could protest that Michelle likely had minions for body disposal, she heard footsteps approaching.

Michelle's cool voice cut in: "The doctor is ready. I'll take you up to her." She eyed Aggie. "You may stay here."

"Fine." Aggie replied. "I'm trusting you with my bestie. But I'll point out that if you hurt her, *I* know people too."

It was total bluster because Aggie's entire network comprised Colin's nerdy friends and Eden's hippie ones.

Michelle's expression turned incredulous. With amusement, she replied, "Duly noted." Her voice was much warmer when she faced Eden and said, "Eden? This way for Dr. Michelson."

She called me Eden. Again!

And just like that, the day was looking up.

After Eden's extensive check-up and scans, which took forever, Phelim asked to speak to her.

Michelle waved them away and murmured something about taking care of the paperwork. Which was code for she was going to pay.

Eden was beyond grateful because she'd seen some pretty high-tech machines this morning and knew the bill wouldn't be pretty. On the other hand, Michelle had caused Eden's injuries with her campaign of terror against Gloria, so fair was fair.

Phelim took Eden into an unused office. He saw that she was seated comfortably, then pulled out a notepad and pen. "I'm real sorry you were hurt," he began, brow furrowing. "It's my mission to find who did it. I've spent most of the mornin' so far tellin' Fixers staff that I don't need help for now. But everyone wants to see you right, and they're all fired up on your behalf."

Eden was taken aback. "Please thank them. Tell them I'm fine—or I will be."

He clicked his pen. "I assume you were attacked at the lot beside the…" Phelim checked his notes, "Unity of Love Praise Temple? Next to Fort Carroll Market."

"Yes," she said in surprise. "How'd you know?"

"The boss said you were headin' to a food market near the impound lot. That's all there is. There's a dry cleaner across the road with a security camera that takes in part of the empty lot. Snakepit's crew is reviewin' footage."

"They are? Thank you."

Phelim tapped his page. "Tell me everythin' about the asshole. I know he's tall, wears a hoodie, military boots, and sunglasses. What else?"

"He's white. Wore aftershave."

"Brand?"

"Don't know. It was old style, or for older men."

"Okay. What else?"

"He spoke weird."

"How so?"

"Um…" Eden frowned. "I'm not sure. I remember thinking it at the time. He said he 'just knew I'd be trouble.'"

"He *knew*." Phelim furrowed his brow. "This was premeditated if he *knew* it."

"Or maybe he said it because I was struggling with him?"

"Hmm. Tell me about his voice again. Was it high, low, accented?"

"It was too low."

"*Too* low? Why?"

"I'm not…sure."

"Think, Lawless. The answer's in that scrambled-egg noggin of yours. He's a big man. They often have low voices. Why's it too low?"

"It sounded…not right. Like in a movie, you think, 'Hey, that voice is fake.'"

"Fake?" He smiled, his pale blue eyes lighting up. "Well, you just cracked the case."

"I did?" Eden asked, baffled.

"Lawless, he *knows* you. Why else alter his voice? To disguise it so you wouldn't recognize him. So, which enemy have you got with his build?"

Eden's mind whirred. She'd made an enemy? Well, a new one, after Michelle?

Wait, was Michelle still her enemy anymore? Hadn't they declared a truce? *Was* it a truce if neither party mentioned it was in place and you had to hear from your best friend there was a cease-fire?

"Lawless? Stay with me here. Who've you pissed off?"

"No one. I mean years ago, sure, when I was doing the hands-on protesting, lots of company bosses had me as their enemy. These days, other people do the protests, I do the masterminding. And, lately, aside from Michelle, I don't really have enemies."

"Shit, seriously? *None?*" Phelim laughed. "I make one a week, easy. And Hastings doesn't count seein' as you two are the sorriest-arsed mortal enemies ever. There's no heart in it." He sighed dramatically. "I swear, it's like you're tapping each other's noses with limp lettuce leaves."

"Fine! I do have another archnemesis. And we hate each other, body and soul."

"Now we're talking." He looked amused now, if surprised. "Okay, so who is this archnemesis?"

"Former mayor of Wingapo. Francine Wilson. I unseated her, remember? Told everyone about it at the Black Rabbit?"

"Ah, her. The cunt-ad lady."

Eden winced at the description, accurate though it was. "Her. Yeah."

"She sure doesn't look huge or male, or like the type to wear military boots."

"No."

"She pay anyone who does fit that bill?" Phelim's craggy brow lifted.

Eden considered that. "Maybe her police chief?" She turned over the idea. "He was her loyal lapdog for years. I'd recognize his voice, so he'd have to disguise it. He always told me my mouth got me in trouble. And he's about the right size."

They stared at each other for a long beat.

Phelim's phone pinged. He glanced at it, frowned, then tapped the screen. "Snakepit's crew has a suspect from the dry-cleaner footage. Is this the fella who attacked you?" He spun his phone around.

It wasn't the clearest screenshot since it was from some distance away. The man was turned, feet wide apart, hands in his hoodie pockets, outside the empty lot. The threat that seeped from the black-and-white image was like being right back there. Eden flattened herself back in her seat with a shudder. Her blood turned to ice. Even just seeing his bulk in half shadow and turned away gave her the creeps. "Yeah."

"Could he also be that police chief?"

Eden forced herself to study the image closely, weighing up what she remembered of Derrick Sharpe. The height and weight were right. She remembered how her attacker had stood, as if he felt important. Like Sharpe. His ego was legend. In the photo, he leaned back a little, legs spaced wide apart, exactly the way Sharpe did.

"Oh goddess. It's him," she whispered. "That's Sharpe."

Phelim's expression didn't change. "Good work." He tapped out a text.

Eden turned to stare out the window. Anything to wipe out the image of the brute.

Clearing his throat, Phelim said, "I've just told the teams we have our perp. Thanks to your ID."

"I didn't do much. He's not too smart if he forgot to look for security cameras, is he?"

"He didn't look for the cameras across the road. However, the Espionage team found the church had a newly busted camera. He thought he'd removed any evidence."

The Espionage team? "Why are you all helping me?" Eden asked, lost.

"Because you're one of us."

Eden shook her head hard. "No. No way."

"I don't mean one of us, like, up to *bad* shit." He rolled his eyes. "We know you're the office Girl Scout. But we all like you, and we protect our own. Simple as that."

There was that word again. "Michelle told me she was *protecting* me by not telling me about what you all do at work. That sounded like BS. She was protecting herself from looking bad."

"Except she's not wrong." He scratched his chin thoughtfully. "We agreed to look out for you after we first got to know you at the Black Rabbit. World's not safe for someone like you, Lawless. And, as it happens, we like you just the way you are. Not a cynical bastard like us. So yeah, we *were* protecting you—from turnin' into us."

Eden took in his sincerity and the way it all made such perfect sense to him. "You weren't all laughing at me?"

"Hell no!" He looked askance. "We were afraid for you. There's nothin' funny about seein' a cute panda amble onto a six-lane highway. You were giving us all indigestion."

"If that's true, why'd Michelle hire me in the first place?"

"Now that, I couldn't tell you. No clue. Probably a whim. Hey, d'ya know your coffee club's still goin'? Daphne Silver's runnin' it these days. My God, it's a disaster, her tryin' to tell us all about fair trade this and that without a lick of your storytellin' ability. And watchin' her attempt to grind beans without makin' a complete mess is hilarious. But that's okay. We're doin' it since you'd want us to. We're like the world's worst tribute band." He laughed heartily and slapped his thigh.

"I can't believe it's still a thing," Eden said in astonishment.

"Of course it is! It's an excuse for us all to get pissed as newts at the pub later." He chuckled, showing he was kidding. "Okay, last thing: Why does a police chief want to beat up your skinny white ass?"

Eden flung up her hands. "You'd have to ask him. So, what happens now? Do we call the cops on him?"

"Nah. We do way better than that." Phelim grinned. "We call the boss on him."

As if on cue, Michelle stuck her head in the room. She glanced at Eden. "Your bill is settled."

"Thank you."

"So." Michelle gave her a long look. "I'm wondering what justice would look like for you regarding your assailant."

"What do you mean? Like how much jail time the guy should get?"

"No, what would *justice* look like." Michelle's expression was intense. "What would you want to happen to him, if you could have anything?"

Suddenly Eden understood what she was getting at. Michelle, who could do anything, wanted to know what The Fixers could do for Eden. "You mean…without police involvement," she asked carefully.

"Yes."

Eden considered that. "In an ideal world, I'd want him to understand how much pain and fear he put me through. The…terror. That the whole time, I had no idea what was next." Her voice shook. "What…*else*…he'd do."

Michelle's jaw clenched briefly.

"I didn't know if I'd live," Eden continued. "Because the whole time, he acted like I was nothing. Vermin." Eden clawed away a rogue tear brusquely. "I'd want him to learn to never do that again. If I'm not the first he's done that to, I really want to be the last."

Michelle spoke, her voice tight. "And would you be content if those two requisites were met and the police weren't involved?"

"Is involving police messier for you?"

"No. Not in this case. But without involving them, I can guarantee justice exactly as you have laid out." Her gaze turned steely.

Eden knew then that justice would be severe. A savage relief filled her. Maybe Eden should be more evolved, above retribution. Would her mom expect that of her? She swallowed. The truth was Sharpe had scared her to her core. He'd frightened her in a way nothing had in her entire life. Nightmares tormented her. She'd awoken this morning gasping in terror when Michelle had shaken her shoulder.

She was filled with so many what-ifs. What if she'd had breakfast yesterday? Then she wouldn't have needed food at that market. What if she'd run the moment he'd asked for a light? What if she'd twisted this way, not that—could she have broken his hold? What if she'd screamed? What if all this was her fault? If she'd never reignited her war with Francine. Or what if she'd never started one with Michelle— the sole reason Eden had been at the impound lot? Recriminations, fears, and uncertainty looped in her head.

But what if Michelle *could* get her justice? Eden would grab that with both hands. Could it drown out the noise and terror rattling her? "Okay," she said. "Yes, we do it your way."

Michelle nodded, approval gleaming in her eye. "May I have permission to examine your medical report? If one is explaining to this individual the error of his ways, I'd like to have a full list of your injuries."

"I don't care who knows what he did to me. I *do* care if he's sorry for it. But I'm not sure how a man like that could feel sorry, given he did it in the first place."

"Oh, he will be." Phelim spoke this time. "And Ms. Hastings? We have an ID."

Michelle's eyes sharpened. "Who?"

"Wingapo Police Chief Derrick Sharpe."

"Motive?" Michelle focused on Eden. "Do you two have a history?"

"No. He harassed me a lot, just minor stuff and empty threats, but it was always him doing Wilson's bidding. He was also who stole my laptop."

"What does Wilson get out of doing this now?" Michelle asked. "Is it retaliation or for some other gain?"

"No idea," Eden said. "All the times she made my life hell before was to get me to leave town. Victory for her was getting me kicked out of college and Dad fired. But actual violence? This is way out of character for her."

"Or she's escalatin'," Phelim said. "Gettin' more vicious."

Eden frowned. "She likes to think she's cleverer than using violence."

"Could Sharpe be acting on his own volition?" Michelle asked. She flicked a loaded look Phelim's way. "For reasons."

"What reasons?" Eden asked.

Phelim looked thoughtful. "Maybe."

"*What* reasons?" Eden repeated.

Michelle sighed. "Last time you left Wingapo, you had no issues leaving town because O'Brian had a security team there. They intercepted Wingapo's police force setting up a roadblock at the border. They cleared your path before you got there."

Eden stared at her, stunned. No wonder it had felt too easy. "Cleared my path how?"

"Incapacitated and removed from the scene," Michelle said.

"Incapacitated?" Eden spun to look at the security chief. "Phelim, by any chance did you and your boys conk a bunch of cops on the head and drag them into the bushes?"

"Ahh…" He gave Michelle a helpless look. "Not into the bushes *exactly*. They were driven a few miles away and dumped."

"How *many* miles away?" she asked silkily.

Phelim coughed. "Close enough that they made it home in time for breakfast."

Given Eden had left Wingapo around midnight, that was not a short walk. Her heart sank. "No wonder he's mad at me. He has a big ego, and you humiliated him. Worse, you did it in front of his own police team. He couldn't attack you in payback, so he went after the person you were protecting." She waved at herself. "I'd say he took it pretty personally."

"As *we* take personally anyone interfering with a Fixers' asset," Michelle cut in, voice hard. "He has no business touching you. None at all."

"I'm not a Fixers' asset anymore, though, am I?" Eden said.

"He doesn't know that," Michelle hissed. "This is unacceptable! I warned her. No one was to touch you. I thought she understood."

"She who?" Eden asked, perplexed.

"The mayor. That night at the Wingapo border, there was a brief… standoff…between her team and mine. We spoke then."

Eden rubbed her head. "Christ. Anything else you've left out?"

"Just that she appeared to have received and understood the message. Now she allows *this*?" Michelle said, eyes flashing with fury. "She was left with no illusions as to how interfering with anyone under my protection was a terrible idea."

My protection? Michelle had all but branded Eden, the way she'd said that. My property. Mine!

Eden wondered how to feel about that. She should be appalled. But the fear and anger in Michelle's eyes seemed to be outrage that Eden had been hurt, not that Michelle had been disobeyed.

"What if *she* didn't allow it," Phelim broke in. "And Sharpe really did just do it on his own, cos he was angry he'd had his ass handed to him? So, I don't know, he tracked Lawless to her friend's place, maybe watched her for a few days, then followed her when she left the impound lot. Probably guessed where she had to be walkin' to since it was around lunchtime, so he drove ahead and lay in wait at the nearest shops for his target."

"He's been watching me for days? Until his *target* was in a place easy to jump?"

Phelim shrugged. "It's what I'd do."

"Find out," Michelle ordered. "And then bring him to me." Her voice was colder than an Arctic wind.

Phelim's eyes took on a cold gleam. "Be my pleasure."

Eden studied them both in alarm. "Um, to be really clear, no one's getting killed, right?"

Phelim gave her such an incredulous look that Eden reddened.

"What part of *bring him to me* did you not follow?" Michelle asked, tone low. "I meant still breathing." After a pause, she added to Phelim, "And in one piece. I'll just be having a little chat with him about his life choices. And I can assure you," she met Eden's eye again, "after we're done, both conditions you require for achieving justice will indeed be met."

Phelim left with a nod.

"As for other matters," Michelle said, "I'd feel a lot better about your safety if you were to remain at my apartment until Mr. O'Brian resolves things with this individual. Sharpe may try again. He can't if you're at my premises where security is in place. You'd be a sitting duck at Ms. Teo's home."

That was probably a reasonable point. But Eden also didn't like feeling her life was out of her hands. Everything seemed to be decided *for* her. Her stubborn streak rose. "What if I'd prefer to stay with Aggie?"

Michelle's face flickered…the faintest hint of dismay…but then it was gone. "As you wish. By all means, damage your ribs further by sleeping on a couch because you find me unsavory. It's your body."

The biting remark sounded harsh, and Eden really wanted to object to the unsavory part. Honestly, she didn't know what she thought of Michelle anymore. It was too big and too hard a question when she was running on emotional fumes and painkillers.

Her lack of reply was clearly taken as agreement by Michelle, who turned, no longer looking at her. "I see. Nonetheless, I'll leave word with my doorman granting you permission to my apartment should you see sense." Her voice was stiff and tight. "Otherwise, I'll alert you when we've dealt with your assailant."

With that, she stalked out of the room.

Chapter 13

The Game's Afoot

An incoming video call from O'Brian interrupted Michelle late the next day. He should have found Sharpe by now. Odd that he hadn't just phoned her.

"Yes?" she said crisply.

O'Brian's eyes darted all about. He appeared to be in a lavish office of some sort. "Um, small problem, boss. The cop's gone to ground. No one's seen him."

"And the trail is cold?" She frowned. Why was she being involved so early into his investigation?

"Not…exactly. I have someone here willing to help. For a price."

Now it all became clear. Michelle switched off video mode and said, "Put Francine Wilson on."

Moments later, the former mayor's smug face filled the screen. "No, not this time, my dear. Full video mode, or I don't help at all."

Michelle glared even though Wilson couldn't see her.

"Fine by me," Wilson said. "I'll leave you and your man to your little hunt. Sharpe's resourceful, though. You won't find him for months."

Sighing, Michelle flicked video back on. "Talk."

"Now isn't that more civilized?" Wilson's gaze raked Michelle. She lifted an eyebrow. "You're younger than I expected. May I have a name?"

Michelle gritted her teeth.

"It's the basis of all good-faith negotiations," Wilson purred.

"Hastings," Michelle ground out. "Now, what do you know? Where is Sharpe?"

"When I found out what he'd done, I allowed him use of one of my untenanted properties. I have so many, and I assumed you'd be looking for him sooner or later."

"And what will it take for us to get the address to his safe house?" Michelle asked sweetly.

"Oh, I can do more than supply an address, Ms. Hastings. I will personally deliver him to you in…DC, was it? I recall you mentioning DC last time we spoke."

A prickle of alarm shot up her spine at the woman's probing. "No need. Hand him over to my man, and we'll be on our way."

"Oh, but I insist."

"Why?" Michelle asked. "Why do you want to see my headquarters?"

"I want to do a lot more than see it." Wilson smiled. Truly, she was an attractive woman with those scarlet lips and olive skin, but her eyes, cold and dark, were disturbingly intense. "My terms are that in exchange for me delivering Chief Sharpe to you, you give me a job at your secret little organization."

"Excuse me?" Michelle couldn't believe her audacity. "You order an attack on an employee and I'm supposed to hire you?"

"First," Wilson said, tone soothing, "Chief Sharpe's actions were his own. I merely capitalized on them when I realized how I could benefit. I don't condone violence. Second, I've been at such a loose end since my mayoral reign came to an abrupt conclusion. And I've replayed our last conversation over and over in my head. The power you have. The people you control. It occurred to me that that was something I'd not only excel at but would enjoy a great deal. I'm exceedingly good at plots and schemes and getting things done. Just ask Eden Lawless." She smirked.

Michelle turned over her claims of innocence. It was possible Sharpe's retribution for a bruised ego had been his idea and Wilson had capitalized on it. Equally it was possible Wilson had masterminded the assault. Either way: Did Michelle want to deal with the devil? Worse, let her inside The Fixers?

"I can't give you a job—" Michelle began.

"Then I can't give you Chief Sharpe. We're done here."

"Wait." Michelle said. "I can't because all hirings and firings are done by my board. It's not my call. But if there's anything else you'd like? Money? An appointment to a prestigious government committee of some sort?" Her eyebrows lifted.

"I'm not so easily bought." Wilson gave her a mocking look. "Get me a meeting with your board. Even if it lasts two minutes and they throw me out, you'll still get Sharpe, and I'll disappear out of your life forever more."

"The board members are protective of their identity. They don't grant meetings with strangers."

"That's your problem, not mine. I'm quite sure a boss has some pull with her own board?" Wilson's eyes glittered. "Use it. Get me that interview and I'll deliver the chief, compliant as a lamb. This is not negotiable. I'll be giving your man my cell number. Text me a time and place or don't contact me again. Good day, Ms. Hastings." Wilson smiled and then the call abruptly ended.

Michelle sat back in disbelief. One question remained: Just how much did she want justice for Eden?

———⊰⊱———

Eden had to admit The Fixers had done an amazing job cleaning up Gloria. The moment she'd climbed out of an Uber at Aggie's place, she was transfixed. Gloria was gleaming! She texted O'Brian her thanks but received no reply. Probably on his way to Wingapo.

She climbed aboard to find her van even more pristine inside than out. Then, still exhausted, she couldn't resist crawling into her bed at the back and curling up. Eden knew she was supposed to be around someone during her recovery, but right now she craved solitude.

Eden woke around four in the afternoon, in pain now that her meds had worn off, and suddenly ravenous. She'd hit up Aggie for snacks and company. She gingerly climbed out and headed for the front door.

Her knocks went unanswered. That was odd—Aggie was a slave to her phone helpline duties on weekdays. After six, she'd sometimes grab takeout, but not this early.

Concern filled her. Cautiously, she rummaged for the spare house key Aggie had given her for emergencies and let herself in.

Kevin the guinea pig burst out of his wide tubing tunnel into a little fenced-off zone. It was like his reception area. The tunnels ran into most rooms throughout Aggie's house, and the adorable guy could be trusted to appear at any moment, requiring attention. He accepted a quick scratch behind his ear, looking delighted.

Bacon, looking floofy and fabulous, appeared a second later and gave Eden a haughty stink eye.

"Oooh, nice to meet you," Eden said. "Any idea where your mom is?"

A bang sounded at the end of the hallway, then a yelp.

Aggie! Eden bolted down the corridor. Visions of Sharpe attacking her filled her head, and she flung open the door she'd heard the cry from.

Not. Sharpe.

"Oh, my eyes!" Eden shrieked, spinning away from the sight of her best friend engaged in…*well*…

A lamp—now on the floor—wasn't the only thing in disarray. *Shit!*

"Glad you two finally got a clue," Eden mumbled to Aggie and Colin and tried to exit the room with her eyes tightly shut. "I thought you were being attacked." She walked into a wall. "Ow! Also, sorry. I'm really freaking sorry."

Aggie snort-giggled. "Um, Edie dearest, try *opening* your eyes to leave."

"No, no, blind is fine. It's all fine! Really." Then she fled the room.

Eden sat on the couch and glared at Kevin and Bacon, who were on their hind feet in the small pen, peering up at her. "Well," she told them ruefully, "*one* of you might have warned me. I mean, that's clearly why you're not hanging out in your mom's bedroom. Don't blame you, either. *Christ.*"

She would never again be able to look Colin in the eye, and that sucked because he'd been helping with her Bring Down the Fixers project.

Maybe they could do all interactions by email in the future?

As for Aggie—well, she'd been covered by Colin's naked body, so no eyefuls there. But still. *Fuck.* His bare ass was seared in her brain.

"Hey, hon?"

Eden looked up to find Aggie, wrapped in a sheet, giving her a sheepish look. A blush reddened her cheeks.

"I'm *so* sorry," Eden said again, her own cheeks warming. "I heard a crash, and I was suddenly afraid you were being attacked now. I'd *never* have just burst in otherwise!"

"Yeah, I figured." Aggie joined her on the couch, looking primed for a toga party. "I'm sorry we scared you."

"Scared, scarred. Tomahtoes, tomaytoes." Eden brightened. "But, hey, what changed? I mean apart from the obvious."

Aggie chuckled. "Well, remember how Irish Dude terrified Colin into a new reality when he dropped off Gloria? After I saw you at the hospital, I went home to find Col still really rattled. I may have given him a few comforting hugs. And one thing led to another."

Eden added that up and factored in the unholy sights she'd just seen. "Wait, have you two been going at it *all day?*"

"We did stop for lunch." Aggie blushed harder. "In our defense, we had a *lot* of time to make up for."

"True." Eden grinned. "I'm pleased for you."

"Me too." Aggie smiled in wonder. "He's the best."

"He is."

"What brings you over? Not that you need a reason, but I got the impression you were staying with Scary Hot Boss?"

Eden's eyebrows lifted. "Not just Hot Boss anymore?"

"Hon, I've met her. Is my description in any way inaccurate?"

No, it probably wasn't—if you didn't know Michelle. "She's… complicated."

"Uh-huh. So do you need to crash here so we can keep an eye on you?" Aggie gave an impish grin. "I'm sure Colin and I can cool our jets."

"Oh no, no, no!" Eden stood abruptly, forgetting her ribs, and instantly regretted it. "Yikes! I mean there is no way I'm going to be a third wheel while you guys work out your kinks. Not *kinks*, I mean... *you know*. Get it out of your system. New lust and all that?"

"New *love* and all that," Aggie correctly gently. "He told me he loves me. I...um...said it back."

"Aggie!" Eden cried in delight. "I'd hug you so hard right now, but that's a terrible idea."

"I'll say. I'd hug you back, and Scary Hot Boss would track me down and flay me alive. I'm too pretty to be flayed."

Eden laughed. "Okay. Anyway, I'll leave you two crazy kids to it."

"Where will you go?" Aggie frowned. "We really don't mind having a break."

"*I* mind. Besides, Gloria's comfy."

"No, you need someone to keep an eye on you, what with all those meds in your system. So, choose: stay here or stay with her. But it's a big no on going it alone. Don't be stubborn, now."

Eden huffed. "Well, I refuse to break up a lovefest, so I suppose it wouldn't kill me to crash at her place. Besides, she owes me."

"She does?"

"Her employees got me beaten up. Sort of," Eden said. "Gloria was towed. My attacker followed me there. By the way, it was Police Chief Sharpe. Wingapo's finest. Remember him?"

"I sure do. He gave me citations for every tiny thing just because you and I were friends. I could have papered a wall with the tickets. He's such a bully. Are you filing a police report?"

"No. Michelle sent O'Brian to deal with him."

Aggie gave a low whistle. "Looks like you've got some serious protection now. I'm glad."

"I..."—well, Eden supposed she had—"guess."

"Which is weird since you've been attacking her company for two months now."

"Yeahhh." Eden scratched her ear.

"Come on, don't tell me that's not weird. You trash her company, then you get attacked, and she...protects you? How does that make sense?"

"It doesn't," Eden had to admit. She'd tied herself up in knots on this very topic. It was so confusing.

"You know, she seems pretty attached to you."

"It's more like I'm someone she sees as her property, and I got messed with. She's proprietorial about her employees."

"You're not her employee. You're the traitor attacking her company."

"Yeah," Eden muttered.

"I'll tell you what," Aggie said. "I'll let this slide for now if you do something for me."

"What?"

"Stay with her until you're past the worst of it. Don't argue. Just do it. After that, when you're feeling a bit better, tell her you care about her. A whole lot."

"Why would I do that?"

"Because you care about her. A whole lot." Aggie gave her a long look.

"Why would I humiliate myself by admitting that to her?" Eden asked, too tired to bother denying it.

"Because she cares about you too."

"Doubtful." Cared that someone messed with her asset, maybe. Not Eden. It was the principle for Michelle. She taught transgressors lessons—as Sharpe was about to find out.

"It's not doubtful at all. That woman was out of her mind with worry for you at the hospital. She wanted to rip my head off when she thought I was about to hug-attack you. And she's sent her man off to get vengeance. That means something. So use this as a way to find out who she really is because right now, I'm just seeing a whole lot of hard-headed nonsense from both of you. And by the time you're back on your feet, you'll be over your little war and ready to negotiate terms."

"My war is not little!" Eden gaped at her. "Her company is evil!"

"Could be. But is she?"

Wasn't *that* the question? Eden was no longer sure.

Colin called plaintively from down the hall: "Aggie?"

"Your man's lonesome." Eden smirked.

Colin padded down the hallway, dressed this time—thank the heavens—looking absolutely blissed out. "Problem?"

Yep, Eden was definitely clearing out of this love shack ASAP. "No, the opposite. Just found out my old boss has called off the dogs on me."

"That's good," Colin said. "Guess she's not entirely heartless, then. Mustn't have liked to heap misery on misery." He waved at her injuries.

"Probably. Yeah." That had to be it. "She's not, um, entirely heartless." Could you be evil but not heartless? Eden wondered if there was a sliding scale for villainy. Like Kinsey.

"Oh?"

"Um," Eden began, "she got me a nice doctor visit. And took me to hospital. Her private hospital."

"Super swanky one," Aggie said. "There was *chrome*."

"And she paid," Eden finished.

Colin tilted his head. "Yeahhhhh. I'd do that for anyone I didn't give two shits about who landed on my doorstep hurt." He grinned.

He was as bad as Aggie. "It's not that so much as…" Eden tried to find the words to explain their odd relationship. "She's annoyed at me, but there's a *line*."

"She paid your medical bills," Colin repeated.

"She feels guilty. Plus, she's rich. You should see where she lives—a twenty-million-dollar apartment! She can afford the bills."

"Still could have outsourced you to someone else," Colin said. "Sent an employee? She didn't."

"I think being loved up is making you see things, buddy," Eden teased, desperate to get him off this topic. "You too." She glanced at Aggie, whose expression said she wasn't buying Eden's argument one bit.

"Maybe." Colin scratched his stomach through his T-shirt. "You hungry? I could whip you up an omelet? It's my specialty." He glanced at Aggie. "Or we could order in?"

"Nah, I'm gonna bail. Things to do," Eden lied. "You should get back to making my best friend very happy." She chuckled.

"Good plan." Aggie grinned.

"Yeah, yeah," Colin said, but the blissed-out look was back. "Whatever."

"I'm really happy for you both. And Aggie, my friend, I'm going to go stay where you suggested but only because I think you two need alone time together. But for the record, I don't agree with your conclusions."

Aggie shrugged. "If I'm wrong, I'm wrong. We'll see."

Chapter 14

Sleeping at The Enemy's

Eden had no intention of staying with Michelle. She'd said that so Aggie wouldn't worry about her, so her friend could get back to lots of making-up-for-lost-time sex. No way was Eden getting in the way of that. And no way was she going to stay with the woman she'd been at war with less than a day ago. Because that would just be weird. All of it was weird.

Eden drove Gloria to a park near Aggie's place. She dug up some protein bars and water from her van's kitchen stores. She'd need to shop for food soon—easier said than done without cash.

That reminded her: Eden logged into her banking app and found her account balance unchanged. Seemed Sharpe had been more about inconveniencing her than committing fraud. That fit. Eden should probably cancel her stolen credit cards. She sighed. *Later*. When she felt less dead.

Munching on her protein bar, Eden watched kids tossing around a football. Her ribs began to hurt. When she finished her food, she tried to do what the doctor had told her: cough gently once an hour and breathe deeply.

Except that just made her ribs hurt more. It was too cold, and she was too sore. So she crawled into her bed and splayed herself like a starfish.

"Just you and me, kid," she told Gloria. "I'll be better soon. Then I'll go for a nice long drive to the middle of nowhere and forget how batshit crazy our time in DC has been."

Eden snuggled deeper into her bed, trying to work out what to do next. Her original plans were in tatters. The journalist she'd been leaking to had been targeted by The Fixers and warned off. Warned in such a way that the woman had *begged* Eden not to give her any more stories. She'd mentioned something about a terrifying Irishman telling her he knew which middle school her kids went to.

Eden sighed. Explaining to the reporter that O'Brian was all bark had been a futile exercise. The woman had been badly shaken. Eden couldn't really blame her. It must have been frightening, her kids being dragged into things. Unfortunately, O'Brian was extremely good at being an enforcer.

Of course, Eden knew other reporters and other ways to get the word out. But she'd already released all the stories she thought needed immediate attention. The rest were too old to be of public interest, too sensitive to reveal, or only affected one random person.

Besides, her heart wasn't really in it anymore. Eden would pause her anti-Fixers campaign while she was healing. She'd reassess later, when everything didn't ache. *And* when that ache didn't extend to still liking a woman who ran an evil business.

Eden supposed it was only natural to like someone who'd rescued you. Someone you felt safe with. Someone you remembered as being witty and amusing and who cared for her grandmother.

Why was everything so confusing and hard? With a sigh, she closed her eyes.

Eden awoke to discover the sky pitch-black. A chill rippled through her. Pain clawed at her, and she hurriedly took more pills. Next, she scrabbled around for an extra blanket, but shivers overtook her. Her core temperature had dropped, and she couldn't stay like this.

Damn it.

Right, just for tonight, she was going to go into debt if she had to and check in at a nice hotel. Warm shower, warm bed, heater, the works. As she slowly climbed into the front seat, she found her phone under a sweater and discovered several missed texts.

The first two were from Aggie, checking that Eden was okay and that "Scary Hot Boss" was looking after her.

She texted back.

I'm fine and fab. You have fun.

Next was O'Brian.

Perp's laying low, but we have a way 2 him now. He's in Wngpo & will stay there. You can relax.—POB

Relief filled her. Wingapo. Far, far away. *Good.*

She also found several texts from Michelle. The first read: *I trust you will sleep well even on that ridiculous couch.*

Eden snorted. How on earth would Michelle know what Aggie's couch was like? Had she asked O'Brian to describe it for her? She was control freak-y enough to.

The next read: *I require a status update. Health okay? Ribs? Bruising?*

And another: *I'm aware we're having differences of opinion on various matters but I'd like to know you're recovering well.*

"Differences of opinion?" That was one way to describe it.

It's not for me, said the next text. *Your doctor is asking for updates.*

Wait, wouldn't Michelle have mentioned that first if the doctor needed information? And wouldn't Dr. Michelson have contacted Eden directly? She had her cell number.

Fine, said the last message. *Ignore me if you wish.*

Eden could hear her petulance. Michelle being petulant was pretty funny, given how uptight and cool she acted at all other times. *Acting* being the operative word. Eden had seen many glimpses under the mask by now and knew there was a lot more going on than cool indifference.

Her final text was the best one. It sounded as if Michelle actually cared.

So sue me if I wanted to ensure a former employee isn't curled up in a ditch in pain somewhere.

Well, *that* was dramatic. If one were indulging in Jewish grandmother stereotypes, Eden might assume Michelle had picked up guilt-tripping from a pro. She made a mental note to ask Hannah sometime, laughed at that thought, then winced. *Ouch!*

Eden couldn't help but notice she was being cited as an ex-employee. Wasn't she a disgraced betrayer of The Fixers?

So…Michelle cared. Warmth spread through her stomach. She glanced at the clock. Nine-thirty. Okay, then. *Fine*. Michelle had won.

With that, Eden decided she might as well be warm while she and Michelle hashed out their "differences of opinion."

Michelle arrived home exhausted. Another late one. Still mopping up Eden's spot fires. It felt worse knowing she really should tell the board. It was well past time to have done so.

Adding misery upon misery, she'd been fretting about Eden all day, and the frustrating woman had not replied once. Michelle had been so close to ordering Tilly to contact Agatha Teo to determine Eden was still alive and infuriating.

Her doorman waved her over. "Ms. Hastings? Uh…You instructed me to allow your friend into your apartment if she returned?"

Michelle stopped dead. "What?"

"She came back. Your friend?" the doorman said.

Michelle's jaw worked at that description. *Friend?* "You're saying she's in my apartment."

"Yes?" His voice hit a worried pitch.

"Good," she said and then dashed for the elevator, heart pounding. What if Eden had returned because she felt unwell? She'd sought Michelle out the first time because she needed safety. What if she'd done so again because something had happened?

To Michelle's great relief, Eden was sprawled out on the couch in purple fuzzy socks and comfy clothes, watching a David Attenborough documentary about penguins.

"I'm glad you came to your senses," Michelle announced by way of hello, dropping her keys in a small, glazed bowl by the door. "You cannot recover adequately on a couch or in a van."

"Well, first, *Hi, Eden, great to see you.*" Eden smiled. "*How are you doing?*"

That gave her pause. "*Hello.*" Michelle repeated, rolling her eyes. "How *are* you?"

"I'm good, thanks for asking." Eden frowned. "Why are you out of breath?" Then a tiny smile curled her lips. "Did you run here to check on me?"

"I thought you might have had a relapse and that was why you'd sought me out," Michelle said, folding her arms.

"You were *worried* about me." Eden's smile turned full-blown. "For the record, I don't need to be beaten up to seek you out."

"That's a new development. I thought I worked for the evil empire?"

"That hasn't changed." Eden sat up, clutching her ribs with a scowl. "But I thought we're having a cease-fire or something."

"Ah." Michelle digested that. "We are? I mean, I'm aware I am. Are you holding fire as well?"

"Yes."

Oh, thank God. "Good," she said evenly as if Eden hadn't just lifted her most pressing burden. "So, how are you feeling?"

"The pain meds are something else." Eden smiled, and then her expression faltered. "You're exhausted. Long day?"

"Not pleasant, no. And, Eden, not that I'm complaining, but I thought you preferred to be on your friend's couch. What's changed?"

"Her couch is great, but Aggie has just discovered sex with the love of her life, Colin, and there's no way I wanna be around for that."

"Ah."

"My van's also comfy, but the doc kept stressing I needed supervision for the first few days."

"So, I'm option three?" Michelle noted dryly.

"Yeah." Eden's grin was so charming, it took the bite out. "I got your text messages. I kind of got a clue from them that maybe you weren't just being polite and actually wanted me here."

"I wouldn't go *that* far," Michelle said, discomfort rising.

Eden's grin widened. "Well, thanks for the offer. By the way, I love your big-screen TV. I'm able to tell the penguins apart. The TV in Gloria is tiny, and they all look like feathered blurs."

"You have a TV in your van?" *Seriously?*

"Not just a TV, a shower, toilet, oven, solar panels, the works. Sometimes I need to be off the grid for weeks. It's amazing how much you can squeeze in when you try. I'm limited only by my imagination, my solar generator…and owning compact stuff."

Michelle didn't want to imagine any of it. "Have you eaten? There's more soup in the freezer if you'd like. Or we can order in."

"I had some more soup earlier, thanks. I hoped that'd be okay. You seemed adamant it was good for me, so I figured you'd want me having more."

"I would. Yes."

"And, hey, I had no idea you had so many varieties of ice cream in the freezer. Like, wow."

"Those are my grandmother's, not mine," Michelle lied through her teeth.

"Sure," Eden said easily, clearly humoring her. "Want to watch penguins with me while you unwind a bit? Stay and tell me about your day."

Michelle froze. This was the most domestic conversation she'd had with any other living soul aside from her grandmother. It was surprisingly nice. "Maybe just for a minute. I have reports to finish up."

She kicked off her shoes, and when Eden drew up her feet to expose a spare sofa seat, Michelle dropped onto it. "As for my day, we had a breakthrough in the hunt for your assailant."

"Yeah, O'Brian texted to say Sharpe's laying low in Wingapo. I'm relieved."

Michelle inhaled. "Francine Wilson is trying to do a prisoner negotiation with us."

Eden blinked. "She *what?*"

"O'Brian went to see if she was behind the attack. Wilson claims she wasn't involved, but as soon as she found out about it, she hid Sharpe in one of her empty properties to use as leverage."

"What leverage?"

"The price for her giving him to us is she gets a job interview."

"You're giving her an interview?"

"No—I cannot hire or fire directly. She'd have to be interviewed by the board."

Eden's hands formed fists. "Giving that power-hungry lunatic any access to more power is a terrible idea! She'd ruin you *and* DC in a matter of months."

"That thought had occurred, yes. But I know the board. They're smart, shrewd men. They'll see right through her games and reject her as unsuitable. We get Sharpe either way."

"You're not seriously considering saying yes?" Eden asked slowly. "It'll mean opening The Fixers up to her scrutiny. She'd use that. Blackmail you. Find a way to come at you again even if the interview is a write-off."

"I'll make her sign the usual nondisclosure forms."

"That worked *so* well on me."

"Only because I chose not to involve the lawyers. You have no idea how much destruction they could have wreaked if I'd given them the go-ahead. Daily fines for noncompliance with our demands, for instance."

"Why didn't you?" Eden studied her closely. "In fact, why did I get the fleas and not the bear attack?"

"Your actions couldn't be ignored. I had to act as CEO. That isn't to say I had to wreak the *worst* havoc on you, though. I chose a middle ground because you hadn't outed The Fixers. Your limiting the harm you inflicted on us gave me some leeway for lighter payback. Had you named us, I'd have had little choice but to unleash the whole arsenal on you."

"Okay, I get that. Why are you helping me now? Asking me to stay? Hunting Sharpe? I can't get my head around it."

"Why do you think?" Michelle asked curiously.

"Are you annoyed Sharpe's messed with someone you see as a Fixers asset? Or feeling guilty because I was only attacked where I was because you'd had Gloria towed?"

"It's not possessiveness *or* guilt," Michelle said waspishly. "If your attack hadn't happened there, it would have happened elsewhere. O'Brian's right—Sharpe had to have been following you."

"So why help me?" Eden persisted. "You could have washed your hands of me when I landed in your lobby."

The thought she could ever have tossed an injured Eden out in the cold to fend for herself was repugnant. Eden needed to be protected from the world, from people like…*well*. Wasn't it ironic that the people she most needed protecting from most wanted to help her? "You truly are infuriating. You can't see… You act as if…" Michelle stopped.

"As if?" Eden asked gently.

"As if you think we see you as disposable. You have many allies at The Fixers—people who care about you. And you dismiss them all as evil." She shot Eden a furious look. "I grant you some of my staff are… ethically challenged…but a lot of it is just the job, pushing boundaries. It doesn't alter their feelings. They're genuinely fond of you. They want you safe. That's *not* guilt, Eden. It's concern. They see you as one of their family."

"You're helping me because *your people* care about my well-being?" Eden hiked an eyebrow. "This is a feel-good exercise you're granting your staff?"

Michelle glowered. "Are you being deliberately obtuse?"

"Are you being deliberately vague?" Eden shot back.

"Fine. *I* don't want you injured either. *Obviously*," Michelle ground out. How could Eden not have worked that out by now? "It's as you said: This is cat and mouse. I didn't want you hurt. That was not my intention at all." She felt stricken at the reminder and covered it up with gruffness. "I lost a year off my life seeing you like that. Don't *ever* do that again."

"Turn up bleeding in your lobby after being jumped by a brute? I have no plans to."

"Good." Michelle narrowed her eyes. "I'll hold you to it."

Eden smiled. "Okay, then."

Michelle gave a curt nod.

"So, Michelle?" Eden leaned closer, eyes intense. "I know someone set me up to see The Fixers a certain way. They showed me the worst

Fixers cases. I've obviously noticed that the list I was given was designed to enrage me so I'd quit. I know that. I was told that was why."

As Michelle had suspected. "Who told you?"

"I promised I wouldn't say."

Her lips thinned. Michelle had a sneaky mole at her workplace and Eden wouldn't reveal their identity? Her mind whirred. Who would want Eden gone from The Fixers badly enough to risk their job to make it happen?

"Who did it is irrelevant," Eden continued. "As the weeks have gone on, I've started to see more clearly. I've noticed, for instance, that the worst jobs were undertaken before you became CEO."

"They were," Michelle agreed.

"I've been seeing a pattern on the cases taken under your reign. Mainly it's entitled assholes behaving badly and screwing over corporations, government committees, other entitled assholes, or family. Yes?"

"That makes up most of the work, I suppose. Yes."

"Right. See, that makes it easier to get my head around. I tell myself I'm going after an evil corporation, not you. Mainly I see it as a client being awful, rather than you being awful."

"You do?" This was a huge surprise. How could Eden simply sidestep Michelle's involvement? Why would she?

"Even though you hurt me greatly." Eden inhaled. "And I know I hurt you too. We both did things on purpose to hurt each other."

Michelle sighed. "Yes."

"I've tried very hard to hate you. It just won't stick. It's impossible." Eden gave her a helpless look. "I'm so close to pushing aside everything about you that I know and focusing only on your goodness."

"My…*goodness*?" Michelle stared at her in astonishment. "Eden, I'm *not* good."

"But I see it." Eden studied her. "Your mask has these cracks. I see them. Your softness when you talk about your safta. The fury you had for the man who hurt his young lover. You protecting me and being so fierce about finding my attacker makes me appreciate you even more. I want to forgive you your role in The Fixers, which I shouldn't. Mom would be so appalled with me. I'm failing in my duty to put the greater good ahead of my personal feelings." Eden bit her lip. "But I can't help how I feel. I look at you and I feel anything but hate. And it's so confusing."

"Rarely is anything an absolute, Eden. Not ideas. Not people. There's nuance. Usually. But not with me. I'm surprised you see something in me that isn't there."

"You mean goodness?" Her expression was gentle.

Michelle exhaled. "Yes." Eden *had* to know this. "That's just *not* in me." Shame filled her at the reminder—not only of the things she'd done but how she looked next to someone decent like Eden—well, when the woman wasn't being blinded by some unrealistic belief in Michelle's nice side.

"You sound so sure," Eden said.

"I *am* sure. I'm also quite sure, deep down, you believe that the greater good comes first. So, by that metric, once you're healed, I suppose you'll resume attacking The Fixers. And my duty will be to try and stop you."

"I suppose." Eden didn't look like her heart was in that idea.

"We do our duties, even if we question them at times."

"You question what you do?" Eden's hopeful gaze burned.

"More and more every day." Michelle briefly closed her eyes. "But it's what I'm trained for. What I'm good for."

"That's not all you're good for." Eden held her eye. "Your brain is incredible. What couldn't you do?"

"I'm a creature of my environment. I was raised in secrets. My father was in the same business. I'm uniquely skilled at playing the games I do."

"Do you…like it?"

Less than ever. The board sniffing around her decisions wasn't helping any more than the constant reminder, thanks to Eden's leaks, that she was doing evil. "I enjoy solving problems no one else can."

"Then solve this problem for me." Eden hesitated. "There's this one case that isn't like the others. My brain can't wrap itself around this, so I'm just going to ask: Michelle, what happened with Catherine Ayers?"

It was like being simultaneously slapped and punched. Michelle snapped her head away, but it was too late. Eden would have seen her fearful reaction. "I can't," she said, voice hoarse. "Not that."

"How can I understand you without knowing the truth? On paper, it reads that you set out to make her fall for you, then ruined her publicly?"

Michelle swallowed. "Yes."

"Which sounds unnecessarily cruel," Eden said evenly. "But nothing I've seen from you is unnecessarily cruel. It's out of character. This changes everything if it's true."

"You mean I really am the villain you've been trying to pretend I'm not?" Michelle's stomach churned. "It *was* unnecessarily cruel. It wasn't out of character. And it's true."

Eden flinched. "What about the rumor that you loved her?"

Alberto's bitter tales had traveled far and wide. Michelle narrowed her eyes.

"See, if those rumors are true, you sound even worse…more calculating," Eden said without accusation. "And that's even more out of character. I can't balance what I know about you and this one case. I can't reconcile the two yous—the you I knew in Wingapo, who I see glimpses of. And the you in the case files: brutal, cold, cruel, ambitious. Which is the real you?"

"Both!" Michelle's voice was harsh. "I hurt Ayers *on purpose*. To further my career. That's all there is. The End!"

"It's not, though, is it? I'm struggling to believe a word of it. Judging by your reaction when I said her name, this wasn't just business. You're traumatized by it."

Michelle glared. "You know *nothing* about it!"

"I agree. That's why I'm asking."

"Drop it."

"I can't."

Michelle scowled. "If you're planning on fixing this by telling her story to the world, she won't talk. There's no making this right. She doesn't want it hashed up again."

"No, I know. That's pretty much what she said when I asked."

"You..." Michelle went cold as stone. "You asked Ayers? You two spoke?"

"Yes. I was going through all the Fixers cases on the USB drive. I reached out to all the victims I found. She was hurt; I offered my help."

"You had *no right!*" Horror filled Michelle. "That poor woman deserves to be left in peace. Hasn't enough been done to her? Didn't I put her through enough?" Her voice cracked.

Even if Eden's motives had been good, it still meant she'd reminded Ayers of the worst pain in her life. She'd been nationally humiliated. Vilified. Demoted from a top Washington correspondent to an LA gossip writer. She'd been made into a punchline for every late-night TV comedian. The pain of that scandal had gone on for over a year and changed Catherine Ayers from charismatic and engaging to cynical and closed off. Even if she'd remade her life now, the scarring had to remain.

"Michelle," Eden said softly. "Do you know what she told me?"

"No!" She dreaded to think. The Caustic Queen's message for Michelle would be vicious and well-deserved. "And I don't want to know. This conversation is *terminated*."

Michelle shot to her feet, unable to keep the anguish from her voice. "I have work to do. You will *not* raise this topic with me again!" With that, she bolted from the room.

Once safely alone, she sucked in deep, ragged lungfuls of breath. Then the tears of regret and shame came. For the first time in years, Michelle was helpless to stop them.

An hour later, Michelle called her grandmother. She desperately needed a friendly voice. An ally she trusted. Not...whatever it was she had with Eden, who at turns saw her as good and evil. She craved the normalcy of her safta.

The old woman was full of beans and gossip on everything she was up to. When she finally ran out of steam, she said, "Okay, bubbeleh, what's wrong?"

"What makes you think something's wrong?" Michelle protested.

"I can hear it in your voice."

"It's...nothing."

"Tell me? I'll decide if it's nothing."

Where to even start? Everything in Michelle's life was secretive. Her FBI work couldn't be shared due to the US Espionage Act of 1917, and The Fixers had her tied by an NDA.

"Eden was attacked," she found herself saying.

"Goodness! No!" Hannah gasped. "Is she all right?"

"Three cracked ribs, terrible bruising, and her throat..." She swallowed. "Choke marks."

"Who would do such a terrible thing to that child?"

Michelle exhaled. "I'm...following a lead."

"*You* are? Did she get hurt in the line of duty, then?"

"In a way."

"I see." Her grandmother sighed. "I wish you wouldn't do such dangerous work. How often did I see all those cuts on you?"

That was different. Her rage room wounds were self-inflicted. "My work's not dangerous."

"Mmm." Her grandmother sounded unconvinced. "I hope you're visiting Eden often? Taking good care of her? I know she means a lot to you."

"She doesn't," Michelle protested. "But I've given her your chicken soup. She loved it."

"Good." Her grandmother sounded brighter. "I'm pleased."

"And...I'm keeping an eye on her here. She's sleeping in my room. I'm in yours. Just until she's a little better."

The silence went so long that Michelle wondered if her safta had gone to make herself a tea.

"Good," Hannah finally repeated. "That is how it should be."

Michelle sat rigid, waiting for Hannah to ask why she had an ex-employee staying with her if she didn't mean a lot.

Instead, sounding all too amused, her safta added, "Are you tucking her in each night?"

Michelle snorted. "No. Because *that* would be highly inappropriate."

Her grandmother cleared her throat. "Did I ever tell you about your great aunt in Boston? Abigail? She lived with her best friend, Mabel, for forty years. Imagine that. Forty years! Two spinsters. Everyone was sad they never married, had families, and so on, but I noticed they never looked unhappy."

Michelle blinked. "Your sister Abigail had a…special friend?"

"Yes, dear. They're buried side by side now, as per their wishes. I made sure of it."

"Well, that's…" Michelle frowned. "How is this relevant?"

"Abigail told me before she passed that Mabel was the love of her life. I'm not talking friendship love." She chortled. "I reminded her that I spent much of my life dancing on stage—and you know what that means."

"I really don't," Michelle said, lost.

"Oh, goodness, so many *creative* types are in dance. Some of my dearest friends were of the lavender persuasion."

"Oh God." Michelle stared at the ceiling. Her safta couldn't possibly be suggesting…

"So I have what they call *The Gaydar*," she said with supreme satisfaction.

Yes, she was. "I…see." Michelle stared miserably at the ceiling some more.

"I saw you in the street once with a woman who ended up all over the news. The way you looked at her? Well, I did understand the divorce with Alberto after that."

Michelle inhaled. She'd known about Catherine? All this time?

"I love you, dear child. Whoever makes you happy makes no difference to me, as long as they are good at heart. I'm not like your parents—so busy clutching pearls about what their friends would say. I just want you happy. This is no life for you—all migraines, loneliness, and misery."

"I'm not…*un*happy." That might just be the biggest lie she'd ever told her grandmother.

The old woman laughed. "Oh heavens, that's a good one."

Grr. Michelle slumped.

"Bubbeleh, the only time you haven't been miserable lately is when you talk to your Eden—or when you talk *about* her. Oh, you kept explaining she's your employee, but I know laughter. I could hear your enjoyment and sense your anticipation when you were due to call her.

You sounded like the woman I haven't seen in a decade. I've missed her."

That her was long gone. "Well, your intel is out of date," Michelle retorted. "Because Eden hasn't been the cause of much enjoyment for me lately. Know what she did after she left my organization? She started feeding the media stories about clients—breaching their privacy."

"Well, now. That's a surprise. Did the clients deserve it?"

"That's hardly the point!"

"I think it's very much the point. She seems a good soul. She wasn't doing it to hurt *you*, was she?"

"No, but I have been running around cleaning up the fallout. She's exhausting, Safta. Maddening!"

"So maddening you've taken her in."

"She was hurt!" Honestly, was Hannah even listening?

"Yes, and I'm very glad you're looking after her." She sounded pleased. "Eden doesn't deserve to be hurt. She's goodness, that one. I can tell. Rare as rare can be."

"She attacked my company," Michelle reminded her, not willing to argue the goodness point because, yes, that was Eden in a nutshell. "Betrayed me."

"Did she, though?"

"Yes!"

"Well, why did you take her in if she's so terrible?"

Michelle could hear the smile in her safta's voice. "I'm rapidly regretting it," she muttered.

"Don't. One thing I know is that doing the right thing is never wrong. But, darling, she believes that too, I just know it. It's why she was hurting those awful clients of yours."

"Why do you think they're awful?"

"Because you didn't argue when I asked if they deserved it. And your Eden wouldn't hurt someone good."

"She hurt me."

And there, into the silence, fell all sorts of awkward, awful truths. If Eden only hurt the bad, and Eden had hurt Michelle, what did that say about Michelle?

The wall clock ticked far too loudly as her safta didn't speak for a moment.

"Oh, bubbeleh," she finally said. "You're being a bit dramatic, aren't you? If she's hurt you, then she's hurt herself, because that woman cares very much for you. It's in her eyes."

Michelle gasped. "That's ridiculous."

"Is it? I not only have an excellent gaydar, I have an excellent sense for who people are. Didn't I tell you Alberto was all wrong for you?"

Michelle mumbled a reply.

"I'm sorry, dear, what was that?"

"I said *yes*."

"Well, now. Could you stop being stubborn, stop blaming your Eden for doing the right thing even if it's making work for you, and sort out your differences? You'd be a wonderful match. I'm never wrong about these things."

Match? Didn't her grandmother hear the part about Eden attacking her company? "She *hurt* me," Michelle repeated quietly.

"In which case I have no doubt whatsoever that you turned around and hurt her back. Am I right?"

Silence fell.

"Well, then," her safta said, "can't you just both call it a tie and move on? Life's too short. Listen to an old woman on this."

"You're not *that* old."

"I'm old enough. When I come home, I expect to find you and Eden thick as thieves again."

"Safta, she thinks I've done terrible things. Hell, an hour ago, I admitted I had. She believes I'm the worst person."

Hannah laughed. "No she doesn't."

"How can you know that?"

"If she did, would she stay? Look at what a person *does*, not what they say. Then you'll see the truth. Don't I always tell you that? Now, darling, I have to go. I love you. Stay out of trouble."

"I make no promises," Michelle grumbled lightly.

"Give my best to Eden too."

Not likely. Michelle had firm plans to avoid the woman for the foreseeable future. Tricky, given she was also anxious that Eden stay under her roof until her ribs were substantially healed.

"I'll take that as agreement." There was faint laughter, and the phone went dead.

How…absurd. As if Eden cared about her. The woman was actively working against her! Although she had committed to a cease-fire. And she had come to her…and said she liked the Michelle she'd met in Wingapo.

All she wanted was to understand the last puzzle piece: Ayers. The problem was, Michelle wasn't sure she *could* share what had happened without breaking inside.

So no, she wasn't going to give that truth up. But one thing she could do instead was give Eden her justice.

She'd probably regret it, but she sent a two-word text to the number Francine Wilson had supplied.

Terms accepted.

Chapter 15
Going With the Tide

Tilly listened as Michelle explained Wilson's terms the next day. Michelle had never seen her so surprised. Ordinarily, she gave little away.

"The mayor," Tilly hissed. "The one we destroyed?"

"The very same," Michelle confirmed. "Apparently she's thinking bigger now." She assigned Tilly the job of liaising with Wilson and the board to find a time and day.

An hour later, Tilly returned and confirmed all parties had agreed to a meeting at the earliest available time, three weeks from now.

The board understood their role was performative—listening to Wilson's pitch before letting her down—in order to give Michelle what she wanted: the man who had attacked a Fixers' operative.

They didn't need to know it was a *former* operative, nor that the person Michelle was protecting was behind the leaks she had yet to inform the board about.

Later, she told herself. She'd notify them once she could assure herself Eden truly was done with outing Fixers' clients. A cease-fire, after all, was no permanent downing of weapons.

Michelle's days were dragging on, even though Eden was no longer attacking The Fixers. Each night, she came home exhausted and more and more stressed about her workload. It was so odd. She'd gone for years not thinking too hard about the morally gray things she did. But ever since Eden had pointed it out, it was all she could see. She wondered why. It's not like Eden had said anything Michelle didn't know.

Was it easier to ignore the unpalatable if everyone else was ignoring it too? And all it took was one person to point, and there it was: something ugly you can never unsee again.

The headaches had been worse lately. They made her grumpier than ever, and everyone except Tilly and O'Brian had been giving her a wide berth.

Things were different at home. At first, the routine had been Eden resting throughout the day. The Fixers' doctor would visit every few days and check there was no pneumonia developing—apparently a potential side effect to rib injuries. Dr. Michelson would test Eden's lung function, assess her pain meds, and make sure she was comfortable.

Now, though, two and a half weeks in, Eden seemed bored. The worst of the pain had receded even though her injury hadn't healed. She'd moved into the downstairs guest bedroom to give Michelle her room back and taken to an assortment of hobbies to amuse herself.

Eden would now greet her with a grin, a dirty martini, and the waft of cooking smells each night. She did it while uttering comically drawled lines such as, "Darling, you're home," straight from a fifties sitcom. The domesticity was both hilarious and warming. Michelle's headaches eased the moment she opened her door.

The quality of meals varied, as Eden only prepared vegetarian dishes, with some vegetables being more alien than others. Not that she'd ever complain. Michelle could see the effort expended. Besides, she'd been starting to look forward to the stories Eden told over dinner, explaining why she'd chosen a dish, which part of the world it was from, and how she'd first come by it.

Initially Michelle had argued they should order takeout to spare Eden's sore ribs. That was pointless. Eden did as Eden did. Michelle may as well argue with the tide.

She understood, though. Eden wanted to do *something* during her day, and right now that meant cooking, watching wildlife documentaries, working on a huge jigsaw puzzle that had appeared on a spare table downstairs, and…filling the house full of plants.

That was the other thing. O'Brian had turned up with a pickup truck loaded up with pots of greenery, and a sheepish grin. "I've been plant-sittin' for her," he told Michelle. "Since you got her to clear out the office?"

Michelle had stared at him for so long, he shifted uneasily.

"Want me to close my eyes while I deliver them?" O'Brian suggested. "We can pretend I never came to your home or know where it is?"

"Yes," Michelle said with a huff. "That would be good."

He grinned. "Sorry I'm invading your castle. Lawless tried fifty different ways to think of how she could get her plants here without any money and without me helping. In the end, I told her I knew you'd rather she didn't hurt herself again and that if I was wrong, I'd suffer the consequences."

"Hmm." Michelle side-eyed him. "Obviously, your life is forfeit if you tell a soul where I live or admit to having put a toe in here."

"Understood, boss." He grinned and mock saluted her. "So…she really didn't tell you her plants were comin'?"

"No," Michelle said, tone clipped. "She *forgot*. Those painkillers do that. She's foggy on some really basic things. *And* she's getting her checkup this minute, so I can't scowl at her while waving pointedly at that greenery."

O'Brian chuckled. "I see your dilemma. But, unlike me, somehow I think she'll live despite her transgressions."

Michelle did not dignify that astute observation with a response.

"Just so you know," he went on, "I offered to let her keep the jungle at our place. Shauna loves it. But Lawless says she misses havin' plants around her way too much."

She missed them? Well. That changed things.

After that, Michelle simply showed him to her lower floor, which contained her guest room, laundry room, and three unused living areas, and told him to store the plants any spot he could find.

She assumed Eden would water them as required and keep them out of her hair. Michelle had no interest in seeing the greenery again.

It reminded her of how the plants had been spread throughout her office once, bringing it to life, and how much she'd secretly adored that.

As the days went by, she kept expecting Eden to comment on O'Brian's delivery, but she never did. Not even an apology for invading Michelle's space unasked. Maddening!

All was forgiven, the moment her former office plant reappeared. The oxalis, with its elegant, butterfly-shaped purple leaves, was simply sitting on her coffee table one day. Her eyes lit up, and she rushed to it and drew in a deep breath. Still the same smell.

Forgetting their unspoken *don't ask, don't notice* plant standoff, Michelle gasped to Eden, "You remembered?"

"That this was your desk plant?" Eden smiled. "Of course. I kept her in my van for ages. When I got extra mad with you, I'd glare at her and say something sarcastic. Then I'd feel bad." She laughed. "Poor little oxalis. After that, I gave her to Shauna to pamper with the rest."

"So why return it now?" Michelle looked up.

"I'm…no longer mad at you." Eden stared at the plant, cheeks reddening. "I think you deserve her back. You missed her."

Michelle digested that. "No longer mad?"

"No. I'm grateful." Eden met her eyes, expression soft. "For everything."

"Well." Michelle didn't know quite how to answer that.

"Thanks for letting me bring my plants here. I really needed their healing energy."

"It was a bit hard to say no when you didn't actually ask," Michelle said lightly.

Eden's face went slack. "I…didn't?" Shock filled her eyes. "Seriously?"

"No." Michelle almost laughed at her horror. "It's fine. I assumed the drugs had addled your brain."

"Oh goddess, I'm sorry! I thought we'd had a whole conversation about it."

"Only in your head, I'm afraid."

Eden looked abashed. Then she brightened. "Okay, I have one way to make it up to you. I've chosen a new plant for you. I put it in your bedroom. I really hope you'll like it."

"But I have this," Michelle pointed at her plant, "which I already like."

"Your oxalis belongs in your office. This new one's for your room."

Without a word, Michelle rose and went to look. There, on the nightstand, perched the most glorious orange flower she'd ever seen in her life. Large but made up of dozens of little petals, it was like happiness personified—so bright and cheerful.

Dear God, she's given me herself in plant form. Michelle snorted.

She rejoined Eden on the couch. "Very friendly looking. What is it?"

"A gerbera. It's a daisy native to South Africa."

"Does it have a meaning?" Flowers often did.

"Uh…" Eden gave a sheepish look. "Well, the common meaning for that color gerbera is energy, warmth, and enthusiasm. And the Celts believed gerberas, in general, lessen sorrows and stress."

"How apt, given my job." Michelle gave Eden a sly look. "So what's the *un*common meaning?"

Eden wiggled in her seat. "Okay, first, I'd like to say I chose it due to the common reason. And maybe a little for the Celtic thing. You needed a pick-me-up."

"Eden…" Michelle drawled.

"Fine." Eden huffed. "Some people give gerberas to declare an attachment to someone. Others say the red or orange varieties convey an unconscious love. Some even claim it means deception or keeping secrets." She drew in a breath. "But to me? I just see joy."

Michelle pictured the beautiful flower. The pop of orange and lime green brightened her sterile bedroom. "Thank you, then, for giving me joy, Eden."

"You're welcome. Now, tell me about your day?" She met Michelle's gaze encouragingly, waiting.

She always did that these days. Asked and waited, looking so interested.

So, Michelle did as Eden asked. She always did that too now.

No point fighting the tide.

The night before Francine Wilson's boardroom meeting, Eden retired early.

Michelle knocked on her bedroom door and stuck her head in when Eden invited her to enter. She leaned against the doorframe and took in the scene. The muted wall TV showed waddling penguins. Eden was curled up with a book in her bed. Something about global warming. Beside it was another one. A lesbian romance, if the seductive cover was anything to go by.

"Chalk and cheese," Michelle suggested with a smile, waving at the two books.

"Work," Eden lifted the one she'd been reading. "Palate cleanser," she pointed at the romance. "For when life gets too depressing and my brain needs a reset."

"Ah."

Eden closed the climate book and inched up into seated position. She didn't pull a pained face for once. That was reassuring.

"One more sleep," Michelle told her as her gaze slid to stare at the penguins, now grouping together for warmth in a snowstorm. "Then you'll have justice."

"Join me?" Eden patted the space beside her.

Michelle slid onto the bed, curling her socked feet under herself, then leaned against the headboard. "Wouldn't want to be the penguins on the outside of that group. The chill factor from the wind would be freezing."

"They rotate. Unlike people—who worm their way into the best position for themselves and stay there, pushing everyone else away." Eden sighed. "On that note, do *not* underestimate Francine Wilson tomorrow."

"It's her who shouldn't underestimate us. She's used to dealing with small-town people easily bought off or threatened. We are the big leagues. She won't know what's hit her."

"Michelle…" Eden edged closer, "she's not like other people. She's empty, soulless, and heartless. Think of the worst person you've ever met and then imagine them times ten. *That's* Francine. It's *you* who needs to be on your toes. Please." Her tone turned beseeching. "If it looks like she's going to win over even one board member, pull the plug on that meeting immediately. I don't need justice that bad."

"She won't win over anyone." Michelle studied the concern radiating from Eden. "To do that, she'd have to get through five smart, cunning, ruthless men who can sniff out pretenders from a mile off. They know what she is. They've been warned she's a schemer. They'll hear her out, then toss her out. Okay?"

Eden still looked worried.

"Hey," Michelle said gently. "Trust me. I've got this."

Eden's eyes closed, and she slid over, resting her cheek on Michelle's shoulder. "Okay." She exhaled.

Michelle couldn't resist sliding fingers through Eden's hair, drifting them behind her ear.

Suddenly the other woman's cheeks reddened, and Eden shifted abruptly away. "Sorry," she mumbled. "I…um…forgot where I was for a second."

Who she was with, she probably meant. Michelle's lips drew down. "Well," she said, snapping her hand back from Eden's hair. "I see." Pain seared through her at the rejection. It wasn't entirely unexpected, though, was it? What had Michelle been thinking, blurring the lines like that? Revealing how she felt?

"No, I don't think you do." Eden's tone was so gentle, it gave Michelle pause. "But we'll talk about all this after the meeting. My plans and what's next."

All this? What plans? It sounded like she was planning on leaving. What else was there to discuss? Eden no longer needed supervision. Dr. Michelson reported she was healing well and didn't need comfortable beds to recover. What was left to keep her here?

What a depressing thought. *No more Eden to come home to?* Her heart squeezed.

Worse, Eden didn't want to stay. Why would she? Certainly, Michelle was no lure; Eden had just made that clear, snatching her hand away.

"You still need security," Michelle tried, hating herself for how desperate she sounded. "From Sharpe."

"Who'll be dealt with tomorrow." Eden eyed her softly. "I can't impose on you forever. I've already taken over your home enough. Your safta must be coming back soon."

One week's time, in fact. "It's not an imposition," Michelle said, feeling sick.

She doesn't want you. She's letting you down gently so she can leave.

"I'm glad I haven't imposed. But you must be missing your meat dishes by now." Eden smiled. "And not having your TVs invaded by wildlife."

"I've gotten used to it. I've learned a lot about snow leopards." Safer grounds. Michelle could do this.

"My favorite animal," Eden said.

"Really? Not penguins?" Michelle asked. She was pleased her voice didn't betray her hurt. "Or pandas?"

"That's your nickname for me, not mine."

"You know about that?"

"Phelim told me. He gave me the sweetest carving of one too."

"O'Brian...carves?"

"Sure does. And his wife's an amazing cook. I've agreed to another dinner with them in a few weeks."

A spike of jealousy pricked Michelle. She was well aware she wasn't good enough to dine with the O'Brians. He'd told her as much, while laughing. Her nostrils flared. So, not only didn't Eden want to be in her orbit, her most loyal of lieutenants didn't want to either.

"I've asked them if I can bring you."

Michelle blinked. "You did?"

"Mmm. I always got the impression you were a bit jealous when I had dinner with them. So I asked." Eden gave the tiniest of shrugs.

"Not *jealous*," Michelle said, lips pursed. "More...unwelcome."

"Well, Shauna was delighted. Can't wait to meet her husband's boss. You're plenty welcome."

"And O'Brian?" She paused. "Phelim," she clarified.

"He said I had to tell you to behave."

Michelle frowned. "What did he mean, exactly?"

"You have to pretend you don't work for an evil corporation, and therefore, by extension, neither does he."

"Ah."

"Don't worry. I'll be there to nudge you if you go all Darth Vadery."

"How...thoughtful." *Lovely; she still thinks I'm evil.*

"Yeah." Eden smiled again. "Now then, want to stay for a bit? I'll even improve your viewing." With that, she reached for the remote.

Penguins were gone, and a murder mystery appeared. It seemed Eden had been paying attention to Michelle's preferences.

"Oooh, Helen Mirren," Eden said enthusiastically. "*Hot.*"

Michelle, still trying to rein in her bruised heart, peered up at Detective Chief Inspector Jane Tennison. "You realize she's fifty-something in this?"

"So?" Eden hunkered into her pillow. "Hot is hot. I don't care about age. I like her attitude."

Michelle swallowed. "Oh." And as she watched, she couldn't disagree. Helen Mirren was *hot*.

That night, Eden couldn't sleep. Not just because tomorrow Michelle was going into battle for her and didn't seem to understand the danger of Francine Wilson.

But also because the skin Michelle had touched still tingled.

Eden sighed. She'd started it. She'd laid her head on Michelle's shoulder without thinking. As one might a friend. Or a confidante.

The moment she'd done so, she'd wanted to sink into Michelle's body, pull her tightly to herself, and stay there. Her stomach had swallowed a whole nest of butterflies when Michelle had responded by touching her hair, gently sliding loose strands behind her ear.

Like a friend. Or a confidante.

Eden's skin had lit on fire. Her breath had caught. She'd realized that she'd arched into Michelle's touch. Not as a friend or a confidante. As a lover. So she'd pulled away, startled by her reaction.

She wished she could rewind time and stay in that delicate moment. Prolong the sensations where walls and masks were gone and all that lay there was the yearning for each other's touch.

Because Eden had felt it: It wasn't just her. Michelle had been drawn in, too, the same as her. There had been a tremor in Michelle's fingers as she'd combed Eden's hair gently and carefully, as if afraid of breaking her.

The tenderness of her actions made Eden crave more. More touches, more soft puffs of air near her ear. More Michelle.

She understood then. Everything. Aggie had been right all along.

I've fallen for her.

And while Eden didn't have the missing piece of the puzzle that was Catherine Ayers, ever since Michelle's gentle fingers had quivered against her skin, Eden no longer cared. Because now she was convinced Michelle was entirely wrong about herself: She wasn't cruel or calculating. If she had hurt her lover on purpose—a distinct possibility—it had been a mistake. Some shocking lapse in judgment—one she'd been torturing herself over for years. No one so traumatized by just hearing Ayers's name could be heartless.

That was the moment Eden reached a conclusion: the Fixers might be evil, but its CEO wasn't.

More than that, Michelle was in so much pain, she couldn't see straight. She couldn't see her own value beyond her professional talents. When Michelle had snatched her hand away, the look on her face radiated shame, loss, embarrassment, and fear that Eden had rejected her.

That was the other thing Eden had learned this evening: Michelle hated herself. She didn't think herself worthy of comfort or love from anyone other than her safta. And that was something Eden absolutely would not let stand.

Tomorrow night, after Michelle finished battling Eden's enemies, Eden would tell her. She would explain that Michelle *was* worthy. Warm. Good. That she was a safe place to curl up in. And that Eden saw her for who she really was.

Chapter 16

The Gray Men

Four men sat before Michelle in the boardroom. She knew their names even though they were referred to as numbers in the minutes Tilly kept.

"One" was Damion Williamson. Ex-deputy director of the CIA. An expert conniver. He could see schemes within schemes.

"Two" was Cole Gilbert—tech billionaire. A clever mind and lateral thinker.

"Three" was Emmett Holt, FBI director…well, until the unfortunate business with MediCache. His public disgrace had made him sharper and harder, more vicious. Michelle was grateful he'd never discovered she'd been the leak.

"Four" was powerbroker Maurice Wagner. The man behind the throne at the White House. He had connections and blackmail files on both sides of the aisle. If you wanted to be president, you needed his nod. Phyllis Kensington counted him as a friend, of course. She was hardly unique. Four had so many presidential contenders sniffing around him that he'd probably lost count.

And "Five." Name unknown. Michelle had never seen him. He was patched into meetings via Skype, although his incoming video stayed black and he made all comments via the chat box to protect his identity.

Obviously the other four knew who he was, but whenever Michelle or anyone outside the inner circle was in attendance, he went into anonymous mode.

Michelle had been alerted two minutes ago that Francine Wilson and Derrick Sharpe had arrived. O'Brian was staying with Sharpe in the foyer during the meeting. Tilly was escorting Wilson to the boardroom.

The moment the former mayor entered the room, the four men stopped and stared, their small talk about the Chinese stock market dying in their throats.

Michelle groaned inwardly at the effect beautiful women could have on the higher functions of men.

Tilly showed Francine to a chair, then made her way to the other end of the table where a sleek laptop sat. She tapped a few buttons, looked up, and said, "Five is patched in and is awaiting the meeting starting. He also asks if anyone else noticed Tencent's takeover bid of Faraday didn't happen?"

Two nodded. "I heard it'll be tomorrow. Paperwork glitch."

Tilly glanced at her screen and then looked up. "He says 'Understood.'" She looked around the table. "Ms. Wilson, would you or anyone else care for a refreshment?"

They all declined.

Before anyone could say anything further, Wilson smiled. "Gentlemen," she began, "and Ms. Hastings, thank you for seeing me on such short notice. I know you must be very busy men." She shot them a dazzling smile, and all four smiled back automatically. "I understand how time-consuming the acquisition of power and control is, so let me be brief."

Michelle drew in a breath. *Here it comes.* Some pitch to be involved in DC's political machinations or networking, maybe? That'd fit.

Instead, Wilson said, "I've called you here because what The Fixers needs is a CEO who is unfettered by limits. Someone not held back by ethical considerations or walking fine lines. Why try so hard not to get your staff arrested when you could do whatever it takes and pay off people to turn a blind eye to the consequences? I speak from experience. Power, gentlemen, comes in seizing the day through strength, not twitching about like timid beetles. You run the world, don't you?" she goaded. "You're masters of industry and capitalism. You are gods among men. Isn't it about time The Fixers and its CEO act like it?"

"You're after *my* job?" Michelle asked, shocked.

Wilson leaned back in her chair, and said, "Yes. And I'll make a better fist of it than a wishy-washy CEO with no stomach for risk. A woman who cost Three his job at the FBI by leaking MediCache's secrets to the press."

Panic shot through her. How could Francine know that?

Everyone gaped.

Three hurled an outraged glare her way. "Is that true?"

Before she could answer, Tilly, eyes darting rapidly across her screen, said, "Five wants to know *how* you come by this theory."

"It's fact, not theory," Wilson said. "I'm now in possession of a *lot* of facts, and every one of them makes Ms. Hastings look terrible."

The next hour was a blur of Wilson raising every mistake, misstep, or unlucky call Michelle had ever made. Wilson knew every skeleton. Every secret. Who had she been speaking to? Alberto? But how had she known to connect with him?

Wilson concluded with: "In case you're wondering how good I am, let me put it this way: I'd never heard of The Fixers until they destroyed my reelection bid. A few months later, I'm sitting here with the powerbrokers of a top-secret organization arguing to run it. *That's* how exceptional I am. And remember my motto: *no limits.*" She sat back and actually smiled at Michelle as though half expecting applause.

"Thank you, Ms. Wilson," One said. His eyebrows were knitted together. "Most…informative. Please wait outside now while we discuss your arguments."

She exited with a swish of black jacket and the swirl of high-end perfume.

Michelle watched her go, cheeks blazing with anger and humiliation. The moment the door snicked shut, she turned on the board, furious. "Surely you can't be planning on replacing me with *her*! She's a scheming psychopath who'll bring you all down with her ambition. Not to mention she's high-profile now due to that national ad campaign. People will be watching her."

"Of course, Ms. Hastings," Two said, tone placating. "We don't even know her. You're a known quantity."

Michelle exhaled. Not exactly a ringing endorsement, but better than nothing.

"But she does raise a good point," One said. "Well, several actually. First, she seems to think you were behind the MediCache story leaking. Is that true?"

"Yes," Three snapped. "Is it?"

Michelle swallowed. *Damn it.* She could deny it, but she was sure Three would investigate. It would be worse if it came out later. Better to own it now. "Yes. Look, we all know the secret of MediCache. It would have compromised the privacy of every American."

Actually, Three had loved that part of it a great deal and was annoyed it had been stopped. His expression turned into a sneer.

"But that wasn't my only concern," Michelle continued. "My other issue was that one of our employees, our then-head of Cybersecurity, Douglas Lesser, who was the brainchild behind the MediCache tech, was also a destructive racist with plans to move into federal politics. He was a loose cannon. He had to be stopped while he still could be."

Three gave her a filthy look. "We are all aware of his personal politics."

Personal politics? Being racist wasn't *politics*! It was a human failing! She gritted her teeth.

"But his views are irrelevant," Three continued. "In fact, if he'd moved into DC politics, that would have been even better for us. Having a man on the inside, highly gifted at hacking computers? The blackmail material alone could have kept us going for years. You threw that away."

Michelle's gaze darted around the table, to see if his views were shared. Of course Three hated the decision she'd made—he'd lost his job over it.

But the others were nodding. The churning in her stomach returned. Couldn't they see the big picture? A racist, computer hacking genius in the highest rungs of politics could ruin careers, maybe even cost lives, if he wanted to. His power would be unfettered.

"Ms. Hastings," One said, "I think Three's point is that Lesser had his issues, but he wasn't afraid of crossing lines. You seemed to be afraid of using his greatest strength—his incredible talent."

"It's not a strength when it's ripe to be misused," Michelle said, dismayed. "His talent just hides a massive deficit in personality, and he uses it as a weapon. Wilson's exactly the same. She mistakes caution for weakness. She wants us to cavalierly intimidate our way to success. She assumes we'll get away with it with payoffs and threats later, when it's simply *not necessary*. We fly under the radar so well, we can get away with virtually anything. Tempting fate just because we can, or to feel important—like *gods*—is a terrible idea! Secrecy means safety. We run at peak efficiency only because no one has leaked our existence."

"Except *someone* has been leaking about us—and rather a lot," Four cut in. "Ms. Hastings, we agreed to this meeting *not* because we wanted to hear out Wilson—although that has been eye-opening—but to discover why you've been hiding these leaks from us."

Tilly broke in. "Five says he's known for over a month about the leaks and is disappointed to have not been officially notified by Ms. Hastings."

And…crap. "I apologize for the delay in conveying the matter to you all," Michelle said. "I'd planned to resolve it myself promptly and report back, after the fact, explaining I'd fixed it."

"*Have* you fixed it?" Three asked, eyes sharp.

"Yes," Michelle said. Well, Eden had called a cease-fire. Close enough for now.

Tilly's eyes darted across her screen. "Five asks if it's true that Wilson's man attacked the woman who leaked our secrets? And if that's true, why are you protecting this Eden Lawless now?"

Michelle paled. How the hell did Five always do that? His network was unparalleled. "She was attacked as a result of working for us. We look after our own."

"Even if our own betrays us?" Three asked.

"I…"

"We're getting off topic," One cut in. "Let's focus on the key thing." His gaze burned a hole into Michelle. "Wilson's not wrong. You're always playing it safe."

"I'm *keeping* us safe," Michelle argued.

"There is such a thing as *too safe*," Three said, a malicious look in his eye. He could smell the blood in the water now. "What about Wilson's suggestion: taking the gloves off and fixing any fallout that comes later."

"Safety has kept you out of headlines and without scrutiny."

"It didn't keep *me* out of the headlines," Three said coldly. "In fact, *you* put me in them."

"We're not arguing about that now." Four lifted a conciliatory hand. "We thank you, Ms. Hastings, for keeping the existence of The Fixers secret. What we *are* wondering is whether maybe your leadership has been *too* cautious of late."

And there it was. They were coming for her.

Tilly flicked her a sad, knowing look.

Great. She smells the blood in the water too. Michelle stared down the men. "Don't do this," she said hoarsely. "It would be a huge error. If you appoint Wilson, this becomes a fiefdom. A dictatorship where she just gets her rocks off on power. She'll destroy The Fixers within six months. Our organization's existence will become public knowledge. That will ruin us."

"We're not replacing you, Ms. Hastings," Four said, tone cajoling in a way that set her teeth on edge. The *yet* was also hanging there. "We're asking you to consider stepping out of your comfort zone. Being…*bold*, as Wilson would be. Can you do that? Consider crossing a few, riskier lines if it means getting the outcome we need?" His bushy white eyebrows lifted.

Tilly spoke: "Five says we also need you to be more up-front with information such as leaks. This has been disappointing. We expect better." She shot Michelle an apologetic look.

The men nodded.

"I'll take your feedback under advisement," Michelle said stiffly. "And may I remind you that hiring and firing is your area. But running The Fixers is my purview."

"Yes, my dear," said One. "*Of course*. We just hoped you'd also accept some input with the benefit of our much greater years of experience and wisdom."

"I'm always open to hearing input," she replied, tone curt.

"And not implementing it," said Three. "Right?"

Michelle gave him a taunting smile because she was so tired of his attitude. He'd hated her long before today but had just stopped hiding it now. "If you want to change how The Fixers is run, then perhaps you *should* consider hiring the dictator from Wingapo."

"That's a little harsh," said Two. "She seems a clever woman to me."

How naive could you get? Had he been watching the same woman? Her games? The danger she presented?

The other men nodded.

Oh, for God's sake. Seriously?

Tilly spoke up. "Five concurs."

Were they blind? Or thinking with the wrong body part? "I can assure you, she's nothing of the sort," Michelle snapped.

"That's your opinion," said Three. "Which we're allowing you to have for now. Perhaps consider our comments with an open mind and try not to be so defensive in the future."

"We could hire her as a political adviser," Two suggested brightly. "It'd be a shame for all that talent to go to waste. POBUD would be a great fit."

The other men agreed with a series of yeses and nods.

"Over my dead body will that woman be on my staff." Michelle spoke softly, her voice so cold it sounded almost dead.

Tilly stared back in shock.

"Really," Three said snidely. "I'm fairly sure hiring and firing is *our* purview."

"On that note," said Four, "How is it Eden Lawless ended up on staff at all without us approving her? We would have flagged her as a potential risk. And we'd have been right, given what followed."

"She was only on probation." Michelle waved her hand. "Not worthy of bothering you all. She did her freelance assignment expertly, then was given a stint in DC in a minor capacity to see if she was suitable for permanent staff before I concluded she wasn't."

The men exchanged glances.

"How did she get any sensitive material to leak?" Tilly asked. "Five says, if she was working for us in a minor capacity, wouldn't she have had no access?"

Michelle sighed. Five never missed a thing. "Alberto Baldoni gave her the intel. He's trying to destroy us."

"*You*, you mean," Three noted sarcastically. "You did humiliate your ex-husband rather badly. Hypothetically speaking, wouldn't it be prudent to remove you to protect us all? Baldoni's agitating stops the moment you're gone."

"Or we get rid of Baldoni." Two's tone was sinister.

"Are you serious?" Michelle demanded furiously. "You want us to add *murder* to our roster? That really would attract the bright glare of scrutiny. I'll quit first."

"Don't bluff," Four said. "And no one's suggesting murder, for God's sake. We're just spit-balling. Tossing out ideas. But tell me," he added, leaning in, "what did you do to Lawless for betraying us?"

"She's been subject to payback by O'Brian's team."

"O'Brian?" He furrowed his brow. "Not Cybersecurity?"

"Correct."

"That seems a light touch. O'Brian's only used for threats, not real action."

"Enough!" Michelle slapped the desk, causing the men to start and Tilly to cock an eyebrow. "Gentlemen, we've established that *how* this company runs is for me to decide. I won't be prosecuted on every little decision. It's bad enough you just let a stranger haul up every perceived misdeed of mine for over an hour without stopping her. You showed me no loyalty. Yet, as your CEO, I've always done what you've asked: I've kept you all in power and free to do whatever you want. How? Because I've kept us a *secret*. This meeting is over. I have a business to run."

"Ms. Hastings," said Two, tone placating, "we're not ungrateful."

"You sound like it." She glared at them.

"We just want you to consider whether maybe being more like Francine Wilson isn't a good thing? Sometimes."

"Only if you want a psychopath running your company."

"Better than a coward," Three muttered.

"Ex-*cuse* me?" Michelle spun to face him. "It's not cowardice to protect you and your interests!"

"No?" Three's words became silky. "I'm just wondering what happened to the woman we promoted? The woman who fucked and manipulated Catherine Ayers like it was *nothing*, tossed away her own marriage just to get ahead. Now *that* woman was cunning and ruthless. Heroic in her ambitions. Impressive."

Silence fell. Everyone was well aware that Catherine Ayers was not a safe topic and that Michelle's hackles were raised over the merest hint of it. Rubbing her nose in it and alluding to her failed marriage too? It was a declaration of war.

The whole room knew it. The other men shifted uncomfortably in their seats, eyes darting about. Tilly suddenly found her laptop fascinating.

Michelle leaped to her feet, leaned across the table toward Three, and enunciated perfectly: "*Fuck. You.*"

Tilly gave the faintest, alarmed headshake of warning.

Too late. She was so over this entire clusterfuck of a meeting. She'd been humiliated and taken to task for difficult decisions she'd made in good faith. It was always so easy in hindsight.

"I'm done here," Michelle growled. "Fire me or not, I no longer care. In the meantime, I have a job to do." With rage crackling through her body, she stormed from the room.

The last sound she heard was Tilly's pained sigh.

Chapter 17
The Funeral Riddle

Michelle stalked out of the boardroom, anger still snapping through her.

Francine Wilson was gazing out at the view and turned, her scarlet lips ticked up into a goading smirk.

"All right," Michelle said wearily, "who briefed you? Who told you all that confidential information?"

"It's a secret." Her smirk widened.

"Alberto?" Michelle would wring his neck this time. Take him to court. Whatever it took. She was so done with his sneaky undermining of her.

"Who?" Wilson looked genuinely baffled. Clearly this wasn't a name she'd heard before.

"Who then?" Three? He hated her enough.

Francine ignored the question. "Thank you for upholding your end of the deal. My end of the deal's sitting in the foyer. Now then—is there a back exit? I intend to take my leave before Chief Sharpe's any the wiser about what I've done."

Michelle paused. "Wait, why does he think he's here?"

"I asked him to be my driver to DC. I explained I get so overwhelmed by the big city." She rolled her eyes. "He's a little…besotted with me. That's been so useful over the years—just a sideways glance and promise of more and he'd do anything."

"*Anything?*" Michelle said suspiciously. "Did he, perhaps, attack Lawless on your orders?"

"Violence is so uncultured. Brutish. Ordinarily, I disdain it."

Michelle's anger rose. "But?"

"But...sometimes extreme times call for extreme measures. This *is* your fault, you know."

"Mine? How!"

"Ever heard of the funeral riddle?" Wilson asked thoughtfully. "A young woman goes to a family funeral, sees the man of her dreams, but doesn't speak to him so doesn't know who he is. Later, she decides she wants to see him again, but how? What does she do?"

Michelle recognized the riddle—a ridiculous social media meme—and what it implied. Her stomach tightened. "She murders a family member in the hope he shows up at the funeral again." Her eyes narrowed. "You wanted to see me again, to work at my organization, but had no way of reaching me. So you attacked Lawless, knowing she was under my protection, and waited to see if I'd show up."

Wilson slow clapped her.

"Ms. Wilson, the funeral riddle is supposed to identify psychopaths."

"Oh, please. It's simply a clever idea I've repurposed. I had no intention of seriously hurting Lawless. I told Sharpe to do just enough damage to get your attention. I ensured he left his fingerprints on her throat to make it clear it wasn't a mugging. I didn't want you to dismiss it as a random incident." Her tone turned mocking. "I needed those big, strong, protective instincts of yours to kick in again. And it worked. Here you are, and here I am!"

Michelle's blood boiled. Eden had been hurt just to get Michelle's attention? "You seriously think those men will give you a job now you've hurt one of our employees *and* trashed their CEO?"

"*Ex*-employee," Wilson corrected, proving her intel was chillingly up to date. She snickered. "Oh, I was most thoroughly briefed."

Michelle really wished murder was legal.

Her thoughts must have leaked a little because Wilson took a nervous step back. "Look, it's unfortunate Lawless got hurt, but it was necessary. I'm goal oriented. She was the price to pay. And, no, I don't know if your board will make me CEO, but I've shot my best shot." Suddenly her expression was all charm. "So, that's that. Your back way out, please?"

Michelle scowled and took Wilson to the trade elevator, then escorted her to the rear door. Pointing to the card reader, Michelle said, "Swipe your visitor pass there, then hand it to me."

Wilson did as instructed and, as she passed, Michelle murmured, "You didn't ask what we're going to do with Sharpe."

"Because I don't care in the least. Do whatever you want." With that, she exited.

Jaw tight, Michelle made her way to the lobby to meet Derrick Sharpe in the flesh.

Chief Sharpe sat, manspreading obnoxiously on the visitor's couch, looking bored, and chewing on a thumb nail. O'Brian lurked at the desk, one eye on Sharpe, while talking to the security guard in low tones. Seeing Michelle's approach, he straightened.

Michelle's gaze flicked over the imposing form of Sharpe. This man…an officer of the law, no less…this lumbering hulk, had laid his meaty hands on Eden? Wrapped them around her slender throat. Eden was a third his weight, if that. And he'd left her unconscious and battered in an empty lot like she was nothing.

Fury burned and burned, and a number of particularly vicious scenarios played out in her head. But no; she and O'Brian had already decided his fate.

Michelle strode over to the seated brute. "Mr. Sharpe," she said curtly.

He blinked up at her in surprise. "Yes?"

"Do you know why you are here?"

"Mayor…Ms. Wilson asked me to be her driver and security escort today."

"That's all she said?"

He nodded slowly. "I thought she might be going somewhere sketchy. Instead, we came here." He sagged at that, as though their modern foyer was far too safe for him to feel in any way heroic.

"I see. You weren't aware *you* were part of a deal she made? Ms. Wilson wanted a meeting with my board and in exchange we got you."

"Me?" He peered at her, then glanced around. His gaze flicked to O'Brian, who had now moved to stand behind Michelle's shoulder. "I...already have a job. I'm good at it. I'm chief of police in Wingapo."

"That's debatable," Michelle snapped.

His expression turned dark. "Ma'am?"

"To be good at being a police chief, aren't you required to uphold the law? Not beat one of my employees and leave her for dead?"

Alarm crossed his face. "The hell? I didn't do that."

"Security footage says otherwise."

"Wait, I wasn't caught on camera."

Christ, the man was stupid.

"I mean, if I did it, which I didn't. You can't prove it. I wasn't there."

"We have footage of you at the scene," Michelle said.

"Bullshit. That camera was destroyed."

So. Stupid. "How do you know a camera was destroyed if you weren't there?"

His mouth closed.

"The church camera was destroyed, yes. Not the dry cleaner's one across the road."

He swallowed.

"So, not only do we have footage of you, but Ms. Wilson outlined your role in great detail."

"She'd never do that." He looked appalled at the thought.

"She brought you here, didn't she? Left you here too." She turned to the guard and called, "Mr. Marshall, what time did Wilson exit our building?"

"Her visitor pass tagged off five minutes ago, ma'am."

Sharpe shot to his feet, betrayal and anger in his eyes. "I'm leaving."

"No. You're not. *Sit.*" Michelle tilted her head toward O'Brian. "Or my head of security will make you."

Sharpe gave her a filthy glare and rose.

O'Brian clapped a hand loudly on Sharpe's shoulder, slamming him back down.

"*Sit*," Michelle repeated. "Or he'll do much worse."

Sharpe hesitated.

Michelle gestured at O'Brian. "You're in the presence of the man whose security team took down you and your officers in Wingapo. I understand you were incapacitated in five minutes. You're not dealing with amateurs. Or civilians."

"*Four* minutes," O'Brian corrected. His voice lowered to dangerous. "Now, keep your ugly arse sat or I won't be so polite next time."

Sharpe instantly stopped moving.

"Mr. Sharpe—" Michelle began.

"*Chief* Sharpe," he spat. "I'll have you fucking arrested. Both of you. For this and what you did to me in Wingapo."

"*Mr.* Sharpe," Michelle said, "the only person about to be arrested is you. We are an organization well connected with everyone in DC, including a number of police chiefs and judges. Worse, you happened to assault someone my head of security is rather fond of." She waved at O'Brian. "And someone I'm fond of too."

She hadn't intended to make that admission and didn't dare look at O'Brian. "You have two choices," she plowed on. "One, you will be given to one of our police associates to be dealt with, along with our security footage and witness statements, including a damning one from the ex-mayor you love so much."

He faltered, shock in his eyes. Well, she might not have Wilson's statement, but psychological warfare was a powerful thing.

"Further," Michelle continued, "everyone in Wingapo will be made aware of your cowardly assault on an unarmed woman. Doubtlessly, your job will be lost, as will be your community's respect for you, your wife's respect." She paused. "It's *so* interesting you have a wife when Ms. Wilson indicated you'd do anything for her because you are *besotted* with her."

He paled. "She said that?"

"Indeed. Oh, we'll let your wife know that too. Full disclosure. So that's option one. Clean house, no secrets, no lies."

"Why would I agree to any of that?" he demanded.

"You wouldn't have to agree to anything. Did you miss the part about where we have judges in our back pocket? Police chiefs? *This* is what your fate is. Your opinion is irrelevant. So," she snapped her fingers, "you'd face a maximum sentence for aggravated assault…"

"Attempted murder," O'Brian corrected.

"I didn't try to murder her!" Sharpe gasped.

"Choke marks say otherwise," O'Brian pointed out.

"That was for *show*!"

"Not what our judge will think," Michelle replied. "You see, the evidence points to you trying to kill her and being interrupted. I have a doctor's report to the effect Lawless was thoroughly choked. Most definitely not *for show*. Now, attempted murder in DC will get you…" She glanced at O'Brian, aware he'd done his research.

"Assault with intent to kill in DC is a max of fifteen years and a $37,500 fine," O'Brian said instantly.

"*Fifteen* years." Michelle clucked. "Goodness, that's quite long, isn't it? You'll be an old man by the time you're out."

Sharpe stared in horror. "What's…" He swallowed. "The other choice?"

"Simple: submit to *our* justice, and we'll let you go afterward."

"You will?" He looked at them skeptically.

"We will. Are you familiar with the concept of an eye for an eye?" Michelle asked sweetly.

His eyes widened.

Michelle pulled folded paper out of her pocket. "This is the list of injuries Eden Lawless sustained at your hands. Three cracked ribs, contusions of the eye socket and cheek, strangulation…and it goes downhill from there." She handed the list to O'Brian, who pocketed it. "Eye for an eye."

Sharpe's gaze darted all around as if expecting a bloodbath to start immediately.

"Oh, not here," Michelle said. "Why should we have to clean up your blood? No, my security chief will drive you to the scene of your crime. He will exact the same punishment on you that you inflicted on Lawless. Next, he will leave you unconscious until it's dark. If you regain consciousness early, you will be rendered unconscious again."

Sharpe's mouth fell open.

"Then you will be required to walk for ten miles, at which point you will be allowed to seek assistance from whomsoever you wish. Bear in mind, you'll be stripped of your phone and wallet first. My security chief will follow you at a distance to make sure you don't cheat and stop or call for help early."

"Ten miles!" he thundered. "No one can walk ten miles all beat up like that!"

"Eden Lawless did," Michelle said coldly. "Astonishing what the human body can do when fueled by determination and adrenaline. That's how far she managed before she found help after *you* brutalized her. What a superhuman feat. Now, it would take a normal person over three hours to walk that route. That's someone healthy and unhurt. I have no idea exactly how long it would take someone badly injured, but tonight we're going to find out." She paused. "Or we can go with the judicial route. Police. Court. Jail. Humiliation. Your choice."

"Who *are* you people?" he rasped out. "And why do you care about Lawless? She's no one!"

"Now, don't you think that's a question you should have asked *before* you did whatever Wilson told you to like a compliant lapdog?"

His expression darkened.

"One more thing." Michelle leaned in and said into his ear, "And this is something men never think about. Women have a fear of walking alone at night because we're not sure if someone's going to leap out and rape us."

He swallowed hard.

"On top of everything else she endured, Lawless would have been terrified of that too. Of course, a big strong man like you—that wouldn't even enter your mind, would it?"

She studied the agreement and disbelief in his eyes.

"But to reenact your victim's night from hell properly, it wouldn't be realistic without that element," Michelle added. "I've decided you should have that fear too. My head of security knows some terrible people. Big brutish ex-convicts whose tastes are...primitive. They don't care who or how they hurt people. You'd be nothing to them. Be aware that one or two of them may be lying in wait for you on your journey. Maybe they'll drag you off into the bushes and fuck you. Maybe you'll get lucky and have enough strength left to fight them off. Who can say? That's the unknown element, isn't it?"

"You wouldn't," he rasped out.

"Me? No. But this is my security chief's operation, and I don't interfere. As I said, he is *very* fond of the young woman you terrorized, so I can't be too sure of his plans. Just be glad I gave you the heads-up. That way, you can keep an ear out for any rustling in the bushes." Michelle paused. "Well, that's everything. So. Are you ready?"

"No," Sharpe said. "I don't… please. I'm sorry. I…I'll tell Lawless I'm sorry. Don't make me do this."

"You're *sorry*?" Finally, Michelle let her white-hot fury show. "So you *don't* want to be left alone with someone far bigger and scarier threatening you harm? I wonder how Ms. Lawless felt? But, unlike you, she didn't know what you were going to do to her, how far you were prepared to go, or where it would end. At least I'm telling you in advance."

A tremor ran through Sharpe.

"I can even give you an exact location," Michelle barreled on. "You'll end up in Fort Washington, exactly ten miles south of the impound lot." She'd worked out the route with O'Brian; it was in the opposite direction of Michelle's home—just to be safe—but the same distance as Eden had walked.

"You'll end up there battered, bleeding, concussed, with three cracked ribs, and quite possibly sexually assaulted," Michelle continued. "But you'll be alive. And then you can put all this behind you as long as you promise never to do it again." She finished in a cheerful tone laced with malice.

He began shaking his head. "No, no, no."

"A bully *and* a coward. How novel." Michelle turned to leave, signaling for O'Brian to take over.

"Why do you even give two shits about that stupid cunt?" Sharpe called after her.

There was an instant thud. And then a louder one.

Michelle spun around to find Chief Sharpe crumpled, unconscious, on the floor. She continued onwards to press the elevator button as she heard O'Brian's amused, muttered: "Oops."

"Just clean up any blood, O'Brian," she said evenly. "This is a place of business."

"Yes, boss." He sounded positively upbeat now. "Sure thing. Then I'll get his ass to that lot to start his justice."

"You do that."

"Um, you know I don't know any rapists, right?" O'Brian called, as an afterthought.

She rolled her eyes. "I would have been disappointed if you did. But the power of suggestion is a terrible thing. He'll be leaping at shadows and twitching like a rabbit for ten long miles."

He snorted.

Michelle glanced over to the security desk. "Mr. Marshall?" she called, as the elevator doors opened. "Delete that footage from the foyer cam. And until Mr. O'Brian is finished down here, restrict access to the ground floor once my elevator has reached its destination." She stepped inside.

His chipper, "Yes ma'am," greeted her ears as the doors slid closed.

Chapter 18
Fired Up

"Well," Tilly said, "*that* was foolish."

Michelle looked up from her desk to find her PA had returned from the boardroom.

The other woman was highly agitated. Tilly slid into the seat opposite and stared at Michelle in disbelief.

"Excuse me?" Michelle said, too surprised to say anything else.

Tilly looked unimpressed. "What were you thinking, challenging the board like that?"

"I was thinking 'How dare they treat me this way? Like a child who needs scolding.'" Michelle glared. "If you don't show people you won't be pushed around, they'll keep doing it."

"Or they'll fire you."

Michelle paused. "What?"

"You had to know they'd push back. Or was that your intention?"

"My..." Michelle inhaled. "I won't tolerate the way they dangled replacing me with Wilson as some threat. Are you saying they're actually doing it? Making that psychopath CEO?"

"All I wanted was an easy life," Tilly muttered.

"You won't get that with Francine Wilson as your boss."

Tilly scoffed. "They weren't serious about her. She was seen as someone useful to snap *you* into line. That whole meeting was about you. Couldn't you see that?"

Michelle blinked.

"They don't want her," Tilly repeated. "They think she's a power-hungry, irritating wannabe."

Well, that was a relief. Michelle relaxed a little.

"She lacks even the basics." Tilly flicked a hand in frustration. "To be a serious contender, the CEO must have three things: connections, ruthlessness, and no exposure risk for The Fixers." She pinned Michelle with a long look. "You had all three. Wilson has only ruthlessness. She will never sit in your chair."

"Good." So...why did Tilly still look so uneasy?

"This meeting was only ever about putting the fear of God into you. To make you more willing to listen to any of their future requests. *That's* the reason the board decided Wilson would be persuaded to make a pitch for the CEO position today, not just any Fixers job, as was her original intention. I was told to brief her on every single failing of yours I knew of in order to thoroughly rattle your cage in that meeting."

"That was *you*?" The treachery felt like acid.

"I carried out the board's decision, yes." Tilly eyed her. "And then, after that whole charade, you're not doing what you were supposed to."

"You mean I've called their bluff? I'm difficult now because I won't be their obedient pet?"

"Essentially."

Michelle wondered how badly that meeting had devolved after she'd left the boardroom. "That must have pissed them off."

"It did. At first. Now, they're glad. It makes it much easier to replace you."

"But you just said..."

"Not with Wilson. But she reminded them of someone else. Someone political, connected, ruthless, and who knows how to keep a secret: Phyllis Kensington."

Phyllis? Oh, hell no!

"It helps she's already friends with Four, who vouched for her," Tilly continued. "And she's recently resigned from politics. She's available. Kensington has agreed to come in for a meeting, but that's just a formality."

Phyllis was having a meeting about becoming CEO? She'd nail it, slippery roach that she was.

"She's heartless," Michelle snapped. "No empathy for others. Same as Francine, but cleverer at hiding it."

Tilly's laugh was dry. "Don't you know that's why they promoted you too? They thought you were a stone-cold bitch for what you did to Ayers. That's the final hiring criteria for CEO: Borderline psychopath. Will do anything, no matter how unethical."

Michelle froze. *That's* why she'd been promoted? They'd thought she was morally bankrupt.

Leaning back in her chair, Tilly gave a dismissive wave. "As you can imagine, they were somewhat dismayed in recent years to discover you had a conscience. It turned out Baldoni was right about you all along. You fell for Ayers. It seems you're skilled at hiding your feelings and clever enough to know when to take the kill shot—just before you were found out. That threw everyone off. You know, I've worked with every one of our CEOs. You are by far the softest, even though you present as the hardest."

"Tilly—"

"No. That is *not* my name."

"It isn't?" Michelle peered at her in astonishment.

"My *name*," she said, "is *Ottilie*. Or Ms. Zimmermann—not that you were ever much interested."

What the hell?

Ottilie narrowed her eyes. "Eden Lawless had barely been here *two minutes* before asking me why everyone was Ms. or Mr. to you, except for me. Why was I not being afforded the respect everyone else was? Even that delinquent in Cybersecurity is called *Mr.* Snakepit." Her eyes flashed.

Michelle's mouth fell open. "I'm sorry. I didn't realize I was offending you. You never said." Her mind raced back to work out how "Tilly" had stuck. "Wait, the previous CEO, he told me you prefer Tilly and I should call you that."

Ottilie rolled her eyes. "Of course. He was a misogynistic, infantilizing sadist who thought it was *hilarious* to use a nickname he knew

I disliked. Probably wanted to see if he could get you to use it too, to keep my irritation going."

"Why did you never say?" Michelle asked, appalled.

"I decided to see how long it'd take you to ask me about my preference. When you never did, I concluded you'd made a choice. That you didn't care, didn't want to know me, and couldn't be bothered getting my name right. It made things easier."

"Made *what* easier?"

Tilly closed her eyes briefly. When she opened them again, she looked different. Older. More authoritative. And her expression was *scorching*.

Michelle had always known her assistant wore her polite, kind, grandmotherly persona as a disguise, but it was gone now, along with her mask of deference, warmth, and gentle sweetness. Raw disdain stared back.

"*Michelle*," Ottilie said, drawing out her first name deliberately. "You are entirely too frustrating. You have made a lot of work for me, and I'm not happy. You weren't supposed to push back today. You were supposed to grasp that your position was in peril and agree to what the board asked. Instead, you backed them into a corner, insulted them, and dared them to fire you. You had to know their egos wouldn't tolerate that. Is that why you did it?" Her eyebrows lifted. "Forced the board to become so angry they'd want to fire you? You'd get a golden handshake that way?"

Had that been what she'd wanted? Subconsciously? For this to all be over?

"Because congratulations, Michelle. You got what you wanted."

"I...What?"

"You're fired." Ottilie folded her arms and glared in displeasure. Her tone was too practiced. She'd said those words before, most likely. Perhaps many times.

Michelle stared. "Who are you? Really?"

"I'm a little surprised you never worked it out. There were so many clues."

Michelle reviewed all their interactions, all the ways her assistant had carried herself with everyone. The way she dealt with the board, that laptop always in front of her, reading out questions, and…

"*Christ.*" Michelle sighed. No wonder Five was always the most knowledgeable board member. It was because Five knew everything Ottilie did. "*You're* Five."

"Well done." The corners of her mouth quirked.

"All those times you read out Five's questions, there was no Skype call, it was just *you* asking. The board knew and played along."

"They enjoyed the charade. Especially whenever I dropped in something about share prices or takeovers or super yachts to sell it."

"Then why are you also a PA if you're jointly in charge of The Fixers?"

"It was decided twenty-seven years ago, when The Fixers was founded, that two things needed to exist: complete deniability for the board should the organization ever be exposed. The only power they'd have was hiring and firing. But since we're also A-Type controlling personalities who wanted to know everything that was happening, we wanted eyes on the ground. I'd just left my position as a department head at the CIA, and I was unknown outside that agency, so it seemed appropriate I'd be the one to go undercover. I didn't mind. I've always liked managing an office."

"You were a spy."

"I prefer 'loyal to the board.'"

"Then it wouldn't have mattered if we were friends or if I'd gotten your name right anyway. You were never loyal to me." Michelle's lips pressed together.

"I was loyal to a point, as long as it didn't conflict with the board or my own situation."

"Good luck managing Phyllis. She won't be easily led."

"That's what all the CEOs think. At first. You were led."

Michelle's eyes widened. "When?"

"Every day. I advised which jobs needed your attention. Which clients were not worth it. I maintained contact with Baldoni for whenever I wanted information leaked to anyone. He was just so eager to stick the knife into you any chance he could get."

"Sounds like him," Michelle muttered.

"Every decision you thought you made was according to my wishes or the board's. I let you have a few victories, ones that mattered to you—such as exposing Lesser and MediCache's secrets—but *I* was running the office, and *you* were implementing my decisions."

"Number Three lost his FBI job due to that MediCache story," Michelle pointed out. "He was humiliated. If you were loyal to the board, why did you allow *that* to happen?"

"An unforeseen side effect. The story was only supposed to bring the tech down. Unfortunately, Ayers and King were a little too good, and their story caused a dragnet effect, pulling in anyone adjacent to it."

Michelle tried to get her head around this. Loyal Tilly. Not loyal and not Tilly. A spy. Who was about to have her hands very full. "It's a terrible idea choosing Kensington. She'll be no better as a CEO than she was as a senator or would have been as president. She's morally bankrupt."

"Is that why you leaked her secrets to DC's political dirt merchants? You worried that she might be president some day?"

Michelle gasped. "How?"

"Simple deduction. Only you had the authority to release Fixers' information about her husband to those men."

Seriously? Had *anything* Michelle done around here ever been a secret?

"We know everyone's secrets," Ottilie said, reading her mind. "Kensington's too, of course. Her appetite for women. Her appetite for you."

What! They'd been so careful. Never any witnesses.

"There's a camera in here." Ottilie pointed to the light fixture above Michelle's desk.

Oh God.

"Your last interaction was…informative. Her husband will be useful too. Should she get too independent, we can keep her leash tight."

Michelle briefly closed her eyes. "So, you humiliated me with Wilson, then fired me when I wasn't cowed, and are now replacing me with someone much more dangerous. But that's okay, because you'll blackmail *her* if she gets out of hand. Is that about it?"

"Exactly." Ottilie studied her. "You weren't a bad CEO, Michelle. Your occasional attacks of conscience were dubious, though, as was your taste in lovers."

"Excuse me?"

"Baldoni, Ayers, Kensington. And now Lawless."

"*Lawless!* We're *not* together. Then or now! That woman tried to bring down my company!"

"And it just made you like her more. Respect her, even." Ottilie tilted her head. "Yes?"

Michelle wanted to protest but couldn't find the words.

"Do you dream of her?" Ottilie asked thoughtfully. "Sorry, but I was the one who ensured she'd no longer dream of you. I like her personally, but she was so unpredictable and needed far too much micromanaging. The needs of the company come first. Lawless was a chaos agent."

A prickle shot through Michelle. "*You* gave Eden that USB drive? You turned her against us?"

"Of course." Tilly brushed her sleeve. "It was physically painful watching you around her, your lack of focus. And she was bumbling around in the dark, giving me so much more work as I hid our true intentions. All I ever wanted was a smooth ride before I retire next year. That's it. Lawless made life so much harder. I gave her a nudge, made her want to resign. You weren't supposed to want to resign too. Or goad the board into firing you, as the case may be."

"And now I'm just…done?" Michelle asked harshly. "No notice?"

"Correct."

Michelle glanced around. Nothing much was worth taking home. She'd left such a small imprint of herself at work. Her gaze drifted to the Degas.

"*That* stays," Ottilie said, tone dry. "*You* go. Also leave your phone, entry key card, and laptop. In exchange for you slipping off gracefully into the night, a sizable payout will be deposited into your bank account. The amount is as per the terms stipulated in your contract in the event your CEO position is terminated early on discretionary grounds.

You'll find it more than generous. Your apartment is, of course, in your name and remains yours in perpetuity. The board would like you to know we're not ungrateful for your years of dedicated service. We also know you are someone who would take our secrets to the grave. Your loyalty is gratefully acknowledged."

A knot of stress in Michelle's chest tightened. This was actually happening. She forced herself to nod.

"One last thing," Ottilie added, suddenly looking uncomfortable. "Since you're no longer CEO, all operations you've ordered will be frozen until they can be assessed for approval by the incoming CEO." Ottilie's words were oddly weighted.

Why was Michelle supposed to care about that now? "O-kay?"

"Including any ops you may have *just* ordered." Ottilie gave her a loaded look.

Understanding hit her at last. "No!"

"It's standard practice with every outgoing CEO."

"Make an exception! You know what Sharpe did. You saw the report, I know you did."

"I did." Ottilie's expression was chilly. "Now that the board knows Lawless was the leak, they can't see how she deserves justice for Sharpe's attack. And certainly not on the company dime."

"What company dime? O'Brian's fists cost nothing!"

"His *time* isn't free."

"*I'll* pay for his time!"

"That's not possible, either. You knew Ms. Lawless was a traitor to our organization when you ordered an employee to punish her attacker. That is unacceptable to the board."

Payback, more likely. Putting Michelle in her place for daring to say "fuck you" to one of them.

"*Please*?" Michelle didn't care how pathetic that sounded.

Ottilie's eyes flew open in surprise.

"You know what happened, how terrifying it must have been. Think of what O'Brian's doing as justice for all the other women who never get it. It's not just some work mission."

"Except it is. I'm sorry. As I say, I like Ms. Lawless personally. I even asked the board to make an exception. I was overruled—as I expected to be, because we are *not* good and don't have altruistic aims. The board has ruled." Ottilie gave her a warning look. "And in case you're planning to call O'Brian and tell him to ignore any new orders, he's already been informed to abort this mission."

Michelle's heart sank. How would she be able to tell Eden she'd failed to get her the justice she'd promised? That Sharpe would get away with hurting her.

There was a knock and one of O'Brian's security guards stuck his head in. "Ms. Zimmermann," the man said. "You asked for an escort of a former employee from the building?"

"Security escort?" Michelle snapped. "For me?"

The man's eyes widened at the implication.

"Just a precaution." Ottilie waved carelessly. "And I'll be staying right with you, just in case."

"I…see." It was standard procedure for any fired employee. With a sigh, Michelle dumped her phone on her desk next to her key card. She pointed to the laptop on her side table to show she'd left it. Then she rummaged through her desk drawers. Nothing of much interest greeted her. In the end, she snagged three packets of Advil and threw them in her handbag. She straightened, looking around one last time.

If she'd thought she'd feel regret or sadness, nothing materialized. All she had was the oddest feeling she didn't know who she was now, where she belonged, or what'd she do next.

"I'm sorry it ended this way," Ottilie said, sounding sincere. "If it helps, you were an efficient CEO. I appreciated that. I enjoyed your clever schemes."

Nothing had ever escaped this woman, had it? "You always kept your secrets close," Michelle said. "I never suspected a thing. I give you kudos for that. Good luck, Ottilie. Of course, with Phyllis Kensington in charge, you'll need a lot more than luck."

And with that she strode from her office for the last time. Behind her, faintly, she heard Ottilie's soft huff of agreement.

Chapter 19

Three Pigeons...and More

Michelle was sick to her stomach by the time she arrived home. On the way, she'd procrastinated, stopping off to buy a new phone and allowing the salesman to drone on about its features before conceding she'd have to face Eden sooner or later.

Now Eden's gentle eyes followed her as Michelle downed one dirty martini, then another, before prepping a third. Eden's soft hand moved to rest lightly on Michelle's, stopping her.

"Hitting the booze this early in the evening? Is it really that bad?"

Michelle couldn't look at her. "It's not good." She slid her hand out from under Eden's and took the martini glass with her as she headed for the balcony. She would just take the edge off and then go inside and stop being such a chickenshit. She'd break the news about Sharpe and watch Eden crumple.

Fuck.

A gust of wind cut through her corporate skirt suit. Michelle shivered.

"Hey, you." Eden's voice sliced into her morose thoughts. "I'm not sure doing an icicle impression is the best idea."

A thick blanket slid over Michelle's shoulders. "Thank you," she murmured, gratefully pulling it tighter.

Eden slid onto the chair beside her. "I figured misery loves company. And blankets."

"Being out here is not good for your ribs." Michelle murmured.

"I have layers on. And it's my cunning plan to lure you back inside. I have veggie lasagna in the oven for dinner."

Michelle wasn't in the mood for food, but Eden's lasagna had grown on her. She always added some unexpected spices to give it an extra kick. Michelle appreciated its uniqueness, although some people would doubtlessly dismiss the flavors as random and chaotic. Of late, Michelle had begun to appreciate "random and chaotic" a great deal. It was just so Eden. So lively. Michelle really hoped her devastating news wouldn't take that spark away.

"That's a big sigh," Eden said.

Michelle took another sip of martini to avoid answering. *Chickenshit.*

"I don't want to pry before you've decompressed, but I'm kind of desperate to know what happened with Francine and the board," Eden said. "Could you at least tell me she didn't win them over?"

Ah. That. "No. Don't worry. Wilson is on her way back to Wingapo. She'll be getting no job offer."

"Oh, thank Christ." Eden exhaled. "I was freaking out for a moment."

Michelle's stomach tightened. "Eden…I have bad news."

Eden stilled. "Oh?"

"The board canceled O'Brian's mission."

Eden's eyes flew open. "Sharpe's not getting punished?"

"No." Michelle's jaw worked. "He's not."

"Oh." Her arms hugged her drawn-up knees. "Damn."

Michelle's heart broke at the small, protective bundle that was now Eden. "I know I promised you justice. I failed."

"Oh," Eden repeated, looking even smaller. She rubbed her eyes, and her hands came away wet.

Michelle had a worrying urge to wrap her into a hug. She didn't do hugs as a rule and definitely not hugs with Eden. They were so uncomfortable and awkward and…vulnerable. Why not just slap a neon sign on your head that reads, *This small, perfect human means so much to me I've wrapped her against my beating heart?*

God, no. But still, Michelle could ache with Eden and wish she could take away her pain.

I'm so sorry.

"What happened?" Eden's voice was unsteady. "I thought the board only hired and fired? The CEO has complete autonomy?"

"Yes."

"Then how could they cancel a mission?"

"They fired me." It hadn't felt real until now. It was like being winded, a moment's shock and then the wash of pain. "When a CEO is fired, all missions are immediately frozen pending review."

Eden gaped. "They *fired* you?"

Michelle's throat tightened. "Yes."

Did Eden think less of her now? Michelle must seem weak to fail not only to punish Sharpe but even to protect her own job. She swung her gaze to the view to avoid the disappointment she'd surely see in Eden's eyes.

Golden lights from the surrounding riverside apartments shimmered across the water, illuminating a few smudges of distant tugboats. It might be beautiful if she didn't feel so sick.

"Michelle?" Eden said. "You mention being fired as an afterthought, behind *I feel bad I couldn't get you justice.* As if avenging me matters more to you than your career!" Her tone was incredulous.

"You deserve justice." Michelle said, tone flat. "It's all I wanted when I woke up today. I'm sorry I failed to get that for you."

"You haven't failed me. You've been doing everything in your power to make it right."

"And now I have no power." Michelle was useless now. Wasn't that the sad truth? It had been nothing for the board to discard her, despite her years of exacting, exemplary work. "I couldn't even save myself. I can't help you now."

"You think I just care about whether you have the power to help me?" Eden studied her face intently. "That your only worth to me is what you can *do* for me? That your only worth is how powerful you are?"

Yes? Michelle didn't say it. But yes.

"You're so wrong, Michelle. I wanted justice but, hey, best-laid plans and all that. Maybe I'll try to bring down Sharpe the old-fashioned way and report him."

"It'll be your word against his, and he's a police chief. That's why I wanted to give you justice myself. It's guaranteed—or it should have been. You deserve that."

Eden considered that. "Yes, I think I do. And *you* deserve to be upset that you were fired. I might hate what your company does, but I can also be furious they've shafted you. Did they give you a reason?"

"I gather I'm not compliant enough." Michelle gave the faintest of shrugs. "And…I may have dented their egos somewhat. It's also possible I swore at one of the board members."

"You *devil*." Eden's lips twitched. "What'd you say?"

"I said—most politely—'Fuck you.'" Now that she said it out loud, it sounded absurd.

Eden laughed. "Oh shit! *Seriously?*"

"Yes." Michelle found a smile whispering at the corners of her own mouth, threatening to be let out. "It wasn't my most evolved moment. My personal assistant almost had a coronary. The whole time, she was shooting me these panicked 'Oh God, *shut up!*' looks, desperately trying to get me to rein my temper in."

Eden was almost wheezing with laughter. "Oh hell, I can picture it—you going off piste and Ottilie's ordered little world crashing down, her easy retirement plans in tatters."

"That's it exactly." Michelle smiled. Ottilie's panic had been rather hilarious in hindsight now that Michelle knew the truth. "God, I never thought I'd find anything humorous about today."

Eden inhaled. "Wait, will you have to give up your apartment now you're fired?"

"No. It was a gift and it's in my name. They can't take it back." That was supremely satisfying at least.

Eden let out a relieved sigh. "That's good. So, why'd you tell a board member to fuck off?"

Michelle sobered. "It turned out the meeting was not to hear out Wilson at all—who by the way made a pitch for *my* job—"

"That conniving little..." Eden's eyes narrowed. "She isn't fit to polish your boots!"

Michelle snorted softly. "Anyway, allowing Wilson to trash me and make a play for my job was intended as a warning so I'd fall into line and know my place, that I'm dispensable and serve at their pleasure. But they're not supposed to backseat drive the CEO, and I don't like bullies. I pushed back, so they fired me."

"Good for you," Eden said firmly. "They'll regret losing you. You're the smartest person there."

No, that was Ottilie. "Well, they didn't want smart. They wanted someone who caves to their authority."

"But why fix what isn't broken?" Eden asked, then stopped abruptly. "And please insert all my usual caveats that *of course* The Fixers remains totally fucked up as a concept, even if it was well run."

"Duly noted," Michelle said dryly. "And I don't think firing me was the original plan."

"Who will they replace you with if not Wilson?"

"Phyllis Kensington."

"The *senator*?" Eden frowned. "Wait, she's the one with the husband who abused his intern, right? Her case was on the USB drive. You were upset about it."

"I still am. The man's callousness was appalling. And Phyllis thought it was wonderful blackmail material to keep her husband in check when she ran for president."

"But I heard she's retiring from politics for family reasons," Eden said.

"If 'family reasons' means that her covering up her husband's misdeeds was leaked to DC's political dirt teams, then, yes, that's accurate."

"So now she needs a new job. Why The Fixers, though?"

"She's ambitious and craves power. If Ottilie wanted the quiet life, she's not going to be getting it now. Phyllis will be exhausting. Trust me, I've seen the woman when she's fired up and furious."

Eden stared at her. "You said Ottilie, not Tilly."

"Ah." Michelle exhaled. "Well, my former PA wasn't shy in sharing her thoughts today. Including her preferred name, that *she* was the one who gave you the USB drive, and that she's a member of The Fixers' board."

Eden's mouth fell open. "She is?"

"Oh, yes. In fact, *she* fired me. I didn't see that coming: sweet Tilly lowering the boom? Although, not so sweet when she drops her act." Michelle couldn't believe she'd never put it together.

"She has a cunning side, yeah," Eden agreed. "That must have been awful for you. You've known her for years, but you didn't *know* her."

"I realized what a pawn I'd been. How Ottilie manipulated my schedule and the clients I took. I felt so foolish. Do you know, she also told me I'd only been promoted to CEO because the board thought I had no empathy. They believed I was emotionless, ruthless, and cold. Being a borderline psychopath is considered desirable."

Eden's mouth formed a perfect "O."

"The board member I cursed threw the Ayers case in my face even though everyone knows not to raise that issue. He discovered at that moment that I am very much *not* emotionless or empathy-free." Michelle paused and added, "The jury's still out on cold. I do concede ruthless, though."

"Michelle, you're not like them."

Surprise washed through her. Of course she was like them!

"And, come on, you aren't emotionless! You cared about *my* well-being even when you hated me."

With a sigh, Michelle admitted, "I never hated you. Your actions caused me no end of headaches, but you personally? No."

"I'm so glad." Eden reached for her hand and gave it a squeeze.

She was so tactile lately. Michelle's fingers tingled under the contact, and she had to focus to hear Eden's next words.

"How are you feeling about losing your job?"

Good question. "Shell-shocked. As ethically dubious as my job was, I enjoyed the problem solving and management side of it. I love efficiency and competence."

Eden smiled knowingly. "You don't say."

"And I'm only human. The power that came with it, being able to threaten the worst individuals with hellfire, always improved my mood." She smiled.

"*Just* the worst?" Eden asked tentatively.

"I'm well aware The Fixers sometimes hurt people who didn't deserve it. I didn't enjoy that aspect. What we did. Or how. It's easier to pretend—for a while—that you aren't doing immoral things when you have a whole circle of people around you who look the other way too."

"Until I pointed it out."

"No, that didn't help. But even before that, it was affecting my health. I've been pushing my reservations aside, trying to live to fight another day, because I had nothing else. I'm not sure which is worse anymore: the fact the job itself can be so reprehensible, or the fact I have nothing without it."

Eden said quietly, "You don't have nothing. You have me."

Michelle looked at her, startled.

"I know I'm a poor substitute for the cool supervillain secret lair you were running," Eden joked. "I can't offer you power or anything close to it. But on the plus side, I come with an oxalis. And I am really loyal when I believe in someone."

The heartfelt words were surely misplaced. "You believe in me? You know what I am. Or was."

"I know exactly who you are." Eden held her gaze. "Like tonight. You were fired from a job that gives you your sense of identity and worth, yet all you could think about was how that would impact me. Despite everything that's happened between us, your first thought was for *me*."

"Well," Michelle said oh-so cleverly.

"You showed me I matter."

"I thought that was obvious." As if Michelle would allow just anyone to stay in her inner sanctum. *Of course* Eden mattered.

"It was and it wasn't obvious." Eden tilted her head. "We're a bit of a contradictory pair. And you can be hard to read."

That was certainly true. Both points. Silence fell.

"Will you be okay?" Michelle asked finally. "Sharpe getting off scot-free must be hard."

"Still worried about me." Eden gave her hand another warm squeeze, and Michelle realized in shock they'd been holding hands all this time. "It's a lot to take in, but I'll process it more later. I don't want to talk about me. What will you do now?"

"I'm not sure." Michelle truly was at a loss. Jobs for spies or managers of covert teams weren't exactly common. "I'm such a creature of secrecy and habit that I'm not sure who I am outside of this business. I'm going to have to start over. Whatever I do next, it will be hard at my age."

"You make yourself sound a hundred." Eden smiled.

"I'm forty-seven, Eden. It's not an age employers look favorably on. And I feel those years every morning when I wake up."

"Oh, please. You're so strong—mind and body. I'd put odds on you winning any contest going."

"I'm afraid I'd only win a battle of wits these days. My body has been screaming at me for over two years to stop the stress I've been putting it through."

"And now you're giving it what it wants. It's a fresh start. You'll finally relax. Actually be happy."

"Happy." Michelle turned that over.

"Have you never been happy?" Eden asked curiously.

Michelle thought back. She was all the way back to her childhood years before Eden tightened the grip on her hand.

"Okay," Eden said. "I can see that's our next life goal for you: be happy."

Our next goal. Her heart lifted. "It feels like a foreign concept. Me and happiness."

"Half the fun will be finding out what brings you joy. I mean, come on—you have money, don't you?" Eden waved at the apartment. "You can go anywhere, do anything. Focus on the fact you're long overdue for a change. Embrace it."

"It'd have been nice if *I'd* been the one to make that choice." Michelle slid her an aggrieved look.

"Are you sure you didn't make it?" Eden lifted an eyebrow. "Because from where I sit, insulting a board member is a fast way to get your ass fired."

Hadn't Ottilie made the same charge?

If Michelle was being completely honest, she'd been itching for a change for a few years. But it was only recently, since Eden had quit, that she'd actively started hating work. Partly because she missed Eden, partly because Eden had tripled her workload, and mainly because Eden's revulsion had held up a mirror as to how terrible The Fixers was. "You might be right."

"I am." Eden's eyes crinkled. "So, in sum, shit happened and now you're free. So you get to kick back, shoot the breeze with me and three pigeons, and decide what's next."

"I have three pigeons?" Michelle's gaze shot around, failing to locate even one.

"You sure do. They're not here right now, but they exist. I've even named them."

"Of course you have." Michelle smiled and felt a wash of serenity. She could get used to this. Sharing time…and pigeons…with Eden. If only she'd stay. "Well, the pigeons put everything into perspective. Thank you."

"No, thank *you*." Eden's tone was sincere. "For everything."

"I didn't do anything. Unfortunately." The weight of Sharpe getting away with his assault settled over her again. How helpless she was now.

Eden's gaze softened. "You tried. Don't dismiss that."

They stared at each other for a few moments until Michelle dragged her gaze back to the river.

"I suppose you're going to go soon." Michelle forced the words out with some difficulty. "But about that—I was wondering if you would consider staying a while longer."

"Longer?" Eden asked curiously. "How long?"

"Just until you're…" Michelle waved at Eden's injured side.

Except Eden's ribs were much better now. She'd mentioned a sharpness when she sat up too suddenly or twisted the wrong way. But pain meds helped. There was nothing keeping her here.

Eden cocked a pointed eyebrow.

"Just until you're sick of me," Michelle amended, aiming for humor. She looked down at their linked fingers. "I don't want you to leave," she murmured.

"Why?" Eden asked carefully. "This can't be about you feeling alone. You have Hannah coming home soon."

"It's not that. I'm used to being alone. So much so, I struggled when my safta moved in because I loved my solitude."

"But weren't you used to living with someone when you were married?"

"We didn't spend much time actually living together. Alberto was forever away on missions, and back then, so was I. When my safta moved in, that was when I noticed how hard I found sharing my home, all day, every day. I got used to it, obviously, but I still struggle with needing alone time. That's why she stays with Rosemary once or twice a year."

"It's good you have something that works for you both," Eden said. "She gets friendship time with someone her age. You get your space."

Michelle nodded, relieved she understood. "I've found, though, it's not been hard having you here. I haven't needed to close the door on the world for a few days and be alone. I may yet need that at some point. It will never be personal, just about recharging my mental batteries. We can make it work." She gave Eden a worried look. "If you'd like."

"What about Hannah?" Eden asked. "This is her home too. I can't just invade, even if I'm out of sight and mind on the lower floor."

As if Eden could ever be "out of mind," even when she was out of sight. She took up too much of Michelle's mental real estate as it was. "My safta would be more than fine if you're here when she returns. She knows you're visiting. She greatly approves."

Eden looked surprised. "Okay, spill. What'd that crafty old woman say?"

Michelle cleared her throat and, as nonchalantly as she could manage, said, "I got a rather random story about how she has excellent gaydar. The gist of it is she hopes we're…closer…than we are." Michelle rolled her eyes in a vain attempt to make it less awkward.

Instead of being shocked, Eden nodded. "That sounds like her. She was dropping vague hints when we Skyped that time. I got the impression she'd decided I'd be 'worthy Michelle Hastings girlfriend material.'"

Michelle swallowed, her mouth far too dry. *Damn it.* Her meddling safta had struck again, forcing things. Eden had to have been uncomfortable as hell.

"Michelle? You okay?" Eden asked. "You look…alarmed?"

"I'm truly sorry about my safta. She can get caught up in her own ideas of what *should* be and pay no attention to what the reality is. Her imagination is vivid. Matchmaking me passes as fun for her."

Eden's face fell. The hand clasping Michelle's suddenly withdrew, leaving her feeling cold.

"Vivid imagination, huh?" Eden asked, brows knitting together.

"Yes?" Michelle asked, a little lost. "That's just my safta. Please don't read anything into her grand pronouncements. She's just being her eccentric self."

"Do you *really* believe she has a vivid imagination? Or do you actually think something else?"

Michelle huffed. Trust Eden to demand the truth like a heat-seeking missile. She shifted uncomfortably. No, Hannah's imagination hadn't been vivid when it came to Michelle, but she wasn't about to air her feelings when they were one-sided. Last night's rejection, Eden pulling away from her, still stung. Michelle wasn't interested in ever feeling that humiliated again.

"Michelle?" Eden prodded.

"Is it wrong to spare you discomfort and reassure you I'm not reading anything into my safta's words?" Michelle asked silkily.

"Is there a reason you won't answer a simple question? Here's another question—*why* do you want me to stay?"

"You need a comfortable space to heal." Michelle couldn't even look at her this time.

Eden paused. "Michelle, why do you want me to stay? Really?"

She was going to *insist* Michelle bared her heart? No matter how foolish her inconvenient feelings? Her lips pursed. "Why? Don't you like it here?"

"Yes." Eden sighed. "A little too much. I've been doing so little protest organization work. My plants have taken over your whole lower floor. My boots are under the bed like they've always lived there. I'm a little too settled."

"Then stay!" Michelle said incredulously. Why was this a problem? "If you like it? Stay."

Eden studied her for a long, long moment. "Not without an honest conversation. I need to understand where we stand with each other. If I've misunderstood things, I have to know. But, equally, I don't like being lied to. Even your tiny white lies of omission."

Michelle sidestepped that landmine. "Why do we even need to talk about anything? Can't things just go on as they have been? What's wrong with that?"

"I *need* to know. Like I label my van Gloria and name your pigeons and know which flower absolutely belongs in your bedroom and which plant belongs by your desk. I need order and certainty and labels for the things that matter to me most because I deal in so much chaos and randomness. But I survive by knowing the things that should be known. Michelle, *you* are one of the things that I must know. Is a relationship something you want with me?"

Something *you* want with me.

Michelle's heart thundered in her ears. Eden demanded she admit a relationship was something she'd thought about when at her most vulnerable? Something Michelle knew full well was absurd because, one, Eden wasn't interested. Two, Eden was good. And three, Michelle's scar tissue was surely too deep and painful to ensure a healthy relationship.

"Why are you asking me to put this out there?" she asked, the cruelty of it creating an ache deep inside. "Why make me say it?" Her hands trembled so she curled them into fists in her lap.

"Because *not* saying it feels like a lie. Acknowledging it is important to me."

Michelle sagged. "I just don't understand why you'd demand this conversation." *When it's not something you want for us. When it's something you've clearly rejected.* "Can't we just ignore…this?" *My inconvenient feelings.*

"No," Eden said quietly. "Because there are only two things I won't tolerate living with: lies and elephants."

"Elephants?" Michelle repeated, baffled.

"You know—the elephant in the room? The thing everyone looks at but doesn't address?"

Michelle's humiliation was inevitable. "Great," she muttered.

Eden's entire face morphed into astonishment. "Oh!"

"What?" Michelle asked acidly. Mortification burned up her throat to her cheeks.

"You…think this is one-sided?" Eden asked in wonder. "That only *you* care?"

That stopped Michelle cold. Her heart contracted. She drew in a ragged breath. "What?"

"You goofball!" Eden punched her arm lightly.

Goof. Ball?

"God, woman! How many ways did you need me to spell it out?" Eden flung her hands up. "I…*like*…you… You know…like Sarah Paulson and Holland Taylor. Anne Lister and Ann Walker. Supergirl and Cat Grant."

Michelle's head snapped up. She didn't watch much television, but was pretty sure from her safta's dubious pop-culture viewing habits that those last two weren't…

"No, no. Don't you deny me that coupling." Eden wagged a finger at her. "Goddess, what did you *think* I meant when I said, 'You don't have nothing, you have me'?"

"You didn't mean that as…friends?" Michelle struggled to make sense of this.

"*No.*" Eden rolled her eyes. "I *didn't.*"

"You think we are more?" she said slowly. "You and me?"

Eden gave her an affectionate, long-suffering look. "Yes: you and me. Don't you feel it? The chemistry?"

It wasn't just her? Eden felt it too?

"Hannah noticed it. I noticed it. Are you saying we're imagining it? That you and I have the same chemistry two *friends* have?"

Michelle had never felt on less certain ground. Eden was gazing at her with such intensity, it was making her brain flail. "How can you be so sure about what you're feeling?" she asked hesitantly. "How do you know this is not just emotions running high after everything we've been through? Being thrown together in a crisis and reaching for the nearest person?"

After all, rescuers could be attractive to the person they saved, even if all Michelle had done was call a doctor and put Eden up for a bit. That's probably all this was.

Eden traced her fingers down Michelle's cheek, leaving trails of fire in their wake. "I know it as surely as I put my head on your shoulder last night and felt things I shouldn't feel for a friend. That truth was so blinding that I came away feeling swallowed whole by it. I'm sorry I pulled away. I'm sorry if you felt unwanted. Nothing could have been further from the truth. But, Michelle, feeling your fingers in my hair, the way you touched me then? I knew you felt something too."

Michelle stared, shocked. Eden *hadn't* been repulsed by her last night? Apparently her blinding epiphanies could be confused with rejection.

Michelle wanted to bang her head against a wall at her obliviousness. Of course, obliviousness was something she was a master at. How many months had she spent ignoring that she found Eden beautiful? Smart. Delightful. Amusing. Someone she loved being around. Someone with whom she had chemistry that was shared and not imagined—vividly or otherwise.

All the time she'd fought herself, she'd never thought Eden saw them as anything but friends.

"There are really only three options going forward." Eden straightened, as if getting down to business. "One, we *are* more than friends and you think we should be more. Two, we are more but you don't want us to take this further. Or three, we are more and you pretend not to see that. But no matter how you look at this, the truth is, Michelle: We *are* more."

Michelle's head buzzed. *Eden's been thinking about us in a relationship?*

"So, I need my certainty, you see," Eden finished. "I need to know what you think we are to each other. We don't have to act on our attraction, but we do have to name it honestly."

Michelle leaped to the next hurdle. "But how would 'we' even work?" she asked. "Our life experiences are so far apart. Do we have anything in common at all? You live in a van and sometimes camp on your best friend's couch! You attend protests and try to end injustice.

I'm the one perpetrating the injustice! Or I was. And look where I live." She waved at her apartment.

"Yet, for all that," Eden countered, "we seem to connect in a space reserved just for us. Your safta says I make you laugh and you haven't done so for years."

Well, there was that. Michelle inhaled. So…Eden wanted more?

Do I want more too? Her breath caught. *Of course I do!* Her heart was not being subtle. It thundered away saying "notice me!" whenever Eden touched her. It made her do ill-conceived, revealing things, such as stroke her hair. Wanting more was not the right question. The answer to that was as plain as the tremble of Michelle's fingers each time Eden carelessly touched her.

Dare I want more?

It was one thing to indulge herself in fun with someone like Phyllis, someone whose heart was as black as her own. But Eden was different—decent and good. Having more wasn't a good idea, for her sake. The woman deserved far better.

Isn't this her choice too? She'll stay if you're honest and name what this is. If you expose your feelings to her.

Michelle winced. She didn't do vulnerable. That was for braver people than her. Besides, she had a terrible track record in relationships.

However, she couldn't deny how much better life had been since Eden had moved in. Even her apartment felt different now. She'd never bothered using the lower floor until Eden showed up. Michelle had always dismissed her downstairs as an overblown indulgence of the original architect/owner who'd combined two floors to make an enormous penthouse suite.

That forgotten floor was now an alluring destination—home to an amusing visitor and a jungle of plants. Michelle sometimes snuck downstairs just to admire the greenery. She'd never admit it to Eden, but it did smell much fresher now.

What a strange place Michelle found herself in: no job, no friends. But she also had a houseguest who'd taught her to breathe again, and who she didn't want to leave.

Oh, Eden. I'm not sure why you'd want me. I'm all wrong for you.

That really was the bottom line. The simplest thing to do would be to emotionally distance herself.

Michelle's brain gave a merry snort at that. *Just like you did after the Wingapo assignment finished? That was some fine walking away there.*

Eden smiled. "I see I've managed to shock you. That has to be a first. I'll leave this with you. Let me know, hey?"

Michelle stared at her, dazed.

"Right now I'm exhausted, and I think you must be too." Eden rose. "Today's been draining. Let's discuss things tomorrow when we're less…on edge."

Michelle nodded. She scooped up the blanket and made a science of folding it. "I'm looking forward to seeing what you've done to the humble lasagna for dinner later."

"If you're counting on *my* cooking to improve our crappy day, I don't think it's that good," Eden joked.

"*You* made it, Eden," Michelle said quietly. "I'd say there's plenty good in it."

Silence stretched out. Michelle glanced up.

Eden's look was a mix between incredulous and warm. She shook her head and left Michelle to pick up the pieces of her mental disarray.

Chapter 20
Unpacked

Early the next day, Michelle was up and at work in her home office, busying herself with filing. Last night's conversation had been a lot. After a sleepless night, she'd concluded she was in no way ready to deal with the emotional eddies of even thinking about a relationship with Eden, no matter how much her treacherous heart begged.

A sharp rap sounded outside her apartment. Michelle frowned and strode to the door.

The building's day doorman, Ryan, stood rigid and tall in his uniform. "Ma'am, sorry to intrude. I couldn't reach you via phone." He held out a small package. "This was left for you with Joe at one a.m. The man said to deliver it to you first thing."

Michelle took it from him. "I have a new phone number now. I'll leave it with you later."

"Thank you, ma'am. That'd be good. Have a nice day."

He left, and Michelle closed the door. She tore the package open, finding a wallet, a note, and a USB drive.

Inside the wallet were Eden's credit cards, driver's license, and some cash. Michelle placed the wallet on her coffee table and opened the note. She recognized O'Brian's messy scrawl.

Boss, hi. Couldn't get you on your phone. I got an abort notice on my mission yesterday. Tilly said the order was correct. It might be correct, but it sure wasn't right.

So I called in sick for the rest of the day and decided that what a fella does on his own time is his own business. And if that means thumping some asshole into the dirt and watching him take a ten-mile hike, that's what I'm going to do.

BTW I did eye for an eye exactly, tempting though it was to...value add. So, mission accomplished.

The asshole folded like a cheap deckchair. The ten miles took him four and a half hours, twitching like a mountain goat the whole time whenever the bushes rustled. Tell Lawless she'd have left his sorry ass in the dust. She won. He lost.

Speaking of Lawless: Didn't want to upset her with sensitive material (see USB drive) if she wasn't up for having it sprung on her in an attachment, so have dropped this off for you to share. Or not.

I also heard some grade-A shite about you being fired. "Time for an exciting new direction," the board's email says.

"Exciting" my Irish arse. Sorry you got axed. Always appreciated the way you treated me. You were good to me—respectful. I won't forget it.

Hope you're both still on for dinner soon. Will text Lawless the details.

—POB

PS to clear up any misunderstandings, I always wanted to have you over before. But as good as you are at extracting information out of people socially, Shauna's WAY better. Now it doesn't matter, does it? You not being my boss anymore means you'll have nothing whatsoever to share about work with my wife. Right?

Michelle snorted and went into her office to find out what was on the drive. After inserting it into her computer, she found a video file.

Derrick Sharpe, covered in dirt, scratches, sweat, and bruises, filled the screen. He had two black eyes and a swollen cheek. He was struggling to lift his head and looked extremely sorry for himself.

He choked out a breath and then howl-sobbed into O'Brian's phone camera. "I'm *sorry*! I promise, I won't do it again! Never!"

Well, he certainly seemed sincere.

"I was wrong to attack an innocent woman," he babbled. "Even if I did it on someone else's orders."

Trust him to hide behind the "just following orders" defense.

Blood trickled from his nose, and he smeared it away with his hand. There was an indignant noise off-screen and Sharpe corrected himself.

"And yes, *I* should've known it was wrong and said no. I'm sorry." His voice hitched and his chin did a wobble. Then tears filled his fearful eyes. "I'm a piece of crap for what I did."

"Phelim *did* it?" a shaky voice whispered from behind her. "He went ahead with it?"

Michelle turned. An ashen Eden filled the doorway. "He did. He ignored orders and carried out the mission."

"Play it again," Eden said flatly. "From the beginning."

Michelle nodded.

Silence fell when the playback finished.

"He's a wreck," Eden said in wonder.

"Bullies often cope poorly with their own medicine. You were nowhere near this condition. *And* it took four and a half hours for him to do the ten-mile walk. To quote O'Brian: Sharpe lost; you won."

Eden fell quiet and then said, "Send me a copy?"

Michelle opened her email program. "What will you do with it?"

"I want to watch him apologize to me hundreds more times to see if that makes any of what I went through better. I want to look in his eyes and see if he's really sorry." There was a raw edge to her voice.

Michelle sent the file.

Eden curled her fingers under Michelle's chin, drawing her head up, and kissed her temple. "Thanks for not arguing. Or telling me it sounds creepy."

Warmth radiated from where Eden's lips had touched. Shock rocketed through Michelle at both the intimate action and the statement. "Why would I think that?"

"I don't know." Eden exhaled. "Maybe *I* think it's creepy."

"What he did was creepy. You're allowed to be angry about it."

"Maybe I wish I was better. I'm sure I should rise above or forgive and forget or go through proper channels." Eden's breathing became harsh. "But for me *that* was justice."

"Yes. It was."

"This is hard for me. I keep trying to be good. And I'm not, am I? Or not good enough. I'm glad Sharpe got hurt. *Glad*," Eden repeated, lips pulling down. "And I'm not sure how to reconcile that with who I'm supposed to be."

"Who are you supposed to be?" Michelle asked gently.

"Phelim keeps calling me a woke, liberal, peace-loving hippie, and I think I fail that. I'm a vengeance-seeking, hurt, pro-vigilante hippie. What happened to Sharpe? That wasn't good or peace-loving. Yet I needed it. And I'm afraid that if I told my mom what I did, she'd reject me."

Michelle drew in a breath. "The way she rejected your father?"

"Yeah." Eden blinked away tears. "So I'm not going to tell her. I don't think she'd understand. She's always morally right on everything, and I fall short."

"There are many ways to be right, Eden. Not just her way."

"No, I'm pretty sure there's just her way," Eden said with certainty.

"Eden, *I* think you were right to want Sharpe physically punished. He won't do it again. You can see it in his eyes. He was done."

"I saw that. And I want to watch it over and over to really take it in." Her voice was small and ashamed when she added, "Part of me is repulsed by that side of me."

"And part of you isn't." Michelle took Eden's hand carefully in her own. "You know, part of me was enraged you betrayed me and my company. Part of me respected you. I *was* right to defend my business interests and go after you. But I was also right to be impressed by someone standing up for her truth. The world comes in so many shades of gray. So do people. I think I appreciate you most for the fact you are a complicated human, just like the rest of us."

"I'm glad you see it that way." Eden still looked disconcerted.

Michelle shrugged. "It's the truth. But, speaking of truth, can I ask you something?"

"Anything."

"Why did you kiss me just now?"

"I...what?" Eden's eyes widened. "I did?"

"Yes." Michelle tapped her temple, which still tingled from the memory.

"Oh." Eden darted a worried glance her way. "Gosh—sorry! I was caught up in the moment. I didn't mean to make you uncomfortable."

"You didn't." Michelle said in surprise. "And that's unexpected for me."

Eden's eyes warmed. "Wow. Soon I'll have you inviting hugs."

Michelle arched an eyebrow. "I'm not a hugger."

"I know, don't worry."

"Good," Michelle said firmly.

"But kisses are okay?" Eden asked cheekily. "I mean, just checking. *For reasons.*"

Michelle was suddenly incapable of getting the alluring image out of her head.

The silence grew uneasy.

"Sorry," Eden rushed in. "Gah! I'm an idiot. If you're not interested in more, I shouldn't be pushing you. That's not fair."

"I never said I wasn't interested," Michelle murmured. "I'm just worried I'd be terrible at all this."

"And by 'all this,' you mean...?" Hope lit her eyes.

"Us."

Eden grinned. "You called us an *us.*"

Michelle sighed. "Well, there *is*...something...here. Obliviousness and denial are officially off the table."

"Oh, yep, I like this you," Eden said, widening her grin.

"Uh-huh," Michelle said dryly.

"So, kisses? Yes or no?" Eden asked hopefully.

"Yes." Michelle blinked. "No. I *meant* no."

"Wow, that cleared things up." Eden's eyes crinkled. "Get back to me on that decision too, okay?"

"Eden? *Why* do you want to date me?" Michelle asked, perplexed. "You know what I've done."

"I know. But you're not your past. You don't even *like* your past. I appreciate that you're trying to be someone better."

"Do you? Have you actually thought it through? All my baggage?"

Eden stared at her as if she were uttering nonsense.

"Remember, I'm much older than you." Michelle slid her a worried look. "Eleven years, in fact."

"Irrelevant," Eden shrugged. "I've dated older women than you."

Michelle paused in surprise. She had? "Until recently, I was evil and a villain. I'm quoting you, by the way."

Eden rolled her eyes. "In hindsight, that's debatable. If you were giving yourself migraines over the unethical demands of your job, I'd say you didn't exactly endorse it."

"I'm…grumpy."

Eden laughed. "No kidding! I *have* worked for you. And lived with you. You're still a pussycat compared to Aggie before her first coffee."

"And smug. *Insufferably* smug."

"I've met your smirks. A-grade, by the way." Eden gave her an amused thumbs-up.

"Antisocial. I don't mix well with others. I fake it expertly. I had to for work."

"As long as you like mixing with me, I don't see the problem."

"I don't think you understand. I have no friends." Michelle paused. "Except, maybe, O'Brian. That's a new development. I've come to appreciate him more and more lately."

"Why don't you have friends?"

Michelle considered how much to reveal. "I used to. They took Alberto's side in the divorce. I can't blame them. Still, afterwards, I didn't want to give anyone else the chance to hurt me again."

"I understand." Eden's eyes were soft and sad. "It's hard to feel safe enough to trust when you're in a dark place."

Michelle digested that awareness. How could Eden really understand? Well, now for the real test. "I…also have self-destructive habits.

Until quite recently, I channeled my anger and other emotions into smashing up mirrors in a rage room."

Eden's eyebrows knotted. "Really?"

"You think less of me now." Michelle's heart sank.

"No. I'm intrigued. I wouldn't mind smashing up some shit sometimes in a controlled environment. Although it seems like a waste of things that could be repurposed," she said, frowning.

Michelle snorted. "Of course you'd say that."

"But my main question is: why mirrors? Aren't those rooms usually about destroying TVs and computers? Things that frustrate the shit out of people? Things they hate?"

"Yes," Michelle said quietly. "Exactly." She waited for Eden to get it. *Things you hate.* Michelle hated herself.

"*Oh.*" Eden gave her a concerned look. "So, why'd you stop going there?"

"Because Phyllis Kensington tried to blackmail me into fucking her, and I decided I was worth more. Admittedly, that was a first for me. My need to vent left when she did."

Eden stared. "You and the senator? But she's so…church and family values and homemade recipes and *conservative!*"

"That *is* her carefully cultivated image. I can assure you the reality is vastly different."

"So she…" Eden paused. "And *you?*"

Michelle sighed. "Yes. Regrettably."

"I'm guessing the 'first' was you saying *no* to her, rather than it being her first sexual approach?"

"We had an…arrangement. By the end of it, I just felt used more than I did her partner. She does that to people—makes everyone a pawn in her games. It started giving me flashbacks to the FBI, when they treated me like a body and little else. In the end, I felt like Phyllis's possession. My mental health was suffering."

"I'm so sorry you were made to feel that way."

"So, in sum," Michelle said, voice thick, "I'm a catch."

Eden straightened. "Well, we haven't been through my issues yet."

Michelle blinked in astonishment. "*Your* issues?"

"What?" Eden asked. "Sure, I didn't run an evil empire, but I have issues too." She began ticking them off. "I can be too trusting. Too insecure about people not wanting to stay with me. I worry they'll leave, and they always do. I sometimes think I'm not good enough to make my girlfriend stay, so I try harder to be better. Which feels a bit tragic to me."

"And yet, here I am, asking you to stay and you're talking about leaving?" Michelle prodded.

"I just want to get it right for once." Eden drew in a breath. "And I don't want to value myself so little that I'll settle for crumbs under the table."

"Living with me is crumbs under the table?" Michelle reeled back, hurt.

"No! Of course not!" Eden looked horrified. "I meant that living with you without you acknowledging that we mean more to each other than friends or housemates sells us both short." Her eyes became imploring. "I don't want either of us to accept less than what we're worth. What *this* is worth."

"I haven't said yes to more yet." Michelle paused. "I have a lot to think about. But will you remember that I haven't said no either?"

"I'll remember." Eden nodded. "Can you remember something too? I'm sorry I ever called you evil. I don't think of you like that and haven't for ages."

Michelle's doubt must have leaked to her face because Eden said, "You can't honestly think I'd stay with someone I think is evil?"

"Well, I just assumed you were being practical," Michelle said, only half joking. "Given the choice between staying with friends who'd just discovered sex with each other or an archnemesis, I'd seriously consider the archnemesis too."

Eden didn't smile at that. "You know, I've had people in my life who everyone said were *so* perfect—so good and pure. They ate, breathed, and associated with only ideologically ethical things. But have you ever tried living with someone like that? It's exhausting. You're constantly on guard—careful of what you're saying and fearful of failing. With you, I get to be me. I don't feel judged. I feel understood. Like this payback with Sharpe. I'd be shamed as a monster if some of my allies and exes knew. Not you."

"I don't know how to feel about that," Michelle said quietly. "I make you feel it's okay to not be good?"

"No, to not be *perfect*. There's a huge difference." Eden sighed. "Look, my mom's perfect, okay? She practices what she preaches too. I love her to pieces. I'm in *awe* of her. But she's hell to live up to and difficult to live with. Not you. You're funny and smart and nonjudgmental."

Well, that felt a little better.

"*And* you sneak downstairs to smell my plants. So I know you have taste." Eden smirked.

What? Michelle thought she'd been subtle. "Okay, since you don't seem to be a fan of denial, I won't *actually* deny that—but can we just pretend I don't do it?"

Eden laughed. "Whatever helps you sleep at night."

Chapter 21

A Good Guest Must...

Eden greeted the return of Michelle's grandma by doing something ambitious, complicated, and foolhardy. She baked. Jewish cookies, to be precise, under Michelle's incredulous eye.

"You know she'll just be happy to see you," Michelle noted as Eden rushed from one end of the kitchen to the other. "Another audience member for her stories."

"And I'll be happy to see her." Eden was speaking faster, eyes darting nervously from her bowl to the recipe. "But a good houseguest brings food! And the Nosher website ranked rugelach as the number one Jewish cookie, so who am I to argue? Pass me the cinnamon?"

"Didn't you bring O'Brian a fiddle-leaf fig?" Michelle slid the cinnamon over.

"And he loved it. It's about tailoring your gift to your host. Or, in this case, the grandmother of the host."

"Technically, since you live here too, doesn't that make you a host?"

Eden paused. "You mean I'm *staying* here. I don't live here. I live in Gloria and sometimes at Aggie's."

Michelle studied the countertop, then started making a tiny mound out of stray flour. "Yes. Until such time as you decide whether you're staying on here or going."

Silence fell. "One sec," Eden said and put the food processor on, smashing walnuts, brown sugar, raisins, and cinnamon to a pulp. Eden stopped blending. "I thought we were waiting for you to decide what *we* are?" she asked gently.

"And you'll leave if I say I'm unwilling to have a relationship with you?" Pain lanced through her at the thought.

"*Is* that your decision?" Eden asked carefully.

"No. I'm still trying to get past all the ways I think I'd ruin this."

"Ah." Eden smiled. "Well, for all you know, *I* could ruin it."

"Doubtful."

Eden tapped the crumbly mixture on top of her rolled dough, smoothing it out. "The other option is I move out and give you space to think. Then we could date like regular people—if and when you're ready. That works too, doesn't it?"

Reaching for a pizza cutter, Eden divided the dough into twelve wedges, then began rolling each one, curling the sweet filling up inside.

"I don't want you to move out." Michelle sighed. "I know this is back to front. Usually people move in *after* they're in relationships."

"We're unusual people." Eden shrugged. "Who cares? It's for us to decide what works best. I'd be more worried about me messing up the rugelach, because what would Hannah think of me then?" Worry darted onto her face.

"I think she's so pleased I've found anyone to put up with me that you could serve her boot leather and she'd still consider you golden."

"Golden, huh?" Eden snorted. "Wait'll she sees my bedhead."

"Wait till you see hers."

Eden smiled, glanced at the recipe, then back up at Michelle. "I guess it's ready. Have mercy on me, universe."

Michelle opened the wall-oven door. A blast of three-fifty-degree heat shot out. "I'm pretty sure the universe loves you. This'll work."

Scooping up the tray, Eden slid it into the oven. Michelle stepped up behind her, hand reaching past Eden's to help her push the heavy door closed.

When Eden turned, she was bracketed by Michelle's body and the arm that was still resting on the door handle.

"Oops. I know you don't like hugs," Eden whispered. "Even impromptu ones."

Michelle didn't move. "I don't think this counts." Her heart was thundering.

"No?" Eden grinned. She slipped both arms around Michelle to loosely hold her. "Oh, well, that's good, then."

Tingles flooded Michelle even as her brain was screaming, *Stop this*! She ignored it and offered a fond huff. "Yes. I suppose it is."

Eden and Hannah hit it off, far beyond Michelle's wildest hopes. Okay, sure, her safta declaring Eden's rugelach the most delicious treat in baking history was a stretch, but those dancing old eyes, filled with affection and humor for both Michelle and Eden, were everything.

They were thick as thieves from the moment they clapped eyes on each other. Days often involved Eden whisking Hannah off to picnic spots and matinée movies. Or curled up on the sofa together watching schlocky female superhero shows.

While they bonded, Michelle put feelers out for new jobs. She'd so far only attracted interest from the CIA and the FBI. She'd turned both down, recoiling at the thought of returning to the secrets game.

Eden, in turn, had suggested something entirely different. "What you need is to feel part of the world at the grassroots level. Hit up a protest or two."

Michelle sometimes tried to picture herself at a protest, holding a Save the Whales sign. *So me.*

"You're smiling," her safta said, joining her on the balcony one sunny morning. "Must be thinking about your Eden."

"Perhaps I'm thinking about my investment portfolio."

"Not unless you have plans to sleep with it later."

"Safta!" Michelle protested.

"What? I might be old, but I'm not blind."

Michelle inhaled. "Does it bother you? That we're…?" *What are we? Between decisions?*

It had been getting harder to dismiss her desire. Harder not to notice how wonderful Eden had felt in her arms against that oven so many weeks ago.

"Why would you two being in the honeymoon phase bother me? I remember how I was with your grandfather. Those were the days. It makes me fantasize about all that flexibility I used to have." Hannah tapped her bad hip.

"No mental pictures, please," Michelle said dryly. "And we're not in the honeymoon phase. We haven't…" *How to phrase it?* She gave a helpless shrug. "We haven't."

"Oh." Hannah looked surprised. "But you want to?"

Michelle tutted. "That is none of your business."

"I don't understand. It's clear it's mutual to my old eyes. You're like a new woman around Eden. Lighter."

Michelle frowned. She was?

"I love Eden, by the way," her safta announced. "Not just because she makes you happy, although that is no small feat. I love her for who she is. Good, through and through."

And yet she's with me. Michelle sighed. "Yes. She is, isn't she?"

Hannah didn't notice her tone, or was choosing not to, as she suddenly shifted topics. "Now then, tell me about this dinner party you're going to tonight? Your former head of security? Won't that be fun!"

Michelle bit her lip. "I haven't been a dinner guest for so long, I'm not sure I remember how."

Hannah smiled. "It'll be fine. Just remember: Who was the FBI's schmoozer at parties? Who could circulate a room and get them to all open up?"

"Don't make me regret telling you that."

Hannah patted her hand. "Just put on your game face, and you'll be amazing."

Chapter 22
Dinner and Insurrections

Dinner was a revelation, Eden thought as she munched through a delicious dish of roasted field mushrooms with blue cheese and spinach. Michelle was treated to roast venison in red wine sauce that by all accounts was blissful.

But the real revelation was watching Michelle. She was utterly charming, able to coax even the littlest O'Brian child out of his shell by asking him about dinosaurs. Michelle made every O'Brian feel important and listened to, and she displayed diplomatic talents Eden had never witnessed before. Oh, she knew from Hannah that this was who Michelle had been at the FBI, but seeing was believing. The woman could *turn it on.*

What Eden had learned most wasn't actually how polished and sociable Michelle could be when she had to but how much out of her comfort zone this was. How much effort it required for her to become this persona. Eden was honored that Michelle had never once hidden who she really was, always being herself with Eden. That made her all kinds of gooey.

Right now, Michelle was charming Shauna with her extensive knowledge of a protest in Shauna's hometown in Cork, Ireland, involving dairy farmers versus an American chemical giant that had tried to build a plant there. Dow Chemicals had lost due to locals protesting it.

The fact Michelle knew any of this amazed Shauna. Eden, however, strongly suspected the chemical giant had hired The Fixers to win over any objectors. One of their rare losses, probably.

"You're so knowledgeable," Shauna exclaimed. "No one around here has ever heard of Cork, let alone our little protest." She nudged her husband. "You never told me your boss was such a well-informed woman."

Phelim merely chewed away on his venison and gave Michelle a knowing look.

"Then again," Shauna went on, "you never tell me anythin' at all, do you now?"

"Don't be too hard on him," Michelle said, smile warm. "He's not allowed to. All staff sign stiff NDAs. They're not even allowed to name their workplace in public."

"Mm. That's what he tells me too. Now then, would you like seconds? Goodness, you need feeding up. Let me get you seconds!"

Before Michelle could protest, Shauna snatched her plate and rushed off to the kitchen.

"Thanks," Phelim said quietly to Michelle. He cast his eye to the end of the table, but his children were paying them no attention. "It helps her to hear that from you."

"Does she know I'm not your boss anymore?"

"I told her. I think she keeps forgetting."

"I see." Michelle leaned back. "Phelim, as much as I loved dinner, I couldn't possibly have seconds."

"About that? She made a whole heap of dessert too."

Michelle gave him a pained look.

"Sorry, she can't help it. When she gets nervous, she cooks."

Eden laughed. "And Michelle cleans. The apartment's gleaming."

"You were nervous?" Phelim asked in surprise. "*You?*"

Michelle shrugged. "Well. A little."

"Gleaaaming," Eden inserted.

Michelle shot her a warning glare.

Eden laughed.

O'Brian chuckled. "Let me talk to Shauna. I'll ask her to give us a little alone time to discuss secret work shite while she puts the kids to bed. I've gotta update you on what's up at the office."

"Oh?" Michelle raised an eyebrow.

"Dying to hear this," Eden said.

"Be right back."

Five minutes later, Phelim launched in. "First things first, boss," he began, "you've been missed."

"Kensington's that bad?" Michelle replied.

"Oh yeah. I don't think people realized how efficiently you kept the ship runnin' until *she* took over."

"What's she been doing?"

"First, she ordered a witch hunt, ta find out who'd leaked her dirt and ruined her political career. When she found out, she tried to get Liam fired. Board refused that since he'd done it on your orders, so she reassigned him to POBUD, right under her nose, so she could regularly point out all his malfunctions."

"She's bullying him," Michelle said dully. "I thought she'd be above that, but apparently her fury at losing her presidential ambitions has fueled a beast."

"Yeah. Then she found a new cause." O'Brian's jaw clenched. "Kensington's been usin' The Fixers to work her way through her list of enemies and hurt them all. Bear attacks. Anyone who's ever pissed her off."

"Oh no," Eden said. "Please tell me they're all assholes, at least? Speaking as the one person here with experience at being attacked by The Fixers?"

"Please," Phelim snorted. "You were gettin' love taps by comparison. And no, some are pretty decent people—by DC standards, at least. She's got our staff diggin' up dirt on them or tryin' to punish them in ways that are really shite." He eyed Michelle pointedly. "Shite even for us."

"Wait," Michelle said, "if the board wasn't going to allow you to attack Sharpe on work time—and by the way, thank you again for doing that anyway…"

"No trouble at all."

Eden squeezed his arm, gratitude filling her once more that he'd put himself on the line for her when he'd been ordered not to. "Thank you, Phelim."

A redness crept into his cheeks. "Really was nothin'."

"My point is," Michelle continued, "the board will not be pleased at all the work resources being used for nonwork reasons."

"No, they sure aren't. I reckon they're rattled given that Tilly—who has to sit in on their meetings—is lookin' about a hundred these days. She's gone all pursed-lipped and grouchy."

"Interesting," Michelle murmured.

"She's been runnin' around, tryin' to make things right, keep the regular work still tickin' over, while havin' to deal with her boss's moods and whims too."

"Ottilie's cracking?" Eden asked. "Seriously?"

"Yeah." He gave them grim looks. "Heard Kensington call Tilly a glorified typist t'other day. I thought she was gonna quit on the spot, she looked so mad. She stormed off for a few hours and came back lookin' even madder. No clue who she complained to, but I'm thinkin' she got no satisfaction."

Michelle's eyes held a fascinated gleam. "You don't say. Who else has Kensington angered?"

"It's a long list. The big one is Snakepit. He was so overworked with her revenge list that he asked if he could hire another hacker. Kensington told him to stop bein' a child demandin' more toys. Then she said somethin' about 'the lazy generation' and laughed at him."

Holy shit. Eden couldn't imagine talking to any employee with such disrespect, let alone someone as unassuming as Snakepit.

"You know, Phelim," Michelle said softly, "I've found it's a *very* bad idea to insult hackers of Snakepit's talent. Douglas Lesser was a god of computers when he worked at The Fixers. Untouchable. And it was *Snakepit* and his friend—two teenagers—who were his downfall. Yet Kensington insults him as if his legitimate request is some childish tantrum? Am I wrong in thinking this could end very badly?"

"Already has." Phelim lowered his voice. "Last time The Fix met at the Black Rabbit, the crap Kensington has been up to was all anyone was discussin'. People compared notes. It became pretty clear there's two factions formin'. Ones who are hopin' she'll be fired soon and life will move on. And t'other one."

"The other one?" Eden asked with interest.

"The ones who don't think they should haveta wait. And given everyone's skills, that group is a mighty dangerous one." He scratched his chin. "When that came to light, the former group decided to decamp. Didn't want to be implicated in whatever may or may not be about to be hatched."

"Did you leave too?" Michelle asked.

Phelim inhaled deeply. "No."

"Why?" Michelle asked evenly. "I never took you as one for orchestrating a mutiny."

"There's been bad things goin' on for years. I didn't speak up. Things that haven't sat right with me." He held Michelle's gaze. "Like threatenin' a reporter about her kids."

Eden swallowed. She'd hated he'd done that, even knowing he hadn't meant it.

Regret crossed Michelle's face. "I'm sorry you did that."

"I'm sorry I did too." Phelim slumped, looking down at his big, scarred hands. "Told myself it was just part of the job. That I knew it was all hot air, so it didn't count. But the reporter lady was so afraid, and I felt like pig shit. That was a real low point for me. Don't get me wrong: I'm still okay with threatenin' total arseholes. They deserve it. But the woman was good. And one of her kids was the same age as Thomas. Started thinkin' how that must have felt for her. Hell, I don't want to be that fella."

Eden grabbed his hand, giving it a squeeze. "Then don't be."

"Sounds easy when you say it. I'll be honest, I've stuck it out this long because of Michelle." His eyes slid to her. "I'm loyal. You were good ta me at a time I needed it. But now there's no need to stay. Kensington's out of control. She's hurtin' everyone because she's angry and she can. I don't have to be loyal to that."

"What would you do if not…" Eden wasn't sure what to call it. *Threatening people into compliance?*

"There's a friend I know, runs a ceramic, wood, and arts shop at t'market. He's been on my case for years to let him sell my carvings and woodwork and so on. Maybe I will. Got some money stashed away now, so I'd be okay if it doesn't take off at first."

"That'd be wonderful!" Eden declared, beaming. "You have so much talent."

"Well," he blushed. "Maybe I—"

"Phelim," Michelle cut in, "I'm pleased you're finding something fulfilling to do with yourself, but can we circle back to the insurrectionist group at the Black Rabbit?"

"Right." He scratched his ear. "So, Liam and Mia are in it. Snakepit too. About eight of us. And someone asks, hypothetically like, 'If someone wanted to destroy The Fixers, what'd be the most effective way?'"

"Why destroy the company?" Michelle asked. "Don't they just want Kensington gone?"

"One or two of them are so mad about how she's treated them, they want ta blow it all up as payback. Metaphorically speakin'. The rest don't. They just want to make things so uncomfortable that the board has to fire its CEO."

"I see," Michelle said. "So what suggestions were made?"

"Someone thought exposin' to the world all the client cases would be feckin' destructive."

"I agree," Eden said. "It's what I've been trying to do. Although there's only nineteen cases on the USB drive I got. I'd need a ton more to really hurt The Fixers."

"Yeah, your name came up." O'Brian nodded. "It was suggested we help you keep doin' that by leaking the rest of the cases to you. CEO'd be gone within the hour if all the client cases hit the media."

Eden glanced at Michelle. It suddenly occurred to her that she had no idea which side Michelle was on. This was a company Michelle had been in charge of for nine years, invested thousands of hours into ensuring it ran efficiently, and here she and Phelim were, casually discussing destroying it.

"Except we discovered it won't work," Phelim continued. "Snakepit told us the system is set up so no one can download more than twenty cases at a time without it bein' automatically flagged to Security, the

CEO, the CEO's assistant, and the board. He can't even open the file to change that limit without it bein' flagged."

"There goes any plans for a big Fixers' takedown," Eden said. "Unless someone wants to leak nineteen cases a time."

"Which ain't happenin'," Phelim said. "Snakepit just quit, and he's the only one in IT who'd look the other way if he kept gettin' suspicious job orders for nineteen files at a time."

"He quit?" Eden sagged. "A shame he didn't download a copy of all those cases before he left."

"He knew that'd get him in deep and immediate shite. Red flags galore. He wouldn't have made it out the door. But he did do somethin' *else* to help." Phelim grinned. "Somethin' that'll fuck them up even more, long-term."

"What could do that?" Eden asked.

Phelim chuckled. "So, when they were all discussin' the best ways to bring down The Fixers, know what the Espionage team said?"

"This'll be good," Eden said.

"Mia told us that the first step in destroyin' a monster is ensurin' it can't hurt you back. She suggested deletin' all our nondisclosure agreements. And Liam said it had to be the lawyers' electronic copies too. And now all the NDAs are gone. Not just at The Fixers. The lawyers' computers were hacked. But no one will realize it until they go looking for an employee's NDA—and they have no reason to. But right now the beast is hobbled. The Fixers can't hurt anyone for revealin' its secrets."

"But I signed a *paper* NDA," Eden said. "There are hard copies."

"Actually," Michelle broke in, "once the paper copies get scanned in, they're shredded to ensure there's no paper trail. The board always insisted the company should be as ghost-like as possible, leaving little hard documentation. Mia's right: The Fixers are defenseless."

"What good is that if we have nothing to expose?" Eden asked.

"You could keep goin' with the cases you do have," Phelim suggested.

"I already leaked the worst ones. The rest is petty stuff. Ethically awful, but it only affects one or two people."

"Mmph." O'Brian frowned. "Maybe the answer will present itself in time."

"Are you going to keep working there?" Eden asked.

"Figured I might see what I can do to help you from the inside before I bail."

Michelle regarded him. "You seem so certain Eden will wish to continue doing this work. What if she doesn't? Will you bring down The Fixers on your own?"

He flicked a surprised glance at Eden. "Sorry I didn't ask what you wanted to do. Are you still doin' this campaign of yours?"

"I hadn't decided," Eden said. "Without fresh material and with my reporter friend quitting on me—"

Guilt crept into Phelim's eyes. "Sorry."

"—I'm not sure where to go from here." Eden turned to Michelle. "It matters a lot to me if I have your support."

"Do you *want* me involved?" Michelle asked neutrally.

"Goddess, yes! Of course." Eden was astonished she'd even ask. "But you haven't said which side you're on."

"You think I'd be on the side of the people who fired me and replaced me with a bullying megalomaniac?" Michelle lifted her eyebrow.

"No, but I think you might have conflicted loyalties. You ran The Fixers for years. You fought tooth and nail to stop me hurting it."

"Tooth and limp lettuce leaf," Phelim inserted helpfully.

"Well, whatever," Eden said with a small grin. "But you fought me. It's not such a stretch to ask: Michelle, whose side are you on in this mutiny?"

"I'd have thought it patently obvious by now. I'm on yours."

Phelim smirked. "You're right. That *was* patently obvious."

Michelle rolled her eyes. She hesitated. "Look, what Kensington is doing is wrong. Terrible. But can you both remember that I've spent a lifetime and two careers dedicated to keeping secrets? You're asking me to change who I am, just like that. *Leak it all*." Her lips thinned. "I don't think like that. I'm too cautious and pragmatic to think this is a wonderful idea. I won't help you—not overtly—but I will not get in your way either. The best I can offer is saying I'm philosophically on your side." She shot a worried look Eden's way. "I'm sorry if that disappoints you."

Eden turned that over with mixed feelings. She supposed something so ingrained in Michelle would be a hard habit to break. "You're used to the shadows. Keeping secrets."

"I'm trying to come around to your position of 'expose everything and stand back', but it's a lot. I've always believed that secrecy keeps people safe. A scattergun approach results in collateral damage. Innocents get hurt. There will be unforeseen consequences. I'm surprised at you, Phelim, not having any qualms about this."

"Oh, I have plenty," he said. "But unlike you, I have a good reason not to miss the secrets. It's been hell not bein' able to be honest with Shauna when she asks, 'How was your day?' I'll look forward to bein' able to answer her honestly: 'Great. I made a side table. Want to see it?'"

"I can see why that will be a wonderful change for you," Michelle noted. "And I'll miss being your boss. Well, I *have* missed it already. You were always efficient and amusing."

"And you were always efficient and terrifying," he shot back. "Well, *I* wasn't terrified. But you had everyone else fooled. I respected that. But I have a question. *You* mightn't be ready to lead the revolution, but can you at least offer some clues on how to get started?"

"What do you mean?" Michelle asked.

"You're in the unique position of havin' the top-drawer intel on The Fixers. Care to share what you think is the key to bringin' it to its knees? Nothin' secret, if you don't want; just throw us a bone." He grinned.

And that was probably the smartest question Eden had ever heard. Michelle, with all her inside information, would know better than anyone multiple ways to destroy her own company.

"Ottilie Zimmerman is the key," Michelle said.

"What?" Phelim's eyebrows knitted. "I told you how everyone's been quittin'. We got no functionin' Cybersecurity or Espionage department, and Tilly's burnin' out. I don't think she'd have patience for any disruptions that add to her workload. She's loyal to the CEO too."

"No. Ottilie's loyal to herself first, then the board, then the CEO. She told me so," Michelle said. "And the day she saunters out the exit, the whole company will fall over."

"What?" Phelim blurted. "She's a PA!"

"No, she's not. I can't tell you everything I know about her because that might put you in a dangerous position—"

"Dangerous? We're talkin' about *Tilly Zimmermann*, right? Types a fierce interoffice memo? Tells you off if you put up personal photos? Lectures you on departmental expenses if you slide a dollar over budget?"

"Yes. She also knows *everything*. She's the glue, the organizer, and the brains, although she hides it well with her officiousness and grandmotherly nonsense. Simply put, she's the smartest person to ever work in that building."

"After you," Phelim corrected, disbelieving.

Michelle shook her head. "No, including me. Including Snakepit, Lesser, Mia, and Liam. Ottilie is the reason The Fixers runs at all. So, if you truly do wish to get on the right side of history—"

"It's time."

"Then you will make it your business to help Ottilie find her way out the door as quickly as possible."

"How?" Phelim asked.

"I don't know. Keep your eyes open. Ask if she needs any help. Play it by ear."

He shrugged. "Okay. Can do."

"And then, when she's gone? They *will* be finished."

"How do you feel about that?" Eden asked curiously.

Michelle looked startled by the question. "Honestly, I'm not sure."

Shauna returned a little later, and they all shared a coffee and dessert.

Well, Michelle tried the dessert but could barely manage more than a few bites. She was too full.

Upon seeing her predicament, Eden surreptitiously helped herself to Michelle's plate. O'Brian's eyebrows shot up to his hairline...such as it was...and would have surely kept climbing if not for gravity.

At the door, they said their goodbyes. While Eden was talking to Shauna, O'Brian drew her close.

"I knew it!" he said softly. "I mean, livin' together cos you felt bad she was hurt was one thing—a highly suspicious thing at that—but dessert sharing?" O'Brian chuckled. "Come on."

"Eden was hungry," Michelle tried.

"That's bollocks." He elbowed her. "You two are on together."

"We're not!" Michelle said hotly.

"Seriously?" He looked askance. "What's in the way?" He frowned. "I'm sure Eden'd be up for it. You must have seen the way she looks at you. Like you're better than beer."

Michelle didn't smile. "Eden is good."

"No shit." He waited expectantly.

"I'm not," Michelle said flatly.

"Ah." Understanding flashed into his eyes.

She didn't say any more.

"Ya know," O'Brian said, "Shauna's about the best human bein' on God's green earth. Her kindness and decency are *unbelievable*. And she chose me. I couldn't believe my damned luck. Do I deserve her? Nope. Am I gonna do everythin' I can to keep her? You bet. On paper, we shouldn't work, but we do. No reason why you'd be bad for Lawless, if that's what you're thinkin'. What if you bring out the best in each other? Don't know till you try. And one thing I know about you, you're determined as all hell when you want somethin' to work. I'd lay good odds on you two. I really would."

Michelle glanced away. Maybe he had a point. There was no denying how good he and Shauna were together. They just *fit*, somehow. Hope dared raise its head. Michelle wasn't fast enough to rein it in before it started cartwheeling around her brain. Perhaps O'Brian was proof this could be done. Could they somehow make this work? Was that insane?

"Don't overthink it," O'Brian added. "And by the way, I'm happy for you. Quality choice. Maybe that crazy hippie'll even get you to relax a bit."

"Unlikely. But she *is* trying. In every sense," Michelle suggested to divert her unease about the topic.

"And you think she's amazin' right down to her ethically-sourced socks."

He was impossible. "What did I say about being cheeky?" she shot back.

He snorted.

Eden finished chatting with Shauna and came over to them. "Dinner was wonderful," she told O'Brian. "Next time, our place, okay?"

Our place? Michelle's stomach did the happiest of little flips. That sounded so…settled.

"Bye, Riverdance," Eden added, grinning.

"Nope. That's still not gonna stick." He wagged a warning finger. Then he gave her a gentle hug in deference to her ribs and Michelle a wave in deference to her dislike of hugs.

In the car on the way home, Eden didn't say much.

"What is it?" Michelle asked as she turned into her building's garage. "Second thoughts about bringing down The Fixers?"

"No."

Michelle brought her Audi to a stop in her personal parking spot. It was dwarfed by the colorful eyesore that was Gloria filling the space beside them. She turned to Eden. "Then what is it?"

Eden's eyes shone with emotion. "I never pictured I'd be with you when I'm planning on destroying your company. I know, I know, you're still processing. But you're not stopping me, are you?"

"I was afraid you'd be upset by me not actively helping." Michelle eyed her. "You're not?"

"It wouldn't be *you* if you didn't have reservations. I expect you to get there in your own time."

Well, that was a relief.

"Or maybe you never will. That's also a possibility."

"I'm a little surprised by how accepting you are about this. I know you don't like us on opposite sides."

"We're not, though. You agree The Fixers is wrong."

"Yes."

"You're only reserving judgment on our *method* of bringing it down."

"I…yes."

"I'm trying to be a better person," Eden said suddenly. "I don't mean by flinging myself into every new cause. I'm trying to be more open to other ways of thinking—as long as no one's hurting people. That's a big one. My do-no-evil clause remains in effect."

"You don't say." Michelle smiled.

Eden smiled back but became serious. "Ever since I started living with you and came to understand you, I've been reevaluating everything I believed about right and wrong. My views have been so rigid. But life's not about seeking perfection, is it? It's about so much more…and so much less. It's understanding people come with flaws. Accepting that you don't throw the whole person out for not thinking or acting in a way *you* would. Life is really about existing in a way that is…kind."

"That may be about as far away from striving for perfection as you can get," Michelle said. "Accepting things as they are."

"Yeah. Isn't that funny?" Eden gazed at her, expression contemplative. "So, here's where I'm at with us: you do you; I'll do me. We can be human and messy and imperfect and silly and wonderful and *ourselves*. We can figure out our crap together. That includes our differences. Okay?"

"I like the sound of that." Even so, Michelle tried to imagine what that would look like in reality. Two such contrasting people, with wildly different philosophies, trying to make sense of things, a…relationship…together. How could it work?

"Are you okay?" Eden asked after a moment. "You look…far away."

"I've been thinking too." Michelle said, ordering her thoughts. "Fretting, really. About what would happen if we did try a relationship. All this time, I've been worried about how I might affect you negatively: scare you off, hurt you, corrupt you somehow. I'm not even sure what half my fears are, but they're *so* strong. But tonight I remembered the day we met. When I asked you about that sculpture in the main office during your interview."

"You asked whether the figure was nude or not, given all the sculpted gauze covering her?"

"Yes. You know, you were the only one to pass my test. Out of everyone I've hired. You were the only one who nailed it."

"Really? No one else thought she was nude?"

"Oh, plenty did. Their views were irrelevant. I argue the opposite of whatever an interviewee says, then I wait to see what they'll do next. Everyone changes their answer to match mine, to ingratiate themselves with a potential boss. Not you, though. You stuck to your guns so stubbornly." Michelle smiled. "You even texted me later: *She's definitely nude!* I laughed so hard that Ottilie burst in, fearing I was having a fit."

Eden grinned. "What does that have to do with us?"

"Don't you see? While you're open to new ideas, no one can change your mind *except you*—even when it's in your interests to do so. You're not easily led."

Eden nodded. "True."

"So it follows, if you want to be good, you will be. If you want to fight injustice, you will. And if you like me, you...like me. You're in, boots and all. *Incorruptible*. End of story."

"Yep." Eden quirked an eyebrow. "That's me."

"That is enormously comforting." Michelle smiled.

Eden's eyebrows shot up in surprise. "Are you saying you want more?"

"Oh, Eden, I've always wanted more. That's not the question." Michelle's gaze settled on Gloria. So many rainbows and painted animals, protest stickers and peace symbols. Chaotic. Eccentric. Beautiful. So Eden. "I'm saying I have a heart that craves more *and* I'm terrified."

Eden inhaled. "Okay?"

"And I'm just working out which will win the race right now. I have so many reservations. But O'Brian reminded me tonight that sometimes even the most unlikely couple can work. Sometimes you just have to dive in and try. See what happens."

"That big ole Irish pussycat is so right." Eden grinned.

"Mmm. I'm so close to saying yes, but I'm still afraid." Michelle hated how vulnerable she sounded, but Eden deserved honesty. "I'm sorry to ask, but can you be patient a little while longer?"

"I *can* be patient," Eden said angelically. "But I should point out that while your heart and brain are arm-wrestling for supremacy, we could be making out."

Michelle inhaled at the vision of the teasing suggestion: Eden's lips on hers, her fingers and tongue playing with Michelle in all sorts of forbidden ways. Her cheeks grew warm.

"You're thinking about it, aren't you?" Eden chuckled.

"What answer will get you to drop the subject?"

"Let me give you something else to think about, then. I've been working out in your building's gym every day as part of my physical therapy. Low-intensity stuff. Don't worry—Dr. Michelson approved it. And I noticed this morning that my biceps are starting to look mighty fine. I'll show them to you sometime. If your heart wins, I mean. If fear wins, you're out of luck." She grinned.

Michelle tried *very* hard not to think of Eden's muscled arms. "You don't play fair," she muttered.

"No," Eden agreed. "I'm a firm believer in going after what I want." Her eyes warmed as she studied Michelle. "And who."

Chapter 23
More

Eden placed her glass under the kitchen's filtered water tap and waited while it quietly filled. The room was dark, given it was almost midnight. She hadn't bothered turning on the light as she could see well enough with the ambient city light from the window—and she was doing her bit for the environment.

It had been a wild few weeks. Discovering Michelle actually thought her feelings were one-sided. And tonight, after dinner at the O'Brians, realizing how close Michelle was to saying yes.

The fridge suddenly opened behind her. Eden spun around.

Michelle was illuminated in the stark fridge light, reaching for a bottled water.

"I don't know why you don't just refill when you have filtered water," Eden said with a smile, turning off the tap and indicating her glass.

Michelle jumped, eyes wide, hand over her chest.

"Sorry! Thought you heard the tap." Eden put down her glass and then froze. *Oh goddess.* Michelle wore a short, emerald-green satin robe that hid little. Or was it silk? Her pale skin seemed to glow against the material. A plunging vee practically demanded closer inspection.

Was she *naked* underneath? Damp hair implied she wasn't long out of the shower. Or had it been a bath? Some indulgent soak while Michelle's tapered neck leaned back, her eyes fluttering closed?

Eden, panicking, tried to wipe that fantasy from her brain. *Are my thoughts written all over my face?*

Michelle, gaze burning and intense, studied Eden with more than her usual scrutiny. Her eyes ran slowly down Eden's body.

Eden glanced at herself. *Oh. Well.* She wasn't exactly overdressed either: tiny, blue cotton bed shorts and an old Wingapo State University tank top.

Michelle's gaze languidly traced her muscled biceps. "I see you didn't exaggerate about the effects of your workouts." Her eyes burned even hotter.

Did she have any idea what that expression was doing?

Michelle slowly put the water bottle back and closed the fridge door.

"Aren't you thirsty?" Eden whispered, confused.

"Yes." Michelle's eyes roamed her body. "Very."

"You can't do that," Eden protested, "if you don't mean it."

"Do...what?" Michelle asked, voice husky.

"You know what," Eden said grumpily. "You can't look at me like *that.*"

"Oh?" Michelle asked softly. She leaned closer. "*How* am I looking at you?"

Eden folded her arms, which only made Michelle's gaze linger on her biceps. "Like you're deciding how to have me. That's not fair if you're not actually going to do it."

The edges of Michelle's lips ticked up. "I see. But if I say yes to us, I *can* look at you like that?"

"You've decided, then?" Eden asked, hope leaking from her voice. "You want more?"

"Yes. I mean," she added teasingly, "*if* you're still interested?"

If? Eden dropped her arms limply to her sides as her brain flailed dramatically. Her hardening nipples stood up and pressed against the cool cotton of her tank top.

"Two extra votes, I see," Michelle noted dryly.

Eden's face turned into a furnace. "Yeah. It's unanimous."

Michelle smiled.

"No more fear, then?" Eden whispered.

"So much it almost chokes me." Michelle swallowed, vulnerability flitting into her eyes. "But equally, I find I can't fight this anymore. If there's one thing I've learned, it's that it's impossible to say no to you. You are a force of nature."

Michelle feathered her fingers through Eden's hair. "You take away my fear, Eden. I'm not brave, but you make me want to be. I don't dare dream, yet you give me hope. I don't want, but you make me crave. You're impossible to resist; so I've decided: I'm not going to." Michelle closed the distance.

The thorough, appreciative kiss felt as if Michelle wanted to savor every moment. Like a chocolate dessert that melted against Eden's lips, it promised so many other delights. Eden couldn't get enough. She tugged Michelle into her arms, pressing together their breasts, bellies, and hips.

Eden's knees wobbled from the sensation of kissing...actually *kissing*...Michelle. The austere, closed-off woman who let no one in, who had such high walls and sharp edges, had opened herself to Eden in an act of trust that was humbling and seriously arousing.

Michelle kissed deeply and with purpose, like someone who'd been denied too long and needed to remember every sensation. She pulled back enough to meet Eden's eyes, her lips parting into a smile. Her hand cupped Eden's cheek gently.

"Tell me that us having more isn't a mistake," Michelle said, expression intense, "and I'll believe you."

The deceptive question stunned Eden. Michelle, who was always so cynical and certain about the world she controlled, had given Eden permission to *remake* it. To convince her. As if Eden had that power.

"It isn't a mistake," she said, lifting her chin. "No way. We're made for each other."

"Okay." Michelle exhaled. Belief replaced the hint of trepidation in her eyes. "*Okay.*"

Eden lifted her hand and let it rest over Michelle's heart. "I've got you." The beating fluttering beneath her hand was so fast.

"Yes." Michelle whispered. "You do."

Eden met her eyes. "Your heart. It's pounding so fast."

"Well," Michelle said, pink flooding her cheeks, "it turns out I'm unaccountably affected by you. Your nearness. The incredible way you kiss."

"Uh...sorry?" Eden offered a crooked grin.

"So you should be," Michelle said with a sniff. "All the hard work I did trying to see you as the pesky irritant and instead all I wanted was..."

Eden held her breath.

Michelle's eyes glowed. "You."

Me. Eden beamed. She loved the sound of that.

"Just don't be smug about it." Michelle's eyes crinkled with amusement.

Eden smiled. She ran her hand across the fabric of Michelle's robe. The sensuousness of the material made her fingers tingle. She ghosted her fingertips down the vee of the garment, allowing her index finger to trail bare skin while the others trailed satin. Definitely satin, as it stayed cool to her touch.

Goosebumps broke out along Michelle's skin. "That feels...incredible," she said, throat tight.

"For me too." Eden cupped Michelle's small breast. It was a lovely handful. With her thumb, she rubbed the nipple through the emerald material, rolling and flicking it until it became even harder.

Eden repeated the action on the other breast. She was a great believer in equality, after all.

Michelle's breathing hitched.

"I love how aroused you are," Eden said as Michelle's eyes darkened with desire.

"That, or it's cold in here."

"Mich-elle," Eden drawled. "It's too late for denial."

"Yes. Habit," Michelle admitted. "Being vulnerable isn't something I'm used to. It feels...dangerous."

"You're safe with me," Eden told her. "Focus on that." She dropped kisses between Michelle's breasts, the creamy slice of skin next to silky green.

"Oh." Michelle's chest rose and fell more quickly.

Eden trailed her lips up Michelle's neck. Then along her jaw. Finally, her lips moved against Michelle's ear. "Just so you know, I heard Hannah's delicate snores on the way to the kitchen. In case you're worried she's about to burst in."

"She sleeps like the dead and never gets up at night," Michelle murmured. "But even so, I have no intention of taking you for the first time up against the fridge."

"Who's to say I won't be the one taking *you*?"

Michelle inhaled sharply. "I'm...used to being in control." She reached for Eden's hip, slipping fingertips beneath the waistband of her shorts.

"Color me shocked." Eden huffed out a laugh. "Christ, this robe is *sinful*. Are you bare underneath?" Her fingers wandered lower. "Naked?"

"I just got out of the bath," Michelle said as Eden tugged the robe open.

She shifted the material off Michelle's shoulders, exposing all of her, which also shifted Michelle's questing fingers.

And *there*. That certainly answered that question. Michelle's pale breasts came into view, along with her flat, pale stomach and a dark, neat thatch of hair. *Beautiful.*

"Oh," Eden whispered in delight. "Thank you, universe." Her hand slipped between Michelle's legs.

Michelle's eyes flew wide. "*Here?*"

"Yes," Eden said. "Well, for starters. So you'll have to be quiet. Can you do that, Michelle?" she asked as her fingers slowly started moving against soft, wet flesh. "Can you be so very, *very* quiet? Can you let me have my way with you? Can you give up that control? For me?"

Michelle swallowed hard. Her body arched into Eden's hand. Then she gave a sharp nod.

"I'll make you feel so good," Eden promised. She leaned in to take Michelle's erect nipple in her mouth and rolled it with her tongue.

Michelle's hand flung backwards and slapped the fridge with a dull thud. Her mouth opened, but no sound came out.

So hot. Eden's fingers slid through Michelle's slick folds. She drew moisture up and trembled at Michelle's soft, strained little gasps. Playing with Michelle's clit lightly, *ever so lightly*, Eden worked to get her to repeat those noises, which were nothing she'd ever heard from Michelle before. The gasps went straight to her own clit.

Michelle's flattened hand against the fridge curled into a tight fist.

Eden increased the pressure. "Is this hard for you? Are you desperate to be in charge? Or desperate to cry out?"

Michelle's nostrils flared. Her eyes lit with a fire that was pure aphrodisiac. She didn't reply.

Circling Michelle's center with the faintest tip of her finger, Eden whispered, "Dying for more? Would you like me inside you?"

Another gasp. Michelle's eyes were pleading.

Eden slid one finger in as deep as it would go. There was no resistance.

Michelle shuddered and shut her eyes.

"You're really wet," Eden murmured her approval. "It's delicious feeling you aroused for me." She teased a second finger at her entrance.

Michelle sank her whole body back against the fridge. There was a soft clatter as fridge magnets fell to the floor along with assorted papers that had been clinging to them.

"Two fingers?" Eden asked.

A tiny little *yes* leaked from Michelle's lips, and her closed eyes tightened.

Eden slipped two fingers inside, the pulsing drawing her deeper.

Michelle spread her legs wider to allow Eden's fingers. Her hand against the fridge flattened and tightened, over and over.

For someone who loved being in control, Michelle had given it up pretty quickly. Her expression was blissed out.

Eden husked in her ear, "I'm going to make you come, Michelle. I'm going to make you tremble. Oh hell, you're so wet. Ready. *Desperate*."

Michelle's eyes flashed open, defiance and desire sparking in them. They said: *just you wait until it's my turn.*

Goddess! Arousal flooded Eden. She was desperate to touch herself. But, no, this wasn't about her. She returned her lips to Michelle's breast, loving it with enthusiasm, and pressed her fingers even deeper inside.

Michelle's thighs began to quiver. Her gasps came faster, head thumping back into the fridge, cords in her throat straining from the effort of not crying out.

Down here, deep between her legs, was so soft, like velvet. Engorged and slippery, pulling in Eden's sliding fingers. Lazily, her other hand brushed Michelle's clit.

"Nnnhh," Michelle gasped. "Oh. *There*."

"Quiet," Eden ordered, although the words had been barely audible. She pressed "there."

Michelle responded with whole-body shudders. Her face lit up, her mouth fell open, and a redness crept up her throat. She rocked with Eden's fingers, pressing her clit harder into Eden's thumb. Sounds of slick wetness filled the air, along with the scent of arousal.

Eden slipped her other hand into Michelle's hair. She'd always loved its glossiness, and now she played with the texture, running the strands between her fingers.

With widening eyes, Michelle quivered, her thighs became taut, and she gritted out, "I don't think I can keep standing. I can't—"

"You can." Eden pressed against her. "I'll pin you to the fridge if I have to until you're a quivering mess." She inhaled sharply at that mental picture. "Goddess, I'd *love* to see you a quivering mess, Michelle. I've thought about you coming undone for weeks."

Michelle's eyes snapped open. "What? You…you imagined me?"

"Yes," Eden admitted. "I've fantasized about you while my hand was between my legs and imagined what you'd look like when you're coming. Do you gasp? Cry out? My fantasies don't do it justice. You're *exquisite*." She slowly withdrew her fingers from inside and slid them up Michelle's folds, coming to rest on her clit.

"Oh!" Michelle gasped. "I'm…it's so sensitive."

Eden lightened her touch. "Next time, I'll use my mouth down here. Can you picture it? Me tonguing you?" Her fingers fluttered against Michelle's clit. "It'll feel so good. Won't it, Michelle?"

Michelle's body arched, trembled, and she gasped, then slammed her hand over her mouth.

Eden leaned into her, keeping her upright, cradling her pussy as Michelle's whole body seemed to turn to liquid.

"God." Michelle closed her eyes briefly and then blinked up at the ceiling. "I can't even…move."

Eden stared in awe. Michelle had let her love her. She'd come under Eden's fingers, her touch. She'd made herself vulnerable to her. She'd made no move to take over, because Eden had asked her not to. That gift was profound. The honor of being allowed to even see Michelle in such a soft, open state was incredible.

She ran slippery fingers up Michelle's body, doing a little loop around her belly button, and then coated her nipple. She leaned in to lick Michelle's essence off it. *Delicious.*

"*God,*" Michelle said with another tremble and a soft sigh. Her whole chest, neck, and cheeks were now flaming red and covered in a faint sheen of perspiration.

Eden lifted her head off Michelle's breast and beamed at her. "Yes?"

"That was…a revelation." Still looking dazed, she straightened, adjusting her robe into something resembling decent, then glanced at the fridge. "I really *did* come for a water. And now I'm entirely dehydrated."

Eden pulled them away from the fridge, drawing Michelle into her arms, then opened the fridge for her. The light came back on, illuminating their disarray. "By all means."

Michelle woke naked in her bed—an uncommon occurrence—with an equally naked arm slung over her waist—an even more uncommon occurrence.

She stretched, studying Eden's arm—beautiful, muscled, and tanned. Erotic memories flooded her. Eden taking her against the fridge, of all places, then suggesting moving them to Michelle's bedroom. After that, there was "naked cuddling," to use Eden's ridiculous term.

Then Eden had kissed Michelle again. She hadn't been prepared for such a kiss. It was so tender and gentle—as if Michelle were an object of great desire. Someone worth worshipping.

And yet, when Michelle's hands had slipped to Eden's body, running under the waistband of her bed shorts, Eden stopped her.

"Tomorrow. I'm too tired tonight. My meds wash me out. Sorry, that's not really sexy, is it?"

And that was when Michelle had remembered to great alarm that she'd forgotten Eden wasn't fully healed.

How had she forgotten? She'd started stuttering out mortified apologies before Eden had kissed her firmly and said, "Michelle, I'm fine. I'd have stopped anything painful. I really am simply tired. Just snuggle me to sleep. Then, tomorrow, I expect some attention too."

Michelle hadn't slept immediately, still overwhelmed. Still throbbing in all the places she hadn't been touched in a while. Actually, had she ever been touched like that? As if she were precious?

Eden's attentions had been so arousing, mapping her with such care and earnestness. But the way she'd looked at Michelle? She wouldn't get over that soon. Eden looked at her as if she were the most desirable, important, worthy woman on earth.

She couldn't wait to reciprocate. But would making love to Eden set back her recovery? That would be unthinkable. Quickly slipping out from under Eden's arm, Michelle rose. After a small hitch, Eden's soft breathing resumed.

Throwing on her robe—now smelling of erotic delights—Michelle collected her phone and stepped into her en suite, gently shutting the door behind her.

"Dr. Michelson," came a tired voice.

"It's Michelle Hastings."

"Ms. Hastings," the doctor said with a sigh. "I don't recognize your number."

"It's new. I've...lost my phone. And this is an urgent matter."

"I figured as much, given it's not even seven. What's up?"

Michelle suddenly stopped, unsure how to phrase the question. This was beyond embarrassing. However, expert knowledge was required, and Michelle was a results-oriented woman. So, she'd just... ask. "Would it be too soon for a patient with three cracked ribs to have sex? And if so, what would be the safest way to minimize injury or pain?" Michelle held her breath.

"A patient with *three cracked ribs*," Dr. Michelson repeated, voice rich with amusement. "By any chance is said patient six weeks through her recovery and staying with you?"

"Perhaps," Michelle said acidly and pursed her lips. There was really no reason for the doctor to turn this into a joke. "Well? What would you advise?"

"If this hypothetical patient feels fine, any movement without pain is okay." There was a pause and Michelle could swear she heard suppressed laughter. "Taking deep breaths is a great exercise for lung capacity and recommended for patients with rib injuries to prevent pneumonia. Screaming is great too. A position with no weight on the injured ribs would be best."

"Screaming?" Michelle repeated dryly.

"I have great faith in your abilities." Dr. Michelson actually snickered this time. "By the way, it's best for the patient to be in control. So it goes at her pace."

How would that be different from last night? Michelle rolled her eyes. It made for a change, though, didn't it? Control was Michelle's domain in the bedroom—until last night, when Eden had simply taken over. "Fine. If it'll help the patient."

"Just don't perform any calisthenics. Ms. Lawless's scans are finally looking satisfactory."

"Who's talking about Ms. Lawless?" Michelle asked, allowing her own humor to edge in.

"Riight." Dr. Michelson's tone was the driest of drawls. "Have fun, you two. Although I'm quite sure you will."

Michelle was far too pleased by getting the green light to care that she was amusing Eden's doctor. Well, former doctor now, she supposed. Obviously, no one had informed Dr. Michelson that Michelle was no longer calling the shots at The Fixers.

"Thanks" was all she said before hanging up, satisfied.

When Michelle returned, Eden watched with sleepy eyes as she slid the phone on her bedside table and shucked her robe.

"Do I wanna know who you were calling at this hour?" Eden mumbled. "Heard voices."

"Dr. Michelson."

Eden's eyes flew open. "Are you okay?"

"More than okay." Michelle climbed into bed, the sheets sliding across her naked skin. "I wanted to be sure what I have in mind for you this morning would be safe."

"Wait, did you just call my doc to see if you could have sex with me safely?"

Michelle smirked. She slid closer and drew Eden into her arms. The feeling of the other woman's soft, warm skin against hers would never get old. "I'm a practical, take-charge woman. So, yes."

"I see." Eden looked in mild shock.

"I needed to know. I wanted an expert opinion, so I asked. Dr. Michelson gave us the go-ahead. That's important information, don't you think?" Michelle's eyebrows lifted.

"You could have just asked me," Eden said.

"And set back your recovery because you were too enthusiastic and we didn't check first?" Michelle murmured into her ear. "Oh no, we're not having that."

Eden blushed. "Did Dr. Michelson laugh hard or just a little?"

"Well, I'm sure she let it out after I hung up. She suggested I let you be in charge. Also? Screaming is good." Michelle supplied her wickedest smile. "That's the one I'll be testing out fully."

"Is that so?" Eden's eyes were wide.

"Mmm." Michelle shifted to hover over Eden's body, all her weight on her forearms. "Are you ready? Because you might be in charge, but that doesn't mean I won't be calling some of the shots."

"Michelle?" Eden said, with a whimper. "I don't want to be in charge right now. I'm *exactly* where I've dreamed of being."

Michelle lowered her lips to Eden's neck and began nibbling. "At my mercy?"

"Y-yes."

"My lips on your nipples?"

Eden gasped. "Fuck."

"My fingers inside you? Or is it my tongue?"

Eden's nostrils flared. "Can we get to one of those sometime soon?"

"Impatient. I thought I might have to work up to that."

"Mich-elle," Eden complained. "Stop teasing. Start *doing*."

Pleased, Michelle pulled back the sheet to reveal Eden's body, then tugged down her shorts. Last night they'd only gotten as far as Eden shedding her tank top. Michelle studied her naked body with interest. Those breasts were as full and gorgeous as she remembered from last night. A faintly rounded stomach led down to the swell of her mound and its glistening curls. *Already wet?* Well, well.

Michelle's hand slowly trailed all over Eden's body until she came to her heat. Sliding her fingers between the folds, she rubbed up the length of Eden's labia.

Eden shuddered. "Oh goddess!"

"You're close, aren't you? How? I've only just started touching you."

"Um…*you're* touching me? And you were fucking me in my dreams last night, so…"

"Ah." Michelle smiled. "Say no more." She slipped a finger inside.

Eden's groan was so deep and aroused, it curled Michelle's toes.

She shifted to straddle one of Eden's thighs, pressing her core into the firm muscle. A bolt of arousal slammed through her. God, to think she'd teased *Eden* about being close. It wouldn't take much.

At the sight of Michelle, Eden's gaze filled with wonder.

Thrills skittered through Michelle. "Is this okay?" she asked, sounding breathless. "Does anything hurt?"

"Hell, no. It's wonderful. I can feel how wet you are."

"Thanks to you. You're beautiful, Eden." Michelle put her weight on one arm and let her other hand tease her lover's clit.

Eden squirmed and arched under her fingers. "Oh!"

Michelle's arousal surged at Eden's pleasure. "Do you want this?" she teased, pressing harder. "Want me?"

"I want you," Eden rasped. "Always have. Even when I hated you, I wanted you. I've never *not* wanted you." Suddenly she stiffened and began to shake. "Oh!"

A rush of moisture coated Michelle's fingers. She thrust harder into Eden's thigh, concentrating on how desirable Eden looked with those unguarded eyes locked on hers.

I love her.

Wait, I do? Michelle froze.

Of course I love Eden. Isn't that obvious?

That thought washed through Michelle, filling her with astonishment. She stopped breathing, stopped thinking, and allowed herself to come.

Eden's hands clenched her trembling thighs. "I could watch you do that forever. You're wonderful."

Michelle slid off, collapsing onto the bed beside Eden. This felt so different. No games. No clever power plays. No mutually assured destruction. Sex without an undertone of dominance? Pleasure for the sake of it? That felt so indulgent and innocent after Phyllis and Alberto.

This was all new territory, which made sense. This was more than sex. The intensity of the experience, the freedom and deep connection frightened her a little. Eden could break her heart so easily—without even trying. Michelle blew her hair out of her eyes and tried to hide how overwhelmed she felt.

"Feeling better?" Eden asked brightly.

"Mmm." Michelle's heart was racing like a thoroughbred.

"Good. Next, ribs willing, I'll slide between your legs and do unspeakable things with my tongue." Eden grinned. "Would you like that?"

Michelle tingled at the thought of it. "Yes. And, um, me too." She quivered more, imagining repaying the favor.

"Great." Eden beamed. "So, just checking in…you're doing okay, right?"

"I am," Michelle drew Eden into her arms. *Christ, I'm taking up hugging.*

Eden wiggled contentedly against her. "I love this."

Me too.

Maybe too much?

Don't hurt me.

Michelle whispered only, "Good."

"I'm hoping we've put your fears aside now?" Eden asked, a tinge of worry in her tone.

Michelle sighed. "My fears will always be here. But for now, they're sitting in the corner of my brain, pouting at me while my hopeful side runs riot. Endorphins are a hell of a thing."

Eden laughed. "Love that. Now then, my sorry body needs another nap before we can see what I can do to make your hopeful side fling glitter in the air. To think you thought *you* were too old for me. What a joke."

"Oh," Michelle said in surprise. She wondered exactly what she'd gotten herself into. And then realized she didn't care. She was all in. No matter how new and terrifying. She was *in*.

Chapter 24
Controlled Demolition

Michelle unlocked her apartment door, groceries balanced on one hip as she opened it. Eden was hauling the rest out of the elevator, chattering about an endangered sloth in the Amazon her mother was championing.

"It's called *Oso perezoso*, which is a super unsexy name for getting public attention," Eden said. "But its alternative is so unfair. Lazy Bear. If I was that sloth, I'd sue my publicist. Hey, why are we stopped?"

Michelle spun to Eden, putting a finger to her own lips, and then gestured at a metal cabinet on a flatbed cart in the apartment's entryway. The cabinet looked expensive. Triple locked. Definitely not Hannah's.

"What is *that*?" Eden whispered, eyes darting to it.

"Good question." Carefully Michelle put down her shopping, gaze tracking the room for anything else that shouldn't be there.

"I hear talking from the balcony," Eden said softly. "Two people."

Michelle stepped in that direction. Hannah and… *oh, for God's sake!* With a growl she stalked over to the balcony door and flung it open.

"Why, Ms. Hastings." Ottilie gave her most grandmotherly smile. "I was just catching up with your safta here. She was filling me in on how your houseguest is all settled in." Her eyes flicked to Eden with a cool awareness. "I'm *so* glad to hear you've healed, Ms. Lawless."

Michelle's jaw worked.

"Ottilie came by an hour ago, darling," Hannah explained. "I told her you were due back soon and asked her in for tea. I was delighted to meet someone from your old office. Especially your assistant, who'd have worked very closely with you."

"Yes." Michelle's gaze bored holes in her former PA. "She did. But that doesn't explain why she's here."

"Oh," Ottilie began brightly, "I had some paperwork to drop off. But then Hannah and I got to talking. You know how it is—two old women with too much time on their hands." She waved as if she were the most harmless soul ever to breathe life.

"So true." Hannah's eyebrow lifted in surprise at the stony expression on Michelle's face—and took the hint. "Well, it's been a delight, Ottilie. Goodness, I've bent your ear off."

She stood and collected a pair of mugs and a plate with crumbs on it. "I'll leave you all to talk shop." Hannah smiled warmly at Ottilie. "It's truly been lovely. Come back some time and visit me."

"I'd love to," Ottilie said. "Thanks so much." She sounded genuine—but that could mean anything.

No one moved or spoke until after Hannah had left. Eden closed the balcony doors behind her, then stood, watching, arms folded.

"Are you threatening my grandmother? Or me?" Michelle demanded. "And how did you get past the front desk, anyway? I live in a secured building!"

"The day I can't talk my way past any front desk is the day I should give up the ghost," Ottilie said with a serene expression, settling into the lounge chair. "All they see is a harmless old lady wanting to catch up with her dearest friend. I am entirely unthreatening." She paused. "*When* I wish to be."

"And now you wish to be?" Michelle glared down at her. "Why are you here? What's my grandmother got to do with anything?"

"Those are very different questions. Honestly, when I knocked on your apartment door, I expected to see you, not Hannah. Who was, in fact, lovely and invited me in, and we had a pleasant chat while I waited. There was no threatening or any intention do so. Now, please sit. You're giving me neck crick."

Michelle sighed, unable to fault her argument, and dropped into the nearest lounge chair. "You have my attention. Proceed."

"Michelle, I have never been your enemy. There's no need for hostility. In fact, I wish to acknowledge how smart it was you sending Mr. O'Brian my way, offering his help. I knew it was you. Who else knows what happens to The Fixers when I leave? You're easing my path out the door, should I face resistance. Yes?"

"Possibly," Michelle conceded. "I didn't tell him you're on the board, by the way. No one else knows that."

"It appears Ms. Lawless does." Ottilie shot Eden a wary look.

"I'm not telling anyone, if that's your concern," Eden said evenly.

"It is a concern, yes." Ottilie straightened. "In a way, that's why I'm here. I have a deal."

"We don't need any deal from The Fixers," Eden said. "You can't do anything to us anymore."

Michelle shot her a warning look.

"If you're alluding to the NDAs, we already know," Ottilie said. "But Mr. Snakepit overlooked one thing."

"You're bluffing!" Eden shot back. "What thing?"

"No denial it was Mr. Snakepit, I see," Ottilie noted conversationally.

At Eden's horrified look, Ottilie waved her hand. "Oh, it was a short suspects list, and he's recently quit, so you didn't exactly drop him in it. Much."

Michelle wished she could warn Eden; Ottilie was too sharp not to seize on any clue.

Eden's shocked expression suggested she'd just come to that conclusion.

"How did you know the NDAs were gone?" Michelle asked.

"Simple. I asked myself what would be the most destructive thing a staff unhappy with new management could do, short of leaking cases. I looked. Sure enough, the NDAs were missing. Same at the lawyers' office. So I suppose those aggrieved by The Fixers now feel free to do anything they want?"

"They can," Michelle taunted.

"Really?" Ottilie reached into a large leather bag beside her chair and pulled out a document. She handed it to Eden. "Recognize this?"

Eden glanced at it and then at Michelle. "It's my NDA—the Fixers' original paper copy. Aren't these supposed to be shredded after being scanned in?"

"That *is* the procedure, yes," Ottilie answered. "And if I'd been a regular assistant, I'd have followed that process. But I'm not, so I didn't. I've kept under lock and key the original of every nondisclosure agreement ever signed. I don't trust the cloud. I knew that if we ever were compromised, our most important weapon is the power to silence our enemies."

Michelle wanted to scream. Just *once*, she'd love to win against the board. Or, really, against Ottilie Zimmermann.

Ottilie retrieved Eden's NDA and slid it back into her bag. "Sorry to disappoint, but you're not bulletproof. My question is, would you like to be?" She clasped her fingers over her stomach, serene as ever.

Michelle frowned. Ottilie held all the cards. They had nothing to offer that she could want, surely? "Go on."

"I'm sure you're aware what's happening at work. We've lost a quarter of staff since the new CEO joined. Some departments are barely functioning. A few have shut down. I'm aware the remaining staff have taken sides and one faction wants Kensington stopped by any means necessary. I'm also aware a subset of that group wants to destroy The Fixers entirely."

"That doesn't bode well for you," Michelle said neutrally.

"No." Ottilie brushed invisible lint off her sensible tweed skirt. "One might think the solution is obvious: fire Kensington, steady the ship."

"Yes. Is there some reason that's not happening?"

"The problem with men with vast amounts of power and money is they become accustomed to being right. Or at least being told they're right. They don't take well to having their noses rubbed in it when they've made a catastrophic error. The board thought they were so smart replacing you with Kensington," Ottilie said, eying Michelle. "The perfect solution."

"I'll bet."

"They didn't listen to my dissenting view, even though I'm the only one on the board who has had to deal with Kensington as a client and often saw her blow into your office and offload her grievances. The board saw only the polished politician."

"They must see the truth now?" Michelle asked. "All those resignations?"

"They're in denial and don't want to admit how wrong they were. They've informed me I'm exaggerating how bad she is because I voted against her hiring. They feel the staff who quit are being petulant and are easily replaced. The latter point is especially false. The espionage team and Mr. Snakepit had unique, advanced skills." Ottilie sighed. "But what would I know?"

Michelle eyed her curiously. "How do we come into this?"

"I wish to retire in peace. I've made a request for early retirement, but the board is refusing to allow it while such uncertainty remains. Yet, they are also refusing to get rid of the rogue element causing that uncertainty. This is *not* acceptable." Ottilie's eyes sharpened.

"Wait, you want *us* to get rid of Kensington?" Michelle asked incredulously.

"No. It's too late anyway. Our star employees are gone for good. It will take forever to headhunt decent replacements. By then, even more staff will have left. The end is so close, but the board willfully refuses to see it. I feel like Cassandra of Greek mythology, warning of a disaster but never believed."

"How do you see it ending?" Eden asked, leaning in. "I have a feeling you'd know better than anyone else."

"Of course I do. There are multiple possible outcomes. I've analyzed them all in detail. It's what I used to do at the CIA after I left field work. I was their best analyst." Ottilie's expression became distant. "I could predict outcomes so accurately that it scared even me. I ended up running my department, I was so good. Those were the days—powerful people actually heeding my warnings."

"Well, we're listening," Michelle said. "What will happen?"

"All right: If I do nothing, in the very near future someone within The Fixers is going to become so enraged by Kensington—if they aren't already—that they will decide to destroy the organization in an explosive and public way. The anger is palpable. It's a powder keg. And the threat is only going to get worse now that a rumor's spread that the NDAs have been wiped."

That was public knowledge?

"Yes," Ottilie said, "word is out. The end will be soon. It'll be a volcanic eruption that will take down everyone. Every employee. Every board member, including me. There's only one solution that sees me left in peace in retirement on a beach sipping mai tais."

"I'm not coming back as CEO," Michelle said quickly. "Just in case that's your path to beach views and overpriced alcohol."

"Well, I don't deny that it was one of the many options I considered, but I knew you wouldn't return. Not now you're under such an ethical influence." Ottilie's words were faintly teasing as her eyes flitted from Michelle to Eden. "You're positively glowing. Both of you. Love is certainly quite a tonic."

Michelle didn't bite on that one. *Always fishing.*

"Let me guess: no more migraines?" Ottilie prodded again. She at least looked genuinely pleased by the idea.

"No," Michelle said. "I'd suggest you take the same medicine—a complete break from working with bastards. Except, you're in deep with them. In fact, you're at the pointy part of reaping what you sow."

"Well, about that? I'll pass." Ottilie shook her head. "I plan to not be around for it. That's where you two come in. While the public destruction of The Fixers is inevitable and I will be powerless to stop it, I'm a firm believer in making lemonade from lemons. That only works if I get in first. So, I've concluded that the best outcome for me is to mastermind a controlled demolition of my organization. I would therefore be in charge of how and who and what gets exposed in a way that protects me and still placates The Fixers' angriest elements. You will assist me with this."

"We will?" Eden cocked an eyebrow. "You've just decided for us?"

"Suddenly *now* you're coy about exposing The Fixers?" Ottilie gave a soft snort. "My dear, you don't have to like it, but our interests align perfectly. Why fight it?"

"We can't expose The Fixers," Michelle broke in. "No one can get access to the full client database. Although I'm sure you know that."

"I know. And even if someone did have the full list of clients, it wouldn't do much good. There's no proof. It's just a list of names and actions requested. It'd be easy for every client to claim it was lies and to threaten expensive lawyers for such an outrageous suggestion. Go after one rich, dangerous individual and it's a risk a newspaper publisher *might* take. Go after a *thousand*? All at once? No one would ever dare print it."

Michelle's heart stopped at the words. She was right.

Eden's face radiated disappointment as she clearly realized it too.

"Okay," Michelle said, "how can you do a controlled demolition of The Fixers if no one will publish the client list—which no one has access to, anyway?"

"I said no one will publish it *without proof*. And I never said I didn't have access to our client list; it's just different than the one Cybersecurity has locked away." Ottilie waved in the direction of the locked cabinet in the entryway. "I brought the client list and proof."

"What proof?" Michelle asked.

"I told you there's a camera above the CEO's desk. There's a microphone in your phone too, which bypasses the white-noise dampening tech in your office and records everything said in there. Who do you suppose downloaded, synced, and backed up the recordings to a data disk each night for years? I've brought you copies of all the CEO/client meeting video footage. You will find powerful and famous people sitting in the visitor's chair asking for reprehensible things. Their faces are visible. Voices are clear. Proof undeniable."

"Oh," Eden gasped. "Wow."

Wow indeed. Ottilie truly had thought of everything.

"You can choose which cases to release." Ottilie looked at Eden. "You might, for example, not include the client who hired you to remove Francine Wilson as mayor of Wingapo."

"Yeah," Eden said. "I don't think that case should be lumped in with evil executives skyrocketing cancer drug prices."

"There, see?" Ottilie said. "You can weed out the cases you deem to be…innocent." She turned to Michelle. "You should know the Ayers case is in there too—the client asking us to destroy her career."

Michelle inhaled. She wasn't sure she could bear watching that footage.

"I know this is a lot to digest. I'll leave the footage here as a sign of good faith."

"I don't get it," Eden said. "How does this help you? Any of it?"

"That's where the NDAs come in. If you do right by me, I'll make sure no one finds out I have them. The Fixers board can never sue you."

"What does 'doing right by you' entail?" Michelle asked carefully.

"When this is out in the world, the media will demand to know who ran the board. I don't want to read my name *anywhere* on that list. I've only ever been some sweet, clueless CEO's assistant who retired shortly before any of this sordid business came out. I am *not* a former board member."

Michelle snorted. "You? Sweet and clueless?"

"You know I can pull that off. Do not test me. And do *not* force me to deliver your NDAs to the board. I will if you out me."

"Let me get this straight," Eden began, "we're supposed to let you off the hook for everything, in exchange for receiving enough dirt to expose The Fixers? But *we* do all the risky stuff and put our necks on the line to implement your secret plan?"

"Yes." Ottilie eyed her.

"Won't the other board members reveal there was a fifth if they get named?"

"No. We have only one code: no one names anyone on the board, *ever*. They also know I have enough dirt on them to ensure they'll never cross me. I can make life much worse for them if they put me in the crosshairs." She smiled angelically. "I'm quite sure they'll be reasonable. So…do we have a deal?"

"I don't like you getting away with everything," Eden said. "You don't even feel bad about it."

"I fought for things to be better," Ottilie said. "Not always, but often. I won every now and then. I refuse to feel bad for not doing better than my best. And I refuse to feel bad for not feeling worse."

"I find it hard to believe you have a conscience at all," Eden said quietly. "How can I believe that?"

"It matters to you that much?" Ottilie asked. "Me feeling bad about my role in The Fixers?"

"If we're letting you get away with all this, then I need to know you're not like them."

"An unethical monster?" Ottilie's lips curled. "Well, on that note, I did bring you a gift. It's been playing on my mind for some time to give it to you because one thing never sat right with me." She reached into her bag, pulled out a document and handed it to Eden. "I have contacts everywhere. I looked into someone for you."

Eden examined the document and frowned. "This is about some old Ponzi property scheme in Maryland? It was in the news when I was a kid."

"Yes—now read the director's list."

Eden blinked. "Francine Wilson? *She* was an original director?"

"Yes. Briefly. That's where she got her startup money to get into property. She cashed out early before there was a whiff of scandal and bribed everyone to bury her name. She evaded prosecutors masterfully. She was smart, but not smart enough, since this document remains. I thought you might appreciate finally being able to beat your old enemy."

"Oh goddess."

"I'm giving you this even if you don't take my deal," Ottilie said. "I don't approve of what happened. I met Sharpe on the day of the boardroom meeting. He was terrifying. A huge brute like that attacking you because Wilson wanted our attention? *Unacceptable*. And frankly, I don't like bullies."

That was rich, given that all The Fixers seemed to do was bully people into doing whatever their clients wanted. Michelle shot her a disbelieving look.

"Yes," Ottilie said with an unguarded flash of irritation, "I'm *well* aware of how that sounds. But I do have a line." Her glare was withering. "Anyone who works as an agent at the CIA or FBI receives an advanced degree in hypocrisy and denial. We have to learn how to cope with doing morally uncomfortable things just to survive. I did. You did. A person *can* work for a problematic organization and still have ethical standards."

She had her there. With a soft sigh, Michelle nodded. "Fine."

Ottilie glanced at Eden. "I hope that answers your question, Ms. Lawless. As to whether I have a conscience or ethics."

Eden was still staring at the document.

"Will you use that?" Michelle asked her.

"Do slugs have four noses?" Eden replied in wonder.

Michelle and Ottilie peered at each other.

"Do they?" Ottilie finally asked.

"Yes!" Eden shook her head. "You two really need to get out into nature more."

"No argument here," Ottilie said. "Roll on, retirement. Hello nature and mai tais. Now, do we have a deal?"

Michelle saw agreement in Eden's eyes.

Good. It was better to sink four out of five board members than none. It wasn't as if they had many other options.

"Yes," Michelle said.

"Excellent. My burner phone's number is with the files. We'll discuss a release schedule that suits me best. I'll see myself out." She rose and then paused, meeting Michelle's eye. "By the way, I found your grandmother to be a complete delight. Please give her my best wishes. If circumstances were different, it would be my pleasure to call on her again. Unfortunately, I doubt I'll be in the US much in the not-too-distant future."

With that, she left.

Chapter 25
Saddest, Loneliest Woman

Ten days later, Michelle lay Eden down in bed and kissed every part of her. She brought her to the edge twice before allowing her to cross and then started all over again. She repeated the process for an hour before Eden whispered, "Hey, honey? I think we should talk."

Michelle didn't want to believe she meant that and trailed her lips back up to Eden's breasts, which she lavished with kisses.

"Michelle. I need you to stop."

With a sigh, Michelle did and flopped over onto her back, flinging an arm across her eyes. "I thought you were having fun."

"Oh, I was. Until I noticed you'd stopped letting me touch you. I started wondering why." Eden curled into her side. "Look at me?"

Michelle wished she could pretend not to hear that too.

"Please?"

With an even heartier sigh, she removed her arm and met Eden's worried expression. "What?"

"You're worthy of being loved too," Eden said. "I know sometimes you go through these dark patches where you seem to think anyone caring about you is too much. Like it feels wrong or undeserved. I don't know what's triggered it this time, but—"

"I watched the video," Michelle said, tone flat. "Well, I watched hundreds of them. And I found the one asking how much it would cost to ruin Catherine's career. It brought back bitter memories."

"Ah." Eden snuggled closer. "You weren't the CEO then, though. You didn't agree to take that case."

"But if I had been, I'd have accepted it. It didn't stand out as being special. I thought nothing of it when they handed the case to me to fulfill."

Eden stroked her arm. "Will you tell me what happened?"

Could she? Michelle's heart started thudding at the thought of Eden knowing the whole, ugly truth. "I made a series of terrible decisions."

"I figured. You hate yourself for them, even a decade later."

"Yes." Michelle's stomach knotted. "I wish I could change many things in my life, but none more than that."

"Please tell me?"

There was something in her tone, a gentle acceptance, that finally made Michelle open up about her worst mistake. And so she told Eden everything. About how the FBI had manipulated her into sleeping with a neo-Nazi. Her parents' shame. The relief at Alberto's acceptance of it and his getting her an interview at The Fixers. She spoke of falling for her target, how impressed she'd been by Ayers. How it was the first time she'd even considered being with a woman.

Michelle grimaced as she laid out Alberto's fury, turning her into an object of ridicule at work. How vulnerable and humiliated she'd been. And...finally...she spoke of her cowardice and betrayal.

Lastly, she told Eden the one thing she'd never faced, so great was her shame. What happened immediately after the Ayers story started unraveling on all the networks.

"I forced myself to sit in the office at work, watching the broadcast streams in full view, volume up high, so there was no mistaking what was on." Michelle ground out the next words. "And then I laughed."

"You *laughed*." Eden's shoulders sank.

"Long and loud." Michelle swallowed. "Until I overheard someone call me 'one cold bitch.'"

"That was your aim," Eden guessed, eyes sad.

"Yes. Then I slipped out, went home, and curled into a ball. Sometimes I think I stayed in that ball for years." She inhaled. "Later, I heard a new rumor. I wasn't weak or soft; I was a stone-cold psycho. Not long after that, I was promoted. And each day, I went to work like I hadn't just destroyed a decent woman who'd done nothing more than have the misfortune to love me."

"Oh goddess." Eden lay her head on Michelle's stomach, and Michelle could feel the wetness of tears. "How awful."

Awful? My shameful behavior towards Catherine? Michelle inhaled sharply.

Eden added, "All of it is awful. How devastated she must have been. How broken you were."

"I couldn't show anyone how I felt, of course," Michelle admitted. "And after that, it became easy to pretend nothing affected me because I was in a dark hole that was getting deeper. I'd lost my friends and family. Hannah moved in, which probably saved my life because by then, I had little interest in getting out of bed or eating. I did both for her sake. But I was indifferent to staying alive. I discovered rage rooms, and they stopped me from doing anything too drastic. It was freeing to be able smash every part of me and scream at the universe."

"I'm sorry," Eden whispered.

"Don't feel sorry for me. The worst part is how unnecessary it was," Michelle said bitterly. "There were so many other ways I could have prevented Catherine Ayers from writing stories the client hated. I didn't intend to destroy her, but that's irrelevant because ultimately, I did. I panicked and *let it happen*. That was *me*. I can't make excuses. And, until quite recently, one of the hardest things for me to do is… laugh." Michelle closed her eyes. "You were right all along about me. I've done such evil. I suppose that's who I am at my core."

"Michelle," Eden said softly. "Evil people don't have regrets. They're glad about what they've done. Proud. They don't torment themselves for years. Yes, of course it was terrible what you did, but it wasn't your plan, and it's in the past. You wouldn't do it again—"

"Of course not!" Michelle said, eyes flashing.

"—And I'm pretty sure you'd have fixed it if you could."

"Actually, I tried. I stumbled across Catherine in Iowa. I gave her a huge story. It was an important one too. It was vital she ran it."

"Okay? That's good, right?"

"Except, the story mattered more than anything else—including how much I wished I could make things right between us."

"I don't understand."

"If I'd approached Catherine in a friendly way, she'd have assumed I was trying to schmooze her again. Trick her. I couldn't allow that story to be dismissed because she didn't trust me. I played the role she *could* trust: I was a bitch." Bile rose at the reminder of Catherine's wounded expression.

"Oh hell." Eden frowned. "Did she run your story?"

"Yes and no. She gave it to Lauren King, her fiancée at the time. It proved she didn't want anything from me. Not even a story that would boost her career into the stratosphere. Or at least return it to where it should have been if not for me." Michelle's lips tightened.

"Maybe she wanted her fiancée to have a big break more than she wanted to big-note herself?"

"But I wanted to help *Catherine*. Not some stranger. I wanted to give it to *her*."

"It doesn't sound like she saw it the way you did. As a gift and an apology," Eden said gently.

"No. Well. It's done now." Michelle grimaced. "These days, I take the view that I did the best I could to make a few things right, and I hope Catherine's okay now. As well as she can be, anyway."

"Would you like to know?" Eden asked. "Remember when I called her up? I asked if she wanted me to reveal to the world what The Fixers had done to her. I offered to keep out the part about her relationship with you. I'd proposed, though, to name you as the reason her career had been destroyed."

"You were going to name me?" Michelle asked, the betrayal stinging.

"I was pretty mad. I'd only just discovered the truth of what The Fixers had done. I didn't know the real story behind Ayers's case, just that you'd ruined her in a sting. So that was the offer I made to her. Ayers would go from a journalist who ran a fake story to a journalist targeted in a calculated plot to ruin her. She'd have everything to gain. And do you know what she said?"

Michelle's heart thundered in her ears. "I imagine it wasn't pretty."

"She said: 'No thanks. I've moved on. I'm happy now. My wife tells me that the last time they met, Michelle was the 'saddest, loneliest woman' she'd ever seen. Maybe one day she'll find peace and happiness. I'm at a point now where I truly hope she does.'"

The silence that followed sounded to Michelle's ears like a bomb going off. She drew in a shocked, sharp breath and tried to calm herself. Her heart seemed to be quivering, like glass at the moment before it shatters.

"Michelle?"

She tried to breathe but couldn't seem to get enough air. Her body was shaking hard enough to break into pieces.

Arms gathered Michelle up and pressed her into warmth, but she couldn't make sense of anything at that moment.

"Michelle? You're okay."

I'm not. I haven't been okay for a long, long time.

Any sadness Michelle ever felt, any despair, she had wrapped up in a tight, little knot inside herself. Emotion couldn't hurt her. She wouldn't let it. If anything threatened her equilibrium, she had her rage room. A way not to think about it.

Except at this moment, all that suppressed sadness and pain was unknotting itself. Michelle gasped in fear. *No! No, no, no. I can't face this. I can't. I'm not strong enough.*

She saw the neo-Nazi standing over her. Naked. Scratching the three-day growth on his weak chin and eyeballing her, his sick little smirk on her. "On your back," he'd said. As if she were nothing.

Michelle had disassociated that day. Her brain had drifted away so as not to think about the awfulness. The knot had tightened, crushing any emotional leakage. And…she'd gotten on her back.

Her mother's disgusted look filled her mind. From when Michelle had found her holding the newspaper photo linking Michelle and *him*. "You're no daughter of mine."

And yet, Michelle could also remember so clearly, when she was a child, her mother smiling and saying, "I'll always love you, my beautiful girl," while affectionately stroking her hair. The sensation of her hair being caressed had always made her feel safe and loved.

Until she remembered her mother's lesson. Love was conditional.

The knot protecting her loosened further, threatening chaos and pain. Michelle trembled. Whimpered.

A hand was stroking her hair.

Don't do that. It reminds me of when…of Mom. Just don't.

Suddenly, she saw herself laughing at a computer screen, a forced, high-pitched jeer. Catherine's horrified face and tight-lipped expression was framed on screen amid a media storm. Braying questions. "No comment," Catherine ground out, eyes wild, looking cornered.

I did that to her. I loved her and still did that.

Love is conditional.

You're no daughter of mine.

On your back.

Michelle curled up into a tight ball, tighter than tight could be.

"Hey, honey? Stay with me," a soft voice whispered in her ear. Michelle's hair was gently stroked. "I've got you. You're safe."

How can I be safe? I never have been before.

A sob filled her, and try as she might, she couldn't stop it. It burst out as the knot in her chest exploded. Michelle turned into her pillow and buried her face in it. A tsunami had overtaken her. It was raw and humiliating. She had no control.

Michelle cried so hard, her ribs began to throb. Her throat ached as if it had forgotten how to cry or didn't know how. Her skin felt too tight.

That warm arm soothed her back as Michelle wept.

"Let it out, honey," Eden whispered. "It's been a long time bottled up. It's okay."

Michelle could smell her. Eden's distinctive scent mixed with her vegan lemon sage shampoo was more reassuring than her words. How could any of this ever be *okay*?

God, Michelle had deliberately and methodically fucked over Catherine Ayers, broken her. And the woman felt sorry for *her*.

She rolled to her side, and Eden slid in behind, spooning her. She was stroking Michelle's hair again.

Don't, Michelle wanted to say. *I hate that. It reminds me.*
Except…that wasn't the reason.
It hurts too much if you don't mean it.
Love is conditional.
Eden's fingers shifted to Michelle's cheek. So tender.
Don't be tender or I'll never stop crying.
"Please tell me what just happened?" Eden asked quietly.
Where to start?
"Catherine didn't want vengeance," Michelle rasped out. "Just hoped I'd be happy one day too. What the hell am I supposed to do with that?"

Eden said nothing for a moment. "I'm starting to think you'd prefer it if Catherine had wanted you destroyed. That way, you'd feel justice had been served. But now you'll always feel you didn't make amends and can never move on."

"Yes," Michelle said with vehemence. "I wish she'd taken your offer."

"Even though everyone in your life, in your family, would learn about The Fixers? How your company hurt people for profit?" Eden asked gently.

"Yes."

"Your safta would find out the truth too."

Michelle rubbed her swollen eyes. "I know."

Eden hesitated. "After I spoke to Catherine, I thought about what she'd said. I pictured your sweet safta's face on learning you did awful things. I worried it would break her. And I worried that would break you. That's far too much breaking for my liking."

Stroking Michelle's arm, Eden continued, "After that, I didn't offer anyone else exposure of The Fixers or you, no matter how hurt or angry I was." Eden sighed. "Which makes me soft, I guess. Mom would be appalled if she knew I'd put my feelings ahead of fixing the world. But…now I think some things are more important."

Michelle leaned over to her bedside table and snagged some tissues. She mopped up the mess she'd made of herself and then turned to meet Eden's eye. "I've had enough. No more."

"No more what?" Eden asked in surprise.

"You were right. No more hating myself for walking past evil and not fixing it. No more."

"What does that mean?"

"No. More. Fixers."

"I thought we'd already agreed to expose them?" Eden asked slowly.

"We had. And it would have ended up with you doing all the upfront work—dealing with the reporters—and me supporting you behind the scenes. Safe in the shadows." Fury filled her. "Well, no more. This is my mess. I'm going to fix it. I'm done being a coward. Done taking the careful, safe approach. And I'm done living in secrets." Michelle drew in a shuddering breath. "I never deserved for Catherine to treat me with compassion. I know that. But I *can* make things better."

"Oh, Michelle." Eden's eyes were bright and pleased.

Michelle tilted her head. "I've also decided what to do next. Even though it'll be as much fun as performing CPR on a cactus."

"Oddly specific but okay." Eden grinned. "We're going to do this!"

"*I'm* going to do it," Michelle corrected gently. "I need to be the one to take a stand and break The Fixers. Of course, I'd never say no to your moral support while I do."

"Always! You never need to ask. I've got your back."

"Yes," Michelle murmured softly. "That's one of the reasons I love you."

Oh! She certainly hadn't meant to reveal that. Not like this. Well, perhaps it was to be expected. Michelle had no more secrets left in her.

"You do?" Eden squeaked in a way so adorably uncool that her cheeks turned bright red.

"Mmm, yes," Michelle declared with complete conviction. "Nicely done, by the way. Complete takeover of your former archnemesis. You win."

"Oh please," Eden said, with a smile so broad it lit her whole face. "It's a little embarrassing how much I was in love with you *while* you were my archnemesis."

Michelle laughed, a warm glow flooding her. "No, you're quite right," she teased. "That *is* embarrassing."

Eden playfully poked her in the ribs. "Rude."

Michelle chuckled before gathering Eden in her arms and kissing her soundly.

Chapter 26

Writing Wrongs

"This was a terrible idea," Michelle announced as they sat in her parked Audi. She glanced up at the sleek DC apartment building in front of them. Black glass made it look even more forbidding. She scowled.

"No, it was a genius idea," Eden said. "*Your* genius idea. Come on." She reached for Michelle's hand and squeezed. "They're waiting for us. I'll be right there with you. It'll be fine."

"Was Lauren skeptical when you made contact? I mean, there's a reason I had to get you to make the call; I'm pretty sure she'd have hung up on me. Last time I saw them, I wasn't polite."

"At first, she was suspicious, but I told her a bit about why you wanted to see them. She called me back after googling me. Says I'm too good for you." Eden frowned. "She's wrong, of course."

"Actually, I'd say that's something Ms. King and I agree on."

"I told her she hadn't even met you yet. The *real* you. Lauren promised to keep an open mind."

Michelle gave her a skeptical look. "You got Lauren King to keep an open mind about me? I swear every time I've met her, she's been three seconds away from ripping my head off."

"That's because you hurt the woman she loves. I get where she's coming from. I'd be pretty mad if someone had hurt you. Anyway, she seems nice enough when she's not in protect-the-queen mode. Now, quit stalling. I'll get the files and meet up with you in a sec."

Michelle knocked on the door to Catherine and Lauren's apartment, nerves making her palms slick. The reporters had both earned reputations for fearlessness at their respective newspapers. Michelle was greatly relieved Catherine had professional respect once more.

The door was answered by Lauren—tall and athletic, with brown hair and watchful eyes—who flicked a glance at Michelle, then looked past her. "Where's your publicist?"

She frowned. "Eden isn't a publicist. And she's grabbing some material we need from the car."

Lauren's eyebrow lifted. "Well, she does a good job at spinning this incredible tale about how you aren't the woman we thought you were." She stepped back. "Catherine's on the balcony. This way."

Lauren led her through a sleek, modern lounge to French doors.

Michelle's heart tightened at the sight of Catherine Ayers, legs stretched out on a lounge chair, a glass of red wine in one hand. She wore faded jeans and a crisp, white button-up under a navy blazer. She was exactly as Michelle remembered her. And yet...not. Older and stiller.

Still so very beautiful. Michelle's heart did its customary lurch of regret and shame. She no longer felt the pull of desire because the guilt was so overwhelming, it drowned everything else out. Besides, her body only seemed to want Eden these days.

"Sit," Lauren waved at an empty lounge chair beside Catherine's. "Drink?"

"No." Michelle swallowed. "Thanks."

"I'll go see if your publicist needs a hand," King said lightly, then disappeared.

"When Lauren said you were coming," Catherine said quietly once she was gone, "I thought she was crazy to allow you here. But she's no fool. She thinks I should hear you out."

"Thank you for seeing me."

Catherine inclined her head. "Lauren tells me you're bringing down The Fixers. You and Eden Lawless."

"No," Michelle said quickly. "Not Eden. Can you leave her out of this?"

"Oh?"

"If there's any blowback, I want it only on me. This is my plan, my doing. If anyone asks if she's your source—and she will be the prime suspect—can you outright say she's not, rather than saying you don't reveal confidential sources?"

"I haven't said yes to the story yet," Catherine said, eyes cool.

"Please, just say yes to that." Michelle sounded pleading. *Ugh*.

"All right." Catherine swirled the wine in her glass. "So...destroying The Fixers: Why? And why now?"

"It's time."

"I'd argue it was time a decade ago."

"Yes. And it was time twenty-seven years ago when the organization was founded. But now I have both the means and the will to do it."

"The *will*." Catherine looked at her properly for the first time, and those still, gray eyes were unsettling. "What's changed?"

"I have."

"Conscience gotten the better of you? Or is it Eden Lawless? I understand she's a social justice advocate. Her mother's River Lawless, the renowned ecowarrior."

Michelle looked at her hands. "Yes."

"So it's a bit hard to do evil when it disappoints your girlfriend?" Catherine suggested dryly.

The biting questions were putting Michelle on edge. She wasn't looking for a fight. "Can we talk about the story now?"

Catherine's gaze sharpened. "You are different, aren't you? Last time we met, you were so...vile."

"I was. I wanted you to do the MediCache story. I was afraid you'd assume I was up to something if I was friendly or charming."

"The way you were friendly and charming when we first met. When you befriended me and then destroyed me."

"Yes," Michelle admitted quietly, guilt churning away hard enough to make butter. "Like that. I didn't want you to feel schmoozed. The MediCache story mattered too much. If it hadn't been run, no one could have stopped the monster that tech would have become."

"That's true." Catherine sighed. "I didn't want to dredge up any of this again. I've moved on. Life's good. I'm content. But Lauren says closure might be a good thing."

"Oh." Michelle sneaked a look at her. Was Catherine still struggling over this?

"Not closure for me." Catherine's look was cutting. "For you. Eden told Lauren your pain and regret prevents you from healing. I found that a little hard to believe. I've never seen a shred of remorse from you. I decided I'd like to see for myself."

"I suppose I deserve that," Michelle said tartly. "Being scrutinized like a museum exhibit. You can laugh at me for being a mess for what I did."

Inhaling sharply, Catherine said, "You're a mess?"

Michelle glared at her, then sagged. "I've regretted what I did to you every day since it happened."

"Well, that makes *everything* all right." Catherine's eyes were half-lidded. "You disappeared. I tore everything apart trying to find you, but you were a ghost. And you ruined me." Her jaw was tight.

"I know." *I ruined myself.*

"I don't understand why. If you cared for me even a little, you wouldn't have. So, my only conclusion is…" She drew in a careful breath. "You didn't care for me at all."

There was a question there. Michelle debated how to answer. It would be so easy to lie, then move on. Hand over the story. Walk away. But…Michelle was done with secrets, and Catherine deserved more than a lie.

"I cared," she said, voice low. "I cared more than was sensible. I cared so much my husband noticed and began wreaking revenge. I cared so much, I became a laughingstock at work. And I cared so much, I panicked and ruined you just to make it all stop. It did. Everything stopped after that." Michelle stared at her fingers, which had become tight tangles.

"Did you…love me?" Catherine asked, expression tight. "Given the cruelty of what you did, I'm thinking no. But Lauren holds a different view."

"I…" *Don't ask me that. Please don't.* "Did." Shame filled Michelle anew, swamping every part of her body. "It wasn't a game, seducing you. I know I said it was, but I'd only intended to befriend you. I failed so completely to keep my attraction at bay. I…fell for you."

There was a long pause. "You were promoted," Catherine finally said. "Baldoni told us that. Promoted for what you did to me. Were you proud of that step up, at least?"

Was she? Michelle's memory of those days, weeks, then months was just bleakness. Sadness. "No," she admitted. "I was honestly just glad when everyone left me alone. That's one upside to being CEO. No one wants to talk to you." Michelle finally met Catherine's eye. "It shouldn't have been that way. It was a terrible thing I did to you. I have no excuse."

"It was cruel," Catherine said, "but you acknowledge that. So are you here today offering The Fixers story in exchange for forgiveness?"

"What? How can I ask for forgiveness? You'd never give it anyway. Nor should you—I'm hardly deserving forgiveness. I'm just relieved to hear you're happy now. I'm hoping the pain from what I did has gone at least."

"I don't think that's possible. It's too deep."

Michelle's heart clenched. Her face fell. "Oh. I'm… Of course."

Catherine regarded her. "But I also meant what I told Eden: I hope you find peace. What you did had to have left a mark. And I don't just mean on me."

Tears filled her eyes, and Michelle snapped her head away. *God, why now?* Ever since she'd told her story to Eden, she'd been unable to stop crying.

Catherine stared, her surprise clear. "You really are different."

An emotional wreck, she probably meant. "You're mocking me," Michelle snapped. "Maybe we should talk about bringing down The Fixers instead. Now that we've covered all my malfunctions."

"Stephanie?"

It took a moment to register that Catherine had used her undercover name, the one Michelle had used with her. "Why would you call me that?"

"I wanted to see if any of her remains in you."

"Her feelings were real. That's where similarities end."

Catherine studied her, then sighed. "I *wasn't* mocking you," she said quietly. "When you left…" She hesitated. "I didn't know anything could hurt like that. I'd never been in love before. You blindsided me. I was at a complete loss."

This time, Michelle couldn't hide the tears. They slipped from her eyes and down her cheeks. "I'm *so* sorry."

"For the first time in years," Catherine said quietly, "I believe you."

A noise behind made them turn. Eden was standing beside Lauren, her gaze worried as she took in Michelle's tear-streaked face.

"Catherine," Lauren said with a sigh, "you weren't supposed to make her cry."

Eden's expression shifted to anger at the flippant remark.

"No," Michelle intervened tiredly. "She didn't. I'm just apparently not cut out for this."

"Apologies?" Lauren asked sweetly.

Eden dug into her pocket and thrust a tissue Michelle's way. She glared at Lauren. "Don't."

"It's fine, Eden." Michelle wiped her eyes, suddenly feeling far too old. "I'm discovering that facing my younger, stupider self is a messier business than I realized."

Eden's hackles went down.

Lauren's expression softened. "Look, sorry," she told Eden. "This is just hard." She waved in Michelle's direction. "Your girlfriend seriously hurt my wife. That makes me want to bawl her out for a bit…but I can also see she got in first."

Great. My self-loathing is apparently visible from outer space. "For the record, I'm highly effective at whatever task I set myself. Up to and including beating myself up," Michelle said dryly.

"I'd say, 'Good,'" Lauren said conversationally, "but that's a bit rude."

"Just a bit." Eden glared and folded her arms.

"Okay." Lauren looked faintly regretful. "It's just—I *really* wish I'd thrown my panda at her at the State Fair."

"You…what?" Eden blinked.

Catherine snorted and it sounded like…laughter?

And suddenly, Michelle couldn't stop her own huff of laughter. She could picture it, Lauren hurling that enormous soft toy she'd clearly won. Michelle absolutely would have deserved it for being a complete ass to both women that day. "Well, I'm quite sure you would have hit me accurately. Baseball star, wasn't it?"

"Softball. As you well know. And damned straight," Lauren confirmed with satisfaction. "Right between the eyes."

"So violent," Michelle shot back, but her lips twitched in amusement. "I should have warned you, Eden. Ms. King has this cowgirl hick streak a mile wide."

"Uh…huh," Eden said, glancing among them all uncertainly.

Catherine smiled. "Eden, I hear you're from a small town in Maryland. Do I want to know how you and Michelle wound up together, given she likes to pretend anyone outside of DC is a yokel?" There was humor in her tone now, and the dark wariness seemed to have shifted from her eyes.

"Oh, well, funny story." Eden bounced on the balls of her feet, grinning. "First, Michelle hired me. Then I found out she ran an evil empire—as you do. I decided to bring it down. She declared war. A thug beat me up—not one of hers—and I went to Michelle's place for help. I never left. And here we are." She beamed.

Silence fell. Lauren and Catherine stared at her in shock, which made Michelle bite back a laugh.

"Oh my God!" Lauren exclaimed. "Are you two *enemies-to-lovers* too? That is such a lesbian thing! I planned my revenge on Catherine in *minute* detail when I worked with her. There was this whole Craigslist thing."

"Oh?" Eden's eyebrows shot up in interest. "What'd you do?"

"I don't think they need to hear all this," Catherine tried in vain.

"I did so much!" Lauren laughed. "And she threatened to get my car clamped a bunch of times, which was so rude! It's a collectible! A 1970 Chevrolet Chevelle SS."

"Really? What color?" Eden's eyes lit up in fascination. "And Michelle got my van towed regularly. It was like her party trick, she did it so often."

Michelle protested, "Excuse me, *context*! We were at war!"

"Blue!" Lauren exclaimed, ignoring Michelle's interruption. "Hotted up for drifting and car chases."

"I can confirm," Catherine said, shuddering. "Unfortunately."

"Now, see, I drive a rainbow," Eden said happily. "A former FedEx van in every color under the sun. Gloria drives like a dopey Smurf."

"Really?" Lauren laughed. "I'd love to see that. Is Gloria outside? Can I see her from here?" She leaned over the balcony railing.

"*I* drove today," Michelle cut in. "I'd never be caught dead in such a ridiculous contraption."

"You sound like Catherine," Lauren retorted before stopping sharply. "*Oh.* I mean…" She glanced to her wife, expression stricken. "I'm not comparing you two."

"It's fine," Catherine said. "Michelle always did have refined taste. She was the one who hooked me on luxury European cars."

"You did?" Eden asked in surprise.

Catherine nodded at the same time Michelle said, "Yes."

An uncomfortable silence fell into this odd place they found themselves—somewhere between old wounds and comfortable familiarity. Okay, so they weren't there yet. Wherever *there* was.

"How do you plan to bring down The Fixers?" Catherine asked, pivoting to a safer topic. "Because if you're planning to give me a bunch of files, I'm going to decline. Not just because such things are easily faked, but because as a victim of The Fixers, I'd be seen as biased. Unless there is iron-clad proof—actual confessions, for example—I can't see how I can get around either of those things."

Eden turned to the door. "Wait one sec." A moment later, she returned, pushing the flatbed cart and cabinet that Ottilie had left them. "On here are several thousand disks containing video files. The footage shows clients meeting The Fixers' CEO. You'll see them ask for what they want done and negotiate a fee for it."

"Holy shit," Lauren sputtered.

"Well." Catherine blinked. "That solves both problems. That really is a confession." She glanced at Michelle. "Are *you* in any of this footage?"

"Not in any identifiable way. All video is shot from above and over the shoulder of the various CEOs. My voice is audible in some files, asking questions of clients, but unless you knew it was me…" Michelle paused. *Would* Catherine name her to the world?

"Are you requesting anonymity, or are you prepared to go on the record publicly?" Catherine asked, divining her thoughts.

"That's up to you." Michelle had decided Catherine could take her pound of flesh if she wanted. "If that's what justice looks like to you, then so be it."

Eden shot her a worried look.

"Your preference," Catherine said, "would be that you're not named, though, correct?"

"I…" Michelle tried to explain how she felt. "I want whatever makes you feel better. If you choose to protect my identity, I'll be glad. I won't deserve it, but, yes, I'll be grateful. If you choose to name me as your source, I'll see it as you punishing me for my past behavior. And that, in its own way, has a degree of satisfaction for me too."

"To have legs, my story will need quotes from someone in management," Catherine said.

"I have included with the files a written Q&A interview with me. It lays out how The Fixers are run, the four members of the board, previous CEOs, how clients find us, and so on. It'd be up to you whether you use my name on those quotes or not."

"It would be a far stronger story with a named source," Lauren argued.

"I'm sure that's true." Michelle rose. "I'm going to leave the decision to you." She glanced at Eden. "Let's go."

"Wait." Catherine held up a hand.

Michelle stopped.

Catherine's jaw worked for a long moment. "It took a lot for you to come here."

Michelle waited for the *but*.

"Thank you."

Oh. Michelle studied Catherine in surprise. "Thank Eden. She convinced me to get out of the car today," she joked stiffly.

Eden pinned a worried gaze on Catherine. "What will you do? Will you name Michelle—hurt her—because she hurt you?"

"That would be fitting, wouldn't it?" Catherine said neutrally.

"Yes," Michelle said. "It would."

"You could have brought me nothing but an apology, you know," Catherine said.

"But then would you have believed my sincerity?" Michelle asked.

Catherine fell silent for a moment. "I think I might have."

"Well, either way, it's an important story. Right up there with the last one I gave you." Michelle schooled from her tone any annoyance that Catherine had given that one away to Lauren.

"This will make a lot of powerful people furious," Catherine said thoughtfully. "Are you ready for that? If I name you, they'll come after you."

"The Fixers should be ended. I brought you the means to do it because I owe you. But I also know you're not going to be corrupted or scared off by the powerful people involved. And I believe that Ms. King would be the same—just in case you're planning on giving my story away again." Michelle straightened. "So that's everything."

"It is," Catherine said, expression intense. "Except for one thing: You asked if I'd ever forgive you. The answer is no. I never will."

Michelle swallowed. She'd known, of course. You don't ruin someone and expect them to ever get over it. But, obviously, based on her own reaction, a small part of her had hoped. She gave a nod of acceptance.

Eden's hand slipped into hers and gave a squeeze.

"But I won't forget you did this either." Catherine held her gaze. "So as of right now? I'll consider us even."

Michelle let out a relieved exhale. "Thank you. My contact details are included with the interview printout. If you need to check a fact or ask a follow-up question, I'll answer." She made it to the front door on less-than-steady legs.

Catherine nodded. "Okay. Thanks."

Shutting the apartment door behind them, Michelle headed to the elevator, feeling freer than she had in a long time. A crushing weight had lifted.

"How's it feel?" Eden asked, eyebrows knitting together. "Laying your ghosts to rest?"

"Did you know," Michelle murmured, "that enemies-to-lovers is a popular thing for lesbians?"

Eden's cheeks went bright red and she grinned. "Oh, yep. I know."

Chapter 27

A Beautiful Heart

Eden called it the lightness of Michelle. It was hard to put into words exactly, but the stiffness was gone from her lover—the rigidity in her back and the way she held herself so erect. The sharpness in Michelle's eyes, well *that* was still there. But, hey, Eden thought it was hot.

"You're staring again," Michelle noted without looking up from her phone. "Should I be worried?"

"Just happy for you." Eden snuggled closer. She'd discovered weeks ago that a balcony lounge chair could fit two. "You're so much less tightly wound since the whole 'Meet the ex' thing."

"'Meet the traumatized victim of my vicious scheming,' you mean."

"I'm sure even Catherine wouldn't categorize it as that anymore."

"Mmm." Michelle put down her phone. "She texted me earlier to tell me the story will be live this evening on the *Sentinel*'s website. Tomorrow for the print edition."

"Oh?" Eden sat up abruptly. "Did she say whether she'll be naming you?"

"No. She did not. Maybe she couldn't resist a *little* payback. Making me fret for weeks might be part of that, I suppose. I don't blame her."

"Or…you didn't ask?"

"Or...that." Michelle huffed. "That reminds me. I've been putting it off, but we have to tell my safta. If I'm going to be named, she needs to be prepared."

"Tell me what?" Hannah stuck her head in. "I heard my name. Are you two up to your schemes again?"

Michelle waved at the lounge chair beside them. "Join us?"

Hannah frowned. "All right, this sounds serious. What is it, bubbeleh?"

"You always wondered what my job entailed." Michelle consulted her watch. "In an hour and twelve minutes, the whole world will know."

Settling deeper onto her chair, Hannah said, "Okay. Tell me."

And so Michelle did. About the clients and their petty, evil, narcissistic demands. The awfulness of some of what they did—from cancer drug price-fixing to crushing a reporter's career.

"The reporter," Hannah said quietly. "That was the woman I saw you with? Years ago? The one you seemed close to."

"Yes. She's also who I've given this story to. She's breaking it tonight."

"You loved this reporter," Hannah said, expression inscrutable.

How does she know that? Eden wondered.

"Yes." Michelle's cheeks, even in the low light, went red.

Eden could feel her nervousness in the way Michelle's whole body tensed. Hannah's opinion meant a great deal to her.

"I see." Hannah looked thoughtful. "Well, that does fill in a few blanks. About why you're so self-destructive. When I moved in, I feared you were going to fade away to nothing. I was desperate to get you to agree to allow me to stay because I worried I'd be going to your funeral if I didn't."

"You moved in to help *me*?" Michelle's mouth fell open. "I was helping *you*! She waved at Hannah's bad hip. "With your mobility issues. You kept falling!"

"Well, I may have exaggerated a little. Yes, I'm a bit unsteady on my feet, but I wasn't too worried. You, though, I was terrified for. I think I moved in just in time too. I'm glad you told me about the journalist. I knew she meant something to you last time you mentioned her, but I'm glad I know."

Michelle rubbed her eyes. "Safta, I just told you about the evil my former organization does, and all you're focused on is a woman from nine years in my past."

"Because she's who upsets you most—what you did to her. Besides, the rest I knew already."

"What?" Eden blurted out at the same time as Michelle.

"Well." Hannah looked suddenly sheepish. "You may have noticed I'm a little nosy."

Michelle frowned. "I keep my paperwork—the sensitive content—under lock and key."

"Of course. But I worked out what Eden was doing in Wingapo by following the election there. That scavenger hunt? Suddenly the mayor's gone—a mayor expected to win? So crafty." She wagged a finger at Eden.

"Thank you." Eden grinned.

"After that, I thought about it. Obviously, someone had paid for the mayor to go. And if that's what happened, what if all your clients were people paying for difficult things to happen? Based on the secrecy and the fact your company gave you this apartment, these were rich and powerful people. One thing I know about rich and powerful people is that they usually aren't either of those due to having done the right thing. It would explain the migraines and stress if your company was expecting you to oversee unethical goings-on."

"How does that make you feel?" Michelle's fingers tightened in Eden's hand. "About me?"

"Sad. I blame the FBI," Hannah said with certainty.

Michelle laughed incredulously. "The FBI!"

"Oh yes," Hannah nodded. "They messed with your head so badly. They made you lose your spark. Your trust for people. When you left there, you were a shell of the warm granddaughter I'd always known, so full of hope. I can see you fell in with a bad crowd, doing more of the same. They took even more from you. I worried you'd be lost forever. The real you."

"This *is* the real me," Michelle said. "We're all the sum of our experiences."

"Dear child, the *real you* hums when you bake cookies with me. You smile. You laugh. You joke. None of these things has happened for years." Hannah glanced at Eden and back. "Until recently. Oh, I've missed you, bubbeleh. It's wonderful you've left those awful people behind and are finding your way back to yourself."

"You really don't hate me for working for them?" Michelle asked. "I *ran* the company, Safta."

"Oh, don't be silly. Of course you didn't. I mentioned I'm nosy? Well, I couldn't resist listening in on your conversation with Ottilie. Smart woman, that one. Sounds like she was the one running things. Oh, I found her fascinating. You know, we share a few things in common. And I'd love to see her crocheted chess pieces some time."

"Her…crocheted *chess pieces*?" Michelle stared.

"Oh yes. Doesn't that sound interesting? Anyway, I'm glad you took her deal. A good way to resolve this business is to put it out in the open and move on. Bright light scares away the cockroaches. They love to hide in shadows. You'll be rid of them all soon."

Silence fell.

"Hannah," Eden said, "you've known about all this since Ottilie's visit?"

"Yes, of course."

"Why didn't you say anything?"

"Oh, well, I'm not one to stick my nose in where it doesn't belong." Michelle snorted.

"Well, all right, I am," Hannah corrected with a smile. "But I hoped you'd tell me in your own time. I suppose an hour before it all goes public still counts as your own time."

"You're really something else," Michelle told her grandmother. "I don't deserve you."

"Of course you do. And you deserve Eden too." Hannah frowned. "What is this nonsense you go on about as if only the most pure and perfect humans deserve love and everyone else can go curl up in a ball of loneliness and cry? *Everyone* deserves to love and be loved. The least of us, the most of us, and everyone in between. And you have my love, sweetheart. Forever."

Michelle swallowed, tears in her eyes. "Thank you."

Eden pulled her close. "I can't improve on Hannah's sentiment, so in the immortal words of Patrick Swayze in *Ghost*, 'Ditto.'"

"Ugh," Michelle said. "You did *not* just ditto me. Or quote Patrick Swayze."

"I sure did. Gotta love the classics." Eden grinned. "And...on a more serious note, this conversation has inspired me. Hannah, you're right: love shouldn't be dependent on whether we've attained some impossible standard of goodness. So..." she sucked in a breath. "I've decided. I'm going to write to my mom. A proper letter, not an email. So she pays attention."

"And tell her what?" Michelle asked, wrapping her arms around Eden.

It was reassuring. Eden inhaled as anxiety coursed through her. "Everything."

The story is out. Catherine didn't name me. I'm safe. The world hasn't ended.

Those thoughts played on a loop in Michelle's head these days. It was all she thought when she woke up and the last thing on her mind when she curled up in bed with Eden.

Headlines about The Fixers' disgraced clients dominated every news service. The videos were everywhere. The public and media couldn't get enough of Fixergate.

How unoriginal. Not even the more correct Fixersgate? Michelle supposed that didn't roll off the tongue, did it?

Public apologies were aired as reputations were shredded and careers ended. Among the ruined were four members of the board of The Fixers, who'd been arrested.

Michelle had half expected her own arrest. Surely someone would reveal her as a former CEO of this toxic company? Her disembodied voice was clear on the leaked video tapes. It would be recognizable to anyone who'd worked at The Fixers.

Yet, no one leaked her name.

Eden told her it was a sign her employees had respected her. Michelle never thought they had. Thanks to Alberto undermining her, she'd gone into the CEO job thinking of her staff as the enemy.

She'd been dead wrong. The most cunning, sly, manipulative group of employees ever assembled had shown their respect for her time in command by keeping the secret.

Alberto hadn't named her either…likely on account of the fact he'd disappeared off the grid just after the story broke. Apparently, he didn't like his chances of not being dragged into the middle of the mess by one of his many enemies.

The fact Phyllis hadn't named Michelle came as an even bigger shock. Perhaps she'd taken her cue from everyone else and was afraid there might be a reason Michelle hadn't been exposed. Or, more likely, Phyllis had so much else on her plate, she hadn't given Michelle a passing thought.

After all, the woman's tape demanding The Fixers cover up her husband's sexual misdeeds was on high news rotation too. Michelle was pleased the young intern's name hadn't been leaked.

O'Brian had been feeding her intel on what was happening inside The Fixers.

Ottilie had retired several weeks ago, exactly one day before Michelle fed the story to Catherine. No one had seen or heard from her since. Probably on some exotic foreign beach indulging in those mai tais.

O'Brian had also resigned, but, unlike Ottilie, had served out two weeks' notice.

As predicted, without Ottilie keeping jobs on track, overseeing departments, and putting out spot fires, everything had fallen over.

Phyllis, now unfettered by her PA, seemed to think losing Ottilie was a gift.

Resignations under Phyllis's reign were at half of all staff before The Fixers finally shut down.

Amid the media frenzy on Fixergate, a small story appeared about a former Wingapo mayor who had been revealed as the mastermind of a historic property Ponzi scheme. Charges were pending for one

Francine Wilson. The story made national news, given her fame from some toxic election ads.

The mug shot of Wilson looking ready to eviscerate police staff for having the temerity to take the unflattering photo had made Eden laugh.

Even funnier had been when Wilson tried to blame it all on recently retired Wingapo Police Chief Derrick Sharpe—only for him to refuse to take the fall. Instead, he came out swinging with a vicious rant that involved a shopping list of all the other crimes Wilson had been up to her neck in.

Had the woman shown her devoted chief even an ounce of loyalty, she might have skated away once more. Wilson would probably end up doing more time than those involved in Fixergate. And so would Sharpe. In his enthusiasm to hurt Wilson, the stupid brute had implicated himself.

Eden stuck her head in the room. "Still in bed? It's a beautiful day out here."

"I am because I can," Michelle admitted lazily. "It's nice not having to be up early anymore."

"I was thinking I should finally take you out in Gloria."

"Is the runner-up prize two trips in Gloria?" Michelle teased.

Eden's phone jangled to life. She glanced at the screen and mouthed: *Aggie*. Answering, Eden listened with widening eyes. "I'll be right there." She hung up and looked at Michelle, shell-shocked.

"What is it?"

"Mom. Mom's at Aggie's place, looking for me. She got my letter." Eden looked ill. "This could be bad."

"Or…it could be okay?"

"You clearly haven't met River Lawless."

"No, but I think I'm about to."

"You don't have to. She might not react well to meeting the woman who headed up The Fixers."

"She knows that?" Michelle's eyebrows shot up.

"It was in my letter. I did tell her everything."

"Then we definitely should meet. There is no way I'm letting you do this alone."

River Lawless looked as if she'd just crawled off a thirty-hour flight instead of the eight-hour one from London. Eden knew that look. She was battle-hardened and ready to push back exhaustion to fight the good fight. She was rummaging through her carry-on luggage, mumbling about finding her phone, when Aggie let Eden and Michelle in.

"Hey. This must be a shock," Aggie whispered.

"Oh yeah. Sorry, she just turned up on your doorstep. I didn't include Michelle's address in my letter, so I guess she had nowhere else to look for me."

Aggie nodded. "She's always welcome, of course. Right, so I'll, ah, leave you guys to it." She bolted down the hall, leaving Eden to her fate.

River looked much the same as ever. Her long brown hair now came with gray streaks, and her sun-weathered, makeup-free face had more lines. But otherwise, this woman in green hemp pants, a matching vest, and a white cotton shirt opened to some Amazonian beads at her throat was the same woman Eden had watched, admired, and loved her whole life.

Here goes nothing. She hesitantly approached her mother, arms out. "Hey, Mom."

Her mother stood abruptly, then engulfed her in her arms and squeezed tight. "Eden! It's good to see you again!"

Well, that didn't sound too bad, did it?

"Although I wish the circumstances were better," River added.

Damn. "Circumstances?"

Stepping away from Eden, River took a few steps toward Michelle. "You must be the CEO of the evil company my daughter has told me so little about."

"I'm a *former* CEO of an evil company," Michelle noted. "In the interests of accuracy."

River glanced at Eden. "When I urged you to take on a terrible, secret organization, I didn't expect you to also find yourself in the thrall of its leader." Her gaze darted back to Michelle.

"It's good to meet you too, Ms. Lawless," Michelle said, her tone bone dry.

River regarded her for a moment. "River, please. I'm not one for honorifics. It's classist."

Michelle shot Eden an amused look.

Eden grinned back.

"I won't ask," River said. "Sit," she declared, dropping to the middle of the couch, neatly removing any chance of Eden sitting next to Michelle for reassurance. "Both of you."

Funny how her mom had managed to take over Aggie's home with so much ease. She could do that to Eden too. She always knew how to make her do anything.

Eden dropped to the cushion on the right of her mother. After a pause, Michelle lowered herself to River's left.

"All right." River turned to Eden. "I came as soon as I got your SOS."

"It wasn't an SOS," Eden protested. "I just thought it was time to tell you what was happening with me."

"It's still not too late." River looked at Michelle. "I presume you haven't married my daughter or anything rash like that?"

"What?" Michelle said, blinking in astonishment. "No. We haven't been dating that long."

"But you're living together, yes?" River asked. "I presume it's not in Eden's van."

Michelle shuddered. "No to the van."

"Yes to the living together," Eden said. "Mom, what's the problem here? Michelle is who gave the story to the press that brought down her own company. She's doing *good*."

"And prior to that?" River prodded. She turned back to Michelle. "Prior to my daughter helping you see the light? Would you say you were *doing good*?"

"No." Michelle admitted. "I wasn't." Her shoulders were tight and she was sitting up too straight, more stressed than Eden had seen her in weeks.

River's lips thinned. "Obviously, your murky past will emerge, and what then?" She turned to Eden. "How will you be placed to deal with that?"

"*How* will it emerge?" Eden asked. "She wasn't named as the source. But we are prepared if it somehow comes out."

"She should be in prison," River said. Her softly delivered words sounded like a slap in the silence. "Right now. For crimes against society."

Michelle went very still. "You seem so very sure of your pronouncement." Her tone was pure ice. "I'm sorry, but who are you in the scheme of things? How do *you* suddenly become my judge and jury?"

"Michelle," Eden said quickly, unnerved by the chill. "Let me handle this. Mom, Michelle has been sick to her stomach about her work for years. She's blown the whistle on it. She's doing everything she can to make this right."

"Make it *right*," River said casually. "That's of comfort to the hundreds of lives she's ruined with The Fixers. Or is it thousands?"

Michelle's nostrils flared.

Eden shot her a warning look, begging her not to respond, before turning back to her mother. "Mom, *stop it*. If you want to punish Michelle, you're too late. She's been punishing herself for years."

"I'd say she's not been doing a very good job if it's taken her *nine years* to do something about her company," River said. "Tell me, Eden. After you realized the evil her company was doing, how long was it before you quit and thought about fighting against it?"

Eden sighed. "Um…an hour?"

"An *hour*." River's eyes radiated danger. "*That* long? I would have taken half a second."

"I know." The worst part was Eden knew she wasn't lying. "But I had to think things through. It was such a shock. I'd had no idea."

"And yet Michelle took *nine years*. Longer, actually…because you mention she worked for The Fixers before she became CEO."

"And I have many regrets," Michelle said sharply. "Are you saying doing the right thing counts for nothing because I didn't do it sooner? By that metric, everyone should be punished for ever making a mistake. Perfection is an impossible standard."

"Everyone *says* that." River's tone was mocking. "It's an excuse to avoid aiming for it. Like Eden's father. Frustrating man. He gave up as soon as he faced a real moral challenge. He just…*gave up*. I can't abide weakness." She turned to look at Eden. "So, here we are. At a crossroads. I need to know, Eden, will *you* abide weakness?"

The tone was so firm, so final, that a skitter went down Eden's back. "What are you saying, Mom?"

"Tell the world Michelle's a former CEO of that disgusting company or I will."

"You have no proof!" Shock prickled along Eden's skin.

"I have your confession letter." River's expression was hooded. "It's all there in black and white."

"That's private!" Betrayal replaced shock. "You wouldn't dare!"

"I absolutely would." River eyed them both. "And Michelle—if you care for my daughter as much as Eden claims you do, you'll break it off with her before you're publicly named. For her sake."

"Mom!" Eden couldn't believe it. "Don't you dare twist her love like that. Trying to emotionally blackmail her is wrong!"

"No, wrong is a daughter of mine living with someone so beyond redemption."

Silence fell.

Michelle's intake of breath was harsh and shaky.

Eden wondered if she believed River's words. Or was she afraid Eden might be swayed? The ultimatum just made her angrier. "Or what?" she snapped. "We love each other. We're not breaking up. What will you do if we call your bluff and say no?"

"I already told you: You would be no daughter of mine."

This time, when the silence fell, it felt like an ice chasm had opened, erupting chilled air, making Eden shiver.

Oh goddess. Had her mom just threatened her with… "You don't mean that," Eden said, voice small. "You can't."

"When have I *ever* said anything I don't mean?" her mother said, eyes flashing. "When? If you weren't so obstinate, you'd see I'm right. That you're good and don't deserve to be with someone so morally crippled."

"All right," Michelle said tiredly. "Stop."

"Ex-cuse me?" River said. "Don't you dare tell me to stop."

Michelle climbed to her feet and came to stand in front of River, looking down at her. Her face was a picture of weariness and pain. "This has gone far enough. Perhaps you're tired, River, and words are being said that can't be unsaid. I've been here before, and I know where it ends."

"What do you mean?" River said. "Where what ends?"

"My parents and I haven't spoken in years because of an argument just like this. They cut me out of their life."

"You probably deserved it," River observed.

"Mom!" Eden glowered at her rudeness.

"I didn't," Michelle said calmly, "but that doesn't matter. There's only one thing that matters here: you *will* regret it if you go ahead with this. Eden's the most stubborn person I know. I suspect you're just like her. Neither of you will back down, and you'll be too proud to walk it back."

Uncertainty flashed into River's eyes. She was listening at least.

"What you're doing here? It's a terrible ultimatum," Michelle continued. "I can tell you love each other. River, you would miss your daughter in a way you can't even imagine. And she would miss you. And for what? Pride? To be *right*? The cost is too high. So, when I say stop, I'm telling you from experience: you do *not* want to go down this path."

River rubbed her eyes. When she lifted her head again, the defiance was gone. "Sit," she begged Michelle. Politely this time.

After a wary moment's pause, Michelle did.

"Are you going to stay with Eden even if your identity is revealed? And vice versa?" River asked. She sounded tired now more than combative.

"Yes," Michelle and Eden said at once.

"You love my daughter?" River asked Michelle.

Michelle folded her arms as if irritated even by the question. "Of course I do."

"And even loving her, you're prepared to have her dragged into a storm of publicity if you're outed as behind The Fixers' story?"

"Mom, that's not fair!" Eden cut in. "It's *my* choice!"

River kept looking at Michelle. "I'd like your answer. Please."

The *please* was unexpected.

"I'll understand if Eden chooses to walk away but, as for me, I'll be at her side," Michelle said. "She is a remarkable woman."

River's reaction was inscrutable. She turned to Eden. "Do you love her?"

"Yes!" Eden scowled.

"Why?"

Silence fell again as Eden tried to put something so big and hard to explain into words. "Because she *sees* me. She likes me exactly as I am. She's smart and safe and beautiful. And most of all, she's kind."

"Kind!" River scoffed. "She hurts people."

"Her *company* hurt people. Michelle tried to minimize the harm. And she *is* kind. To her grandmother. To me. She's protective too. I was attacked, Mom. I didn't tell you because I didn't want to upset you. But it was by one of Francine's men, on her orders. Remember that police chief? Derrick Sharpe? He kicked the crap out of me, punched me, and left me unconscious in the middle of nowhere."

"What?" River's eyes widened. "Oh, my goddess!"

"I dragged myself to Michelle's apartment. It took hours. Do you get what that means? I was barely conscious; we were at *war* with each other. She was my *enemy*. But I knew she'd be a safe place to go. And without hesitation, she took me in and looked after me. I felt so protected."

Michelle's cheeks took on a pink tinge.

"So yeah," Eden finished. "She's kind."

River's concerned eyes raked Eden. "Are you okay now?"

"More or less. It was a painful recovery. I still get nightmares sometimes."

"I've had multiple run-ins with Sharpe," River said, lips pursed. "He tried to intimidate me many times because of my activist work. Or yours."

"I'm sorry," Eden said, appalled. *That bastard.* "I didn't know."

"I didn't want you to. It's a mother's job to keep her child safe." River inhaled. "But Sharpe is someone no one can be protected from. He's corrupt and…he's terrifying."

"He's a bully," Michelle said. "And like most bullies, he crumpled when faced with the same medicine."

"What do you mean?" River asked in confusion.

"I had him punished," Michelle said, tone cold. "He won't hurt anyone else."

"You had him *punished*?" River's tone was deceptively soft. "How?"

"I put him through everything he put your daughter through." Then Michelle explained in detail what that meant, including giving Sharpe three cracked ribs and one terrifying forced hike.

The room was so quiet, Eden could have sworn she heard Aggie's office clock ticking from three rooms away.

Eden swallowed. Her mother stood up *against* violence. It was one of her pet causes. This might end very badly.

River's breathing became harsh. She reached over to Michelle, placed a hand on hers, and said, "Thank you for protecting my daughter when I couldn't. When *no one* could." River removed her hand and ran her fingers down her pants, smoothing them. It was her anxious tic. "But honestly, I can't endorse violence."

It was the least convincing Eden had ever heard her.

"He was a brute," Michelle said flatly. "He deserved the eye for an eye he received."

River shifted uncomfortably. "Vigilante justice, though…" She faded out.

Eden turned her whole body to face her mom. "I don't care if it's wrong, but I'm glad Sharpe got payback. After years of abusing people, he learned what it felt like to be *that* afraid. I know that probably makes me a terrible person, but I can't help how I feel."

River's hands turned into fists. "Sometimes…" she admitted quietly, "I feel that way too."

What?

Eden's eyes flew wide open. "Mom?"

"Sometimes I get so angry over the injustice I see all around me that I want the powerful people doing it to suffer the way their victims have." There were tears in her eyes. "And I *know* I'm wrong for it. But sometimes…that's what I feel. I can't blame you for feeling it too. If

I wasn't a pacifist, I'd want Sharpe dead for what he did to you. But I am, and I can't wish that. I'm hardly a paragon of virtue, am I?"

Eden slid an arm around her. "Thank you for saying that. I always feel like such a failure next to you. Not living up to your standards."

"Maybe we all are," River said. "Perfection is hard work."

"Or impossible work," Michelle murmured.

"Maybe," River conceded. "I have firm principles. Eden's father called them rigid, but I've lived by them my whole life. I've always believed I can't weaken on even one or they'll *all* crumble. That's my deepest fear, how close I am to failing."

"But you're so strong!" Eden protested. "You always do what's right."

"Do I?" River sighed. "Even now, I feel a murderous rage towards Sharpe. Some pacifist I am."

"You're human," Michelle said simply. "And a protective mom."

"Mmm." River sighed. "Well." She glanced at Eden. "I'm glad you had someone to go to, someone who made you feel safe. Not everyone has that, sadly."

"Do you…" Eden paused. "Not have anyone safe to go to?"

"No, but it's usually fine. I'm extremely self-sufficient." River shook her head. "You know what's silly? The older I get, the more I forget the bad things your father did and I remember only the good. Up until he started drinking, he made me feel wonderfully safe."

"Same," Eden said. "He was a safe place for me back then too."

"After he showed himself for who he was," River said, "a man who wouldn't stand by his own daughter because he wanted to protect his job, I was devastated by his weakness. I'd believed we were the same, but we weren't. I was also so relieved I had you, Eden. We had the same vision for justice."

"I'm not like you, though," Eden said. "I don't have your clarity of vision. I make all these mistakes."

"Like sleeping with the enemy?" River asked gently, an eyebrow lifting.

Eden's stomach clenched. "Michelle is not a mistake and she's *not* my enemy. Haven't you been listening? Even when I was trying to ruin her company, she helped me. She is the greatest ally anyone could have.

She keeps fighting despite everything. She makes mistakes—big ones, bad ones. And she gets up again and keeps trying to do better. I know you hate who she was, but you can't just cancel a person who's trying hard to make things right. How does *that* make sense?"

Michelle shot her a grateful look.

River threw up her hands. "I just wish you'd found a nice, sweet girl to change the world with. Why not Aggie? Didn't I beg you two to date in college?"

"Um, Mom? Aggie's straight! And in love with Colin. Remember?"

"Oh. Right. Well, a mother can dream."

"You're probably the only mother dreaming their kid would get into a lesbian relationship with her best friend," Eden muttered.

"Well, I'm no homophobe. Even if I can't remember everyone's preferences." She almost smiled. Then it faded. "Michelle? I wasn't there that night to help Eden. I'm grateful you were. Thank you for protecting her."

"I'd say 'anytime,'" Michelle said quietly, "but I'm praying there won't be a repeat performance."

"Praying?" River's head snapped around to study her closely. "Please tell me you're not some traditional theist? I really *will* have to put my foot down if you're a conservative, judgmental sort from the fire-and-brimstone crowd. Religion should never be used as a weapon. I won't have ancient-tome thumpers with all their puritanical nonsense in my family."

"I'm Jewish," Michelle said, looking amused by the rant. "The *regular* kind."

"The 'bakes good cookies and looks after her safta' kind," Eden inserted.

"Oh, well." River looked thoughtful. "I do appreciate a good kichel."

"My grandmother makes the best," Michelle said conversationally. "Eden is mastering a fine rugelach."

"Really?" River cocked her head. "What type? With raisins?"

"Yes," Eden said, suddenly confused about this random tangent.

"Ahhh." River's eyes turned misty. "I stayed at a kibbutz once that had the most divine rugelach."

"I could make you some," Eden suggested. "I'm sure they're not as good, but…" She petered out, realizing she'd just invited her mother to Michelle's apartment, when Michelle didn't like anyone knowing where she lived.

"That's a good idea," Michelle said, apparently understanding her pause. "You must come over. I'm sure my grandmother would love to meet you. Hannah thinks the world of Eden."

"Well, then yes." River nodded. "All right. I'd like that."

"Mom?" Eden asked. "You won't really out Michelle as the source, will you? She's trying to fix things. How will hurting her help that?"

River's gaze drifted to Michelle and back to Eden. "I won't. Of course I won't. I was angry and worried when I said that. I thought you'd caught yourself up in some Svengali situation. I feared someone cunning and clever was taking advantage of you. I always worried your kind heart would be used and abused. I can see, though, Michelle is protective of you and cares a great deal about you."

"I do," Michelle confirmed.

"Good, good." River looked thoughtful. "You know, I think I'll take a raincheck on the rugelach. I'm suddenly interested in a road trip to Wingapo. Since I'm in the same state for once."

"Mom!" Eden exclaimed. "You're going to visit Dad!"

"Nonsense," River said with a carefree wave. "I'm just going to take in some old sights. And if he happens to be in front of me, wellll, I won't *not* say hello."

"He's staying with Mayor Boone and his wife."

"Yes, so you said on your call. It's so pretty out there. Sophia Boone has the most beautiful garden I've ever seen. She's been working on it for so long. I wouldn't mind catching up with her, having an iced tea on her porch, and just gazing at it."

Eden burst into laughter.

"What?" River asked, perplexed.

"Sorry, if only you knew how much fuss Mrs. Boone's garden created. It's the reason I met Michelle in the first place. Never mind. You go and see Mrs. Boone and gaze at her flowers. Say hello to Dad for me while you're there."

"Of course, sweetheart. Although I'm sure he's just the same as he always was." She rolled her eyes, but a familiar fond look was threatening to appear.

"No," Eden said quietly. "He's better. More reflective. Calm. But you'll understand when you see him. Do you know he forgave Francine Wilson? For everything she's done to us?"

"Oh goddess," River muttered. "Seriously? That's just too much. How did I ever get caught up with such a bleeding-heart liberal?"

Eden laughed so hard her sides ached. Her mother, the actual *pinup* for bleeding-heart liberals, had asked that? The woman was wearing hemp pants, for heaven's sake. "Yeah, Mom. No idea how you two fell for each other. It's a complete mystery."

"Well," River said straightening. "At least you two, I understand." She waved a finger between them.

"You do?" Michelle asked, confusion lining her features.

"Now I've had a chance to talk to you both, it's obvious. Eden has a beautiful heart. And you, Michelle, ache to have one too."

Michelle swallowed.

Eden blinked back tears. Her Mom was so close to the truth. "Mom? Michelle's heart might be a little battered and bruised right now…but it's already beautiful. And that's why I love her."

Epilogue

"Tell me again why I'm doing this?" Michelle asked. "I've faced down terrorists, I'll have you know. I've been attacked by bodyguards and threatened by assassins. I once endured a four-hour political speech that turned into a diatribe on shingles. None of those gave me this much indigestion."

"And yet you're scared of a little rainbow van?" Eden smirked, then paused. "Wait, *assassins*?"

"Well, only one. An Australian, so she's miles away. And don't worry—we reached an understanding."

"*She?*"

Michelle pressed her lips together, looking regretful at revealing that much. Her expression said that this was the end of that line of conversation.

Fine. "Come on, get in," Eden said and grinned at the most incongruous sight: Michelle, with her natural elegance and designer jeans and blouse, about to crawl into a beat-up hippie van.

"Do I have to?" Michelle looked dubious.

"Yes, you do." Eden suppressed a laugh.

Michelle huffed but slid into Gloria's front seat.

"There, now," Eden said, joining her on the driver's side. "Isn't this nice?"

"That largely depends on one's definition of *nice*. Remind me why I'm doing this again?"

"Because it's the first anniversary of the day we met. I've decided that special date means *you* get a ride in Gloria. Aren't you lucky!"

"I swear, if you tell O'Brian about this…"

"Yes, yes, he'll have blackmail material for life. Although, I think he's a little too busy now with his carving projects."

"I never knew my favorite enforcer hid such a creative soul. Did you see his first show sold out?"

"I saw." Eden beamed. She decided not to tell Michelle just how many pieces would be coming to their apartment. Maybe when that beautiful fruit bowl arrived, Eden would reveal its maker.

Michelle gave her a knowing look. "Do I want to know how much of it *you* bought?"

"He's very talented," Eden said, admitting nothing. "Hey, Shauna has invited us over again on the eleventh."

"Well. I suppose we should go."

She sounded so casual, but Eden knew that look—she couldn't wait to catch up with Phelim again. Especially his family. Thomas, his youngest boy, had become absolutely besotted with Michelle. His "Aunty Mishy" was now his favorite visitor of all—a development about which Michelle was entirely too smug—on account of her knowing random dinosaur trivia.

"I'll have to get Thomas that complete 3D printed dinosaur set we saw last week," Michelle said thoughtfully.

"Michelle," Eden said in exasperation, "you are not going to spend three thousand dollars on a five-year-old. Besides, the other little O'Brians will get jealous."

"I suppose." Michelle pursed her lips. "Well, I'll think of something." She had a glint in her eye that said little Thomas Seamus O'Brian was about to be exceedingly happy with his Aunty Mishy.

They headed off at a slow, rumbling pace to let Michelle get used to the van.

"Where's Hannah today?" Eden asked. "She was acting all Secret Squirrel on me when I asked her plans at breakfast."

"I'm not officially supposed to know," Michelle said, "but I gather she's meeting her favorite new friend."

Eden frowned. "Is Rosemary in town? I thought she never left Florida?"

"No, not that friend. The other one. She of the cryptic postcards."

"Ahhh."

Every few weeks or so, Hannah had been receiving postcards from all over the world. Always a beach scene, often with a drink in the photo. And the handwriting, so very familiar to Eden, was Ottilie's.

The retired PA hadn't been lying when she'd said she'd greatly enjoyed Hannah's company. The two had become close pen pals. Whenever Ottilie was in DC, she'd drop a hint or two as to where she'd be and let Hannah puzzle it out.

"I'm not sure why Ottilie bothers with the cloak-and-dagger nonsense anymore," Eden said. "The news cycle has moved on. No one ever named a fifth board member. She won the game."

"I'm glad someone won the game because it was a pretty savage one," Michelle said. "Thirty-two people in prison, including Kensington's husband and various heads of government agencies. It's been quite the purge. And I'm pretty sure Ottilie does the cloak-and-dagger routine because she knows my safta loves it. Being sent an 'assignation' and clues on where to meet? It keeps Hannah young, and Ottilie knows it."

"Probably." Eden nodded. "Ottilie truly is the queen of reading people."

"Mmm. Well, speaking of winning things, did you see that news story saying Catherine's Fixergate series is a lock for a Pulitzer?" Michelle asked. "The winner won't be announced for a while, but it sounds promising."

"Really? Good for her." Eden loved seeing how relaxed Michelle was when she mentioned Catherine these days. No more tight shoulders or clenched jaw. "Nice."

"It is." Michelle smiled. "I sent her a text along the lines of 'Congratulations and I hope you win.' I didn't expect to hear back. It was Lauren who replied a few days later."

"Oh no." Eden winced. "Was she hilariously rude or just slightly rude?"

Michelle pulled out her phone. "She wrote, 'You're still an asshole to me, but FYI, you're officially off our supreme shit list. You're on the regular shit list. Oh, and please tell Eden I'd love to see Gloria some time. I'll bring my Beast.—The 'Iowan hick'." Michelle peered closer at her screen. "After that there's a fist emoji, a car emoji, and a flame emoji."

"Poetic," Eden said. "That probably counts as friendly from Lauren, all things considered."

Michelle snorted. "I agree."

"How are you finding my van so far?"

Michelle glanced around, as if she'd forgotten she was in Gloria... or was surprised she hadn't been attacked by small creatures yet. "It's adequate."

"That's good. You know, I've been thinking."

"Now I'm afraid," Michelle deadpanned.

Eden rolled her eyes. "Since you've had a nice long vacation from work, you must be looking for a new challenge, right? I'm wondering how you'd feel about saving the world, one cause at a time, with me?"

"I can't see myself waving protest signs, knee-deep in rainforest. And I'm not sure my Audi would appreciate going off-road."

"Yeah, we're not going to be saving anything with your Audi in the picture because you'll keep being confused as someone from Corporate at protest sites." Eden laughed.

"That won't be a problem because I'm not going to *be* at any protest sites in the first place."

"Oh?" Eden sagged. Damn. She'd had visions of them being an unstoppable team. "Right."

"No, because an effective office manager can do so without leaving home." Michelle's eyes twinkled. "I knew you were going to ask me, by the way. I've been giving it some thought."

"Oh!" Eden grinned at her. "So you'll help? I have some great causes and amazing clients. You can pick the ones you like most."

"Actually, what you need is a good manager to make your many causes run smoothly. I can do that for you. I've looked at the model of business you run. It's very dependent on *you* doing everything. That's not practical. What if you can't do all the physical demands? Or you can't be everywhere at once? Or you want a break to stay in bed with your demanding lover?" Michelle's lips quirked.

"A very valid concern." Eden chuckled. "What did you conclude?"

"I've worked out a way to streamline the processes and outsource your concepts without you needing to physically be at every protest and cause you're championing."

"Outsourcing?" Eden frowned. "To who?"

"I'm getting to that. But first, have you considered expanding your reach and your brand to *individuals* seeking justice as well as groups? Think of it like a…reverse Fixers model. This time, the underdog gets the help instead of the powerful. Cases that get swept under the rug but deserve justice. Especially cases where someone with power is targeting someone with none."

"I love it! But how can we expand? Right now, it's just me and a few of my friends I use from time to time to help, such as Aggie and Colin."

"Same principle as that. Between my contacts' skills and all the people who owe me favors, most issues would be dealt with rather quickly. I've already reached out to several former Fixers employees to see if they'd be willing to help your justice cause on a freelance basis. Just putting in a few hours here and there as needed."

"Really?" Eden held her breath. "Did any say yes?"

"They all did. I've had confirmations from Mia, Liam, Daphne, Snakepit, and O'Brian to be on your books casually for a basic fee, plus expenses and coffee club meetups. They were most insistent on that last point. Apparently, it was the deal closer. The Espionage pair offered to work for free as long as there was coffee."

Eden couldn't believe it. These people were the best of the best and were offering their services just to basically…catch up again? "Oh wow! And this is a *brilliant* idea. A reverse Fixers? This is so great! *And* we're getting the band back together. No one will stop us now!" Eden drummed her fingers on the steering wheel.

"So, as I say, you'd choose which causes and clients you want the team to focus on," Michelle said. "I'll be happy to oversee your employees and do the paperwork. I could work from our new office, which in the short term would be the downstairs floor of our apartment now that you've moved to my room."

"You've thought of everything." Eden grinned happily. "This is going to be epic."

"Not *quite* everything. If we're expanding your mission, you need a good name. Something catchy."

Eden nodded. She was so right. "What about Panda Justice!"

Michelle snorted. "I'm *not* going to be a manager of something called Panda Justice. I'll never be able to show my face again."

"Are you sure?" Eden batted her eyes at her. "Wait'll you see the logo I'll get made up. I know this environmentalist from San Diego who's a genius at graphic art. You'll see."

"Except people will assume you're trying to get justice for pandas."

"Oh." Good point. "The Right Side! Since I'm about doing the right thing for people."

"That could sound like you're running a conservative political movement."

"Shit. Yeah. Okay. Um…The Bright Side!"

"A movie."

Eden pouted. "Damn. This is hard."

"What about The Eden Justice Project? It's beautiful and simple—just like you."

"Did you just call me simple?" Eden's lips curled.

"*And* beautiful." Michelle's eyes were bright with amusement.

"I'll call that a working title. We'll get our team in and brainstorm together. Over organic coffee, of course. Fair trade. Something really awesome to commemorate our new venture." Eden bounced lightly in her seat. "I love it! You're a genius. Wow. I can't wait."

"Apparently, you'll have to wait because we're driving somewhere right now. Where *exactly* still remains a mystery." Michelle lifted her eyebrows in question.

"Ahhh, but Gloria is lovely to drive in, isn't she?"

"She isn't *un*comfortable," Michelle conceded.

"See!" Eden grinned from ear to ear. "Knew you'd love her. That matters because the drive today is a long one."

"Where *are* we going?"

"Wingapo."

Michelle groaned. "Why?"

"We're going to look at Sophia Boone's garden. She's invited us. And how can I say no to the wife of the mayor of my hometown? The woman who brought us together."

"Simply: 'Mrs. Boone? No.'"

"It truly is an amazing garden, you'll see. And we'll be staying at Melba's B&B tonight. Wait'll you try her son's food. It's divine. And if you're *very* good, I'll introduce you to my dad."

"I thought this was supposed to be a *special* occasion," Michelle teased.

"My mom'll be there too. She wanted to watch Francine's and Sharpe's trials. And she's been visiting Wingapo quite a lot lately."

"See my last comment." Michelle paused. "Wait…are your dad and mom…"

"No! At least, I don't think so? They've become friends again, though. It's really sweet. I think Mom really does miss Dad's safe vibe. He's always had that. He's a warm, secure person to be around."

"I can understand being drawn to warmth and security," Michelle mused. "Although heaven only knows why I stick with you," she teased. "You're also a chaos agent, remember? Isn't that what Ottilie called you?"

"Yup. And you're The Fixer."

"I was."

"No. You are. You fixed so much for me. My happiness. My sense of belonging. And my feeling that I had to be lacking something because I was never enough to stay for. You make me feel like I'm all someone could ever want."

"Well, you are." Michelle smiled. "Of course, you still have ridiculous taste in vans."

Eden smiled back. "If you behave yourself, I'll let you find out what it's like to make love in the back of my van. It's an *experience*. Memoir-worthy."

Michelle huffed. "Eden? I'm about to turn forty-eight. My back isn't made for makeshift beds in vans. Are you trying to turn me into your archnemesis again? Because this sounds a lot like a villain origin story."

Eden laughed hard. "Oh goddess. I love you."

"And I love you." Michelle looked ridiculously pleased.

Eden gave her a soft smile. "You are, hands down, my favorite archnemesis of them all."

Other Books from Ylva Publishing

www.ylva-publishing.com

The Red Files
(*On the Record series – Book 1*)
Lee Winter

ISBN: 978-3-96324-534-3
Length: 304 pages (103,000 words)

Ambitious journalist Lauren King is stuck reporting on the vapid LA social scene's gala events while sparring with her rival—icy ex-Washington correspondent Catherine Ayers. Then a curious story unfolds before their eyes, involving a business launch, thirty-four prostitutes, and a pallet of missing pink champagne. Can the warring pair join together to unravel an incredible story?

Rival reporters team up for the story of their careers in this lesbian romantic suspense filled with humor, twists, and one fierce ice queen.

Under Your Skin
(*On the Record series – Book 2*)
Lee Winter

ISBN: 978-3-96324-026-3
Length: 332 pages (111,000 words)

What do a food-delivery robot, a face from the past, and plans to microchip veterans have in common? Caustic DC bureau chief Catherine Ayers would love to know but she and Lauren King are busy wedding planning in Iowa. That means a lot of beefy brothers, a haughty cat, and a sharp-tongued Meemaw. But she's sure she can play nice. Well, pretty sure.

Ice queen Ayers and Iowan girl King are back chasing a crazy story and planning one big fat wedding in this lesbian romance sequel to The Red Files.

Chemistry
Rachael Sommers

ISBN: 978-3-96324-679-1
Length: 276 pages (92,000 words)

Disillusioned Eva never imagined she'd wind up as a high school teacher in her hometown, or worse, suffer the boundless enthusiasm of new colleague, Lily. Their clashing arguments lead to sparks and then the impossible…attraction. But how can two such different people ever work?

An opposites-attract, ice queen lesbian romance about finding the softest of hearts behind the highest walls.

Truth and Measure
(The Carlisle series – Book 1)

Roslyn Sinclair
ISBN: 978-3-96324-644-9
Length: 376 pages (120,000 words)

What happens when the world's fiercest fashion editor learns she's pregnant and her assistant is the only one she can turn to? This shocking moment throws them into an intimacy neither ever imagined. Everything will work out—if they don't do anything ridiculous. Like fall in love.

This wildly popular age-gap lesbian romance mixes humor and chaos with self-discovery.

About Lee Winter

Lee Winter is an award-winning veteran newspaper journalist who has lived in almost every Australian state, covering courts, crime, news, features, and humour writing. Now a full-time author and part-time editor, Lee is also a 2015 and 2016 Lambda Literary Award finalist and has won several Golden Crown Literary Awards. She lives in Western Australia with her long-time girlfriend, where she spends much time ruminating on her garden, US politics, and shiny, new gadgets.

CONNECT WITH LEE
Website: www.leewinterauthor.com

Chaos Agent
© 2023 by Lee Winter

ISBN: 978-3-96324-749-1

Available in e-book and paperback formats.

Published by Ylva Publishing, legal entity of Ylva Verlag, e.Kfr.

Ylva Verlag, e.Kfr.
Owner: Astrid Ohletz
Am Kirschgarten 2
65830 Kriftel
Germany

www.ylva-publishing.com

First edition: 2023

No part of this book may be reproduced, scanned, or distributed in any printed or electronic form without permission. Please do not participate in or encourage piracy of copyrighted materials in violation of the author's rights. Thank you for respecting the hard work of this author.

This is a work of fiction. Names, characters, places, and incidents either are a product of the author's imagination or are used fictitiously, and any resemblance to locales, events, business establishments, or actual persons—living or dead—is entirely coincidental.

Credits
Edited by Alissa McGowan and Michelle Aguilar
Cover Design and Print Layout by Streetlight Graphics

Printed in Great Britain
by Amazon